Space Odyssey

Space
Odyssey

GALLERY BOOKS
An Imprint of W. H. Smith Publishers Inc.
112 Madison Avenue
New York City 10016

First published in Great Britain in 1984 by
Octopus Books Limited

This edition published in the USA in 1987 by
Gallery Books
An imprint of W.H. Smith Publishers, Inc.
112 Madison Avenue, New York, New York 10016

Reprinted 1989
Copyright © 1984 selection, illustration and arrangement
Octopus Books Limited

Illustrations by Angela Barrett

ISBN 0 8317 7988 8

Printed in Czechoslovakia

Contents

Harrison Bergeron

KURT VONNEGUT JR

THE YEAR WAS 2081, and everybody was finally equal. They weren't only equal before God and the law, they were equal every which way. Nobody was smarter than anybody else; nobody was better looking than anybody else; nobody was stronger or quicker than anybody else. All this equality was due to the 211th, 212th and 213th Amendments to the Constitution, and to the unceasing vigilance of agents of the United States Handicapper General.

Some things about living still weren't quite right, though. April, for instance, still drove people crazy by not being spring time. And it was in that clammy month that the H-G men took George and Hazel Bergeron's fourteen-year-old son, Harrison, away.

It was tragic, all right, but George and Hazel couldn't think about it very hard. Hazel had a perfectly average intelligence, which meant she couldn't think about anything except in short bursts. And George, while his intelligence was way above normal, had a little mental handicap radio in his ear – he was required by law to wear it at all times. It was tuned to a government transmitter, and every twenty seconds or so, the transmitter would send out some sharp noise to keep people like George from taking unfair advantage of their brains.

George and Hazel were watching television. There were tears on Hazel's cheeks, but she'd forgotten for the moment what they were about, as the ballerinas came to the end of a dance.

A buzzer sounded in George's head. His thoughts fled in panic, like bandits from a burglar alarm.

'That was a real pretty dance, that dance they just did,' said Hazel.

'Huh?' said George.

'That dance – it was nice,' said Hazel.

'Yup,' said George. He tried to think a little about the ballerinas. They weren't really very good – no better than anybody else would have been, anyway. They were burdened with sashweights and bags of birdshot, and their faces were masked, so that no one, seeing a free and graceful gesture or a pretty face, would feel like something the cat dragged in. George was toying with the vague notion that maybe dancers shouldn't be handicapped. But he didn't get very far with it before another noise in his ear

9

radio scattered his thoughts.

George winced. So did two out of the eight ballerinas.

Hazel saw him wince. Having no mental handicap herself, she had to ask George what the latest sound had been.

'Sounded like somebody hitting a milk bottle with a ball-pen hammer,' said George.

'I'd think it would be real interesting, hearing all the different sounds,' said Hazel, a little envious. 'The things they think up.'

'Um,' said George.

'Only, if I was Handicapper General, you know what I would do?' said Hazel. Hazel, as a matter of fact, bore a strong resemblance to the Handicapper General, a woman named Diana Moon Glampers. 'If I was Diana Moon Glampers,' said Hazel, 'I'd have chimes on Sunday – just chimes. Kind of in honour of religion.'

'I could think if it was just chimes,' said George.

'Well – maybe make 'em real loud,' said Hazel. 'I think I'd make a good Handicapper General.'

'Good as anybody else,' said George.

'Who knows better'n I do what normal is?' said Hazel.

'Right,' said George. He began to think glimmeringly about his abnormal son who was now in jail, about Harrison, but a twenty-one gun salute in his head stopped that.

'Boy!' said Hazel, 'that was a doozy, wasn't it?'

It was such a doozy that George was white and trembling, and tears stood on the rims of his red eyes. Two of the eight ballerinas had collapsed to the studio floor, were holding their temples.

'All of a sudden you look so tired,' said Hazel. 'Why don't you stretch out on the sofa, so's you can rest your handicap bag on the pillows, honeybunch.' She was referring to the forty-seven pounds of birdshot in a canvas bag, which was padlocked around George's neck. 'Go on and rest the bag for a while,' she said. 'I don't care if you're not equal to me for a while.'

George weighed the bag with his hands. 'I don't mind it,' he said. 'I don't notice it any more. It's just part of me.'

'You have been so tired lately – kind of wore out,' said Hazel. 'If there was just some way we could make a little hole in the bottom of the bag, and just take out a few of them lead balls. Just a few.'

'Two years in prison and two-thousand dollars fine for every ball I took out,' said George, 'I don't call that a bargain.'

'If you could just take a few out when you came home from work,' said Hazel. 'I mean – you don't compete with anybody around here. You just set around.'

'If I tried to get away with it,' said George, 'then other people'd get away with it – and pretty soon we'd be right back to the dark ages again, with everybody competing against everybody else. You wouldn't like that, would you?'

'I'd hate it,' said Hazel.

'There you are,' said George. 'The minute people start cheating on laws, what do you think happens to society?'

If Hazel hadn't been able to come up with an answer to this question, George couldn't have supplied one. A siren was going off in his head.

'Reckon it'd fall all apart,' said Hazel.

'What would?' said George blankly.

'Society,' said Hazel uncertainly. 'Wasn't that what you just said?'

'Who knows?' said George.

The television programme was suddenly interrupted for a news bulletin. It wasn't clear at first as to what the bulletin was about, since the announcer, like all announcers, had a serious speech impediment. For about half a minute, and in a state of high excitement, the announcer tried to say, 'Ladies and gentlemen – '

He finally gave up, handed the bulletin to a ballerina to read.

'That's all right,' Hazel said of the announcer, 'he tried. That's the big thing. He tried to do the best he could with what God gave him. He should get a nice raise for trying so hard.'

'Ladies and gentlemen – ' said the ballerina, reading the bulletin. She must have been extraordinarily beautiful, because the mask she wore was hideous. And it was easy to see that she was the strongest and most graceful of all the dancers, for her handicap bags were as big as those worn by two-hundred-pound men.

And she had to apologize at once for her voice, which was a very unfair voice for a woman to use. Her voice was a warm, luminous, timeless melody. 'Excuse me – ' she said, and she began again, making her voice absolutely uncompetitive.

'Harrison Bergeron, age fourteen,' she said in a grackle squawk, 'has just escaped from jail, where he was held on suspicion of plotting to overthrow the government. He is a genius and an athlete, is under-handicapped, and is extremely dangerous.'

A police photograph of Harrison Bergeron was flashed on the screen – upside down, then sideways, upside down again, then right-side up. The picture showed the full length of Harrison against a background calibrated in feet and inches. He was exactly seven feet tall.

The rest of Harrison's appearance was Halloween and hardware. Nobody had ever borne heavier handicaps. He had outgrown hindrances faster than the H-G men could think them up. Instead of a little ear radio for a mental handicap, he wore a tremendous pair of earphones, and spectacles with thick, wavy lenses besides. The spectacles were intended not only to make him half blind, but to give him whanging headaches besides.

11

Scrap metal was hung all over him. Ordinarily, there was a certain symmetry, a military neatness to the handicaps issued to strong people, but Harrison looked like a walking junkyard. In the race of life, Harrison carried three hundred pounds.

And to offset his good looks, the H-G men required that he wear at all times a red rubber ball for a nose, keep his eyebrows shaved off, and cover his even white teeth with black caps at snaggle-tooth random.

'If you see this boy,' said the ballerina, 'do not – I repeat, do not – try to reason with him.'

There was the shriek of a door being torn from its hinges.

Screams and barking cries of consternation came from the television set. The photograph of Harrison Bergeron on the screen jumped again and again, as though dancing to the tune of an earthquake.

George Bergeron correctly identified the earthquake, and well he might have – for many was the time his own home had danced to the same crashing tune. 'My God!' said George. 'That must be Harrison!'

The realization was blasted from his mind instantly by the sound of an automobile collision in his head.

When George could open his eyes again, the photograph of Harrison was gone. A living, breathing Harrison filled the screen.

Clanking, clownish, and huge, Harrison stood in the centre of the studio. The knob of the uprooted studio door was still in his hand. Ballerinas, technicians, musicians and announcers cowered on their knees before him, expecting to die.

'I am the Emperor!' cried Harrison. 'Do you hear? I am the Emperor! Everybody must do what I say at once!' He stamped his foot and the studio shook.

'Even as I stand here,' he bellowed, 'crippled, hobbled, sickened – I am a greater ruler than any man who ever lived! Now watch me become what I *can* become!'

Harrison tore the straps of his handicap harness like wet tissue paper, tore straps guaranteed to support five thousand pounds.

Harrison's scrap-iron handicaps crashed to the floor.

Harrison thrust his thumbs under the bar of the padlock that secured his head harness. The bar snapped like celery. Harrison smashed his headphones and spectacles against the wall.

He flung away his rubber-ball nose, revealed a man that would have awed Thor, the god of thunder.

'I shall now select my Empress!' he said, looking down on the cowering people. 'Let the first woman who dares rise to her feet claim her mate and her throne!'

A moment passed, and then a ballerina arose, swaying like a willow.

Harrison plucked the mental handicap from her ear, snapped off her physical handicaps with marvellous delicacy. Last of all, he removed her mask.

She was blindingly beautiful.

'Now – ' said Harrison, taking her hand. 'Shall we show the people the meaning of the word dance? Music!' he commanded.

The musicians scrambled back into their chairs, and Harrison stripped them of their handicaps, too. 'Play your best,' he told them, 'and I'll make you barons and dukes and earls.'

The music began. It was normal at first – cheap, silly, false. But Harrison snatched two musicians from their chairs, waved them like batons as he sang the music as he wanted it played. He slammed them back into their chairs.

The music began again, and was much improved.

Harrison and his Empress merely listened to the music for a while – listened gravely, as though synchronizing their heart beats with it.

They shifted their weight to their toes.

Harrison placed his big hands on the girl's tiny waist, letting her sense the weightlessness that would soon be hers.

And then, in an explosion of joy and grace, into the air they sprang!

Not only were the laws of the land abandoned, but the law of gravity and the laws of motion as well.

They reeled, whirled, swivelled, flounced, capered, gambolled and spun.

They leaped like deer on the moon.

The studio ceiling was thirty feet high, but each leap brought the dancers nearer to it.

It became their obvious intention to kiss the ceiling.

They kissed it.

And then, neutralizing gravity with love and pure will, they remained suspended in air inches below the ceiling, and they kissed each other for a long, long time.

It was then that Diana Moon Glampers, the Handicapper General, came into the studio with a double-barrelled ten-gauge shot-gun. She fired twice, and the Emperor and the Empress were dead before they hit the floor.

Diana Moon Glampers loaded the gun again. She aimed it at the musicians and told them they had ten seconds to get their handicaps back on.

It was then that the Bergerons' television tube burned out.

Hazel turned to comment about the blackout to George. But George had gone out into the kitchen for a can of beer.

George came back in with the beer, paused while a handicap signal shook him up. And then he sat down again. 'You been crying?' he said to Hazel, watching her wipe her tears.

13

'Yup,' she said.

'What about?' he said.

'I forget,' she said. 'Something real sad on television.'

'What was it?' he said.

'It's kind of mixed up in my mind,' said Hazel.

'Forget sad things,' said George.

'I always do,' said Hazel.

'That's my girl,' said George. He winced. There was the sound of a riveting gun in his head.

'Gee – I could tell that one was a doozy,' said Hazel.

'You can say that again,' said George.

'Gee –' said Hazel – 'I could tell that one was a doozy.'

The Engine at Heartspring's Centre

ROGER ZELAZNY

LET ME TELL YOU OF THE creature called the Bork. It was born in the heart of a dying sun. It was cast forth upon this day from the river of past/ future as a piece of time pollution. It was fashioned of mud and aluminium, plastic and some evolutionary distillate of seawater. It had spun dangling from the umbilical of circumstance till, severed by its will, it had fallen a lifetime or so later, coming to rest on the shoals of a world where things go to die. It was a piece of a man in a place by the sea near a resort grown less fashionable since it had become a euthanasia colony.

Choose any of the above and you may be right.

Upon this day, he walked beside the water, poking with his forked, metallic stick at the things the last night's storm had left: some shiny bit of detritus useful to the weird sisters in their crafts shop, worth a meal there or a dollop of polishing rouge for his smoother half; purple seaweed for a salty chowder he had come to favour: a buckle, a button, a shell; a white chip from the casino.

The surf foamed and the wind was high. The heavens were a blue-grey wall, unjointed, lacking the graffiti of birds or commerce. He left a jagged track and one footprint, humming and clicking as he passed over the pale sands. It was near to the point where the fork-tailed icebirds paused for several days – a week at most – in their migrations. Gone now, portions of the beach were still dotted with their rust-coloured droppings. There he saw the girl again, for the third time in as many days. She had tried before to speak with him, to detain him. He had ignored her for a number of reasons. This time, however, she was not alone.

She was regaining her feet, the signs in the sand indicating flight and collapse. She had on the same red dress, torn and stained now. Her black hair – short, with heavy bangs – lay in the only small disarrays of which it was capable. Perhaps thirty feet away was a young man from the Centre, advancing towards her. Behind him drifted one of the seldom seen dispatch-machines – about half the size of a man and floating that same distance above the ground, it was shaped like a tenpin, and silver, its bulbous head-end faceted and illuminated, its three ballerina skirts

15

tinfoil-thin and gleaming, rising and falling in rhythms independent of the wind.

Hearing him, or glimpsing him peripherally, she turned away from her pursuers, said, 'Help me' and then she said a name.

He paused for a long while, although the interval was undetectable to her. Then he moved to her side and stopped again.

The man and the hovering machine halted also.

'What is the matter?' he asked, his voice smooth, deep, faintly musical.

'They want to take me,' she said.

'Well?'

'I do not wish to go.'

'Oh. You are not ready.'

'No, I am not ready.'

'Then it is a simple matter. A misunderstanding.'

He turned towards the two.

'There has been a misunderstanding,' he said. 'She is not ready.'

'This is not your affair, Bork,' the man replied. 'The Centre has made its determination.'

'Then it will have to re-examine it. She says that she is not ready.'

'Go about your business, Bork.'

The man advanced. The machine followed.

The Bork raised his hands, one of flesh, the others of other things.

'No,' he said.

'Get out of the way,' the man said. 'You are interfering.'

Slowly, the Bork moved towards them. The lights in the machine began to blink. Its skirts fell. With a sizzling sound it dropped to the sand and lay unmoving. The man halted, drew back a pace.

'I will have to report this – '

'Go away,' said the Bork.

The man nodded, stooped, raised the machine. He turned and carried it off with him, heading up the beach, not looking back. The Bork lowered his arms.

'There,' he said to the girl. 'You have more time.'

He moved away then, investigating shell-shucks and driftwood.

She followed him.

'They will be back,' she said.

'Of course.'

'What will I do then?'

'Perhaps by then you will be ready.'

She shook her head. She laid her hand on his human part.

'No,' she said. 'I will not be ready.'

'How can you tell, now?'

'I made a mistake,' she said. 'I should never have come here.'

He halted and regarded her.

16

'That is unfortunate,' he said. 'The best thing that I can recommend is to go and speak with the therapists at the Centre. They will find a way to persuade you that peace is preferable to distress.'

'They were never able to persuade you,' she said.

'I am different. The situation is not comparable.'

'I do not wish to die.'

'Then they cannot take you. The proper frame of mind is prerequisite. It is right there in the contract – Item Seven.'

'They can make mistakes. Don't you think they ever make a mistake? They get cremated the same as the others.'

'They are most conscientious. They have dealt fairly with me.'

'Only because you are virtually immortal. The machines short out in your presence. No man could lay hands on you unless you willed it. And did they not try to dispatch you in a state of unreadiness?'

'That was the result of a misunderstanding.'

'Like mine?'

'I doubt it.'

He drew away from her, continuing on down the beach.

'Charles Eliot Borkman,' she called.

That name again.

He halted once more, tracing lattices with his stick, poking out a design in the sand.

Then, 'Why did you say that?' he asked.

'It is your name, isn't it?'

'No,' he said. 'That man died in deep space when a liner was jumped to the wrong co-ordinates, coming out too near a star gone nova.'

'He was a hero. He gave half his body to the burning, preparing an escape boat for the others. And he survived.'

'Perhaps a few pieces of him did. No more.'

'It *was* an assassination attempt, wasn't it?'

'Who knows? Yesterday's politics are not worth the paper wasted on its promises, its threats.'

'He wasn't just a politician. He was a statesman, a humanitarian. One of the very few to retire with more people loving him than hating him.'

He made a chuckling noise.

'You are most gracious. But if that is the case, then the minority still had the final say. I personally think he was something of a thug. I am pleased, though, to hear that you have switched to the past tense.'

'They patched you up so well that you could last forever. Because you deserved the best.'

'Perhaps I already have. What do you want of me?'

'You came here to die and you changed your mind – '

'Not exactly. I've just never composed it in a fashion acceptable under the terms of Item Seven. To be at peace – '

17

'And neither have I. But I lack your ability to impress this fact on the Centre.'

'Perhaps if I went there with you and spoke to them ...'

'No,' she said. 'They would only agree for so long as you were about. They call people like us life-malingerers and are much more casual about the disposition of our cases. I cannot trust them as you do without armour of my own.'

'Then what would you have me do – girl?'

'Nora. Call me Nora. Protect me. That is what I want. You live near here. Let me come stay with you. Keep them away from me.'

He poked at the pattern, began to scratch it out.

'You are certain that this is what you want?'

'Yes. Yes, I am.'

'All right. You may come with me, then.'

So Nora went to live with the Bork in his shack by the sea. During the weeks that followed, on each occasion when the representatives from the Centre came about, the Bork bade them depart quickly, which they did. Finally, they stopped coming by.

Days, she would pace with him along the shores and help in the gathering of driftwood, for she liked a fire at night, and while heat and cold had long been things of indifference to him, he came in time and his fashion to enjoy the glow.

And on their walks he would poke into the dank trash heaps the sea had lofted and turn over stones to see what dwelled beneath.

'God! What do you hope to find in that?' she said, holding her breath and retreating.

'I don't know,' he chuckled. 'A stone? A leaf? A door? Something nice. Like that.'

'Let's go watch the things in the tidepools. They're clean, at least.'

'All right.'

Though he ate from habit and taste rather than from necessity, her need for regular meals and her facility in preparing them led him to anticipate these occasions with something approaching a ritualistic pleasure. And it was later still after an evening's meal, that she came to polish him for the first time. Awkward, grotesque – perhaps it could have been. But as it occurred, it was neither of these. They sat before the fire, drying, warming, watching, silent. Absently, she picked up the rag he had let fall to the floor and brushed a fleck of ash from his flame-reflecting side. Later, she did it again. Much later, and this time with full attention, she wiped all the dust from the gleaming surface before going off to her bed.

One day she asked him, 'Why did you buy the one-way ticket to this place and sign the contract, if you did not wish to die?'

'But I did wish it,' he said.

'And something changed your mind after that? What?'

'I found here a pleasure greater than that desire.'

'Would you tell me about it?'

'Surely. I found this to be one of the few situations – perhaps the only – where I can be happy. It is in the nature of the place itself: departure, a peaceful conclusion, a joyous going. Its contemplation here pleases me, living at the end of entropy and seeing that it is good.'

'But it doesn't please you enough to undertake the treatment yourself?'

'No. I find in this a reason for living, not for dying. It may seem a warped satisfaction. But then, I am warped. What of yourself?'

'I just made a mistake. That's all.'

'They screen you pretty carefully, as I recall. The only reason they made a mistake in my case was that they could not anticipate anyone finding in this place an inspiration to go on living. Could your situation have been similar?'

'I don't know. Perhaps ...'

On days when the sky was clear they would rest in the yellow warmth of the sun, playing small games and sometimes talking of the birds that passed and of the swimming, drifting, branching, floating and flowering things in their pools. She never spoke of herself, saying whether it was love, hate, despair, weariness or bitterness that had brought her to this place. Instead, she spoke of those neutral things they shared when the day was bright; and when the weather kept them indoors she watched the fire, slept or polished his armour. It was only much later that she began to sing and to hum, small snatches of tunes recently popular or tunes quite old. At these times, if she felt his eyes upon her she stopped abruptly and turned to another thing.

One night then, when the fire had burned low, as she sat buffing his plates, slowly, quite slowly, she said in a soft voice, 'I believe that I am falling in love with you.'

He did not speak, nor did he move. He gave no sign of having heard.

After a long while, she said, 'It is most strange, finding myself feeling this way – here – under these circumstances ...'

'Yes,' he said, after a time.

After a long while, she put down the cloth and took hold of his hand – the human one – and felt his grip tighten upon her own.

'Can you?' she said, much later.

'Yes. But I would crush you, little girl.'

She ran her hands over his plates, then back and forth from flesh to metal. She pressed her lips against his only cheek that yielded.

'We'll find a way,' she said, and of course they did.

In the days that followed she sang more often, sang happier things and did not break off when he regarded her. And sometimes he would awaken

19

from the light sleep that even he required, awaken and through the smallest aperture of his lens note that she lay there or sat watching him, smiling. He sighed occasionally for the pure pleasure of feeling the rushing air within and about him, and there was a peace and a pleasure come into him of the sort he had long since relegated to the realms of madness, dream and vain desire. Occasionally, he even found himself whistling.

One day as they sat on a bank, the sun nearly vanished, the stars coming on, the deepening dark was melted about a tiny wick of falling fire and she let go of his hand and pointed.

'A ship,' she said.

'Yes,' he answered, retrieving her hand.

'Full of people.'

'A few, I suppose.'

'It is sad.'

'It must be what they want, or what they want to want.'

'It is still sad.'

'Yes. Tonight. Tonight it is sad.'

'And tomorrow?'

'Then too, I daresay.'

'Where is your old delight in the graceful end, the peaceful winding-down?'

'It is not on my mind so much these days. Other things are there.'

They watched the stars until the night was all black and light and filled with cold air. Then, 'What is to become of us?' she said.

'Become?' he said. 'If you are happy with things as they are, there is no need to change them. If you are not, then tell me what is wrong.'

'Nothing,' she said. 'When you put it that way, nothing. It was just a small fear – a cat scratching at my heart, as they say.'

'I'll scratch your heart myself,' he said, raising her as if she were weightless.

Laughing, he carried her back to the shack.

It was out of a deep, drugged-seeming sleep that he dragged himself/ was dragged much later, by the sound of her weeping. His timesense felt distorted, for it seemed an abnormally long interval before her image registered, and her sobs seemed unnaturally drawn out and far apart.

'What – is – it?' he said, becoming at that moment aware of the faint, throbbing, pinprick after-effect in his biceps.

'I did not – want you to – awaken,' she said. 'Please go back to sleep.'

'You are from the Centre, aren't you?'

She looked away.

'It does not matter,' he said.

'Sleep. Please. Do not lose the – '

' – requirements of Item Seven,' he finished. 'You always honour a contract, don't you?'

'That is not all that it was – to me.'

'You meant what you said, that night?'

'I came to.'

'Of course you would say that now. Item Seven – '

'You bastard!' she said, and she slapped him.

He began to chuckle, but it stopped when he saw the hypodermic on the table at her side. Two spent ampoules lay with it.

'You didn't give me two shots,' he said, and she looked away. 'Come on.' He began to rise. 'We've got to get you to the Centre. Get the stuff neutralized. Get it out of you.'

She shook her head.

'Too late – already. Hold me. If you want to do something for me, do that.'

He wrapped all of his arms about her and they lay that way while the tides and the winds cut, blew and ebbed, grinding their edges to an ever more perfect fineness.

I think –

Let me tell you of the creature called the Bork. It was born in the heart of a dying star. It was a piece of man and pieces of many other things. If the things went wrong, the man-piece shut them down and repaired them. If he went wrong, they shut him down and repaired him. It was so skilfully fashioned that it might have lasted forever. But if part of it should die the other pieces need not cease to function, for it could still contrive to carry on the motions the total creature had once performed. It is a thing in a place by the sea that walks beside the water, poking with its forked, metallic stick at the other things the waves have tossed. The human piece, or a piece of the human piece, is dead.

Choose any of the above.

Twilight

JOHN W. CAMPBELL

'SPEAKING OF HITCH-HIKERS,' said Jim Bendell in a rather bewildered way,
'I picked up a man the other day that certainly was a queer cuss.' He
laughed, but it wasn't a real laugh. 'He told me the queerest yarn I ever
heard. Most of them tell you how they lost their good jobs and tried to
find work out here in the wide spaces of the West. They don't seem to
realize how many people we have out here. They think all this great
beautiful country is uninhabited.'

Jim Bendell's a real estate man, and I knew how he could go on. That's
his favourite line, you know. He's real worried because there's a lot of
homesteading plots still open out in our state. He talks about the
beautiful country, but he never went further into the desert than the edge
of town. 'Fraid of it actually. So I sort of steered him back on the track.

'What did he claim, Jim? Prospector who couldn't find land to
prospect?'

'That's not very funny, Bart. No; it wasn't only what he claimed. He
didn't even claim it, just said it. You know, he didn't say it was true, he
just said it. That's what gets me. I know it ain't true, but the way he said
it – Oh, I don't know.'

By which I knew he didn't. Jim Bendell's usually pretty careful about
his English – real proud of it. When he slips, that means he's disturbed.
Like the time he thought the rattlesnake was a stick of wood and wanted
to put it on the fire.

Jim went on: And he had funny clothes, too. They looked like silver,
but they were soft as silk. And at night they glowed just a little.

I picked him up about dusk. Really picked him up. He was lying off
about ten feet from the South Road. I thought, at first, somebody had hit
him, and then hadn't stopped. Didn't see him very clearly, you know. I
picked him up, put him in the car, and started on. I had about three
hundred miles to go, but I thought I could drop him at Warren Spring
with Doc Vance. But he came to in about five minutes, and opened his
eyes. He looked straight off, and he looked first at the car, then at the
Moon. 'Thank God!' he says, and then looks at me. It gave me a shock.
He was beautiful. No; he was handsome.

He wasn't either one. He was magnificent. He was about six feet two, I think, and his hair was brown, with a touch of red-gold. It seemed like fine copper wire that's turned brown. It was crisp and curly. His forehead was wide, twice as wide as mine. His features were delicate, but tremendously impressive; his eyes were grey, like etched iron, and bigger than mine – a lot.

That suit he wore – it was more like a bathing suit with pyjama trousers. His arms were long and muscled smoothly as an Indian's. He was white, though, tanned lightly with a golden, rather than a brown tan.

But he was magnificent. Most beautiful man I ever saw. I don't know, damn it!

'Hello!' I said. 'Have an accident?'

'No; not this time, at least.'

And his voice was magnificent, too. It wasn't an ordinary voice. It sounded like an organ talking, only it was human.

'But maybe my mind isn't quite steady yet. I tried an experiment. Tell me what the date is, year and all, and let me see,' he went on.

'Why – December 9, 1932,' I said.

And it didn't please him. He didn't like it a bit. But the wry grin that came over his face gave way to a chuckle.

'Over a thousand –' he says reminiscently. 'Not as bad as seven million. I shouldn't complain.'

'Seven million what?'

'Years,' he said, steadily enough. Like he meant it. 'I tried an experiment once. Or I will try it. Now I'll have to try again. The experiment was – in 3059. I'd just finished the release experiment. Testing space then. Time – it wasn't that, I still believe. It was space. I felt myself caught in that field, but I couldn't pull away. Field gamma-H 481, intensity 935 in the Pellman range. It sucked me in, and I went out.

'I think it took a short cut through space to the position the solar system will occupy. Through a higher dimension, effecting a speed exceeding light and throwing me into the future plane.'

He wasn't telling me, you know. He was just thinking out loud. Then he began to realize I was there.

'I couldn't read their instruments, seven million years of evolution changed everything. So I overshot my mark a little coming back. I belong in 3059.

'But tell me, what's the latest scientific invention of this year?'

He startled me so, I answered almost before I thought.

'Why, television, I guess. And radio and airplanes.'

'Radio – good. They will have instruments.'

'But see here – who are you?'

'Ah – I'm sorry. I forgot,' he replied in that organ voice of his. 'I am Ares Sen Kenlin. And you?'

'James Waters Bendell.'

23

'Waters – what does that mean? I do not recognize it.'

'Why – it's a name, of course. Why should you recognize it?'

'I see – you have not the classification, then. "Sen" stands for science.'

'Where did you come from, Mr Kenlin?'

'Come from?' He smiled, and his voice was slow and soft. 'I came out of space across seven million years or more. They had lost count – the men had. The machines had eliminated the unneeded service. They didn't know what year it was. But before that – my home is in Neva'th City in the year 3059.'

That's when I began to think he was a nut.

'I was an experimenter,' he went on. 'Science, as I have said. My father was a scientist, too, but in human genetics. I myself experiment. He proved his point, and all the world followed suit. I was the first of the new race.

'The new race – oh, holy destiny – what has – what will –

'What is its end? I have seen it – almost. I saw them – the little men – bewildered – lost. And the machines. Must it be – can't anything sway it?

'Listen – I heard this song.'

He sang the song. Then he didn't have to tell me about the people. I knew them. I could hear their voices, in the queer, crackling, un-English words. I could read their bewildered longings. It was in a minor key, I think. It called, it called and asked, and hunted hopelessly. And over it all the steady rumble and whine of the unknown, forgotten machines.

The machines that couldn't stop, because they had been started, and the little men had forgotten how to stop them, or even what they were for, looking at them and listening – and wondering. They couldn't read or write any more, and the language had changed, you see, so that the phonic records of their ancestors meant nothing to them.

But that song went on, and they wondered. And they looked out across space and they saw the warm, friendly stars – too far away. Nine planets they knew and inhabited. And locked by infinite distance, they couldn't see another race, a new life.

And through it all – two things. The machines. Bewildered forgetfulness. And maybe one more. Why?

That was the song, and it made me cold. It shouldn't be sung around people of today. It almost killed something. It seemed to kill hope. After that song – I – well, I believed him.

When he finished the song, he didn't talk for a while. Then he sort of shook himself.

You won't understand (he continued). Not yet – but I have seen them. They stand about, like misshapen men with huge heads. But their heads contain only brains. They had machines that could think – but somebody turned them off a long time ago, and no one knew how to start them again. That was the trouble with them. They had wonderful brains. Far

24

better than yours or mine. But it must have been millions of years ago when they were turned off, too, and they just haven't thought since then. Kindly little people. That was all they knew.

When I slipped into that field it grabbed me like a gravitational field whirling a space transport down to a planet. It sucked me in – and through. Only the other side must have been seven million years in the future. That's where I was. It must have been in exactly the same spot on Earth's surface, but I never knew why.

It was night then, and I saw the city a little way off. The Moon was shining on it, and the whole scene looked wrong. You see, in seven million years, men had done a lot with the positions of the planetary bodies, what with moving space liners, clearing lanes through the asteroids, and such. And seven million years is long enough for natural things to change positions a little. The Moon must have been fifty thousand miles farther out. And it was rotating on its axis. I lay there awhile and watched it. Even the stars were different.

There were ships going out of the city. Back and forth, like things sliding along a wire, but there was only a wire of force, of course. Part of the city, the lower part, was brightly lighted with what must have been mercury vapour glow, I decided. Blue-green. I felt sure men didn't live there – the light was wrong for eyes. But the top of the city was so sparsely lighted.

Then I saw something coming down out of the sky. It was brightly lighted. A huge globe, and it sank straight to the centre of the great black-and-silver mass of the city.

I don't know what it was, but even then I knew the city was deserted. Strange that I could even imagine that, I who had never seen a deserted city before. But I walked the fifteen miles over to it and entered it. There were machines going about the streets, repair machines, you know. They couldn't understand that the city didn't need to go on functioning, so they were still working. I found a taxi machine that seemed fairly familiar. It had a manual control that I could work.

I don't know how long that city had been deserted. Some of the men from the other cities said it was a hundred and fifty thousand years. Some went as high as three hundred thousand years. Three hundred thousand years since human foot had been in that city. The taxi machine was in perfect condition, functioned at once. It was clean, and the city was clean and orderly. I saw a restaurant and I was hungry. Hungrier still for humans to speak to. There were none, of course, but I didn't know.

The restaurant had the food displayed directly, and I made a choice. The food was three hundred thousand years old, I suppose, I didn't know, and the machines that served it to me didn't care, for they made things synthetically, you see, and perfectly. When the builders made those cities, they forgot one thing. They didn't realize that things shouldn't go on forever.

It took me six months to make my apparatus. And near the end I was ready to go; and, from seeing those machines go blindly, perfectly, on in orbits of their duties with the tireless, ceaseless perfection their designers had incorporated in them, long after those designers and their sons, and their sons' sons had no use for them –

When Earth is cold, and the Sun has died out, those machines will go on. When Earth begins to crack and break, those perfect, ceaseless machines will try to repair her –

I left the restaurant and cruised about the city in the taxi. The machine had a little, electric-power motor, I believe, but it gained its power from the great central power radiator. I knew before long that I was far in the future. The city was divided into two sections, a section of many strata where machines functioned smoothly, save for a deep humming beat that echoed through the whole city like a vast unending song of power. The entire metal framework of the place echoed with it, transmitted it, hummed with it. But it was soft and restful, a reassuring beat.

There must have been thirty levels above ground, and twenty more below, a solid block of metal walls and metal floors and metal and glass and force machines. The only light was the blue-green glow of the mercury vapour arcs. The light of mercury vapour is rich in high-energy-quanta, which stimulate the alkali metal atoms to photo-electric activity. Or perhaps that is beyond the science of your day? I have forgotten.

But they had used that light because many of their worker machines needed sight. The machines were marvellous. For five hours I wandered through the vast power plant on the very lowest level, watching them, and because there was motion, and that pseudo-mechanical life, I felt less alone.

The generators I saw were a development of the release I had discovered – when? The release of the energy of matter, I mean, and I knew when I saw that for what countless ages they could continue.

The entire lower block of the city was given over to the machines. Thousands. But most of them seemed idle, or, at most, running under light load. I recognized a telephone apparatus, and not a single signal came through. There was no life in the city. Yet when I pressed a little stud beside the screen on one side of the room, the machine began working instantly. It was ready. Only no one needed it any more. The men knew how to die, and be dead, but the machines didn't.

Finally I went up to the top of the city, the upper level. It was a paradise.

There were shrubs and trees and parks, glowing in the soft light that they had learned to make in the very air. They had learned it five million years or more before. Two million years ago they forgot. But the machines didn't, and they were still making it. It hung in the air, soft, silvery light, slightly rosy, and the gardens were shadowy with it. There were no machines here now, but I knew that in daylight they must come out and work on those gardens, keeping them a paradise for masters who had died, and stopped moving, as they could not.

In the desert outside the city it had been cool, and very dry. Here the air was soft, warm and sweet with the scent of blooms that men had spent several hundreds of thousands of years perfecting.

Then somewhere music began. It begun in the air, and spread softly through it. The Moon was just setting now, and as it set, the rosy-silver glow waned and the music grew stronger.

It came from everywhere and from nowhere. It was within me. I do not know how they did it. And I do not know how such music could be written.

Savages make music too simple to be beautiful, but it is stirring. Semisavages write music beautifully simple, and simply beautiful. Your Negro music was your best. They knew music when they heard it and sang it as they felt it. Semicivilized people write great music. They are proud of their music, and make sure it is known for great music. They make it so great it is top-heavy.

I had always thought our music good. But that which came through the air was the song of triumph, sung by a mature race, the race of man in its full triumph! It was man singing his triumph in majestic sound that swept me up; it showed me what lay before me; it carried me on.

And it died in the air as I looked at the deserted city. The machines should have forgotten that song. Their masters had, long before.

I came to what must have been one of their homes; it was a dimly-seen doorway in the dusky light, but as I stepped up to it, the lights which had not functioned in three hundred thousand years illuminated it for me with a green-white glow, like a firefly, and I stepped into the room beyond. Instantly something happened to the air in the doorway behind me; it was as opaque as milk. The room in which I stood was a room of metal and stone. The stone was some jet-black substance with the finish of velvet, and the metals were silver and gold. There was a rug on the floor, a rug of just such material as I am wearing now, but thicker and softer. There were divans about the room, low and covered with these soft metallic materials. They were black and gold and silver, too.

I had never seen anything like that. I never shall again, I suppose, and my language and yours were not made to describe it.

The builders of that city had right and reason to sing that song of sweeping triumph, triumph that swept them over the nine planets and the fifteen habitable moons.

But they weren't there any more, and I wanted to leave. I thought of a plan and went to a subtelephone office to examine a map I had seen. The old World looked much the same. Seven or even seventy million years don't mean much to old Mother Earth. She may even succeed in wearing down those marvellous machine cities. She can wait a hundred million or a thousand million years before she is beaten.

I tried calling different city centres shown on the map. I had quickly learned the system when I examined the central apparatus.

I tried once – twice – thrice – a round dozen times. Yawk City, Lunon City, Paree, Shkago, Singpor, others. I was beginning to feel that there were no more men on all earth. And I felt crushed, as at each city the machines replied and did my bidding. The machines were there in each of those far vaster cities, for I was in the Neva City of their time. A small city. Yawk City was more than eight hundred kilometers in diameter.

In each city I tried several numbers. Then I tried San Frisco. There was some one there, and a voice answered and the picture of a human appeared on the little glowing screen. I could see him start and stare in surprise at me. Then he started speaking to me. I couldn't understand, of course. I can understand your speech, and you mine, because your speech of this day is largely recorded on records of various types and has influenced our pronunciation.

Some things are changed; names of cities, particularly because the names of cities are apt to be polysyllabic, and used a great deal. People tend to elide them, shorten them. I am in – Nee-vah-dah – as you would say? We say only Neva. And Yawk State. But it is Ohio and Iowa still. Over a thousand years, effects were small on words, because they were recorded.

But seven million years had passed, and the men had forgotten the old records, used them less as time went on, and their speech varied till the time came when they could no longer understand the records. They were not written any more, of course.

Some men must have arisen occasionally among that last of the race and sought for knowledge, but it was denied them. An ancient writing can be translated if some basic rule is found. An ancient voice though – and when the race has forgotten the laws of science and the labour of mind.

So his speech was strange to me as he answered over that circuit. His voice was high in pitch, his words liquid, his tones sweet. It was almost a song as he spoke. He was excited and called others. I could not understand them, but I knew where they were. I could go to them.

So I went down from the paradise gardens, and as I prepared to leave, I saw dawn in the sky. The strange-bright stars winked and twinkled and faded. Only one bright rising star was familiar – Venus. She shone golden now. Finally, as I stood watching for the first time that strange heaven, I began to understand what had first impressed me with the wrongness of the view. The stars, you see, were all different.

In my time – and yours, the solar system is a lone wanderer that by chance is passing across an intersection point of Galactic traffic. The stars we see at night are the stars of moving clusters, you know. In fact our system is passing through the heart of the Ursa Major group. Half a dozen other groups centre within five hundred light-years of us.

But during those seven millions of years, the Sun had moved out of the group. The heavens were almost empty to the eye. Only here and there shone a single faint star. And across the vast sweep of black sky swung the band of the Milky Way. The sky was empty.

That must have been another thing those men meant in their songs – felt in their hearts. Loneliness – not even the close, friendly stars. We have stars within half a dozen light-years. They told me that their instruments, which gave directly the distance to any star, showed that the nearest was one hundred and fifty light-years away. It was enormously bright. Brighter even than Sirius of our heavens. And that made it even less friendly, because it was a blue-white supergiant. Our sun would have served as a satellite for that star.

I stood there and watched the lingering rose-silver glow die as the powerful blood-red light of the Sun swept over the horizon. I knew by the stars now, that it must have been several millions of years since my day; since I had last seen the Sun sweep up. And that blood-red light made me wonder if the Sun itself was dying.

An edge of it appeared, blood-red and huge. It swung up, and the colour faded, till in half an hour it was the familiar yellow-gold disc.

It hadn't changed in all that time.

I had been foolish to think that it would. Seven million years – that is nothing to Earth, how much less to the Sun? Some two thousand thousand thousand times it had risen since I last saw it rise. Two thousand thousand thousand days. If it had been that many years – I might have noticed a change.

The universe moves slowly. Only life is not enduring; only life changes swiftly. Eight short millions of years. Eight days in the life of Earth – and the race was dying. It had left something; machines. But they would die, too, even though they could not understand. So I felt. I – may have changed that. I will tell you. Later.

For when the Sun was up, I looked again at the sky and the ground, some fifty floors below. I had come to the edge of the city.

Machines were moving on that ground, levelling it, perhaps. A great wide line of grey stretched off across the level desert straight to the east. I had seen it glowing faintly before the Sun rose – a roadway for ground machines. There was no traffic on it.

I saw an airship slip in from the east. It came with a soft, muttering whine of air. Like a child complaining in sleep; it grew to my eyes like an expanding balloon. It was huge when it settled in a great port-slip in the city below. I could hear now the clang and mutter of machines, working

29

on the materials brought in, no doubt. The machines had ordered raw materials. The machines in other cities had supplied. The freight machines had carried them here.

San Frisco and Jacksville were the only two cities on North America still used. But the machines went on in all the others, because they couldn't stop. They hadn't been ordered to.

Then high above, something appeared, from the city beneath me, from a centre section, three small spheres rose. They, like the freight ship, had no visible driving mechanisms. The point in the sky above, like a black star in a blue space, had grown to a moon. The three spheres met it high above. Then together they descended and lowered into the centre of the city, where I could not see them.

It was freight transport from Venus. The one I had seen land the night before had come from Mars, I learned.

I moved after that and looked for some sort of a taxi-plane. They had none that I recognized in scouting about the city. I searched the higher levels, and here and there saw deserted ships, but far too large for me, and without controls.

It was nearly noon – and I ate again. The food was good.

I knew then that this was a city of the dead ashes of human hopes. The hopes not of *a* race, not the whites, nor the yellow, nor the blacks, but the human race. I was mad to leave the city. I was afraid to try the ground road to the west, for the taxi I drove was powered from some source in the city, and I knew it would fail before many miles.

It was afternoon when I found a small hangar near the outer wall of the vast city. It contained three ships. I had been searching through the lower strata of the human section – the upper part. There were restaurants and shops and theatres there. I entered one place where, at my entrance, soft music began, and colours and forms began to rise on a screen before me.

They were the triumph songs in form and sound and colour of a mature race, a race that had marched steadily upward through five millions of years – and didn't see the path that faded out ahead, when they were dead and stopped, and the city itself was dead – but hadn't stopped. I hastened out of there – and the song that had not been sung in three hundred thousand years died behind me.

But I found the hangar. It was a private one, likely. Three ships. One must have been fifty feet long and fifteen in diameter. It was a yacht, a space yacht, probably. One was some fifteen feet long and five feet in diameter. That must have been the family air machine. The third was a tiny thing, little more than ten feet long and two in diameter. I had to lie down within it, evidently.

There was a periscope device that gave me a view ahead and almost directly above. A window that permitted me to see what lay below – and a device that moved a map under a frosted-glass screen and projected it onto the screen in such a way that the cross-hairs of the screen always marked my position.

I spent half an hour attempting to understand what the makers of that ship had made. But the men who made that were men who held behind them the science and knowledge of five million years and the perfect machines of those ages. I saw the release mechanism that powered it. I understood the principles of that and, vaguely, the mechanics. But there were no conductors, only pale beams that pulsed so swiftly you could hardly catch the pulsations from the corner of the eye. They had been glowing and pulsating, some half dozen of them, for three hundred thousand years at least; probably more.

I entered the machine, and instantly half a dozen more beams sprang into being; there was a slight suggestion of a quiver, and a queer strain ran through my body. I understood in an instant, for the machine was resting on gravity nullifiers. That had been my hope when I worked on the space fields I discovered after the release.

But they had had it for millions of years before they built that perfect deathless machine. My weight entering it had forced it to readjust itself and simultaneously to prepare for operation. Within, an artificial gravity equal to that of Earth had gripped me, and the neutral zone between the outside and the interior had caused the strain.

The machine was ready. It was fully fuelled. You see they were equipped to tell automatically their wants and needs. They were almost living things, every one. A caretaker machine kept them supplied, adjusted, even repaired them when need be, and when possible. If it was not, I learned later, they were carried away in a service truck that came automatically; replaced by an exactly similar machine; and carried to the shops where they were made, and automatic machines made them over.

The machine waited patiently for me to start. The controls were simple, obvious. There was a lever at the left that you pushed forward to move forward, pulled back to go back. On the right a horizontal, pivoted bar. If you swung it left, the ship spun left; if right, the ship spun right. If tipped up, the ship followed it, and likewise for all motions other than backward and forward. Raising it bodily raised the ship, as depressing it depressed the ship.

I lifted it slightly, a needle moved a bit on a gauge comfortably before my eyes as I lay there, and the floor dropped beneath me. I pulled the other control back, and the ship gathered speed as it moved gently out into the open. Releasing both controls into neutral, the machine continued till it stopped at the same elevation, the motion absorbed by air friction. I turned it about, and another dial before my eyes moved, showing my position. I could not read it, though. The map did not move, as I had hoped it would. So I started toward what I felt was west.

31

I could feel no acceleration in that marvellous machine. The ground simply began leaping backward, and in a moment the city was gone. The map unrolled rapidly beneath me now, and I saw that I was moving south of west. I turned northward slightly, and watched the compass. Soon I understood that, too, and the ship sped on.

I had become too interested in the map and compass, for suddenly there was a sharp buzz and, without my volition, the machine rose and swung to the north. There was a mountain ahead of me; I had not seen, but the ship had.

I noticed then what I should have seen before – two little knobs that could move the map. I started to move them and heard a sharp clicking, and the pace of the ship began decreasing. A moment and it had steadied at a considerably lower speed, the machine swinging to a new course. I tried to right it, but to my amazement the controls did not affect it.

It was the map, you see. It would either follow the course, or the course would follow it. I had moved it and the machine had taken over control of its own accord. There was a little button I could have pushed – but I didn't know. I couldn't control the ship until it finally came to rest and lowered itself to a stop six inches from the ground in the centre of what must have been the ruins of a great city. Sacramento probably.

I understood now, so I adjusted the map for San Frisco, and the ship went on at once. It steered itself around a mass of broken stone, turned back to its course, and headed on, a bullet-shaped, self-controlled dart.

It didn't descend when it reached San Frisco. It simply hung in the air and sounded a soft musical hum. Twice. Then I waited, too, and looked down.

There were people here. I saw the humans of that age for the first time. They were little men – bewildered – dwarfed, with heads disproportionately large. But not extremely so.

Their eyes impressed me most. They were huge, and when they looked at me there was a power in them that seemed sleeping, but too deeply to be roused.

I took the manual controls then and landed. And no sooner had I got out, than the ship rose automatically and started off by itself. They had automatic parking devices. The ship had gone to a public hangar, the nearest, where it would be automatically serviced and cared for. There was a little call set I should have taken with me when I got out. Then I could have pressed a button and called it to me – wherever I was in that city.

The people about me began talking – singing almost – among themselves. Others were coming up leisurely. Men and women – but there seemed no old and few young. What few young there were, were treated almost with respect, carefully taken care of lest a careless footstep on their toes or a careless step knock them down.

There was reason, you see. They lived a tremendous time. Some lived as long as three thousand years. Then – they simply died. They didn't grow old, and it never had been learned why people died as they did. The heart stopped, the brain ceased thought – and they died. But the young children, children not yet mature, were treated with the utmost care. But one child was born in the course of a month in that city of one hundred thousand people. The human race was growing sterile.

And I have told you that they were lonely? Their loneliness was beyond hope. For, you see, as man strode toward maturity, he destroyed all forms of life that menaced him. Disease. Insects. Then the last of the insects, and finally the last of the man-eating animals.

The balance of nature was destroyed then, so they had to go on. It was like the machines. They started them – and now they can't stop. They started destroying life – and now it wouldn't stop. So they had to destroy weeds of all sorts, then many formerly harmless plants. Then the herbivora, too, the deer and the antelope and the rabbit and the horse. They were a menace, they attacked man's machine-tended crops. Man was still eating natural foods.

You can understand. The thing was beyond their control. In the end they killed off the denizens of the sea, also, in self-defence. Without the many creatures that had kept them in check, they were swarming beyond bounds. And the time had come when synthetic foods replaced natural. The air was purified of all life about two and a half million years after our day, all microscopic life.

That meant that the water, too, must be purified. It was – and then came the end of life in the ocean. There were minute organisms that lived on bacterial forms, and tiny fish that lived on the minute organisms, and small fish that lived on the tiny fish, and the big fish that lived on the small fish – and the beginning of the chain was gone. The sea was devoid of life in a generation. That meant about one thousand and five hundred years to them. Even the sea plants had gone.

And on all Earth there was only man and the organisms he had protected – the plants he wanted for decoration, and certain ultra-hygienic pets, as long-lived as their masters. Dogs. They must have been remarkable animals. Man was reaching his maturity then, and his animal friend, the friend that had followed him through a thousand millenniums to your day and mine, and another four thousand millenniums to the day of man's early maturity, had grown in intelligence. In an ancient museum – a wonderful place, for they had, perfectly preserved, the body of a great leader of mankind who had died five and a half million years before I saw him – in that museum, deserted then, I saw one of those canines. His skull was nearly as large as mine. They had simple ground machines that dogs could be trained to drive, and they held races in which the dogs drove those machines.

33

Then man reached his full maturity. It extended over a period of a full million years. So tremendously did he stride ahead, the dog ceased to be a companion. Less and less were they wanted. When the million years had passed, and man's decline began, the dog was gone. It had died out.

And now this last dwindling group of men still in the system had no other life form to make its successor. Always before when one civilization toppled, on its ashes rose a new one. Now there was but one civilization, and all other races, even other species, were gone save in the plants. And man was too far along in his old age to bring intelligence and mobility from the plants. Perhaps he could have in his prime.

Other worlds were flooded with man during that million years – the million years. Every planet and every moon of the system had its quota of men. Now only the planets had their populations, the moons had been deserted. Pluto had been left before I landed, and men were coming from Neptune, moving in toward the Sun, and the home planet, while I was there. Strangely quiet men, viewing, most of them, for the first time, the planet that had given their race life.

But as I stepped from that ship and watched it rise away from me, I saw why the race of man was dying. I looked back at the faces of those men, and on them I read the answer. There was one single quality gone from the still-great minds – minds far greater than yours or mine. I had to have the help of one of them in solving some of my problems. In space, you know, there are twenty coordinates, ten of which are zero, six of which have fixed values, and the four others represent our changing, familiar dimensions in space-time. That means that integrations must proceed in not double, or triple, or quadruple – but ten integrations.

It must have taken me too long. I would never have solved all the problems I must work out. I could not use their mathematics machines; and mind, of course, were seven million years in the past. But one of those men was interested and helped me. He did quadruple and quintuple integration, even quadruple integration between varying exponential limits – in his head.

When I asked him to. For the one thing that had made man great had left him. As I looked in their faces and eyes on landing I knew it. They looked at me, interested at this rather unusual-looking stranger – and went on. They had come to see the arrival of a ship. A rare event, you see. But they were merely welcoming me in a friendly fashion. They were not curious! Man had lost the instinct of curiosity.

Oh, not entirely! They wondered at the machines, they wondered at the stars. But they did nothing about it. It was not wholly lost to them yet, but nearly. It was dying. In the six short months I stayed with them, I learned more than they had learned in the two or even three thousand years they had lived among the machines.

Can you appreciate the crushing loneliness it brought to me? I, who love science, who see in it, or have seen in it, the salvation, the raising of mankind – to see those wondrous machines, of man's triumphant maturity, forgotten and misunderstood. The wondrous, perfect machines that tended, protected, and cared for those gentle, kindly people who had – forgotten.

They were lost among it. The city was a magnificent ruin to them, a thing that rose stupendous about them. Something not understood, a thing that was of the nature of the world. It was. It had not been made; it simply was. Just as the mountains and the deserts and the waters of the seas.

Do you understand – can you see that the time since those machines were new was longer than the time from our day to the birth of the race? Do we know the legends of our first ancestors? Do we remember their lore of forest and cave? The secret of chipping a flint till it had a sharp-cutting edge? The secret of trailing and killing a saber-toothed tiger without being killed oneself?

They were now in similar straits, though the time had been longer, because the language had taken a long step toward perfection, and because the machines maintained everything for them through generation after generation.

Why, the entire planet of Pluto had been deserted – yet on Pluto the largest mines of one of their metals were located; the machines still functioned. A perfect unity existed throughout the system. A unified system of perfect machines.

And all those people knew was that to do a certain thing to a certain lever produced certain results. Just as men in the Middle Ages knew that to take a certain material, wood, and place it in contact with other pieces of wood heated red, would cause the wood to disappear, and become heat. They did not understand that wood was being oxidized with the release of the heat of formation of carbon dioxide and water. So those people did not understand the things that fed and clothed and carried them.

I stayed with them there for three days. And then I went to Jacksville. Yawk City, too. That was enormous. It stretched over – well, from well north of where Boston is today to well south of Washington – that was what they called Yawk City.

I never believed that, when he said it, said Jim, interrupting himself. I knew he didn't. If he had I think he'd have bought land somewhere along there and held for a rise in value. I know Jim. He'd have the idea that seven million years was something like seven hundred, and maybe his great-grandchildren would be able to sell it.

Anyway, went on Jim, he said it was all because the cities had spread so. Boston spread south. Washington, north. And Yawk City spread all over. And the cities between grew into them.

And it was all one vast machine. It was perfectly ordered and perfectly neat. They had a transportation system that took me from the North End to the South End in three minutes. I timed it. They had learned to neutralize acceleration.

Then I took one of the great space lines to Neptune. There were still some running. Some people, you see, were coming the other way.

The ship was huge. Mostly it was a freight liner. It floated up from Earth, a great metal cylinder three quarters of a mile long, and a quarter of a mile in diameter. Outside the atmosphere it began to accelerate. I could see Earth dwindle. I have ridden one of our own liners to Mars, and it took me, in 3048, five days. In half an hour on this liner Earth was just a star, with a smaller, dimmer star near it. In an hour we passed Mars. Eight hours later we landed on Neptune. M'reen was the city. Large as the Yawk City of my day – and no one living there.

The planet was cold and dark – horribly cold. The sun was a tiny, pale disc, heatless and almost lightless. But the city was perfectly comfortable. The air was fresh and cool, moist with the scent of growing blossoms, perfumed with them. And the whole giant metal framework trembled just slightly with the humming, powerful beat of the mighty machines that had, made and cared for it.

I learned from records I deciphered, because of my knowledge of the ancient tongue that their tongue was based on, and the tongue of that day when man was dying, that the city was built three million, seven hundred and thirty thousand, one hundred and fifty years after my birth. Not a machine had been touched by the hand of man since that day.

Yet the air was perfect for man. And the warm, rose-silver glow hung in the air and supplied the only illumination.

I visited some of their other cities where there were men. And there, on the retreating outskirts of man's domain, I first heard The Song of Longings, as I called it.

And another, The Song of Forgotten Memories. Listen:

He sang another of those songs. There's one thing I know, declared Jim. That bewildered note was stronger in his voice, and by that time I guess I pretty well understood his feelings. Because, you have to remember, I heard it only secondhand from an ordinary man, and Jim had heard it from an eye-and-ear witness that was not ordinary, and heard it in that organ voice. Anyway, I guess Jim was right when he said: 'He wasn't any ordinary man.' No ordinary man could think of those songs. They weren't right. When he sang that song, it was full of more of those plaintive minors. I could feel him searching his mind for something he had forgotten, something he desperately wanted to remember – something he knew he should have known – and I felt it eternally elude him. I felt it get further away from him as he sang. I heard that lonely, frantic searcher attempting to recall that thing – that thing that would save him.

And I heard him give a little sob of defeat – and the song ended. Jim tried a few notes. He wasn't a good ear for music – but that was too powerful to forget. Just a few hummed notes. Jim hasn't much imagination, I guess, or when that man of the future sang to him he would have gone mad. It shouldn't be sung to modern men; it isn't meant for them. You've heard those heart-rendering cries some animals give, like human cries, almost? A loon, now – he sounds like a lunatic being murdered horribly.

That's just unpleasant. That song made you feel just exactly what the singer meant – because it didn't just sound human – it was human. It was the essence of humanity's last defeat, I guess. You always feel sorry for the chap who loses after trying hard. Well, you could feel the whole of humanity trying hard – and losing. And you knew they couldn't afford to lose, because they couldn't try again.

He said he'd been interested before. And still not wholly upset by these machines that couldn't stop. But that was too much for him.

I knew after that, he said, that these weren't men I could live among. They were dying men, and I was alive with the youth of the race. They looked at me with the same longing, hopeless wonder with which they looked at the stars and the machines. They knew what I was, but couldn't understand.

I began to work on leaving.

It took six months. It was hard because my instruments were gone, of course, and theirs didn't read in the same units. And there were few instruments, anyway. The machines didn't read instruments; they acted on them. They were sensory organs to them.

But Reo Lantal helped where he could. And I came back.

I did just one thing before I left that may help. I may even try to get back there sometime. To see, you know.

I said they had machines that could really think? But that someone had stopped them a long time ago, and no one knew how to start them?

I found some records and deciphered them. I started one of the last and best of them and started it on a great problem. It is only fitting it should be done. The machine can work on it, not for a thousand years, but for a million, if it must.

I started five of them actually, and connected them together as the records directed.

They are trying to make a machine with something that man had lost. It sounds rather comical. But stop to think before you laugh. And remember that Earth as I saw it from the ground level of Neva City just before Reo Lantal threw the switch.

Twilight – the sun has set. The desert out beyond, in its mystic, changing colours. The great, metal city rising straight-walled to the human city above, broken by spires and towers and great trees with scented blossoms. The silvery-rose glow in the paradise of gardens above.

And all the great city-structure throbbing and humming to the steady gentle beat of perfect, deathless machines built more than three million years before – and never touched since that time by human hands. And they go on. The dead city. The men that have lived, and hoped, and built – and died to leave behind them those little men who can only wonder and look and long for a forgotten kind of companionship. They wander through the vast cities their ancestors built, knowing less of them than the machines themselves.

And the songs. Those tell the story best, I think. Little, hopeless, wondering men amid vast unknowing, blind machines that started three million years before – and just never know how to stop. They are dead – and can't die and be still.

So I brought another machine to life, and set it to a task which, in time to come, it will perform.

I ordered it to make a machine which would have what man had lost. A curious machine.

And then I wanted to leave quickly and go back. I had been born in the first full light of man's day. I did not belong in the lingering, dying glow of man's twilight.

So I came back. A little too far back. But it will not take me long to return – accurately this time.

'Well, that was his story.' Jim said. 'He didn't *tell* me it was true – didn't say anything about it. And he had me thinking so hard I didn't even see him get off in Reno when we stopped for gas.

'But – he wasn't an ordinary man,' repeated Jim, in a rather belligerent tone.

Jim claims he doesn't believe the yarn, you know. But he does; that's why he always acts so determined about it when he says the stranger wasn't an ordinary man.

No, he wasn't, I guess. I think he lived and died, too, probably, sometime in the thirty-first century. And I think he saw the twilight of the race, too.

38

Mysterious Doings in the Metropolitan Museum

FRITZ LEIBER

THE TOP HALF OF THE blade of grass growing in a railed plot beside the Metropolitan Museum of Art in Manhattan said, 'Beetles! You'd think they were the Kings of the World, the way they carry on!'

The bottom half of the blade of grass replied, 'Maybe they are. The distinguished writer of supernatural horror stories H.P. Lovecraft said in *The Shadow Out of Time* there would be a "hardy Coleopterous species immediately following mankind," to quote his exact words. Other experts say all insects, or spiders, or rats will inherit the Earth, but old H.P.L. said hardy coleopts.'

'Pedant!' the top half mocked. '"Coleopterous species"! Why not just say "beetles" or "bugs"? Means the same thing.'

'You favour long words as much as I do,' the bottom half replied imperturbably, 'but you also like to start arguments and employ a salty, clipped manner of speech which is really not your own – more like that of a death-watch beetle.'

'I call a spade a spade,' the top half retorted. 'And speaking of what spades delve into (a curt kenning signifying the loamy integument of Mother Earth), I hope we're not mashed into it by gunboats the next second or so. Or by beetle-crushers, to coin a felicitous expression.'

Bottom explained condescendingly. 'The president and general secretary of the Coleopt Convention have a trusty corps of early-warning beetles stationed about to detect the approach of gunboats. A Coleopterous Dewline.'

Top snorted, 'Trusty! I bet they're all goofing off and having lunch at Schrafft's.'

'I have a feeling it's going to be a great con,' bottom said.

'I have a feeling it's going to be a lousy, fouled-up con,' top said. 'Everybody will get connec. The Lousicon – how's that for a name?'

'Lousy. Lice have their own cons. They belong to the orders *Psocoptera, Anoplura,* and *Mallophaga,* not to the godlike, shining order *Coleoptera.*'

'Scholiast! Paranoid!'

The top and bottom halves of the blade of grass broke off their polemics, panting.

39

The beetles of all Terra, but especially the United States, were indeed having their every-two-years world convention, their Biannual Bug Thing, in the large, railed-off grass plot in Central Park, close by the Metropolitan Museum of Art, improbable as that may seem and just as the grassblade with the split personality had said.

Now, you may think it quite impossible for a vast bunch of beetles, ranging in size from nearly microscopic ones to unicorn beetles two and one-half inches long, to hold a grand convention in a dense urban area without men becoming aware of it. If so, you have seriously underestimated the strength and sagacity of the coleopterous tribe and overestimated the sensitivity and eye for detail of Homo sapiens – Sap for short.

These beetles had taken security measures to awe the CIA and NKVD, had those fumbling human organizations been aware of them. There was indeed a Beetle Dewline to warn against the approach of gunboats – which are, of course, the elephantine, leather-armoured feet of those beetle-ignoring, city-befuddled giants, men. In case such veritable battleships loomed nigh, all accredited beetles had their directives to dive down to the grass-roots and harbour there until the all-clear sounded on their ESP sets.

And should such a beetle-crusher chance to alight on a beetle or beetles, well, in case you didn't know it, beetles are dymaxion-built ovoids such as even Buckminster Fuller and Frank Lloyd Wright never dreamed of, crush-resistant to a fabulous degree and able to endure such saturation shoe-bombings without getting the least crack in their resplendent carapaces.

So cast aside doubts and fears. The beetles were having their world convention exactly as and where I've told you. There were bright-green ground beetles, metallic wood-boring beetles, yellow soldier beetles, gorgeous ladybird beetles and handsome and pleasing fungus beetles just as brilliantly red, charcoal-grey blister beetles, cryptic flower beetles of the scarab family with yellow hieroglyphs imprinted on their shining green backs, immigrant and affluent Japanese beetles, snout beetles, huge darksome stag and horn beetles, dogbane beetles like fire opals, and even that hyper-hieroglyphed rune-bearing yellow-on-blue beetle wonder of the family *Chysomelidae* and subfamily *Chrysomelinae Calligrapha serpentina*. All of them milling about in happy camaraderie, passing drinks and bons mots, as beetles will. Scuttling, hopping, footing the light fantastic, and even in sheer exuberance lifting their armoured carapaces to take short flights of joy on their retractable membranous silken wings like glowing lace on the lingerie of Viennese baronesses.

And not just U.S. beetles, but coleopts from all over the world – slant-eyed Asian beetles in golden robes, North African beetles in burnished burnooses, South African beetles wild as fire ants with great Afro hairdos, smug English beetles, suave Continental bugs, and brilliantly clad billionaire Brazilian beetles and fireflies constantly dancing the carioca and sniffing ether and generously spraying it at other beetles in intoxicant mists. Oh, a grandsome lot.

Not that there weren't flies in the benign ointment of all this delightful coleopterous sociability. Already the New York City cockroaches were out in force, picketing the convention because they hadn't been invited. Round and round the sacred grass plot they tramped, chanting labour-slogans in thick Semitic accents and hurling coarse working-class epithets.

'But of course we couldn't have invited them even if we'd wanted to,' explained the Convention's general secretary, a dapper click beetle, in fact an eyed elater of infinite subtlety and resource in debate and tactics. As the book says, 'If the eyed elater falls on its back, it lies quietly for perhaps a minute. Then, with a loud click, it flips into the air. If it is lucky, it lands on its feet and runs away; otherwise it tries again.' And the general secretary had a million other dodges as good or better. He said now, 'But we couldn't have invited them even if we'd wanted to because cockroaches aren't true beetles at all, aren't *Coleoptera*; they belong to the order *Orthoptera*, the family *Blattidae* – *blat* to them! Moreover, many of them are mere German (German-Jewish, maybe?) Croton bugs, dwarfish in stature compared to American cockroaches, who all once belonged to the Confederate Army.'

In seconds the plausible slander was known by insect grapevine to the cockroaches. Turning the accusation to their own Wobbly purposes, they began rudely to chant in unison as they marched, 'Blat, blat, go the *Blattidae!*'

Also, several important delegations of beetles had not yet arrived, including those from Bangladesh, Switzerland, Iceland and Egypt.

But despite all these hold-ups and disturbances, the first session of the Great Coleopt Congress got off to a splendid start. The president, a portly Colorado potato beetle resembling Grover Cleveland, rapped for order. Whereupon row upon row of rainbow-hued beetles rose to their feet amidst the greenery and sonorously sang – drowning out even the guttural *blats* of the crude cockroaches – the chief beetle anthem:

> 'Beetles are not dirty bugs,
> Spiders, scorpions or slugs.
> Heroes of the insect realms,
> They sport winged burnished helms.
> They are shining and divine.
> They are kindly and just fine.
> Beetles do not bite or sting.
> They love almost everything.'

41

They sang it to the melody of the Ode to Joy in the last movement of Beethoven's Ninth.

The session left many beetle wives, larval children, husbands and other nonvoting members at loose ends. But provision had been made for them. Guided by a well-informed though somewhat stuffy scribe beetle, they entered the Metropolitan Museum for a conducted tour designed for both entertainment and cultural enrichment.

While the scribe beetle pointed out notable items of interest and spoke his educational but somewhat long-winded pieces, they scuttled all over the place, feeling out the forms of great statues by crawling over them and revelling inside the many silvery suits of medieval armour.

Most gunboats didn't notice them at all. Those who did were not in the least disturbed. Practically all gunboats – though they dread spiders and centipedes and loathe cockroaches – like true beetles, as witness the good reputation of the ladybug, renowned in song and story for her admirable mother love and fire-fighting ability. These gunboats assumed that the beetles were merely some new educational feature of the famed museum, or else an artistry of living arabesques.

When the touring beetles came to the Egyptian Rooms, they began to quiet down, entranced by art most congenial to coleopts by reason of its antiquity and dry yet vivid precision. They delighted in the tiny, toylike tomb ornaments and traced out the colourful murals and even tried to decipher the cartouches and other hieroglyphs by walking along their lines, corners and curves. The absence of the Egyptian delegation was much regretted. They would have been able to answer many questions, although the scribe beetle waxed eloquent and performed prodigies of impromptu scholarship.

But when they entered the room with the sign reading SCARABS, their awe and admiration knew no bounds. They scuttled softer than mice in feather slippers. They drew up silently in front of the glass cases and gazed with wonder and instinctive reverence at the rank on rank of jewel-like beetle forms within. Even the scribe beetle had nothing to say.

Meanwhile, back at the talkative grassblade, the top half, who was in fact a purple boy tiger beetle named Speedy, said, 'Well, they're all off to a great start, I don't think. This promises to be the most fouled-up convention in history.'

'Don't belittle,' reproved the bottom half, who was in reality a girl American burying beetle named Big Yank. 'The convention is doing fine – orderly sessions, educational junkets, what more could you ask?'

'Blat, blat, go the *Blattidae*!' Speedy commented sneeringly. 'The con's going to hell in a beetle basket. Take that sneaky click beetle who's general secretary – he's up to no good, you can be sure. An insidious insect, if I ever knew one. An eyed elater – who'd he ever elate? And that

42

potato bug who's president – a bleedin' plutocrat. As for that educational junket inside the museum, you just watch what happens!'

'You really do have an evil imagination,' Big Yank responded serenely.

Despite their constant exchange of persiflage, the boy and girl beetles were inseparable pals who'd had many an exciting adventure together. Speedy was half an inch long, a darting purple beauty most agile and difficult for studious gunboats to catch. Big Yank was an inch long, gleaming black of carapace with cloudy red markings. Though quick to undermine and bury small dead animals to be home and food for her larvae, Big Yank was not in the least morbid in outlook.

Although their sex was different and their companionship intimate, Speedy and Big Yank had never considered having larvae together. Their friendship was of a more manly or girlish character and very firm-footed, all twelve of them.

'You really think something *outré* is going to happen inside the museum?' Big Yank mused.

'It's a dead certainty,' Speedy assured her.

In the SCARAB room silent awe had given way to whispered speculation. Exactly what and/or who were those gemlike beetle forms arranged with little white cards inside the glass-walled cases? Even the scribe-beetle guide found himself wondering.

It was a highly imaginative twelve-spotted cucumber beetle of jade-green who came up with the intriguing notion that the scarabs were living beetles rendered absolutely immobile by hypnosis or drugs and imprisoned behind walls of thick glass by the inscrutable gunboats, who were forever doing horrendous things to beetles and other insects. Gunboats were the nefarious giants, bigger than Godzilla, of beetle legend. Anything otherwise nasty and inexplicable could be attributed to them.

The mood of speculation now changed to one of lively concern. How horrid to think of living, breathing beetles doped and brainwashed into the semblance of death and jailed in glass by gunboats for some vile purpose! Something must be done about it.

The junketing party changed its plans in a flash, and they all scuttled swifter than centipedes back to the convention, which was deep into such matters as Folk Remedies for DDT, Marine Platforms to Refuel Transoceanic Beetle Flights, and Should There Be a Cease Fire Between Beetles and *Blattidae*? (who still went 'Blat, blat!').

The news brought by the junketters tabled all that and electrified the convention. The general secretary eyed elater was on his back three times running and then on his feet again – click, click, click, click, click, *click*! The president Colorado potato beetle goggled his enormous eyes. It was decided by unanimous vote that the imprisoned beetles must be rescued

43

at once. Within seconds Operation Succour was under way.

A task force of scout, spy, and tech beetles was swiftly told off and dispatched into the museum to evaluate and lay out the operation. They confirmed the observations and deductions of the junketters and decided that a rare sort of beetle which secretes fluoric acid would be vital to the caper.

A special subgroup of these investigators traced out by walking along them the characters of the word SCARAB. Their report was as follows:

'First you got a Snake character, see?' (That was the s.)

'Then you get a Hoop Snake with a Gap.' (That was the c.)

'Then Two Snakes Who Meet in the Night and have Sexual Congress.' (That was the A.)

'Next a Crooked Hoop Snake Raping an Upright or Square Snake.' (The R.)

'Then a repeat of Two Snakes Who Meet in the Night, et cetera.' (The second A.)

'Lastly Two Crazy Hoop Snakes Raping a Square Snake.' (The B.)

'Why all this emphasis on snakes and sex we are not certain.

'We suggest the Egyptian delegation be consulted as soon as it arrives.'

Operation Succour was carried out that night.

It was a complete success.

Secreted fluoric acid ate small round holes in the thick glass of all the cases. Through these, every last scarab in the Egyptian Rooms was toted by carrying beetles – mostly dung beetles – down into deep beetle bunkers far below Manhattan and armoured against the inroads of cockroaches.

Endless attempts to bring the drugged and hypnotized beetles back to consciousness and movement were made. All failed.

Undaunted, the beetles decided simply to venerate the rescued scarabs. A whole new beetle cult sprang up around them.

The Egyptian delegation arrived, gorgeous as pharaohs, and knew at once what had happened. However, they decided to keep this knowledge secret for the greater good of all beetledom. They genuflected dutifully before the scarabs just as did the beetles not in the know.

The cockroaches had their own theories, but merely kept up their picketing and their chanting of 'Blat, blat, go the *Blattidae.*'

Because of their theories, however, one fanatical Egyptian beetle went bats and decided that the scarabs were indeed alive though drugged and that the whole thing was part of a World Cockroach Plot carried out by commando Israeli beetles and their fellow travellers. His wild mouthings were not believed.

Human beings were utterly puzzled by the whole business. The curator of the Met and the chief of the New York detectives investigating

44

the burglary stared at the empty cases in stupid wonder.

'Godammit,' the detective chief said. 'When you look at all those little holes, you'd swear the whole job had been done by beetles.'

The curator smiled sourly.

Speedy said, 'Hey, this skyrockets us beetles to the position of leading international jewel thieves.'

For once Big Yank had to agree. 'It's just too bad the general public, human and coleopterous, will never know,' she said wistfully. Then, brightening, 'Hey, how about you and me having another adventure?'

'Suits,' said Speedy.

The Crystal Egg

H.G. WELLS

THERE WAS, UNTIL A year ago, a little and very grimy-looking shop near Seven Dials, over which, in weather-worn yellow lettering, the name of 'C. Cave, Naturalist and Dealer in Antiquities,' was inscribed. The contents of its window were curiously varied. They comprised some elephant tusks and an imperfect set of chessmen, beads and weapons, a box of eyes, two skulls of tigers and one human, several moth-eaten stuffed monkeys (one holding a lamp), an old-fashioned cabinet, a fly-blown ostrich egg or so, some fishing-tackle, and an extraordinarily dirty, empty glass fish-tank. There was also, at the moment the story begins, a mass of crystal, worked into the shape of an egg and brilliantly polished. And at that two people, who stood outside the window, were looking, one of them a tall, thin clergyman, the other a black-bearded young man of dusky complexion and unobtrusive costume. The dusky young man spoke with eager gesticulation, and seemed anxious for his companion to purchase the article.

While they were there, Mr Cave came into his shop, his beard still wagging with the bread and butter of his tea. When he saw these men and the object of their regard, his countenance fell. He glanced guiltily over his shoulder, and softly shut the door. He was a little old man, with pale face and peculiar watery blue eyes; his hair was a dirty grey, and he wore a shabby blue frock-coat, an ancient silk hat, and carpet slippers very much down at heel. He remained watching the two men as they talked. The clergyman went deep into his trouser pocket, examined a handful of money, and showed his teeth in an agreeable smile. Mr Cave seemed still more depressed when they came into the shop.

The clergyman, without any ceremony, asked the price of the crystal egg. Mr Cave glanced nervously towards the door leading into the parlour, and said five pounds. The clergyman protested that the price was high, to his companion as well as to Mr Cave – it was, indeed, very much more than Mr Cave had intended to ask, when he had stocked the article – and an attempt at bargaining ensued. Mr Cave stepped to the shop-door, and held it open. 'Five pounds is my price,' he said, as though he wished to save himself the trouble of unprofitable discussion. As he did so, the upper portion of a woman's face appeared above the blind in the glass upper panel of the door leading into the parlour, and stared

46

curiously at the two customers. 'Five pounds is my price,' said Mr Cave, with a quiver in his voice.

The swarthy young man had so far remained a spectator, watching Cave keenly. Now he spoke. 'Give him five pounds,' he said. The clergyman glanced at him to see if he were in earnest, and, when he looked at Mr Cave again, he saw that the latter's face was white. 'It's a lot of money,' said the clergyman, and, diving into his pocket, began counting his resources. He had little more than thirty shillings, and he appealed to his companion, with whom he seemed to be on terms of considerable intimacy. This gave Mr Cave an opportunity of collecting his thoughts, and he began to explain in an agitated manner that the crystal was not, as a matter of fact, entirely free for sale. His two customers were naturally surprised at this, and inquired why he had not thought of that before he began to bargain. Mr Cave became confused, but he stuck to his story, that the crystal was not in the market that afternoon, that a probable purchaser of it had already appeared. The two, treating this as an attempt to raise the price still further, made as if they would leave the shop. But at this point the parlour door opened, and the owner of the dark fringe and the little eyes appeared.

She was a coarse-featured, corpulent woman, younger and very much larger than Mr Cave; she walked heavily, and her face was flushed. 'That crystal *is* for sale,' she said. 'And five pounds is a good enough price for it. I can't think what you're about, Cave, not to take the gentleman's offer!'

Mr Cave, greatly perturbed by the irruption, looked angrily at her over the rims of his spectacles, and, without excessive assurance, asserted his right to manage his business in his own way. An altercation began. The two customers watched the scene with interest and some amusement, occasionally assisting Mrs Cave with suggestions. Mr Cave hard driven, persisted in a confused and impossible story of an enquiry for the crystal that morning, and his agitation became painful. But he stuck to his point with extraordinary persistence. It was the young Oriental who ended this curious controversy. He proposed that they should call again in the course of two days – so as to give the alleged inquirer a fair chance. 'And then we must insist,' said the clergyman. 'Five pounds.' Mrs Cave took it on herself to apologize for her husband, explaining that he was sometimes 'a little odd,' and as the two customers left, the couple prepared for a free discussion of the incident in all its bearings.

Mrs Cave talked to her husband with singular directness. The poor little man, quivering with emotion, muddled himself between his stories, maintaining on the one hand that he had another customer in view, and on the other asserting that the crystal was honestly worth ten guineas. 'Why did you ask five pounds?' said his wife. '*Do* let me manage my business my own way!' said Mr Cave.

Mr Cave had living with him a step-daughter and a step-son, and at supper that night the transaction was re-discussed. None of them had a high opinion of Mr Cave's business methods, and this action seemed a culminating folly.

'It's my opinion he's refused that crystal before,' said the step-son, a loose-limbed lout of eighteen.

'But *Five Pounds!*' said the step-daughter, an argumentative young woman of six-and-twenty.

Mr Cave's answers were wretched; he could only mumble weak assertions that he knew his own business best. They drove him from his half-eaten supper into the shop, to close it for the night, his ears aflame and tears of vexation behind his spectacles. 'Why had he left the crystal in the window so long? The folly of it!' That was the trouble closest in his mind. For a time he could see no way of evading sale.

After supper his step-daughter and step-son smartened themselves up and went out and his wife retired upstairs to reflect upon the business aspects of the crystal, over a little sugar and lemon and so forth in hot water. Mr Cave went into the shop, and stayed there until late, ostensibly to make ornamental rockeries for gold-fish cases but really for a private purpose that will be better explained later. The next day Mrs Cave found that the crystal had been removed from the window, and was lying behind some second-hand books on angling. She replaced it in a conspicuous position. But she did not argue further about it, as a nervous headache disinclined her from debate. Mr Cave was always disinclined. The day passed disagreeably. Mr Cave was, if anything, more absent-minded than usual, and uncommonly irritable withal. In the afternoon, when his wife was taking her customary sleep, he removed the crystal from the window again.

The next day Mr Cave had to deliver a consignment of dog-fish at one of the hospital schools, where they were needed for dissection. In his absence Mrs Cave's mind reverted to the topic of the crystal, and the methods of expenditure suitable to a windfall of five pounds. She had already devised some very agreeable expedients, among others a dress of green silk for herself and a trip to Richmond, when a jangling of the front door bell summoned her into the shop. The customer was an examination coach who came to complain of the non-delivery of certain frogs asked for the previous day. Mrs Cave did not approve of this particular branch of Mr Cave's business, and the gentleman, who had called in a somewhat aggressive mood, retired after a brief exchange of words – entirely civil so far as he was concerned. Mrs Cave's eye then naturally turned to the window; for the sight of the crystal was an assurance of the five pounds and of her dreams. What was her surprise to find it gone!

She went to the place behind the locker on the counter, where she had discovered it the day before. It was not there; and she immediately began an eager search about the shop.

When Mr Cave returned from his business with the dog-fish, about a quarter to two in the afternoon, he found the shop in some confusion, and his wife, extremely exasperated and on her knees behind the counter, routing among his taxidermic material. Her face came up hot and angry over the counter, as the jangling bell announced his return, and she forthwith accused him of 'hiding it'.

'Hid *what*?' asked Mr Cave.

'The crystal!'

At that Mr Cave, apparently much surprised, rushed to the window. 'Isn't it here?' he said. 'Great Heavens! what has become of it?'

Just then, Mr Cave's step-son re-entered the shop from the inner room – he had come home a minute or so before Mr Cave – and he was blaspheming freely. He was apprenticed to a second-hand furniture dealer down the road, but he had his meals at home, and he was naturally annoyed to find no dinner ready.

But, when he heard of the loss of the crystal, he forgot his meal, and his anger was diverted from his mother to his step-father. Their first idea, of course, was that he had hidden it. But Mr Cave stoutly denied all knowledge of its fate – freely offering his bedabbled affidavit in the matter – and at last was worked up to the point of accusing, first, his wife and then his step-son of having taken it with a view to a private sale. So began an exceedingly acrimonious and emotional discussion, which ended for Mrs Cave in a peculiar nervous condition midway between hysterics and amuck, and caused the step-son to be half-an-hour late at the furniture establishment in the afternoon. Mr Cave took refuge from his wife's emotions in the shop.

In the evening the matter was resumed, with less passion and in a judicial spirit, under the presidency of the step-daughter. The supper passed unhappily and culminated in a painful scene. Mr Cave gave way at last to extreme exasperation, and went out banging the front door violently. The rest of the family, having discussed him with the freedom his absence warranted, hunted the house from garret to cellar, hoping to light upon the crystal.

The next day the two customers called again. They were received by Mrs Cave almost in tears. It transpired that no one *could* imagine all that she had stood from Cave at various times in her married pilgrimage. ... She also gave a garbled account of the disappearance. The clergyman and the Oriental laughed silently at one another, and said it was very extraordinary. As Mrs Cave seemed disposed to give them the complete history of his life they made to leave the shop. Thereupon Mrs Cave, still clinging to hope, asked for the clergyman's address, so that, if she could get anything out of Cave, she might communicate it. The address was duly given, but apparently was afterwards mislaid. Mrs Cave can remember nothing about it.

In the evening of that day, the Caves seem to have exhausted their emotions, and Mr Cave, who had been out in the afternoon, supped in a gloomy isolation that contrasted pleasantly with the impassioned controversy of the previous days. For some time matters were very badly strained in the Cave household, but neither crystal nor customer reappeared.

Now, without mincing the matter, we must admit that Mr Cave was a liar. He knew perfectly well where the crystal was. It was in the rooms of Mr Jacoby Wace, Assistant Demonstrator at St Catherine's Hospital, Westbourne Street. It stood on the sideboard partially covered by a black velvet cloth, and beside a decanter of American whisky. It is from Mr Wace, indeed, that the particulars upon which this narrative is based were derived. Cave had taken off the thing to the hospital hidden in the dog-fish sack, and there had pressed the young investigator to keep it for him. Mr Wace was a little dubious at first. His relationship to Cave was peculiar. He had a taste for singular characters, and he had more than once invited the old man to smoke and drink in his rooms, and to unfold his rather amusing views of life in general and of his wife in particular. Mr Wace had encountered Mrs Cave, too, on occasions when Mr Cave was not at home to attend to him. He knew the constant interference to which Cave was subjected, and having weighed the story judicially, he decided to give the crystal a refuge. Mr Cave promised to explain the reasons for his remarkable affection for the crystal more fully on a later occasion, but he spoke distinctly of seeing visions therein. He called on Mr Wace the same evening.

He told a complicated story. The crystal he said had come into his possession with other oddments at the forced sale of another curiosity dealer's effects, and not knowing what its value might be, he had ticketed it at ten shillings. It had hung upon his hands at that price for some months, and he was thinking of 'reducing the figure', when he made a singular discovery.

At that time his health was very bad – and it must be borne in mind that, throughout all this experience, his physical condition was one of ebb – and he was in considerable distress by reason of the negligence, the positive ill-treatment even, he received from his wife and step-children. His wife was vain, extravagant, unfeeling, and had a growing taste for private drinking; his step-daughter was mean and over-reaching; and his step-son had conceived a violent dislike for him, and lost no chance of showing it. The requirements of his business pressed heavily upon him, and Mr Wace does not think that he was altogether free from occasional intemperance. He had begun life in a comfortable position, he was a man of fair education, and he suffered, for weeks at a stretch, from melancholia and insomnia. Afraid to disturb his family, he would slip quietly from his wife's side, when his thoughts became intolerable, and wander about the house. And about three o'clock one morning, late in August, chance directed him into the shop.

The dirty little place was impenetrably black except in one spot, where he perceived an unusual glow of light. Approaching this, he discovered it to be the crystal egg, which was standing on the corner of the counter towards the window. A thin ray smote through a crack in the shutters, impinged upon the object, and seemed as it were to fill its entire interior.

It occurred to Mr Cave that this was not in accordance with the laws of optics as he had known them in his younger days. He could understand the rays being refracted by the crystal and coming to a focus in its interior, but this diffusion jarred with his physical conceptions. He approached the crystal nearly, peering into it and round it, with a transient revival of the scientific curiosity that in his youth had determined his choice of a calling. He was surprised to find the light not steady, but writhing within the substance of the egg, as though that object was a hollow sphere of some luminous vapour. In moving about to get different points of view, he suddenly found that he had come between it and the ray, and that the crystal none the less remained luminous. Greatly astonished, he lifted it out of the light ray and carried it to the darkest part of the shop. It remained bright for some four or five minutes, when it slowly faded and went out. He placed it in the thin streak of daylight, and its luminousness was almost immediately restored.

So far, at least, Mr Wace was able to verify the remarkable story of Mr Cave. He has himself repeatedly held this crystal in a ray of light (which had to be of a less diameter than one millimetre). And in a perfect darkness, such as could be produced by velvet wrapping, the crystal did undoubtedly appear very faintly phosphorescent. It would seem, however, that the luminousness was of some exceptional sort, and not equally visible to all eyes; for Mr Harbinger – whose name will be familiar to the scientific reader in connection with the Pasteur Institute – was quite unable to see any light whatever. And Mr Wace's own capacity for its appreciation was out of comparison inferior to that of Mr Cave's. Even with Mr Cave the power varied very considerably: his vision was most vivid during states of extreme weakness and fatigue.

Now from the outset this light in the crystal exercised an irresistible fascination upon Mr Cave. And it says more for his loneliness of soul than a volume of pathetic writing could do, that he told no human being of his curious observations. He seems to have been living in such an atmosphere of petty spite that to admit the existence of a pleasure would have been to risk the loss of it. He found that as the dawn advanced, and the amount of diffused light increased, the crystal became to all appearance non-luminous. And for some time he was unable to see anything in it, except at night-time, in dark corners of the shop.

But the use of an old velvet cloth, which he used as a background for a collection of minerals, occurred to him, and by doubling this, and putting it over his head and hands, he was able to get a sight of the luminous movement within the crystal even in the day-time. He was very cautious lest he should be thus discovered by his wife, and he practised this occupation only in the afternoons, while she was asleep upstairs, and then circumspectly in a hollow under the counter. And one day, turning the crystal about in his hands, he saw something. It came and went like a flash, but it gave him the impression that the object had for a moment opened to him the view of a wide and spacious and strange country; and turning it about, he did, just as the light faded, see the same vision again.

Now, it would be tedious and unnecessary to state all the phases of Mr Cave's discovery from this point. Suffice that the effect was this: the crystal, being peered into at an angle of about 137 degrees from the direction of the illuminating ray, gave a clear and consistent picture of a wide and peculiar country-side. It was not dream-like at all; it produced a definite impression of reality, and the better the light the more real and solid it seemed. It was a moving picture: that is to say, certain objects moved in it, but slowly in an orderly manner like real things, and, according as the direction of the lighting and vision changed, the picture changed also. It must, indeed, have been like looking through an oval glass at a view, and turning the glass about to get at different aspects.

Mr Cave's statements, Mr Wace assures me, were extremely circumstantial, and entirely free from any of that emotional quality that taints hallucinatory impressions. But it must be remembered that all the efforts of Mr Wace to see any similar clarity in the faint opalescence of the crystal were wholly unsuccessful, try as he would. The difference in intensity of the impressions received by the two men was very great, and it is quite conceivable that what was a view to Mr Cave was a mere blurred nebulosity to Mr Wace.

The view, as Mr Cave described it, was invariably of an extensive plain, and he seemed always to be looking at it from a considerable height, as if from a tower or a mast. To the east and to the west the plain was bounded at a remote distance by vast reddish cliffs, which reminded him of those he had seen in some picture; but what the picture was Mr Wace was unable to ascertain. These cliffs passed north and south – he could tell the points of the compass by the stars that were visible of a night – receding in an almost illimitable perspective and fading into the mists of the distance before they met. He was nearer the eastern set of cliffs, on the occasion of his first vision the sun was rising over them, and black against the sunlight and pale against their shadow appeared a multitude of soaring forms that Mr Cave regarded as birds. A vast range of buildings spread below him; he seemed to be looking down upon them; and, as they approached the blurred and refracted edge of the picture, they became indistinct. There were also trees curious in shape, and in colouring, a deep mossy green and an exquisite grey, beside a wide and shining canal. And something great and brilliantly coloured flew across the picture. But the first time Mr Cave saw these pictures he saw only in flashes, his hands shook, his head moved, the vision came and went, and grew foggy and indistinct. And at first he had the greatest difficulty in finding the picture again once the direction of it was lost.

His next clear vision, which came about a week after the first, the interval having yielded nothing but tantalising glimpses and some useful experience, showed him the view down the length of the valley. The view was different, but he had a curious persuasion, which his subsequent observations abundantly confirmed, that he was regarding this strange world from exactly the same spot, although he was looking in a different direction. The long façade of the great building, whose roof he had looked down upon before, was now receding in perspective. He recognized the roof. In the front of the façade was a terrace of massive proportions and extraordinary length, and down the middle of the terrace, at certain intervals, stood huge but very graceful masts, bearing small shiny objects which reflected the setting sun. The import of these small objects did not occur to Mr Cave until some time after, as he was describing the scene to Mr Wace. The terrace overhung a thicket of the most luxuriant and graceful vegetation, and beyond this was a wide grassy lawn on which certain broad creatures, in form like beetles but enormously larger reposed. Beyond this again was a richly decorated causeway of pinkish stone; and beyond that, and lined with dense *red* weeds, and passing up the valley exactly parallel with the distant cliffs, was a broad and mirror-like expanse of water. The air seemed full of squadrons of great birds, manoeuvring in stately curves; and across the river was a multitude of splendid buldings, richly coloured and glittering with metallic tracery and facets, among a forest of moss-like and lichenous trees. And suddenly something flapped repeatedly across the vision, like the fluttering of a jewelled fan or the beating of a wing, and a face, or rather the upper part of a face with very large eyes, came as it were close to his own and as if on the other side of the crystal. Mr Cave was so startled and so impressed by the absolute reality of these eyes, that he drew his head back from the crystal to look behind it. He had become so absorbed in watching that he was quite surprised to find himself in the cool darkness of his little shop, with its familiar odour of methyl, mustiness, and decay. And, as he blinked about him, the glowing crystal faded, and went out.

Such were the first general impressions of Mr Cave. The story is curiously direct and circumstantial. From the outset, when the valley first flashed momentarily on his senses, his imagination was strangely affected, and, as he began to appreciate the details of the scene he saw, his wonder rose to the point of a passion. He went about his business listless and distraught, thinking only of the time when he should be able to return to his watching. And then a few weeks after his first sight of the valley came the two customers, the stress and excitement of their offer, and the narrow escape of the crystal from sale, as I have already told.

Now while the thing was Mr Cave's secret, it remained a mere wonder, a thing to creep to covertly and peep at, as a child might peep upon a forbidden garden. But Mr Wace has, for a young scientific investigator, a particularly lucid and consecutive habit of mind. Directly the crystal and its story came to him, and he had satisfied himself, by seeing the phosphorescence with his own eyes, that there really was a certain evidence for Mr Cave's statements, he proceeded to develop the matter systematically. Mr Cave was only too eager to come and feast his eyes on this wonderland he saw, and he came every night from half-past eight until half-past ten, and sometimes, in Mr Wace's absence, during the day. On Sunday afternoons, also, he came. From the outset Mr Wace made copious notes, and it was due to his scientific method that the relation between the direction from which the initiating ray entered the crystal and the orientation of the picture was proved. And, by covering the crystal in a box perforated only with a small aperture to admit the exciting ray, and by substituting black holland for his buff blinds, he greatly improved the conditions of the observations; so that in a little while they were able to survey the valley in any direction they desired.

So having cleared the way, we may give a brief account of this visionary world within the crystal. The things were in all cases seen by Mr Cave and the method of working was invariably for him to watch the crystal and report what he saw, while Mr Wace (who as a science student had learnt the trick of writing in the dark) wrote a brief note of his report. When the crystal faded, it was put into its box in the proper position and the electric light turned on. Mr Wace asked questions, and suggested observations to clear up difficult points. Nothing, indeed, could have been less visionary and more matter-of-fact.

The attention of Mr Cave had been speedily directed to the bird-like creatures he had seen so abundantly present in each of his earlier visions. His first impression was soon corrected, and he considered for a time that they might represent a diurnal species of bat. Then he thought, grotesquely enough, that they might be cherubs. Their heads were round, and curiously human, and it was the eyes of one of them that had so startled him on his second observation. They had broad, silvery wings, not feathered, but glistening almost as brilliantly as new-killed fish and with the same subtle play of colour, and these wings were not built on the plan of bird-wing, or bat, Mr Wace learned, but supported by curved ribs radiating from the body. (A sort of butterfly wing with curved ribs seems best to express their appearance.) The body was small, but fitted with two bunches of prehensile organs, like long tentacles, immediately under the mouth. Incredible as it appeared to Mr Wace, the persuasion at last became irresistible, that it was these creatures which owned the great quasi-human buildings and the magnificent garden that made the broad valley so splendid. And Mr Cave perceived that the buildings, with other peculiarities, had no doors, but that the great circular windows, which opened freely, gave the creatures egress, and entrance. They would alight upon their tentacles, fold their wings to a smallness almost rod-like, and hop into the interior. But among them was a multitude of smaller-winged creatures, like great dragon-flies and moths and flying beetles, and across the greensward brilliantly-coloured gigantic ground-beetles crawled lazily to and fro. Moreover, on the causeways and terraces, large-headed creatures similar to the greater winged flies, but wingless, were visible, hopping busily upon their hand-like tangle of tentacles.

Allusion has already been made to the glittering objects upon masts that stood upon the terrace of the nearer building. It dawned upon Mr Cave, after regarding one of these masts very fixedly on one particularly vivid day, that the glittering object there was a crystal exactly like that into which he peered. And a still more careful scrutiny convinced him that each one in a vista of nearly twenty carried a similar object.

Occasionally one of the large flying creatures would flutter up to one, and, folding its wings and coiling a number of its tentacles about the mast, would regard the crystal fixedly for a space, – sometimes for as long as fifteen minutes. And a series of observations, made at the suggestion of Mr Wace, convinced both watchers that, so far as this visionary world was concerned, the crystal into which they peered actually stood at the summit of the end-most mast on the terrace, and that on one occasion at least one of these inhabitants of this other world had looked into Mr Cave's face while he was making these observations.

So much for the essential facts of this very singular story. Unless we dismiss it all as the ingenious fabrication of Mr Wace, we have to believe one of two things: either that Mr Cave's crystal was in two worlds at once, and that, while it was carried about in one, it remained stationary in the other, which seems altogether absurd; or else that it had some peculiar relation of sympathy with another and exactly similar crystal in this other world, so that what was seen in the interior of the one in this world was, under suitable conditions, visible to an observer in the corresponding crystal in the other world; and *vice versa*. At present, indeed, we do not know of any way in which two crystals could so come *en rapport*, but nowadays we know enough to understand that the thing is not altogether impossible. This view of the crystals as *en rapport* was the supposition that occurred to Mr Wace, and to me at least it seems extremely plausible. . . .

And where was this other world? On this, also, the alert intelligence of Mr Wace speedily threw light. After sunset, the sky darkened rapidly – there was a very brief twilight interval indeed – and the stars shone out. They were recognizably the same as those we see, arranged in the same constellations. Mr Cave recognized the Bear, the Pleiades, Aldebaran, and Sirius: so that the other world must be somewhere in the solar system, and, at the utmost, only a few hundreds of millions of miles from our own. Following up this clue, Mr Wace learned that the midnight sky was a darker blue even than our midwinter sky, and that the sun seemed a little smaller. *And there were two small moons!* 'like our moon but smaller, and quite differently marked,' one of which moved so rapidly that its motion was clearly visible as one regarded it. These moons were never high in the sky, but vanished as they rose; that is, every time they revolved they were eclipsed because they were so near their primary planet. And all this answers quite completely, although Mr Cave did not know it, to what must be the condition of things on Mars.

Indeed, it seems an exceedingly plausible conclusion that peering into this crystal Mr Cave did actually see the planet Mars and its inhabitants. And, if that be the case, then the evening star that shone so brilliantly in the sky of that distant vision was neither more nor less than our own familiar earth.

For a time the Martians – if they were Martians – do not seem to have known of Mr Cave's inspection. Once or twice one would come to peer, and go away very shortly to some other mast, as though the vision was unsatisfactory. During this time Mr Cave was able to watch the proceedings of these winged people without being disturbed by their attentions, and, although his report is necessarily vague and fragmentary, it is nevertheless very suggestive. Imagine the impression of humanity a Martian observer would get who, after a difficult process of preparation and with considerable fatigue to the eyes, was able to peer at London from the steeple of St Martin's Church for stretches, at longest, of four minutes at a time. Mr Cave was unable to ascertain if the winged Martians were the same as the Martians who hopped about the causeways and terraces, and if the latter could put on wings at will. He several times saw certain clumsy bipeds, dimly suggestive of apes, white and partially translucent, feeding among certain of the lichenous trees, and once some of these fled before one of the hopping, round-headed Martians. The latter caught one in its tentacles, and then the picture faded suddenly and left Mr Cave most tantalizingly in the dark. On another occasion a vast thing, that Mr Cave thought at first was some gigantic insect, appeared advancing also the causeway beside the canal with extraordinary rapidity. As this drew nearer Mr Cave perceived that it was a mechanism of shining metals and of extraordinary complexity. And then, when he looked again, it had passed out of sight.

After a time Mr Cave aspired to attract the attention of the Martians, and the next time that the strange eyes of one of them appeared close to the crystal Mr Cave cried out and sprang away, and they immediately turned on the light and began to gesticulate in a manner suggestive of signalling. But when at last Mr Cave examined the crystal again the Martian had departed.

Thus far these observations had progressed in early November, and then Mr Cave, feeling that the suspicions of his family about the crystal were allayed, began to take it to and fro with him in order that, as occasion arose in the daytime or night, he might comfort himself with what was fast becoming the most real thing in his existence.

In December Mr Wace's work in connection with a forthcoming examination became heavy, the sittings were reluctantly suspended for a week, and for ten or eleven days – he is not quite sure which – he saw nothing of Cave. He then grew anxious to resume these investigations, and, the stress of his seasonal labours being abated, he went down to Seven Dials. At the corner he noticed a shutter before a bird fancier's window, and then another at a cobbler's. Mr Cave's shop was closed.

He rapped and the door was opened by the step-son in black. He at once called Mrs Cave, who was, Mr Wace could not but observe, in cheap but ample widow's weeds of the most imposing pattern. Without any great surprise Mr Wace learnt that Cave was dead and already buried. She was in tears, and her voice was a little thick. She had just returned from Highgate. Her mind seemed occupied with her own prospects and the honourable details of the obsequies, but Mr Wace was at last able to learn the particulars of Cave's death. He had been found dead in his shop in the early morning, the day after his last visit to Mr Wace, and the crystal had been clasped in his stone-cold hands. His face was smiling, said Mrs Cave, and the velvet cloth from the minerals lay on the floor at his feet. He must have been dead five or six hours when he was found.

This came as a great shock to Wace, and he began to reproach himself bitterly for having neglected the plain symptoms of the old man's ill-health. But his chief thought was of the crystal. He approached that topic in a gingerly manner, because he knew Mrs Cave's peculiarities. He was dumbfounded to learn that it was sold. '

Mrs Cave's first impulse, directly Cave's body had been taken upstairs, had been to write to the mad clergyman who had offered five pounds for the crystal, informing him of its recovery; but after a violent hunt in which her daughter joined her, they were convinced of the loss of his address. As they were without the means required to mourn and bury Cave in the elaborate style the dignity of an old Seven Dials inhabitant demands, they had appealed to a friendly fellow-tradesman in Great Portland Street. He had very kindly taken over a portion of the stock at a valuation. The valuation was his own and the crystal egg was included in one of the lots. Mr Wace, after a few suitable consolatory observations, a little off-handedly proffered perhaps, hurried at once to Great Portland Street. But there he learned that the crystal egg had already been sold to a tall, dark man in grey. And there the material facts in this curious, and to me at least very suggestive story come abruptly to an end. The Great Portland Street dealer did not know who the tall dark man in grey was, nor had he observed him with sufficient attention to describe him minutely. He did not even know which way this person had gone after leaving the shop. For a time Mr Wace remained in the shop, trying the dealer's patience with hopeless questions, venting his own exasperation. And at last, realizing abruptly that the whole thing had passed out of his hands, had vanished like a vision of the night, he returned to his own rooms, a little astonished to find the notes he had made still tangible and visible upon his untidy table.

His annoyance and disappointment were naturally very great. He made a second call (equally ineffectual) upon the Great Portland Street dealer, and he resorted to advertisements in such periodicals as were likely to come into the hands of a bric-a-brac collector. He also wrote letters to *The Daily Chronicle* and *Nature*, but both those periodicals, suspecting a hoax, asked him to reconsider his action before they printed, and he was advised that such a strange story, unfortunately so bare of supporting evidence, might imperil his reputation as an investigator. Moreover, the calls of his proper work were urgent. So that after a month or so, save for an occasional reminder to certain dealers, he had reluctantly to abandon the quest for the crystal egg, and from that day to this it remains undiscovered. Occasionally however, he tells me, and I can quite believe him, he has bursts of zeal in which he abandons his more urgent occupation and resumes the search.

Whether or not it will remain lost for ever, with the material and origin of it, are things equally speculative at the present time. If the present purchaser is a collector, one would have expected the inquiries of Mr Wace to have reached him through the dealers. He has been able to discover Mr Cave's clergyman and 'Oriental' – no other than the Rev James Parker and the young Prince of Bosso-Kuni in Java. I am obliged to them for certain particulars. The object of the Prince was simply curiosity – and extravagance. He was so eager to buy, because Cave was so oddly reluctant to sell. It is just as possible that the buyer in the second instance was simply a casual purchaser and not a collector at all, and the crystal egg, for all I know, may at the present moment be within a mile of me, decorating a drawing-room or serving as a paper-weight – its remarkable functions all unknown. Indeed, it is partly with the idea of such a possibility that I have thrown this narrative into a form that will give it a chance of being read by the ordinary consumer of fiction.

. My own ideas in the matter are practically identical with those of Mr Wace. I believe the crystal on the mast in Mars and the crystal egg of Mr Cave's to be in some physical, but at present quite inexplicable, way *en rapport*, and we both believe further that the terrestrial crystal must have been – possibly at some remote date – sent hither from that planet, in order to give the Martians a near view of our affairs. Possibly the fellows to the crystals in the other masts are also on our globe. No theory of hallucination suffices for the facts.

The Gioconda of the Twilight Noon

J.G. BALLARD

'THOSE CONFOUNDED GULLS!' Richard Maitland complained to his wife. 'Can't you drive them away?'

Judith hovered behind the wheelchair, her hands glancing around his bandaged eyes like nervous doves. She peered across the lawn to the river bank. 'Try not to think about them, darling. They're just sitting there.'

'Just? That's the trouble!' Maitland raised his cane and struck the air vigorously. 'I can feel them all out there, watching me!'

They had taken his mother's house for his convalescence, partly on the assumption that the rich store of visual memories would in some way compensate for Maitland's temporary blindness – a trivial eye injury had become infected, eventually requiring surgery and a month's bandaged darkness. However, they had failed to reckon with the huge extension of his other senses. The house was five miles from the coast, but at low tide a flock of the greedy estuarine birds would fly up the river and alight on the exposed mud fifty yards from where Maitland sat in his wheelchair in the centre of the lawn. Judith could barely hear the gulls, but to Maitland their ravenous pecking filled the warm air like the cries of some savage Dionysian chorus. He had a vivid image of the wet banks streaming with the blood of thousands of dismembered fish.

Fretting impotently to himself, he listened as their voices suddenly fell away. Then, with a sharp sound like tearing cloth, the entire flock rose into the air. Maitland sat up stiffly in the wheelchair, the cane clasped like a cudgel in his right hand, half-expecting the gulls to swerve down on to the placid lawn, their fierce beaks tearing at the bandages over his eyes.

As if to conjure them away, he chanted aloud:

> 'The nightingales are singing near
> The Convent of the Sacred Heart,
> And sang within the bloody wood
> When Agamemnon cried aloud . . .!'

During the fortnight since his return from the hospital Judith had read most of the early Eliot aloud to him. The flock of unseen gulls seemed to come straight out of that grim archaic landscape.

The birds settled again, and Judith took a few hesitant steps across the

59

lawn, her dim form interrupting the even circle of light within his eyes. 'They sound like a shoal of piranha,' he said with a forced laugh. 'What are they doing – stripping a bull?'

'Nothing, dear, as far as I can see. . . .' Judith's voice dipped on this last word. Even though Maitland's blindness was only temporary – in fact, by twisting the bandages he could see a blurred but coherent image of the garden with its willows screening the river – she still treated him to all the traditional circumlocutions, hedging him with the elaborate taboos erected by the seeing to hide them from the blind. The only real cripples, Maitland reflected, were the perfect in limb.

'Dick, I have to drive into town to collect the groceries. You'll be all right for half an hour?'

'Of course. Just sound the horn when you come back.'

The task of looking after the rambling country house single-handed – Maitland's widowed mother was on a steamer cruise in the Mediterranean – limited the time Judith could spend with him. Fortunately his long familiarity with the house saved her from having to guide him around it. A few rope hand-rails and one or two buffers of cotton wool taped to dangerous table corners had been enough. Indeed, once upstairs Maitland moved about the winding corridors and dark back staircases with more ease than Judith, and certainly with far more willingness – often in the evening she would go in search of Maitland and be startled to see her blind husband step soundlessly from a doorway two or three feet from her as he wandered among the old attics and dusty lofts. His rapt expression, as he hunted some memory of childhood, reminded her in a curious way of his mother, a tall, handsome woman whose bland smile always seemed to conceal some potent private world.

To begin with, when Maitland had chafed under the bandages, Judith had spent all morning and afternoon reading the newspapers aloud to him, then a volume of poems and even, heroically, the start of a novel, *Moby Dick*. Within a few days, however, Maitland had come to terms with his blindness, and the constant need for some sort of external stimulation faded. He discovered what every blind person soon finds out – that its external optical input is only part of the mind's immense visual activity. He had expected to be plunged into a profound Stygian darkness, but instead his brain was filled with a ceaseless play of light and colour. At times, as he lay back in the morning sunlight, he would see exquisite revolving patterns of orange light, like huge solar discs. These would gradually recede to brilliant pinpoints, shining above a veiled landscape across which dim forms moved like animals over an African veldt at dusk.

At other times forgotten memories impinged themselves on this screen, what he assumed to be visual relics of his childhood long buried in his mind.

It was these images, with all their tantalizing associations, that most intrigued Maitland. By letting his mind drift into reverie he could almost summon them at will, watching passively as these elusive landscapes materialized like visiting spectres before his inner eye. One in particular, composed of fleeting glimpses of steep cliffs, a dark corridor of mirrors and a tall, high-gabled house within a wall, recurred persistently, although its unrelated details owed nothing to his memory. Maitland tried to explore it, fixing the blue cliffs or the tall house in his mind and waiting for their associations to gather. But the noise of the gulls and Judith's to and fro movements across the garden distracted him.

''Bye, darling! See you later!'

Maitland raised his cane in reply. He listened to the car move off down the drive, its departure subtly altering the auditory profile of the house. Wasps buzzed among the ivy below the kitchen windows, hovering over the oil stains in the gravel. A line of trees swayed in the warm air, muffling Judith's last surge of acceleration. For once the gulls were silent. Usually this would have roused Maitland's suspicions, but he lay back, turning the wheels of the chair so that he faced the sun.

Thinking of nothing, he watched the aureoles of light mushroom soundlessly within his mind. Occasionally the shifting of the willows or the sounds of a bee bumping around the glass water jug on the table beside him would end the sequence. This extreme sensitivity to the faintest noise or movement reminded him of the hypersensitivity of epileptics, or of rabies victims in their grim terminal convulsions. It was almost as if the barriers between the deepest level of the nervous system and the external world had been removed, those muffling layers of blood and bone, reflex and convention. . . .

With a barely perceptible pause in his breathing, Maitland relaxed carefully in the chair. Projected on to the screen within his mind was the image he had glimpsed before, of a rocky coastline whose dark cliffs loomed through an off-shore mist. The whole scene was drab and colourless. Overhead low clouds reflected the pewter surface of the water. As the mist cleared he moved nearer the shore, and watched the waves breaking on the rocks. The plumes of foam searched like white serpents among the pools and crevices for the caves that ran deep into the base of the cliff.

Desolate and unfrequented, the coast reminded Maitland only of the cold shores of Tierra del Fuego and the ships' graveyards of Cape Horn, rather than of any memories of his own. Yet the cliffs drew nearer, rising into the air above him, as if their identity reflected some image deep within Maitland's mind.

Still separated from them by the interval of grey water, Maitland followed the shoreline, until the cliffs divided at the mouth of a small estuary. Instantly the light cleared. The water within the estuary glowed with an almost spectral vibrancy. The blue rocks of the surrounding cliffs, penetrated by small grottoes and caverns, emitted a soft prismatic light, as if illuminated by some subterranean lantern.

Holding this scene before him, Maitland searched the shores of the estuary. The caverns were deserted, but as he neared them the luminous archways began to reflect the light like a hall of mirrors. At the same time he found himself entering the dark, high-gabled house he had seen previously, and which had now superimposed itself on his dream. Somewhere within it, masked by the mirrors, a tall, green-robed figure watched him, receding through the caves and groins. . . .

A motor-car horn sounded, a gay succession of toots. The gravel grating beneath its tyres, a car swung into the drive.

'Judith here, darling,' his wife called. 'Everything all right?'

Cursing under his breath, Maitland fumbled for his cane. The image of the dark coast and the estuary with its spectral caves had gone. Like a blind worm, he turned his blunted head at the unfamiliar sounds and shapes in the garden.

'Are you all right?' Judith's footsteps crossed the lawn. 'What's the matter, you're all hunched up – have those birds been annoying you?'

'No, leave them.' Maitland lowered his cane, realizing that although not visibly present in his inward vision, the gulls had played an oblique role in its creation. The foam-white sea-birds, hunters of the albatross. . . .

With an effort he said: 'I was asleep.'

Judith knelt down and took his hands. 'I'm sorry. I'll ask one of the men to build a scare-crow. That should – – '

'No!' Maitland pulled his hands away. 'They're not worrying me at all.' Levelling his voice, he said: 'Did you see anyone in the town?'

'Dr Phillips. He said you should be able to take off the bandages in about ten days.'

'Good. There's no hurry, though. I want the job done properly.'

After Judith had walked back Maitland tried to return to his reverie, but the image remained sealed behind the screen of his consciousness.

At breakfast the next morning Judith read him the mail.

'There's a postcard from your mother. They're near Malta, somewhere called Gozo.'

'Give it to me.' Maitland felt the card in his hands. 'Gozo – that was Calypso's island. She kept Ulysses there for seven years, promised him eternal youth if he'd stay with her forever.'

'I'm not surprised.' Judith inclined the card towards her. 'If we could spare the time you and I should go there for a holiday. Wine-dark seas, a sky like heaven, blue rocks. Bliss.'

'Blue?'

'Yes. I suppose it's the bad printing. They can't really be like that.'

'They are, actually.' Still holding the card, Maitland went out into the garden, feeling his way along the string guide-rail. As he settled himself in the wheelchair he reflected that there were other correspondences in the graphic arts. The same blue rocks and spectral grottoes could be seen in

Leonardo's *Virgin of the Rocks*, one of the most forbidding and most enigmatic of his paintings. The madonna sitting on a bare ledge by the water beneath the dark overhang of the cavern's mouth was like the presiding spirit of some enchanted marine realm, waiting for those cast on to the rocky shores of this world's end. As in so many of Leonardo's paintings, all its unique longings and terrors were to be found in the landscape in the background. Here, through an archway among the rocks, could be seen the crystal blue cliffs that Maitland had glimpsed in his reverie.

'Shall I read it out to you?' Judith had crossed the lawn.

'What?'

'Your mother's postcard. You're holding it in your hand.'

'Sorry. Please do.'

As he listened to the brief message, Maitland waited for Judith to return to the house. When she had gone he sat quietly for a few minutes. The distant sounds of the river came to him through the trees, and the faint cry of gulls swooping on to the banks further down the estuary.

This time, almost as if recognizing Maitland's need, the vision came to him quickly. He passed the dark cliffs, and the waves vaulting into the cave mouths, and then entered the twilight world of the grottoes beside the river. Outside, through the stone galleries, he could see the surface of the water glittering like a sheet of prisms, the soft blue light reflected in the vitreous mirrors which formed the cavern walls. At the same time he sensed that he was entering the high-gabled house, whose surrounding wall was the cliff face he had seen from the sea. The rock-like vaults of the house glowed with the olive-black colours of the marine deeps, and curtains of old lace-work hung from the doors and windows like ancient nets.

A staircase ran through the grotto, its familiar turnings leading to the inner reaches of the cavern. Looking upwards, he saw the green-robed figure watching him from an archway. Her face was hidden from him, veiled by the light reflected off the damp mirrors on the walls. Impelled forward up the steps, Maitland reached towards her, and for an instant the face of the figure cleared. . . .

'Judith!' Rocking forward in his chair, Maitland searched helplessly for the water jug on the table, his left hand drumming at his forehead in an attempt to drive away the vision and its terrifying lamia.

'Richard! What is it?'

He heard his wife's hurried footsteps across the lawn, and then felt her hands steadying his own.

'Darling, what on earth's going on? You're pouring with perspiration!'

That afternoon, when he was left alone again, Maitland approached the dark labyrinth more cautiously. At low tide the gulls returned to the mud flats below the garden, and their archaic cries carried his mind back into its deeps like mortuary birds bearing away the body of Tristan. Guarding himself and his own fears, he moved slowly through the luminous chambers

63

of the subterranean house, averting his eyes from the green-robed enchantress who watched him from the staircase.

Later, when Judith brought his tea to him on a tray, he ate carefully, talking to her in measured tones.

'What did you see in your nightmare?' she asked.

'A house of mirrors under the sea, and a deep cavern,' he told her. 'I could see everything, but in a strange way, like the dreams of people who have been blind for a long time.'

Throughout the afternoon and evening he returned to the grotto at intervals, moving circumspectly through the outer chambers, always aware of the robed figure waiting for him in the doorway to its innermost sanctum.

The next morning Dr Phillips called to change his dressing.

'Excellent, excellent,' he commented, holding his torch in one hand as he retaped Maitland's eyelids to his cheeks. 'Another week and you'll be out of this for good. At least you know what it's like for the blind.'

'One can envy them,' Maitland said.

'Really?'

'They see with an inner eye, you know. In a sense everything is more real.'

'That's a point of view.' Dr Phillips replaced the bandages. He drew the curtains. 'What have you seen with your's?'

Maitland made no reply. Dr Phillips had examined him in the darkened study, but the thin torch beam and the few needles of light around the curtains had filled his brain like arc lights. He waited for the glare to subside, realizing that his inner world, the grotto, the house of mirrors and the enchantress, had been burned out of his mind by the sunlight.

'They're hypnagogic images,' Dr Phillips remarked, fastening his bag. 'You've been living in an unusual zone, sitting around doing nothing but with your optic nerves alert, a no-man's land between sleep and consciousness. I'd expect all sorts of strange things.'

After he had gone Maitland said to the unseen walls, his lips whispering below the bandages: 'Doctor, give me back my eyes.'

It took him two full days to recover from this brief interval of external light. Laboriously, rock by rock, he re-explored the hidden coastline, willing himself through the enveloping sea-mists, searching for the lost estuary.

At last the luminous beaches appeared again.

'I think I'd better sleep alone tonight,' he said. 'I'll use mother's room.'

'Of course, Richard. What's the matter?'

'I suppose I'm restless. I'm not getting much exercise and there are only three days to go. I don't want to disturb you.'

He found his own way into his mother's bedroom, glimpsed only occasionally during the years since his marriage. The high bed, the deep rustle of silks and the echoes of forgotten scents carried him back to his earliest childhood. He lay awake all night, listening to the sounds of the river reflected off the cut-glass ornaments over the fireplace.

At dawn, when the gulls flew up from the estuary, he visited the blue grottoes again, and the tall house in the cliff. Knowing its tenant now, the green-robed watcher on the staircase, he decided to wait for the morning light. Her beckoning eyes, the pale lantern of her smile, floated before him.

However, after breakfast Dr Phillips returned.

'Right,' he told Maitland briskly, leading him in from the lawn. 'Let's have those bandages off.'

'For the last time, Doctor?' Judith asked. 'Are you sure?'

'Certainly. We don't want this to go on for ever, do we?' He steered Maitland into the study. 'Sit down here, Richard. You draw the curtains, Judith.'

Maitland stood up, feeling for the desk. 'But you said it would take three more days, Doctor.'

'I dare say. But I didn't want you to get over-excited. What's the matter? You're hovering about like an old woman. Don't you want to see again?'

'See?' Maitland repeated numbly. 'Of course.' He subsided limply into a chair as Dr Phillips' hands unfastened the bandages. A profound sense of loss had come over him. 'Doctor, could I put it off for – – '

'Nonsense. You can see perfectly. Don't worry, I'm not going to fling back the curtains. It'll be a full day before you can see freely. I'll give you a set of filters to wear. Anyway, these dressings let through more light than you imagine.'

At eleven o'clock the next morning, his eyes shielded only by a pair of sunglasses, Maitland walked out on to the lawn. Judith stood on the terrace, and watched him make his way around the wheelchair. When he reached the willows she called: 'All right, darling? Can you see me?'

Without replying, Maitland looked back at the house. He removed the sunglasses and threw them aside on to the grass. He gazed through the trees at the estuary, at the blue surface of the water stretching to the opposite bank. Hundreds of gulls stood by the water, their heads turned in profile to reveal the full curve to their beaks. He looked over his shoulder at the high-gabled house, recognizing the one he had seen in his dream. Everything about it, like the bright river which slid past him, seemed dead.

Suddenly the gulls rose into the air, their cries drowning the sounds of Judith's voice as she called again from the terrace. In a dense spiral, gathering itself off the ground like an immense scythe, the gulls wheeled into the air over his head and swirled over the house.

Quickly Maitland pushed back the branches of the willows and walked down on to the bank.

A moment later, Judith heard his shout above the cries of the gulls. The sound came half in pain and half in triumph, and she ran down to the trees uncertain whether he had injured himself or discovered something pleasing.

Then she saw him standing on the bank, his head raised to the sunlight, the bright carmine on his cheeks and hands, an eager, unrepentant Oedipus.

65

The Tunnel under the World

FREDERIK POHL

ON THE MORNING OF June the 15th, Guy Burckhardt woke up screaming out of a dream.

It was more real than any dream he had ever had in his life. He could still hear and feel the sharp, ripping-metal explosion, the violent heave that had tossed him furiously out of bed, the searing wave of heat.

He sat up convulsively and stared, not believing what he saw, at the quiet room and the bright sunlight coming in the window.

He croaked, 'Mary?'

His wife was not in the bed next to him. The covers were tumbled and awry, as though she had just left it, and the memory of the dream was so strong that instinctively he found himself searching the floor to see if the dream explosion had thrown her down.

But she wasn't there. Of course she wasn't, he told himself, looking at the familiar vanity and slipper chair, the uncracked window, the unbuckled wall. It had only been a dream.

'Guy?' His wife was calling him querulously from the foot of the stairs. 'Guy, dear, are you all right?'

He called weakly, 'Sure.'

There was a pause. Then Mary said doubtfully, 'Breakfast is ready. Are you sure you're all right? I thought I heard you yelling – '

Burckhardt said more confidently, 'I had a bad dream, honey. Be right down.'

In the shower, punching the lukewarm-and-cologne he favoured, he told himself that it had been a beaut of a dream. Still, bad dreams weren't unusual, especially bad dreams about explosions. In the past thirty years of H-bomb jitters, who had not dreamed of explosions?

Even Mary had dreamed of them, it turned out, for he started to tell her about the dream, but she cut him off. 'You *did?*' Her voice was astonished. 'Why, dear, I dreamed the same thing! Well, almost the same thing. I didn't actually *hear* anything. I dreamed that something woke me up, and then there was a sort of quick bang, and then something hit me on the head. And that was all. Was yours like that?'

Burckhardt coughed. 'Well, no,' he said. Mary was not one of these strong-as-a-man, brave-as-a-tiger women. It was not necessary, he

66

thought, to tell her all the little details of the dream that made it seem so real. No need to mention the splintered ribs, and the salt bubble in his throat, and the agonized knowledge that this was death. He said, 'Maybe there really was some kind of explosion downtown. Maybe we heard it and it started us dreaming.'

Mary reached over and patted his hand absently. 'Maybe,' she agreed. 'It's almost half past eight, dear. Shouldn't you hurry? You don't want to be late to the office.'

He gulped his food, kissed her, and rushed out – not so much to be on time as to see if his guess had been right.

But downtown Tylerton looked as it always had. Coming in on the bus, Burckhardt watched critically out of the window, seeking evidence of an explosion. There wasn't any. If anything, Tylerton looked better than it ever had before: it was a beautiful crisp day, the sky was cloudless, the buildings were clean and inviting. They had, he observed, steamblasted the Power & Light Building, the town's only skyscraper – that was the penalty of having Contro Chemicals main plant on the outskirts of town; the fumes from the cascade stills left their mark on stone buildings.

None of the usual crowd was on the bus, so there wasn't anyone Burckhardt could ask about the explosion. And by the time he got out at the corner of Fifth and Lehigh and the bus rolled away with a muted diesel moan, he had pretty well convinced himself that it was all imagination.

He stopped at the cigar stand in the lobby of his office building, but Ralph wasn't behind the counter. The man who sold him his pack of cigarettes was a stranger.

'Where's Mr Stebbins?' Burckhardt asked.

The man said politely, 'Sick, sir. He'll be in tomorrow. A pack of Marlins today?'

'Chesterfields,' Burckhardt corrected.

'Certainly, sir,' the man said. But what he took from the rack and slid across the counter was an unfamiliar green-and-yellow pack.

'Do try these, sir,' he suggested. 'They contain an anti-cough factor. Ever notice how ordinary cigarettes make you choke every once in a while?'

Burckhardt said suspiciously. 'I never heard of this brand.'

'Of course not. They're something new.' Burckhardt hesitated, and the man said persuasively, 'Look, try them out at my risk. If you don't like them, bring back the empty pack and I'll refund your money. Fair enough?'

Burckhardt shrugged. 'How can I lose? But give me a pack of Chesterfields, too, will you?'

He opened the pack and lit one while he waited for the elevator. They weren't bad, he decided, though he was suspicious of cigarettes that had the tobacco chemically treated in any way. But he didn't think much of Ralph's stand-in; it would raise hell with the trade at the cigar stand if the man tried to give every customer the same high-pressure sales talk.

The elevator door opened with a low-pitched sound of music. Burckhardt and two or three others got in and he nodded to them as the door closed. The thread of music switched off and the speaker in the ceiling of the cab began its usual commercials.

No, not the *usual* commercials, Burckhardt realized. He had been exposed to the captive-audience commercials so long that they hardly registered on the outer ear any more, but what was coming from the recorded programme in the basement of the building caught his attention. It wasn't merely that the brands were mostly unfamiliar; it was a difference in pattern.

There were jingles with an insistent, bouncy rhythm, about soft drinks he had never tasted. There was a rapid patter dialogue between what sounded like two ten-year-old boys about a candy bar, followed by an authoritative bass rumble: 'Go right out and get a DELICIOUS Choco-Bite and eat your TANGY Choco-Bite *all up*. That's *Choco-Bite!*' There was a sobbing female whine: I *wish* I had a Feckle Freezer! I'd do *anything* for a Feckle Freezer!' Burckhardt reached his floor and left the elevator in the middle of the last one. It left him a little uneasy. The commercials were not for familiar brands; there was no feeling of use and custom to them.

But the office was happily normal – except that Mr Barth wasn't in. Miss Mitkin, yawning at the reception desk, didn't know exactly why. 'His home phoned, that's all. He'll be in tomorrow.'

'Maybe he went to the plant. It's right near his house.'

She looked indifferent. 'Yeah.'

A thought struck Burckhardt. 'But today is June the 15th! It's quarterly tax return day – he has to sign the return!'

Miss Mitkin shrugged to indicate that that was Burckhardt's problem, not hers. She returned to her nails.

Thoroughly exasperated, Burckhardt went to his desk. It wasn't that he couldn't sign the tax returns as well as Barth, he thought resentfully. It simply wasn't his job, that was all; it was a responsibility that Barth, as office manager for Contro Chemicals' downtown office, should have taken.

He thought briefly of calling Barth at his home or trying to reach him at the factory, but he gave up the idea quickly enough. He didn't really care much for the people at the factory and the less contact he had with them the better. He had been to the factory once, with Barth: it had been a confusing and, in a way, a frightening experience. Barring a handful of executives and engineers, there wasn't a soul in the factory – that is, Burckhardt corrected himself, remembering what Barth had told him, not a *living* soul – just the machines.

According to Barth, each machine was controlled by a sort of computer which reproduced, in its electronic snarl, the actual memory and mind of a human being. It was an unpleasant thought. Barth, laughing, had assured him that there was no Frankenstein business of robbing graveyards and implanting brains in machines. It was only a matter, he said, of transferring a man's habit patterns from brain cells to vacuum-tube cells. It didn't hurt the man and it didn't make the machine into a monster.

But they made Burckhardt uncomfortable all the same.

He put Barth and the factory and all his other little irritations out of his mind and tackled the tax returns. It took him until noon to verify the figures – which Barth could have done out of his memory and his private ledger in ten minutes, Burckhardt resentfully reminded himself.

He sealed them in an envelope and walked out to Miss Mitkin. 'Since Mr Barth isn't here, we'd better go to lunch in shifts,' he said. 'You can go first.'

'Thanks.' Miss Mitkin languidly took her bag out of the desk drawer and began to apply make-up.

Burckhardt offered her the envelope. 'Drop this in the mail for me, will you? Uh – wait a minute. I wonder if I ought to phone Mr Barth to make sure. Did his wife say whether he was able to take phone calls?'

'Didn't say.' Miss Mitkin blotted her lips carefully with a Kleenex. 'Wasn't his wife, anyway. It was his daughter who called and left the message.'

'The kid?' Burckhardt frowned. 'I thought she was away at school.'

'She called, that's all I know.'

Burckhardt went back to his own office and stared distastefully at the unopened mail on his desk. He didn't like nightmares; they spoiled his whole day. He should have stayed in bed, like Barth.

A funny thing happened on his way home. There was a disturbance at the corner where he usually caught his bus – someone was screaming something about a new kind of deep-freeze – so he walked an extra block. He saw the bus coming and started to trot. But behind him, someone was calling his name. He looked over his shoulder; a small harried-looking man was hurrying towards him.

Burckhardt hesitated, and then recognized him. It was a casual acquaintance named Swanson. Burckhardt sourly observed that he had already missed the bus.

He said, 'Hello.'

Swanson's face was desperately eager. 'Burckhardt?' he asked inquiringly, with an odd intensity. And then he just stood there silently, watching Burckhardt's face with a burning eagerness that dwindled to a faint hope and died to a regret. He was searching for something, waiting for something, Burckhardt thought. But whatever it was he wanted,

Burckhardt didn't know how to supply it.

Burckhardt coughed and said again, 'Hello, Swanson.'

Swanson didn't even acknowledge the greeting. He merely sighed a very deep sigh.

'Nothing doing,' he mumbled, apparently to himself. He nodded abstractedly to Burckhardt and turned away.

Burckhardt watched the slumped shoulders disappear in the crowd. It was an *odd* sort of day, he thought, and one he didn't much like. Things weren't going right.

Riding home on the next bus, he brooded about it. It wasn't anything terrible or disastrous; it was something out of his experience entirely. You live your life, like any man, and you form a network of impressions and reactions. You *expect* things. When you open your medicine chest, your razor is expected to be on the second shelf; when you lock your front door, you expect to have to give it a slight extra tug to make it latch.

It isn't the things that are right and perfect in your life that make it familiar. It is the things that are just a litle bit wrong – the sticking latch, the light switch at the head of the stairs that needs an extra push because the spring is old and weak, the rug that unfailingly skids underfoot.

It wasn't just that things were wrong with the pattern of Burckhardt's life; it was that the *wrong* things were wrong. For instance, Barth hadn't come into the office, yet Barth *always* came in.

Burckhardt brooded about it through dinner. He brooded about it, despite his wife's attempt to interest him in a game of bridge with the neighbours, all through the evening. The neighbours were people he liked – Anne and Farley Dennerman. He had known them all their lives. But they were odd and brooding, too, this night and he barely listened to Dennerman's complaints about not being able to get good phone service or his wife's comments on the disgusting variety of television commercials they had these days.

Burckhardt was well on the way to setting an all-time record for continuous abstraction when, around midnight, with a suddenness that surprised him – he was strangely *aware* of it happening – he turned over in his bed and, quickly and completely, fell asleep.

On the morning of June the 15th, Burckhardt woke up screaming.

It was more real than any dream he had ever had in his life. He could still hear the explosion, feel the blast that crushed him against a wall. It did not seem right that he should be sitting bolt upright in bed in an undisturbed room.

His wife came pattering up the stairs. 'Darling!' she cried. 'What's the matter?'

He mumbled, 'Nothing. Bad dream.'

She relaxed, hand on heart. In an angry tone, she started to say: 'You gave me such a shock – '

But a noise from outside interrupted her. There was a wail of sirens and a clang of bells; it was loud and shocking.

The Burckhardts stared at each other for a heartbeat, then hurried fearfully to the window.

There were no rumbling fire engines in the street, only a small panel truck, cruising slowly along. Flaring loudspeaker horns crowned its top. From them issued the screaming sounds of sirens, growing in intensity, mixed with the rumble of heavy-duty engines and the sound of bells. It was a perfect record of a fire engine arriving at a four-alarm blaze.

Burckhardt said in amazement, 'Mary, that's against the law! Do you know what they're doing? They're playing records of a fire. What are they up to?'

'Maybe it's a practical joke,' his wife offered.

'Joke? Waking up the whole neighbourhood at six o'clock in the morning?' He shook his head. 'The police will be here in ten minutes,' he predicted. 'Wait and see.'

But the police weren't – not in ten minutes, or at all. Whoever the pranksters in the car were, they apparently had a police permit for their games.

The car took a position in the middle of the block and stood silent for a few minutes. Then there was a crackle from the speaker, and a giant voice chanted:

'Feckle Freezers!
Feckle Freezers!
Gotta have a
Feckle Freezer!
Feckle, Feckle, Feckle,
Feckle, Feckle, Feckle – '

It went on and on. Every house on the block had faces staring out of windows by then. The voice was not merely loud; it was nearly deafening.

Burckhardt shouted to his wife, over the uproar, 'What the hell is a Feckle Freezer?'

'Some kind of a freezer, I guess, dear,' she shrieked back unhelpfully.

Abruptly the noise stopped and the truck stood silent. It was a still misty morning; the sun's rays came horizontally across the rooftops. It was impossible to believe that, a moment ago, the silent block had been bellowing the name of a freezer.

'A crazy advertising trick,' Burckhardt said bitterly. He yawned and turned away from the window. 'Might as well get dressed. I guess that's the end of – '

The bellow caught him from behind; it was almost like a hard slap on

71

the ears. A harsh, sneering voice, louder than the archangel's trumpet, howled:

'Have you got a freezer? *It stinks!* If it isn't a Feckle Freezer, *it stinks!* If it's a last year's Feckle Freezer, *it stinks!* Only this year's Feckle Freezer is any good at all! You know who owns an Ajax Freezer? Fairies own Ajax Freezers! You know who owns a Triplecold Freezer? Commies own Triplecold Freezers! Every freezer but a brand-new Feckle Freezer *stinks!*'

The voice screamed inarticulately with rage. 'I'm warning you! Get out and buy a Feckle Freezer right away! Hurry up! Hurry for Feckle! Hurry for Feckle! Hurry, hurry, hurry, Feckle, Feckle, Feckle, Feckle, Feckle, Feckle...'

It stopped eventually. Burckhardt licked his lips. He started to say to his wife, 'Maybe we ought to call the police about – ' when the speakers erupted again. It caught him off guard; it was intended to catch him off guard. It screamed:

'Feckle, Feckle, Feckle, Feckle, Feckle, Feckle, Feckle, Feckle. Cheap freezers ruin your food. You'll get sick and throw up. You'll get sick and die. Buy a Feckle, Feckle, Feckle, Feckle! Ever take a piece of meat out of the freezer you've got and see how rotten and mouldy it is? Buy a Feckle, Feckle, Feckle, Feckle, Feckle. Do you want to eat rotten, stinking food? Or do you want to wise up and buy a Feckle, Feckle, Feckle – '

That did it. With fingers that kept stabbing the wrong holes, Burckhardt finally managed to dial the local police station. He got a busy signal – it was apparent that he was not the only one with the same idea – and while he was shakingly dialling again, the noise outside stopped.

He looked out the window. The truck was gone.

Burckhardt loosened his tie and ordered another Frosty-Flip from the waiter. If only they wouldn't keep the Crystal Café so *hot!* The new paint job – searing reds and blinding yellows – was bad enough, but someone seemed to have the delusion that this was January instead of June; the place was a good ten degrees warmer than outside.

He swallowed the Frosty-Flip in two gulps. It had a kind of peculiar flavour, he thought, but not bad. It certainly cooled you off, just as the waiter had promised. He reminded himself to pick up a carton of them on the way home; Mary might like them. She was always interested in something new.

He stood up awkwardly as the girl came across the restaurant towards him. She was the most beautiful thing he had ever seen in Tylerton. Chin-height, honey-blonde hair, and a figure that – well, it was all hers. There was no doubt in the world that the dress that clung to her was the only thing she wore. He felt as if he were blushing as she greeted him.

'Mr Burckhardt.' The voice was like distant tomtoms. 'It's wonderful of you to let me see you, after this morning.'

He cleared his throat. 'Not at all. Won't you sit down, Miss – '

'April Horn,' she murmured, sitting down – beside him, not where he had pointed on the other side of the table. 'Call me April, won't you?'

She was wearing some kind of perfume. Burckhardt noted with what little of his mind was functioning at all. It didn't seem fair that she should be using perfume as well as everything else. He came to with a start and realized that the waiter was leaving with an order for *filets mignon* for two.

'Hey!' he objected.

'Please, Mr Burckhardt.' Her shoulder was against his, her face was turned to him, her breath was warm, her expression was tender and solicitous. 'This is all on the Feckle Corporation. Please let them – it's the *least* they can do.'

He felt her hand burrowing into his pocket.

'I put the price of the meal into your pocket,' she whispered conspiratorially. 'Please do that for me, won't you? I mean I'd appreciate it if you'd pay the waiter – I'm old-fashioned about things like that.'

She smiled meltingly, then became mock-businesslike. 'But you must take the money,' she insisted. 'Why, you're letting Feckle off lightly if you do! You could sue them for every nickel they've got, disturbing your sleep like that.'

With a dizzy feeling, as though he had just seen someone make a rabbit disappear into a top hat, he said, 'Why, it really wasn't so bad, uh, April. A little noisy, maybe, but – '

'Oh, Mr Burckhardt!' The blue eyes were wide and admiring. 'I *knew* you'd understand. It's just that – well, it's such a *wonderful* freezer that some of the outside men get carried away, so to speak. As soon as the main office found out about what happened, they sent representatives around to every house on the block to apologize. Your wife told us where we could phone you – and I'm so very pleased that you were willing to let me have lunch with you, so that I could apologize, too. Because truly, Mr Burckhardt, it is a *fine* freezer.

'I shouldn't tell you this, but – ' the blue eyes were shyly lowered – 'I'd do almost anything for Feckle Freezers. It's more than a job to me.' She looked up. She was enchanting. 'I bet you think I'm silly, don't you?'

Burckhardt coughed. 'Well, I – '

'Oh, you don't want to be unkind!' She shook her head. 'No, don't pretend. You think it's silly. But really, Mr Burckhardt, you wouldn't think so if you knew more about the Feckle. Let me show you this little booklet – '

Burckhardt got back from lunch a full hour later. It wasn't only the girl who delayed him. There had been a curious interview with a little man named Swanson, whom he barely knew, who had stopped him with desperate urgency on the street – and then left him cold.

But it didn't matter much. Mr Barth, for the first time since

Burckhardt had worked there, was out for the day – leaving Burckhardt stuck with the quarterly tax returns.

What did matter, though, was that somehow he had signed a purchase order for a twelve-cubic-foot Feckle Freezer, upright model, self-defrosting, list price $625, with a ten per cent 'courtesy' discount – 'Because of that *horrid* affair this morning, Mr Burckhardt,' she had said.

And he wasn't sure how he could explain it to his wife.

He needn't have worried. As he walked in the front door, his wife said almost immediately, 'I wonder if we can't afford a new freezer, dear. There was a man here to apologize about that noise and – well, we got to talking and – '

She had signed a purchase order, too.

It had been the damnedest day, Burckhardt thought later, on his way up to bed. But the day wasn't done with him yet. At the head of the stairs, the weakened spring in the electric light switch refused to click at all. He snapped it back and forth angrily, and, of course, succeeded in jarring the tumbler out of its pins. The wires shorted and every light in the house went out.

'Damn!' said Guy Burckhardt.

'Fuse?' His wife shrugged sleepily: 'Let it go till the morning, dear.'

Burckhardt shook his head. 'You go back to bed. I'll be right along.'

It wasn't so much that he cared about fixing the fuse, but he was too restless for sleep. He disconnected the bad switch with a screwdriver, stumbled down into the black kitchen, found the flashlight and climbed gingerly down the cellar stairs. He located a spare fuse, pushed an empty trunk over to the fuse box to stand on, and twisted out the old fuse.

When the new one was in, he heard the starting click and steady drone of the refrigerator in the kitchen overhead.

He headed back to the steps, and stopped.

Where the old trunk had been, the cellar floor gleamed oddly bright. He inspected it in the flashlight beam. It was metal!

'Son of a gun,' said Guy Burckhardt. He shook his head unbelievingly. He peered closer, rubbed the edges of the metallic patch with his thumb and acquired an annoying cut – the edges were *sharp*.

The stained cement floor of the cellar was a thin shell. He found a hammer and cracked it off in a dozen spots – everywhere was metal.

The whole cellar was a copper box. Even the cement-brick walls were false fronts over a metal sheath!

Baffled, he attacked on of the foundation beams. That, at least, was real wood. The glass in the cellar windows was real glass.

He sucked his bleeding thumb and tried the base of the cellar stairs. Real wood. He chipped at the bricks under the oil burner. Real bricks. The retaining walls, the floor – they were faked.

It was as though someone had shored up the house with a frame of

74

metal and then laboriously concealed the evidence.

The biggest surprise was the upside-down boat hull that blocked the rear half of the cellar, relic of a brief home workship period that Burckhardt had gone through a couple of years before. From above, it looked perfectly normal. Inside, though, where there should have been thwarts and seats and lockers, there was a mere tangle of braces, rough and unfinished.

'But I *built* that!' Burckhardt exclaimed, forgetting his thumb. He leaned against the hull dizzily, trying to think this thing through. For reasons beyond his comprehension, someone had taken his boat and his cellar away, maybe his whole house, and replaced them with a clever mock-up of the real thing.

'That's crazy,' he said to the empty cellar. He stared around in the light of the flash. He whispered, 'What in the name of Heaven would anybody do that for?'

Reason refused an answer; there wasn't any reasonable answer. For long minutes, Burckhardt contemplated the uncertain picture of his own sanity.

He peered under the boat again, hoping to reassure himself that it was a mistake, just his imagination. But the sloppy, unfinished bracing was unchanged. He crawled under for a better look, feeling the rough wood incredulously. Utterly impossible!

He switched off the flashlight and started to wriggle out. But he didn't make it. In the moment between the command to his legs to move and the crawling out, he felt a sudden draining weariness flooding through him.

Consciousness went – not easily, but as though it were being taken away, and Guy Burckhardt was asleep.

On the morning of June the 16th, Guy Burckhardt woke up in a cramped position huddled under the hull of the boat in his basement – and raced upstairs to find it was June the 15th.

The first thing he had done was to make a frantic, hasty inspection of the boat hull, the faked cellar floor, the imitation stone. They were all as he had remembered them – all completely unbelievable.

The kitchen was its placid, unexciting self. The electric clock was purring soberly around the dial. Almost six o'clock, it said. His wife would be waking at any moment.

Burckhardt flung open the front door and stared out into the quiet street. The morning paper was tossed carelessly against the steps – and as he retrieved it, he noticed that this was the 15th day of June.

But that was impossible. *Yesterday* was the 15th of June. It was not a date one would forget – it was quarterly tax-return day.

He went back into the hall and picked up the telephone; he dialled for

Weather Information, and got a well-modulated chant: '– and cooler, some showers. Barometric pressure thirty point zero four, rising ... United States Weather Bureau forecast for June the 15th. Warm and sunny, with high around – '

He hung the phone up. June the 15th.

'Holy heaven!' Burckhardt said prayerfully. Things were very odd indeed. He heard the ring of his wife's alarm and bounded up the stairs.

Mary Burckhardt was sitting upright in bed with the terrified, uncomprehending stare of someone just waking out of a nightmare.

'Oh!' she gasped, as her husband came in the room. 'Darling, I just had the most *terrible* dream! It was like an explosion and – '

'Again?' Burckhardt asked, not very sympathetically. 'Mary, something's funny! I *knew* there was something wrong all day yesterday and – '

He went on to tell her about the copper box that was the cellar, and the odd mock-up someone had made of his boat. Mary looked astonished, then alarmed, then placatory and uneasy.

She said, 'Dear, are you *sure?* Because I was cleaning that old trunk out just last week and I didn't notice anything.'

'Positive!' said Guy Burckhardt. 'I dragged it over to the wall to step on it to put a new fuse in after we blew the lights out and – '

'After we what?' Mary was looking more than merely alarmed.

'After we blew the lights out. You know, when the switch at the head of the stairs stuck. I went down to the cellar and – '

Mary sat up in bed. 'Guy, the switch didn't stick. I turned out the lights myself last night.'

Burckhardt glared at his wife. 'Now I *know* you didn't! Come here and take a look!'

He stalked out to the landing and dramatically pointed to the bad switch, the one that he had unscrewed and left hanging the night before ...

Only it wasn't. It was as it had always been. Unbelieving, Burckhardt pressed it and the lights sprang up in both halls.

Mary, looking pale and worried, left him to go down to the kitchen and start breakfast. Burckhardt stood staring at the switch for a long time. His mental processes were gone beyond the point of disbelief and shock; they simply were not functioning.

He shaved and dressed and ate his breakfast in a state of numb introspection. Mary didn't disturb him; she was apprehensive and soothing. She kissed him goodbye as he hurried out to the bus without another word.

Miss Mitkin, at the reception desk, greeted him with a yawn. 'Morning,' she said drowsily. 'Mr Barth won't be in today.'

Burckhardt started to say something, but checked himself. She would not know that Barth hadn't been in yesterday, either, because she was tearing a June the 14th pad off her calendar to make way for the 'new' June the 15th sheet.

He staggered to his own desk and stared unseeingly at the morning's mail. It had not even been opened yet, but he knew that the Factory Distributors envelope contained an order for twenty thousand feet of the new acoustic tile, and the one from Finebeck & Sons was a complaint.

After a long while, he forced himself to open them. They were.

By lunchtime, driven by a desperate sense of urgency, Burckhardt made Miss Mitkin take her lunch hour first – the June-fifteenth-that-was-yesterday *he* had gone first. She went, looking vaguely worried about his strained insistence, but it made no difference to Burckhardt's mood.

The phone rang and Burckhardt picked it up abstractedly. 'Contro Chemicals Downtown, Burckhardt speaking.'

The voice said, 'This is Swanson,' and stopped.

Burckhardt waited expectantly, but that was all. He said, 'Hello?'

Again the pause. Then Swanson asked in sad resignation, 'Still nothing, eh?'

'Nothing what? Swanson, is there something you want? You came up to me yesterday and went through this routine. You – '

The voice crackled: 'Burckhardt! Oh, my good heavens, *you remember!* Stay right there – I'll be down in half an hour!'

'What's this all about?'

'Never mind,' the little man said exultantly. 'Tell you about it when I see you. Don't say any more over the phone – somebody may be listening. Just wait there. Say, hold on a minute. Will you be alone in the office?'

'Well, no. Miss Mitkin will probably – '

'Hell. Look, Burckhardt, where do you eat lunch? Is it good and noisy?'

'Why I suppose so. The Crystal Café. It's just about a block – '

'I know where it is. Meet you in half an hour!' And the receiver clicked.

The Crystal Café was no longer painted red, but the temperature was still up. And they had added piped-in music interpersed with commercials. The advertisements were for Frosty-Flip, Marlin Cigarettes – 'They're sanitized,' the announcer purred – and something called Choco-Bite candy bars that Burckhardt couldn't remember ever having heard of before. But he heard more about them quickly enough.

While he was waiting for Swanson to show up, a girl came through the restaurant with a tray of tiny scarlet-wrapped candies.

'Choco-Bites are *tangy*,' she was murmuring as she came close to his table. 'Choco-Bites are *tangier* than tangy!'

Burckhardt, intent on watching for the strange little man who had phoned him, paid little attention. But as she scattered a handful of the confections over the table next to his, smiling at the occupants, he caught a glimpse of her and turned to stare.

'Why, Miss Horn!' he said.

The girl dropped her tray of candies.

Burckhardt rose, concerned over the girl. 'Is something wrong?'

But she fled.

The manager of the restaurant was staring suspiciously at Burckhardt, who sank back in his seat and tried to look inconspicuous. He hadn't insulted the girl! Maybe she was just a very strictly reared young lady, he thought – in spite of the long bare legs under the cellophane skirt – and when he addressed her, she thought he was a masher.

Ridiculous idea. Burckhardt scowled uneasily and picked up his menu.

'Burckhardt!' It was a shrill whisper.

Burckhardt looked up over the top of his menu, startled. In the seat across from him, the little man named Swanson was sitting, tensely poised.

'Burckhardt!' the little man whispered again. 'Let's get out of here! They're on to you now. If you want to stay alive, come on!'

There was no arguing with the man. Burckhardt gave the hovering manager a sick apologetic smile and followed Swanson out. The little man seemed to know where he was going. In the street, he clutched Burckhardt by the elbow and hurried him off down the block.

'Did you see her?' he demanded. 'That Horn woman, in the phone booth? She'll have them here in five minutes, believe me, so hurry it up!'

Although the street was full of people and cars, nobody was paying any attention to Burckhardt and Swanson. The air had a nip in it – more like October than June, Burckhardt thought, in spite of the weather bureau. And he felt like a fool, following this mad little man down the street, running away from some 'them' towards – towards what? The little man might be crazy, but he was afraid. And the fear was infectious.

'In here!' panted the little man.

It was another restaurant – more of a bar, really, and a sort of second-rate place that Burckhardt never had patronized.

'Right straight through,' Swanson whispered; and Burckhardt, like a biddable boy, sidestepped through the mass of tables to the far end of the restaurant.

It was L-shaped, with a front on two streets at right angles to each other. They came out on the side street, Swanson staring coldly back at the question-looking cashier, and crossed to the opposite sidewalk.

They were under the marquee of a movie theatre. Swanson's expression began to relax.

'Lost them!' he crowed softly. 'We're almost there.'

He stepped up to the window and bought two tickets. Burckhardt trailed him into the theatre. It was a weekday matinee and the place was almost empty. From the screen came sounds of gunfire and horses' hoofs.

A solitary usher, leaning against a bright brass rail, looked briefly at them and went back to staring boredly at the picture as Swanson led Burckhardt down a flight of carpeted marble steps.

They were in the lounge and it was empty. There was a door for men and one for ladies; and there was a third door, marked MANAGER in gold letters. Swanson listened at the door, and gently opened it and peered inside.

'Okay,' he said, gesturing.

Burckhardt followed him through an empty office, to another door – a closet, probably, because it was unmarked.

But it was no closet. Swanson opened it warily, looked inside, then motioned Burckhardt to follow.

It was a tunnel, metal-walled, brightly lit. Empty, it stretched vacantly away in both directions from them.

Burckhardt looked wondering around. One thing he knew and knew full well:

No such tunnel belonged under Tylerton.

There was a room off the tunnel with chairs and a desk and what looked like television screens. Swanson slumped in a chair, panting.

'We're all right for a while here,' he wheezed. 'They don't come here much any more. If they do, we'll hear them and we can hide.'

'Who?' demanded Burckhardt.

The little man said, 'Martians!' His voice cracked on the word and the life seemed to go out of him. In morose tones, he went on: 'Well, I think they're Martians. Although you could be right, you know; I've had plenty of time to think it over these last few weeks, after they got you, and it's possible they're Russians after all. Still – '

'Start from the beginning. Who got me when?'

Swanson sighed. 'So we have to go through the whole thing again. All right. It was about two months ago that you banged on my door, late at night. You were all beat up – scared silly. You begged me to help you – '

'*I* did?'

'Naturally you don't remember any of this. Listen and you'll understand. You were talking a blue streak about being captured and threatened and your wife being dead and coming back to life, and all kinds of mixed-up nonsense. I thought you were crazy. But – well, I've always had a lot of respect for you. And you begged me to hide you and I have this darkroom, you know. It locks from the inside only. I put the lock on myself. So we went in there – just to humour you – and along about midnight, which was only fifteen or twenty minutes after, we passed out.'

'Passed out?'

Swanson nodded. 'Both of us. It was like being hit with a sandbag. Look, didn't that happen to you again last night?'

79

'I guess it did,' Burckhardt shook his head uncertainly.

'Sure. And then all of a sudden we were awake again, and you said you were going to show me something funny, and we went out and bought a paper. And the date on it was June the 15th.'

'June the 15th? But that's today! I mean –'

'You got it, friend. It's *always* today!'

It took time to penetrate.

Burckhardt said wonderingly, 'You've hidden out in that darkroom for how many weeks?'

'How can I tell? Four or five, maybe. I lost count. And every day the same – always the 15th of June, always my landlady, Mrs Keefer, is sweeping the front steps, always the same headline in the papers at the corner. It gets monotonous, friend.'

It was Burckhardt's idea and Swanson despised it, but he went along. He was the type who always went along.

'It's dangerous,' he grumbled worriedly. 'Suppose somebody comes by? They'll spot us and –'

'What have we got to lose?'

Swanson shrugged. 'It's dangerous,' he said again. But he went along.

Burckhardt's idea was very simple. He was sure of only one thing – the tunnel went somewhere. Martians or Russians, fantastic plot or crazy hallucination, whatever was wrong with Tylerton had an explanation, and the place to look for it was at the end of the tunnel.

They jogged along. It was more than a mile before they began to see an end. They were in luck – at least no one came through the tunnel to spot them. But Swanson had said that it was only at certain hours that the tunnel seemed to be in use.

Always the 15th of June. Why? Burckhardt asked himself. Never mind the how. *Why?*

And falling asleep, completely involuntarily – everyone at the same time, it seemed. And not remembering, never remembering anything – Swanson had said how eagerly he saw Burckhardt again, the morning after Burckhardt had incautiously waited five minutes too many before retreating into the darkroom. When Swanson had come to, Burckhardt was gone. Swanson had seen him in the street that afternoon, but Burckhardt had remembered nothing.

And Swanson had lived his mouse's existence for weeks, hiding in the woodwork at night, stealing out by day to search for Burckhardt in pitiful hope, scurrying around the fringe of life, trying to keep from the deadly eyes of *them*.

Them. One of 'them' was the girl named April Horn. It was by seeing her walk carelessly into a telephone booth and never come out that Swanson had found the tunnel. Another was the man at the cigar stand in

Burckhardt's office building. There were more, at least a dozen that Swanson knew of or suspected.

They were easy enough to spot, once you knew where to look – for they, alone in Tylerton, changed their roles from day to day. Burckhardt was on that 8.51 bus, every morning of every-day-that-was-June-the-15th, never different by a hair or a moment. But April Horn was sometimes gaudy in the cellophane skirt, giving away candy or cigarettes; sometimes plainly dressed; sometimes not seen by Swanson at all.

Russians? Martians? Whatever they were, what could they be hoping to gain from this mad masquerade?

Burckhardt didn't know the answer – but perhaps it lay beyond the door at the end of the tunnel. They listened carefully and heard distant sounds that could not quite be made out, but nothing that seemed dangerous. They slipped through.

And, through a wide chamber and up a flight of steps, they found they were in what Burckhardt recognized as the Contro Chemicals plant.

Nobody was in sight. By itself, that was not so very odd – the automatized factory had never had many persons in it. But Burckhardt remembered, from his single visit, the endless, ceaseless busyness of the plant, the valves that opened and closed, the vats that emptied themselves and filled themselves and stirred and cooked and chemically tested the bubbling liquids they held inside themselves. The plant was never populated, but it was never still.

Only – now it *was* still. Except for the distant sounds, there was no breath of life in it. The captive electronic minds were sending out no commands; the coils and relays were at rest.

Burckhardt said, 'Come on.' Swanson reluctantly followed him through the tangled aisles of stainless steel columns and tanks.

They walked as though they were in the presence of the dead. In a way, they were, for what were the automatons that once had run the factory, if not corpses? The machines were controlled by computers that were really not computers at all, but the electronic analogues of living brains. And if they were turned off, were they not dead? For each had once been a human mind.

Take a master petroleum chemist, infinitely skilled in the separation of crude oil into its fractions. Strap him down, probe into his brain with searching electronic needles. The machine scans the patterns of the mind, translates what it sees into charts and sine waves. Impress the same waves on a robot computer and you have your chemist. Or a thousand copies of your chemist, if you wish, with all of his knowledge and skill, and no human limitations at all.

Put a dozen copies of him into a plant and they will run it all, twenty-four hours a day, seven days of every week, never tiring, never overlooking anything, never forgetting...

Swanson stepped up closer to Burckhardt. 'I'm scared,' he said.

They were across the room now and the sounds were louder. They were not machine sounds, but voices; Burckhardt moved cautiously up to a door and dared to peer around it.

It was a smaller room, lined with television screens, each one – a dozen or more, at least – with a man or woman sitting before it, staring into the screen and dictating notes into a recorder. The viewers dialled from scene to scene; no two screens ever showed the same picture.

The pictures seemed to have little in common. One was a store, where a girl dressed like April Horn was demonstrating home freezers. One was a series of shots of kitchens. Burckhardt caught a glimpse of what looked like the cigar stand in his office building.

It was baffling and Burckhardt would have loved to stand there and puzzle it out, but it was too busy a place. There was the chance that someone would look their way or walk out and find them.

They found another room. This one was empty. It was an office, large and sumptuous. It had a desk, littered with papers. Burckhardt stared at them, briefly at first – then, as the words on one of them caught his attention, with incredulous fascination.

He snatched up the topmost sheet, scanned it, and another, while Swanson was frenziedly searching through the drawers.

Burckhardt swore unbelievingly and dropped the papers to the desk.

Swanson, hardly noticing, yelped with delight: 'Look!' He dragged a gun from the desk. 'And it's loaded, too!'

Burckhardt stared at him blankly, trying to assimilate what he had read. Then, as he realized what Swanson had said, Burckhardt's eyes sparked. 'Good man!' he cried. 'We'll take it. We're getting out of here with that gun, Swanson. And we're going to the police! Not the cops in Tylerton, but the FBI maybe. Take a look at this!'

The sheaf he handed Swanson was headed: 'Test Area Progress Report. Subject: Marlin Cigarettes Campaign.' It was mostly tabulated figures that made little sense to Burckhardt and Swanson, but at the end was a summary that said:

Although Test 47–K3 pulled nearly double the number of new users of any of the other tests conducted, it probably cannot be used in the field because of local sound-truck control ordinances.

The tests in the 47–K12 group were second best and our recommendation is that retests be conducted in this appeal, testing each of the three best campaigns with and without the addition of sampling techniques.

An alternative suggestion might be to proceed directly with the top appeal in the K12 series, if the client is unwilling to go to the expense of additional tests.

All of these forecast expectations have an 80% probability of being within one-half of one per cent of results forecast, and more than 99% probability of coming within 5%.

Swanson looked up from the paper into Burckhardt's eyes. 'I don't get it,' he complained. Burckhardt said, 'I do not blame you. It's crazy, but it fits the facts, Swanson, *it fits the facts*. They aren't Russians and they aren't Martians. These people are advertising men! Somehow – heaven knows how they did it – they've taken Tylerton over. They've got us, all of us, you and me and twenty or thirty thousand other people, right under their thumbs.

'Maybe they hypnotize us and maybe it's something else; but however they do it, what happens is that they let us live a day at a time. They pour advertising into us the whole damned day long. And at the end of the day, they see what happened – and then they wash the day out of our minds and start again the next day with different advertising.'

Swanson's jaw was hanging. He managed to close it and swallow. 'Nuts!' he said flatly.

Burckhardt shook his head. 'Sure, it sounds crazy – but this whole thing is crazy. How else would you explain it? You can't deny that most of Tylerton lives the same day over and over again. You've *seen* it. And that's the crazy part and we have to admit that that's true – unless *we* are the crazy ones. And once you admit that somebody, somehow, knows how to accomplish that, the rest of it makes all kinds of sense.

'Think of it, Swanson! They test every last detail before the spend a nickel on advertising! Do you have any idea what that means? Lord knows how much money is involved, but I know for a fact that some companies spend twenty or thirty million dollars a year on advertising. Multiply it, say, by a hundred companies. Say that every one of them learns how to cut its advertising cost by only ten per cent. And that's peanuts, believe me!

'If they know in advance what is going to work, they can cut their costs in half – maybe to less than half, I don't know. But that is saving two or three hundred million dollars a year – and if they pay only ten or twenty per cent of that for the use of Tylerton, it's still dirt cheap for them and a fortune for whoever took over Tylerton.'

Swanson licked his lips. 'You mean,' he offered hesitantly, 'that we're a – well, a kind of captive audience?'

Burckhardt frowned. 'Not exactly.' He thought for a minute. 'You know how a doctor tests something like penicillin? He sets up a series of little colonies of germs on gelatine discs and he tries the stuff on one after another, changing it a little each time. Well, that's us – we're the germs, Swanson. Only it's even more efficient than that. They don't have to test more than one colony, because they can use it over and over again.'

It was too hard for Swanson to take in. He only said: 'What do we do about it?'

'We go to the police. They can't use human beings for guinea pigs!'

'How do we get to the police?'

Burckhardt hesitated. 'I think – ' he began slowly. 'Sure. This place is the office of somebody important. We've got a gun. We will stay right here until he comes along. And he'll get us out of here.'

Simple and direct. Swanson subsided and found a place to sit, against the wall, out of sight of the door. Burckhardt took up a position behind the door itself –

And waited.

The wait was not as long as it might have been. Half an hour, perhaps. Then Burckhardt heard approaching voices and had time for a swift whisper to Swanson before he flattened himself against the wall.

It was a man's voice, and a girl's. The man was saying, ' – reason why you couldn't report on the phone? You're ruining your whole day's test! What the devil's the matter with you, Janet?'

'I'm sorry, Mr Dorchin,' she said in a sweet, clear tone. 'I thought it was important.'

The man grumbled, 'Important! One lousy unit out of twenty-one thousand.'

'But it's the Burckhardt one, Mr Dorchin. Again. And the way he got out of sight, he must have had some help.'

'All right, all right. It doesn't matter, Janet; the Choco-Bite pro-gramme is ahead of schedule anyhow. As long as you're this far, come on in the office and make out your worksheet. And don't worry about the Burckhardt business. He's probably just wandering around. We'll pick him up tonight and – '

They were inside the door. Burckhardt kicked it shut and pointed the gun.

'That's what you think,' he said triumphantly.

It was worth the terrified hours, the bewildered sense of insanity, the confusion and fear. It was the most satisfying sensation Burckhardt had ever had in his life. The expression on the man's face was one he had read about but never actually seen: Dorchin's mouth fell open and his eyes went wide, and though he managed to make a sound that might have been a question, it was not in words.

The girl was almost as surprised. And Burckhardt, looking at her, knew why her voice had been so familiar. The girl was the one who had introduced herself to him as April Horn.

Dorchin recovered himself quickly. 'Is this the one?' he asked sharply.

The girl said, 'Yes.'

Dorchin nodded. 'I take it back. You were right. Uh, you – Burckhardt. What do you want?'

Swanson piped up, 'Watch him! He might have another gun.'

'Search him then,' Burckhardt said. 'I'll tell you what we want, Dorchin. We want you to come along with us to the FBI and explain to them how you can get away with kidnapping twenty thousand people.'

'Kidnapping?' Dorching snorted. 'That's ridiculous, man! Put that gun away – you can't get away with this!'

Burckhardt hefted the gun grimly. 'I think I can.'

Dorchin looked furious and sick – but, oddly, not afraid. 'Damn it –' he started to bellow, then closed his mouth and swallowed. 'Listen,' he said persuasively, 'you're making a big mistake. I haven't kidnapped anybody, believe me!'

'I don't believe you,' said Burckhardt bluntly. 'Why should I?'

'But it's true! Take my word for it!'

Burckhardt shook his head. 'The FBI can take your word if they like. We'll find out. Now how do we get out of here?'

Dorchin opened his mouth to argue.

Burckhardt blazed: 'Don't get in my way! I'm willing to kill you if I have to. Don't you understand that? I've gone through two days of hell and every second of it I blame on you. Kill you? It would be a pleasure and I don't have a thing in the world to lose! Get us out of here!'

Dorchin's face went suddenly opaque. He seemed about to move; but the blonde girl he had called Janet slipped between him and the gun.

'Please!' she begged Burckhardt. 'You don't understand. You mustn't shoot!'

'*Get out of my way!*'

'But, Mr Burckhardt –'

She never finished. Dorchin, his face unreadable, headed for the door. Burckhardt had been pushed one degree too far. He swung the gun, bellowing. The girl called out sharply. He pulled the trigger. Closing on him with pity and pleading in her eyes, she came again between the gun and the man.

Burckhardt aimed low instinctively, to cripple, not to kill. But his aim was not good.

The pistol bullet caught her in the pit of her stomach.

Dorchin was out and away, the door slamming behind him, his footsteps racing into the distance.

Burckhardt hurled the gun across the room and jumped to the girl.

Swanson was moaning, 'That finishes us, Burckhardt. Oh, why did you do it? We could have got away. We should have gone to the police. We were practically out of here! We –'

Burckhardt wasn't listening. He was kneeling beside the girl. She lay flat on her back, arms helter-skelter. There was no blood, hardly any sign of the wound; but the position in which she lay was one that no living human being could have held.

Yet she wasn't dead.

She wasn't dead – and Burckhardt, frozen beside her, thought: *She isn't alive, either.*

There was no pulse, but there was a rhythmic ticking of the

outstretched fingers of one hand.

There was no sound of breathing, but there was a hissing, sizzling noise.

The eyes were open and they were looking at Burckhardt. There was neither fear nor pain in them, only a pity deeper than the Pit.

She said, through lips that writhed erratically, 'Don't – worry, Mr Burckhardt. I'm – all right.'

Burckhardt rocked back on his haunches, staring. Where there should have been blood, there was a clean break of a substance that was not flesh; and a curl of thin golden-copper wire.

Burckhardt moistened his lips.

'You're a robot,' he said.

The girl tried to nod. The twitching lips said, 'I am. And so are you.'

Swanson, after a single inarticulate sound, walked over to the desk and sat staring at the wall. Burckhardt rocked back and forth beside the shattered puppet on the floor. He had no words.

The girl managed to say, 'I'm – sorry all this happened.' The lovely lips twisted into a rictus sneer, frightening on that smooth young face, until she got them under control. 'Sorry,' she said again. 'The – nerve centre was right about where the bullet hit. Makes it difficult to – control this body.'

Burckhardt nodded automatically, accepting the apology. Robots. It was obvious, now that he knew it. In hindsight, it was inevitable. He thought of his mystic notions of hypnosis or Martians or something stranger still – idiotic, for the simple fact of created robots fitted the facts better and more economically.

All the evidence had been before him. The automatized factory, with its transplanted minds – why not transplant a mind into a humanoid robot, give it its original owner's features and form?

Could it know that it was a robot?

'All of us,' Burckhardt said, hardly aware that he spoke out loud. 'My wife and my secretary and you and the neighbours. All of us the same.'

'No.' The voice was stronger. 'Not exactly the same, all of us. I chose it, you see. I – ' this time the convulsed lips were not a random contortion of the nerves – 'I was an ugly woman, Mr Burckhardt, and nearly sixty years old. Life had passed me. And when Mr Dorchin offered me the chance to live again as a beautiful girl, I jumped at the opportunity. Believe me, I *jumped*, in spite of its disadvantages. My flesh body is still alive – it is sleeping, while I am here. I could go back to it. But I never do.'

'And the rest of us?'

'Different, Mr Burckhardt. I work here. I'm carrying out Mr Dorchin's orders, mapping the results of the advertising tests, watching you and the others live as he makes you live. I do it by choice, but you have no choice. Because, you see, you are dead.'

'Dead?' cried Burckhardt; it was almost a scream.

The blue eyes looked at him unwinkingly and he knew that it was no lie. He swallowed, marvelling at the intricate mechanisms that let him swallow, and sweat, and eat.

He said: 'Oh. The explosion in my dream.'

'It was no dream. You are right – the explosion. That was real and this plant was the cause of it. The storage tanks let go and what the blast didn't get, the fumes killed a little later. But almost everyone died in the blast, twenty-one thousand persons. You died with them and that was Dorchin's chance.'

'The damned ghoul!' said Burckhardt.

The twisted shoulders shrugged with an odd grace. 'Why? You were gone. And you and all the others were what Dorchin wanted – a whole town, a perfect slice of America. It's as easy to transfer a pattern from a dead brain as a living one. Easier – the dead can't say no. Oh, it took work and money – the town was a wreck – but it was possible to rebuild it entirely, especially because it wasn't necessary to have all the details exact.

'There were the homes where even the brains had been utterly destroyed, and those are empty inside, and the cellars that needn't be too perfect, and the streets that hardly matter. And anyway, it only had to last for one day. The same day – June the 15th – over and over again; and if someone finds something a little wrong, somehow, the discovery won't have time to snowball, wreck the validity of the tests, because all errors are cancelled out at midnight.'

The face tried to smile. 'That's the dream, Mr Burckhardt, that day of June the 15th, because you never really lived it. It's a present from Mr Dorchin, a dream that he gives you and then takes back at the end of the day, when he has all his figures on how many of you responded to what variation of which appeal, and the maintenance crews go down the tunnel to go through the whole city, washing out the new dream with their little electronic drains, and then the dream starts all over again. On June the 15th.

'Always June the 15th, because June the 14th is the last day any of you can remember alive. Sometimes the crews miss someone – as they missed you, because you were under your boat. But it doesn't matter. The ones who are missed give themselves away if they show it – and if they don't, it doesn't affect the test. But they don't drain us, the ones of us who work for Dorchin. We sleep when the power is turned off, just as you do. When we wake up, though, we remember.' The face contorted wildly. 'If I could only forget!'

Burckhardt said unbelievingly, 'All this to sell merchandise! It must have cost millions!'

The robot called April Horn said, 'It did. But it has made millions for Dorchin, too. And that's not the end of it. Once he finds the master words that make people act, do you suppose he will stop with that? Do you suppose –'

The door opened, interrupting her. Burckhardt whirled. Belatedly remembering Dorchin's flight, he raised the gun.

'Don't shoot,' ordered the voice calmly. It was not Dorchin; it was another robot, this one not disguised with the clever plastics and cosmetics, but shining plain. It said metallically: 'Forget it, Burckhardt. You're not accomplishing anything. Give me that gun before you do any more damage. Give it to me *now*.'

Burckhardt bellowed angrily. The gleam on this robot torso was steel; Burckhardt was not at all sure that his bullets would pierce it, or do much harm if they did. He would have put it on the test –

But from behind him came a whimpering, scurrying whirl-wind; its name was Swanson, hysterical with fear. He catapulted into Burckhardt and sent him sprawling, the gun flying free.

'Please!' begged Swanson incoherently, prostrate before the steel robot. 'He would have shot you – please don't hurt me! Let me work for you, like that girl. I'll do anything, anything you tell me –'

The robot voice said, 'We don't need your help.' It took two precise steps and stood over the gun – and spurned it, left it lying on the floor.

The wrecked blonde robot said, without emotion, 'I doubt that I can hold out much longer, Mr Dorchin.'

'Disconnect if you have to,' replied the steel robot.

Burckhardt blinked. 'But you're not Dorchin!'

The steel robot turned deep eyes on him. 'I am,' it said. 'Not in the flesh – but this is the body I am using at the moment. I doubt that you can damage this one with the gun. The other robot body was more vulnerable. Now will you stop this nonsense? I don't want to have to damage you; you're too expensive for that. Will you just sit down and let the maintenance crews adjust you?'

Swanson grovelled. 'You – you won't punish us?'

The steel robot had no expression, but its voice was almost surprised. 'Punish you?' it repeated on a rising tone. 'How?'

Swanson quivered as though the word had been a whip; but Burckhardt flared: 'Adjust *him*, if he'll let you – but not me! You're going to have to do me a lot of damage, Dorchin. I don't care what I cost or how much trouble it's going to be to put put me back together again. But I'm going out of that door! If you want to stop me, you'll have to kill me. You won't stop me any other way!'

The steel robot took a half-step towards him, and Burckhardt involuntarily checked his stride. He stood poised and shaking, ready for death, ready for attack, ready for anything that might happen.

Ready for anything except what did happen. For Dorchin's steel body merely stepped aside, between Burckhardt and the gun, but leaving the door free.

'Go ahead,' invited the steel robot. 'Nobody's stopping you.'

Outside the door, Burckhardt brought up sharp. It was insane of Dorchin to let him go! Robot or flesh, victim or beneficiary, there was nothing to stop him from going to the FBI or whatever law he could find away from Dorchin's synthetic empire, and telling his story. Surely the corporation who paid Dorchin for test results had no notion of the ghoul's technique he used; Dorchin would have to keep it from them, for the breath of publicity would put a stop to it. Walking out meant death, perhaps – but at that moment in his pseudo-life, death was no terror for Burckhardt.

There was no one in the corridor. He found a window and stared out of it. There was Tylerton – an ersatz city, but looking so real and familiar that Burckhardt almost imagined the whole episode a dream. It was no dream, though. He was certain of that in his heart and equally certain that nothing in Tylerton could help him now.

It had to be the other direction.

It took him a quarter of an hour to find a way, but he found it – skulking through the corridors, dodging the suspicion of footsteps, knowing for certain that his hiding was in vain, for Dorchin was undoubtedly aware of every move he made. But no one stopped him, and he found another door.

It was a simple enough door from the inside. But when he opened it and stepped out, it was like nothing he had ever seen.

First there was light – brilliant, incredible, blinding light. Burckhardt blinked upward, unbelieving and afraid.

He was standing on a ledge of smooth, finished metal. Not a dozen yards from his feet, the ledge dropped sharply away; he hardly dared approach the brink, but even from where he stood he could see no bottom to the chasm before him. And the gulf extended out of sight into the glare on either side of him.

No wonder Dorchin could so easily give him his freedom! From the factory, there was nowhere to go – but how incredible this fantastic gulf, how impossible the hundred white and blinding suns that hung above!

A voice by his side said inquiringly, 'Burckhardt?' And thunder rolled the name, mutteringly soft, back and forth in the abyss before him.

Burckhardt wet his lips. 'Y-yes?' he croaked.

'This is Dorchin. Not a robot this time, but Dorchin in the flesh, talking to you on a hand mike. Now you have seen, Burckhardt. Now will you be reasonable and let the maintenance crews take over?'

Burckhardt stood paralysed. One of the moving mountains in the blinding glare came towards him.

It towered hundreds of feet over his head; he stared up at its top, squinting helplessly into the light.

It looked like –

Impossible!

The voice in the loudspeaker at the door said, 'Burckhardt?' But he was unable to answer.

A heavy rumbling sigh. 'I see,' said the voice. 'You finally understand. There's no place to go. You know it now. I could have told you, but you might not have believed me, so it was better for you to see it yourself. And after all, Burckhardt, why would I reconstruct a city just the way it was before? I'm a businessman; I count costs. If a thing has to be full-scale, I build it that way. But there wasn't any need to in this case.'

From the mountain before him, Burckhardt helplessly saw a lesser cliff descend carefully towards him. It was long and dark, and at the end of it was whiteness, five-fingered whiteness...

'Poor little Burckhardt,' crooned the loudspeaker, while the echoes rumbled through the enormous chasm that was only a workshop. 'It must have been quite a shock for you to find out you were living in a town built on a table top.'

It was the morning of June the 15th, and Guy Burckhardt woke up screaming out of a dream.

It had been a monstrous and incomprehensible dream, of explosions and shadowy figures that were not men and terror beyond words.

He shudderd and opened his eyes.

Outside his bedroom window, a hugely amplified voice was howling.

Burckhardt stumbled over to the window and stared outside. There was an out-of-season chill to the air, more like October than June; but the scene was normal enough – except for the sound-truck that squatted at the kerbside halfway down the block. Its speaker horns blared:

'Are you a coward? Are you a fool? Are you going to let crooked politicians steal the country from you? NO! Are you going to put up with four more years of graft and crime? NO! Are you going to vote straight Federal Party all up and down the ballot? YES! *You just bet you are!*'

Sometimes he screams, sometimes he wheedles, threatens, begs, cajoles ... but his voice goes on and on through one June the 15th after another.

The Coffin Cure

ALAN E. NOURSE

WHEN THE DISCOVERY was announced, it was Dr Chauncey Patrick Coffin who announced it. He had, of course, arranged with uncanny skill to take most of the credit for himself. If it turned out to be greater than he had hoped, so much the better. His presentation was scheduled for the last night of the American College of Clinical Practioners' annual meeting, and Coffin had fully intended it to be a bombshell.

It was. Its explosion exceeded even Dr Coffin's wilder expectations, which took quite a bit of doing. In the end he had waded through more newspaper reporters than medical doctors as he left the hall that night. It was a heady evening for Chauncey Patrick Coffin, MD.

Certain others were not so delighted with Coffin's bombshell.

'It's idiocy!' young Dr Philip Dawson wailed in the laboratory conference room the next morning. 'Blind, screaming idiocy. You've gone out of your mind – that's all there is to it. Can't you see what you've done? Aside from selling your colleagues down the river, that is?' He clenched the reprint of Coffin's address in his hand and brandished it like a broadsword. ' "Report on a Vaccine for the Treatment and Cure of the Common Cold," by C.P. Coffin, *et al*. That's what it says – *et al*. My idea in the first place. Jake and I both pounding our heads on the wall for eight solid months – and now you sneak it into publication a full year before we have any business publishing a word about it.'

'Really, Phillip!' Dr Chauncey Coffin ran a pudgy hand through his snowy hair. 'How ungrateful! I thought for sure you'd be delighted. An excellent presentation, I must say – terse, succinct, unequivocal. –' he raised his hand – 'but *generously* unequivocal, you understand. You should have heard the ovation – they nearly went wild! And the look on Underwood's face! Worth waiting twenty years for.'

'And the reporters,' snapped Phillip. 'Don't forget the reporters.' He whirled on the small dark man sitting quietly in the corner. 'How about that, Jake? Did you see the morning papers? This thief not only steals our work, he splashes it all over the countryside in red ink.'

Dr Jacob Miles coughed apologetically. 'What Phillip is so stormed up about is the prematurity of it all,' he said to Coffin. 'After all, we've hardly had an acceptable period of clinical trial.'

'Nonsense,' said Coffin, glaring at Phillip. 'Underwood and his men were ready to publish their discovery within another six weeks. Where would we be then? How much clinical testing do you want? Phillip, you had the worst cold of your life when you took the vaccine. Have you had any since?'

'No, of course not,' said Phillip, peevishly.

'Jacob, how about you? Any sniffles?'

'Oh, no. No colds.'

'Well, what about those six hundred students from the University? Did I misread the reports on them?'

'No – 98 per cent cured of active symptoms within twenty-four hours. Not a single recurrence. The results were just short of miraculous.' Jake hesitated. 'Of course, it's only been a month. . . .'

'Month, year, century! Look at them! Six hundred of the world's most luxuriant colds, and now not even a sniffle.' The chubby doctor sank down behind the desk, his ruddy face beaming. 'Come, now, gentlemen, be reasonable. Think positively! There's work to be done, a great deal of work. They'll be wanting me in Washington, I imagine. Press conference in twenty minutes. Drug houses to consult with. How dare we stand in the path of Progress? We've won the greatest medical triumph of all times – the conquering of the Common Cold. We'll go down in history!'

And he was perfectly right on one point, at least.

They did go down in history.

The public response to the vaccine was little less than monumental. Of all the ailments that have tormented mankind through history none was ever more universal, more tenacious, more uniformly miserable than the common cold. It was a respecter of no barriers, boundaries, or classes; ambassadors and chambermaids snuffled and sneezed in drippy-nosed unanimity. The powers in the Kremlin sniffed and blew and wept genuine tears on draughty days, while senatorial debates on earth-shaking issues paused reverently upon the unplugging of a nose, the clearing of a rhinorrheic throat. Other illnesses brought disability, even death in their wake; the common cold merely brought torment to the millions as it implacably resisted the most superhuman of efforts to curb it.

Until that chill, rainy November day when the tidings broke to the world in four-inch banner heads:

COFFIN NAILS LID ON COMMON COLD
'No More Coughin'' States Co-Finder of Cure
SNIFFLES SNIPED: SINGLE SHOT TO SAVE SNEEZERS

In medical circles it was called the Coffin Multicentric Upper Respiratory Virus-Inhibiting Vaccine; but the papers could never stand for such high-sounding names, and called it, simply, 'The Coffin Cure.'

Below the banner heads, world-renowned feature writers expounded in reverent terms the story of the leviathan struggle of Dr Chauncey Patrick Coffin (*et al.*) in solving this riddle of the ages: how, after years of failure, they ultimately succeeded in culturing the causative agent of the common cold, identifying it not as a single virus or group of viruses, but as a multicentric virus complex invading the soft mucous linings of the nose, throat and eyes, capable of altering its basic molecular structure at any time to resist efforts of the body from within, or the physician from without, to attack and dispel it; how the hypothesis was set forth by Dr Phillip Dawson that the virus could be destroyed only by an antibody which could 'freeze' the virus-complex in one form long enough for normal body defences to dispose of the offending invader; the exhausting search for such a 'crippling agent', and the final crowning success after injecting untold gallons of cold-virus material into the hides of a group of cooperative and forbearing dogs (a species which never suffered from colds, and hence endured the whole business with an air of affectionate boredom).

And finally, the testing. First, Coffin himself (who was suffering a particularly horrendous case of the affliction he sought to cure); then his assistants Phillip Dawson and Jacob Miles; then a multitude of students from the University – carefully chosen for the severity of their symptoms, the longevity of their colds, their tendency to acquire them on little or no provocation, and their utter inability to get rid of them with any known medical programme.

They were a sorry spectacle, those students filing through the Coffin laboratory for three days in October: wheezing like steam shovels, snorting and sneezing and sniffling and blowing, coughing and squeaking, mute appeals glowing in their blood-shot eyes. The researchers dispensed the materials – a single shot in the right arm, a sensitivity control in the left.

With growing delight they then watched as the results came in. The sneezing stopped; the sniffling ceased. A great silence settled over the campus, in the classrooms, in the library, in classic halls. Dr Coffin's voice returned (rather to the regret of his fellow workers) and he began bouncing about the laboratory like a small boy at a fair. Students by the dozen trooped in for check-ups with noses dry and eyes bright.

In a matter of days there was no doubt left that the goal had been reached.

'But we have to be *sure*,' Phillip Dawson had cried cautiously. 'This was only a pilot test. We need mass testing now, on an entire community. We should go to the West Coast and run studies there – they have a different breed of cold out there, I hear. We'll have to see how long the immunity lasts, make sure there are no unexpected side effects. . . .' And muttering to himself, he fell to work with pad and pencil, calculating the programme to be undertaken before publication.

But there were rumours. Underwood at Standford, they said, had already completed his tests and was preparing a paper for publication in a matter of months. Surely with such dramatic results on the pilot tests *something* could be put into print. It would be tragic to lose the race for the sake of a little unnecessary caution . . .

Phillip Dawson was adamant, but he was a voice crying in the wilderness. Chauncey Patrick Coffin was boss.

Within a week even Coffin was wondering if he had bitten off just a trifle too much. They had expected that demand for the vaccine would be great – but even the grisly memory of the early days of the Salk vaccine had not prepared them for the mobs of sneezing, wheezing red-eyed people bombarding them for the first fruits.

Clear-eyed young men from the Government Bureau pushed through crowds of local townspeople, lining the streets outside the Coffin laboratory, standing in pouring rain to raise insistent placards.

Seventeen pharmaceutical houses descended like vultures with production plans, cost-estimates, colourful graphs demonstrating proposed yield and distribution programmes. Coffin was flown to Washington, where conferences laboured far into the night as demands pounded their doors like a tidal wave.

One laboratory promised the vaccine in ten days; another said a week. The first actually appeared in three weeks and two days, to be soaked up in the space of three hours by the thirsty sponge of cold-weary humanity. Express planes were dispatched to Europe, to Asia, to Africa with the precious cargo, a million needles pierced a million hides, and with a huge, convulsive sneeze mankind stepped forth into a new era.

There were abstainers of course. There always are.

'It doesn't bake eddy differets how much you talk,' Ellie Dawson cried hoarsely, shaking her blonde curls. 'I dod't wadt eddy cold shots.'

'You're being totally unreasonable,' Phillip said, glowering at his wife in annoyance. She wasn't the sweet young thing he had married, not this evening. Her eyes were puffy, her nose red and dripping. 'You've had this cold for two solid months now, and there just isn't any sense to it. It's making you miserable. You can't eat, you can't breathe, you can't sleep.'

'I dod't wad't eddy cold shots,' she repeated stubbornly.

'But why not? Just one little needle, you'd hardly feel it.'

'But I dod't like deedles!' she cried, bursting into tears. 'Why dod't you leave be alode? Go take your dasty old deedles ad stick theb id people that wadt theb.'

'Aw, Ellie – –'

'I dod't care, *I dod't like deedles!*' she wailed, burying her face in his shirt.

He held her close, making comforting little noises. It was no use, he reflected sadly. Science just wasn't Ellie's long suit; she didn't know a cold vaccine from a case of smallpox, and no appeal to logic or common sense could surmount her irrational fear of hypodermics. 'All right, nobody's

94

going to make you do anything you don't want to,' he said.

'Ad eddyway, thik of the poor tissue baducfacturers,' she sniffled, wiping her nose with a pink facial tissue. 'All their little childred starvig to death.'

'Say, you *have* got a cold,' said Philip, sniffing. 'You've got on enough perfume to fell an ox.' He wiped away tears and grinned at her. 'Come on now, fix your face. Dinner at the Driftwood? I hear they have marvellous lamb chops.'

It was a mellow evening. The lamb chops were delectable – the tastiest lamb chops he had ever eaten, he thought, even being blessed with as good a cook as Ellie for a spouse. Ellie dripped and blew continuously, but refused to go home until they had taken in a movie, and stopped by to dance a while. 'I hardly ever gedt to see you eddy bore,' she said. 'All because of that dasty bedicide you're givig people.'

It was true, of course. The work at the lab was endless. They danced, but came home early nevertheless. Phillip needed all the sleep he could get.

He woke once during the night to a parade of sneezes from his wife, and rolled over, frowning sleepily to himself. It was ignominious, in a way – his own wife refusing the fruit of all those months of work.

And cold or no cold, she surely was using a whale of a lot of perfume.

He awoke, suddenly, began to stretch, and sat bolt upright in bed, staring wildly about the room. Pale morning sunlight drifted in the window. Downstairs he heard Ellie stirring in the kitchen.

For a moment he thought he was suffocating. He leaped out of bed, stared at the vanity table across the room. '*Somebody's spilled the whole damned bottle――*'

The heavy sick-sweet miasma hung like a cloud around him, drenching the room. With every breath it grew thicker. He searched the table top frantically, but there were no empty bottles. His head began to spin from the sickening effluvium.

He blinked in confusion, his hand trembling as he lit a cigarette. No need to panic, he thought. She probably knocked a bottle over when she was dressing. He took a deep puff, and burst into a paroxysm of coughing as acrid fumes burned down his throat to his lungs.

'Ellie!' He rushed into the hall, still coughing. The match smell had given way to the harsh, caustic stench of burning weeds. He stared at his cigarette in horror and threw it into the sink. The smell grew worse. He threw open the hall closet, expecting smoke to come billowing out. 'Ellie! Somebody's burning down the house!'

'Whadtever are you talking about?' Ellie's voice came from the stair well. 'It's just the toast I burned, silly.'

He rushed down the stairs two at a time – and nearly gagged as he reached the bottom. The smell of hot, rancid grease struck him like a solid wall. It was intermingled with an oily smell of boiled and parboiled coffee, overpowering in its intensity. By the time he reached the kitchen he was holding his nose, tears pouring from his eyes. *'Ellie, what are you doing in here?'*

She stared at him. 'I'b baking breakfast.'

'But don't you *smell* it?'

'Sbell whadt?' said Ellie.

On the stove the automatic percolator was making small, promising noises. In the frying-pan four sunnyside eggs were sizzling; half a dozen strips of bacon drained on a paper towel on the sideboard. It couldn't have looked more innocent.

Cautiously, Phillip released his nose, sniffed. The stench nearly choked him. 'You mean you don't smell anything *strange?*'

'I dod't sbell eddythig, period,' said Ellie defensively.

'The coffee, the bacon – *come here a minute.*'

She reeked – of bacon, of coffee, of burned toast, but mostly of perfume. 'Did you put on any fresh perfume this morning?'

'Before breakfast? Dod't be ridiculous.'

'Not even a drop?' Phillip was turning very white.

'Dot a drop.'

He shook his head. 'Now, wait a minute. This must be all in my mind. I'm – just imagining things, that's all. Working too hard, hysterical reaction. In a minute it'll go away.' He poured a cup of coffee, added cream and sugar.

But he couldn't get close enough to taste it. It smelled as if it had been boiling three weeks in a rancid pot. It was the smell of coffee, all right, but a smell that was fiendishly distorted, overpoweringly, nauseatingly magnified. It pervaded the room and burned his throat and brought tears gushing to his eyes.

Slowly, realization began to dawn. He spilled the coffee as he set the cup down. The perfume. The coffee. The cigarette. . . .

'My hat,' he choked. 'Get me my hat. I've got to get to the laboratory.'

It got worse all the way downtown. He fought down waves of nausea as the smell of damp, rotting earth rose from his front yard in a grey cloud. The neighbour's dog dashed out to greet him, exuding the great-grandfather of all doggy odours. As Phillip waited for the bus, every passing car fouled the air with noxious fumes, gagging him, doubling him up with coughing as he dabbed at his streaming eyes.

Nobody else seemed to notice anything wrong at all.

The bus ride was a nightmare. It was a damp, rainy day; the inside of the bus smelled like the men's locker room after a big game. A bleary-eyed man with three-day's stubble on his chin flopped down in the seat next to him, and Phillip reeled back with a jolt to the job he had held in his student days, cleaning vats in the brewery.

'It'sh a great morning,' Bleary-eyes breathed at him, 'huh, Doc?' Phillip blanched. To top it, the man had had a breakfast of salami. In the seat ahead, a fat man held a dead cigar clamped in his mouth like a rank growth. Phillip's stomach began rolling; he sank his face into his hand, trying unobtrusively to clamp his nostrils. With a groan of deliverance he lurched off the bus at the laboratory gate.

He met Jake Miles coming up the steps. Jake looked pale, too pale.

'Morning,' Phillip said weakly. 'Nice day. Looks like the sun might come through.'

'Yeah,' said Jake. 'Nice day. You – uh – feel all right this morning?'

'Fine, fine.' Phillip tossed his hat in the closet, opened the incubator on his culture tubes, trying to look busy. He slammed the door after one whiff and gripped the edge of the work table with whitening knuckles. 'Why?'

'Oh, nothing. Thought you looked a little peaked, was all.'

They stared at each other in silence. Then, as though by signal, their eyes turned to the office at the end of the lab.

'Coffin come in yet?'

Jake nodded. 'He's in there. He's got the door locked.'

'I think he's going to have to open it,' said Phillip.

A grey-faced Dr Coffin unlocked the door, backed quickly toward the wall. The room reeked of kitchen deodorant. 'Stay right where you are,' Coffin squeaked. 'Don't come a step closer. I can't see you now. I'm – I'm busy, I've got work that has to be done – – '

'You're telling *me*,' growled Phillip. He motioned Jake into the office and locked the door carefully. Then he turned to Coffin. 'When did it start for you?'

Coffin was trembling. 'Right after supper last night. I thought I was going to suffocate. Got up and walked the streets all night. My God, what a stench!'

'Jake?'

Dr Miles shook his head. 'Sometime this morning, I don't know when. I woke up with it.'

'That's when it hit me,' said Phillip.

'But I don't understand,' Coffin howled. 'Nobody else seems to notice anything – – '

'Yet,' said Phillip, 'we were the first three to take the Coffin Cure, remember? You, and me and Jake. Two months ago.'

Coffin's forehead was beaded with sweat. He stared at the two men in growing horror. '*But what about the others?*' he whispered.

'I think,' said Phillip, 'that we'd better find something spectacular to do in a mighty big hurry. That's what I think.'

Jake Miles said, 'The most important thing right now is secrecy. We mustn't let a word get out, not until we're absolutely certain.'

'But what's *happened?*' Coffin cried. 'These foul smells, everywhere. You, Phillip, you had a cigarette this morning. I can smell it clear over here, and it's bringing tears to my eyes. And if I didn't know better I'd swear neither of you had had a bath in a week. Every odour in town has suddenly turned foul – – '

'*Magnified*, you mean,' said Jake. 'Perfume still smells sweet – there's just too much of it. The same with cinnamon; I tried it. Cried for half an hour, but it still smelled like cinnamon. No, I don't think the *smells* have changed any.'

'But what, then?'

'Our noses have changed, obviously.' Jake paced the floor in excitement. 'Look at our dogs! They've never had colds – and they practically live by their noses. Other animals – all dependent on their senses of smell for survival – and none of them ever have anything even vaguely reminiscent of a common cold. The multicentric virus hits primates only – *and it reaches its fullest parasitic powers in man alone!*'

Coffin shook his head miserably. 'But why this horrible stench all of a sudden? I haven't had a cold in weeks – – '

'Of course not! That's just what I'm trying to say,' Jake cried. 'Look, why do we have any sense of smell at all? Because we have tiny olfactory nerve endings buried in the mucous membrane of our noses and throats. But we have always had the virus living there, too, colds or no colds, throughout our entire lifetime. Its *always* been there, anchored in the same cells, parasitizing the same sensitive tissues that carry our olfactory nerve endings, numbing them and crippling them, making them practically useless as sensory organs. No wonder we never smelled anything before! Those poor little nerve endings never had a chance!'

'Until we came along in our shining armour and destroyed the virus,' said Phillip.

'Oh, we didn't destroy it. We merely stripped it of a very slippery protective mechanism against normal body defences.' Jake perched on the edge of the desk, his dark face intense. 'These two months since we had our shots have witnessed a battle to the death between our bodies and the virus. With the help of the vaccine, our bodies have won, that's all – stripped away the last vestiges of an invader that has been almost a part of our normal physiology since the beginning of time. And now for the first time those crippled little nerve endings are just beginning to function.'

'God help us,' Coffin groaned. 'You think it'll get worse?'

'And worse. And still worse,' said Jake.

'I wonder,' said Phillip slowly, 'what the anthropologists will say.'

'What do you mean?'

'Maybe it was just a single mutation somewhere back there. Just a tiny change of cell structure or metabolism that left one line of primates vulnerable to an invader no other would harbour. Why else should man have begun to flower and blossom intellectually – grow to depend so much on his brains instead of his brawn that he could rise above all others? What better reason than because somewhere along the line in the world of fang and claw *he suddenly lost his sense of smell?*'

They stared at each other. 'Well, he's got it back again now,' Coffin wailed, 'and he's not going to like it a bit.'

'No, he surely isn't,' Jake agreed. 'He's going to start looking very quickly for someone to blame, I think.'

They both looked at Coffin.

'Now don't be ridiculous, boys,' said Coffin, turning white. 'We're in this together. Phillip, it was your idea in the first place – you said so yourself! You can't leave me now – –'

The telephone jangled. They heard the frightened voice of the secretary clear across the room. 'Dr Coffin? There was a student on the line just a moment ago. He – he said he was coming up to see you. Now, he said, not later.'

'I'm busy,' Coffin sputtered. 'I can't see anyone. And I can't take any calls.'

'But he's already on his way up,' the girl burst out. 'He was saying something about tearing you apart with his bare hands.'

Coffin slammed down the receiver. His face was the colour of lead. 'They'll crucify me!' he sobbed. 'Jake – Phillip – you've got to help me.'

Phillip sighed and unlocked the door. 'Send a girl down to the freezer and have her bring up all the live cold virus she can find. Get us some inoculated monkeys and a few dozen dogs.' He turned to Coffin. 'And stop snivelling. You're the big publicity man around here; you're going to handle the screaming masses, whether you like it or not.'

'But what are you going to do?'

'I haven't the faintest idea,' said Phillip, 'but whatever I do is going to cost you your shirt. We're going to find out how to catch cold again if we have to die.'

It was an admirable struggle, and a futile one. They sprayed their noses and throats with enough pure culture of virulent live virus to have condemned an ordinary man to a lifetime of sneezing, watery-eyed misery. They didn't develop a sniffle between them. They mixed six different strains of virus and gargled the extract, spraying themselves and every inoculated monkey they could get their hands on with the vile-smelling stuff. Not a sneeze. They injected it hypodermically, intradermally, subcutaneously, intramuscularly, and intravenously. They drank it. They bathed in the stuff.

But they didn't catch a cold.

'Maybe it's the wrong approach,' Jake said one morning. 'Our body defences are keyed up to top performance right now. Maybe if we break them down we can get somewhere.'

They plunged down that alley with grim abandon. They starved themselves. They forced themselves to stay awake for days on end, until exhaustion forced their eyes closed in spite of all they could do. They carefully devised vitamin-free, protein-free, mineral-free diets that tasted like library paste and smelled worse. They wore wet clothes and sopping shoes to work, turned off the heat and threw windows open to the raw winter air. Then they re-sprayed themselves with the live cold virus and waited reverently for the sneezing to begin.

It didn't. They stared at each other in gathering gloom. They'd never felt better in their lives.

Except for the smells, of course. They'd hoped that they might, presently, get used to them. They didn't. Every day it grew a little worse. They began smelling smells they never dreamed existed – noxious smells, cloying smells, smells that drove them gagging to the sinks. Their nose-plugs were rapidly losing their effectiveness. Mealtimes were nightmarish ordeals; they lost weight with alarming speed.

But they didn't catch cold.

'*I* think you should all be locked up,' Ellie Dawson said severely as she dragged her husband, blue-faced and shivering, out of an icy shower one bitter morning. 'You've lost your wits. You need to be protected against yourselves, that's what you need.'

'You don't understand,' Phillip moaned. 'We've *got* to catch cold.'

'Why?' Ellie snapped angrily. 'Suppose you don't – what's going to happen?'

'We had three hundred students march on the laboratory today,' Phillip said patiently. 'The smells were driving them crazy, they said. They couldn't even bear to be close to their best friends. They wanted something done about it, or else they wanted blood. Tomorrow we'll have them back and three hundred more. And they were just the pilot study! What's going to happen when fifteen million people find their noses going bad on them?' He shuddered. 'Have you seen the papers? People are already going around sniffing like bloodhounds. And *now* we're finding out what a thorough job we did. We can't crack it, Ellie. We can't even get a toe-hold. Those antibodies are just doing too good a job.'

'Well, maybe you can find some unclebodies to take care of them,' Ellie offered vaguely.

'Look, don't make bad jokes — '

'I'm not making jokes! All I want is a husband back who doesn't complain about how everything smells, and eats the dinners I cook, and doesn't stand around in cold showers at six in the morning.'

'I know it's miserable,' he said helplessly. 'But I don't know how to stop it.'

He found Jake and Coffin in tight-lipped conference when he reached the lab. 'I can't do it any more,' Coffin was saying. 'I've begged them for time. I've threatened them. I've promised them everything but my upper plate. I can't face them again, I just can't.'

'We only have a few days left,' Jake said grimly. 'If we don't come up with something, we're goners.'

Phillip's jaw suddenly sagged as he stared at them. 'You know what I think?' he said suddenly. 'I think we've been prize idiots. We've gotten so rattled we haven't used our heads. And all the time it's been sitting there blinking at us!'

'What are you talking about?' snapped Jake.

'Unclebodies,' said Phillip.

'Oh, great God!'

'No, I'm serious.' Phillip's eyes were very bright. 'How many of those students do you think you can corral to help us?'

Coffin gulped. 'Six hundred. They're out there in the street right now, howling for a lynching.'

'All right, I want them in here. And I want some monkeys. Monkeys with colds, the worse colds the better.'

'Do you have any idea what you're doing?' asked Jake.

'None in the least,' said Phillip happily, 'except that it's never been done before. But maybe it's time we tried following our noses for a while.'

The tidal wave began to break two days later . . . only a few people here, a dozen there, but enough to confirm the direst newspaper predictions. The boomerang was completing its circle.

At the laboratory the doors were kept barred, the telephones disconnected. Within, there was a bustle of feverish – if odorous – activity. For the three researchers, the olfactory acuity had reached agonizing proportions. Even the small gas masks Phillip had devised could no longer shield them from the constant barrage of violent odours.

But the work went on in spite of the smell. Truckloads of monkeys arrived at the lab – cold-ridden monkeys, sneezing, coughing, weeping, wheezing monkeys by the dozen. Culture trays bulged with tubes, overflowed the incubators and work tables. Each day six hundred angry students paraded through the lab, arms exposed, mouths open, grumbling but cooperating.

At the end of the first week, half the monkeys were cured of their colds and were quite unable to catch them back; the other half had new colds and couldn't get rid of them. Phillip observed this fact with grim satisfaction, and went about the laboratory mumbling to himself.

Two days later he burst forth jubilantly, lugging a sad-looking puppy under his arm. It was like no other puppy in the world. This puppy was sneezing and snuffling with a perfect howler of a cold.

The day came when they injected a tiny droplet of milky fluid beneath the skin of Phillip's arm, and then got the virus spray and gave his nose and throat a liberal application. Then they sat back and waited.

They were still waiting three days later.

'It was a great idea,' Jake said gloomily, flipping a bulging notebook closed with finality. 'It just didn't work, was all.'

Phillip nodded. Both men had grown thin, with pouches under their eyes. Jake's right eye had begun to twitch uncontrollably whenever anyone came within three yards of him. 'We can't go on like this, you know. The people are going wild.'

'Where's Coffin?'

'He collapsed three days ago. Nervous prostration. He kept having dreams about hangings.'

Phillip sighed. 'Well, I suppose we'd better just face it. Nice knowing you, Jake. Pity it had to be this way.'

'It was a great try, old man. A great try.'

'Ah, yes. Nothing like going down in a blaze of — — '

Phillip stopped dead, his eyes widening. His nose began to twitch. He took a gasp, a larger gasp, as a long-dead reflex came sleepily to life, shook its head, reared back . . .

Phillip sneezed.

He sneezed for ten minutes without a pause, until he lay on the floor blue-faced and gasping for air. He caught hold of Jake, wringing his hand as tears gushed from his eyes. He gave his nose an enormous blow, and headed shakily for the telephone.

'It was a sipple edough pridciple,' he said later to Ellie as she spread mustard on his chest and poured more warm water into his foot bath. 'The Cure itself depedded upod it – the adtiged-adtibody reactoid. We had the adtibody agaidst the virus, all ridght; what we had to find was sobe kide of adtibody agaidst the *adtibody*.' He sneezed violently, and poured in nose drops with a happy grin.

'Will they be able to make it fast enough?'

'Just aboudt fast edough for people to get good ad eager to catch cold agaid,' said Phillip. 'There's odly wud little hitch . . .'

Ellie Dawson took the steaks from the grill and set them, still sizzling, on the dinner table. 'Hitch?'

Phillip nodded as he chewed the steak with a pretence of enthusiasm. It tasted like slightly damp K-ration.

'This stuff we've bade does a real good job. Just a little too good.' He wiped his nose and reached for a fresh tissue.

'I bay be wrog, but I thik I've got this cold for keeps,' he said sadly. 'Udless I cad fide ad adtibody agaidst the adtibody agaidst the adtibody — — '

Castaway

ARTHUR C. CLARKE

'Most of the matter in the universe is at temperatures so high that no chemical compounds can exist, and the atoms themselves are stripped of all but their inner electron screens. Only on those incredibly rare bodies known as planets can the familiar elements and their combinations exist and, in all still rarer cases, give rise to the phenomenon known as life.' – *Practically any astronomy book of the early 20th Century.*

THE STORM WAS STILL rising. He had long since ceased to struggle against it, although the ascending gas streams were carrying him into the bitterly cold regions ten thousand miles above his normal level. Dimly he was aware of his mistake: he should never have entered the area of disturbance, but the spot had developed so swiftly that there was now no chance of escape. The million-miles-an-hour wind had seized him as it rose from the depths and was carrying him up the great funnel it had torn in the photosphere – a tunnel already large enough to engulf a hundred worlds.

It was very cold. Around him carbon vapour was condensing in clouds of incandescent dust, swiftly torn away by the raging winds. This was something he had never met before, but the short-lived particles of solid matter left no sensation as they whipped through his body. Presently they were no more than glowing streamers far below, their furious movement foreshortened to a gentle undulation.

He was now at a truly enormous height, and his velocity showed no signs of slackening. The horizon was almost fifty thousand miles away, and the whole of the great spot lay visible beneath. Although he possessed neither eyes nor organs of sight, the radiation patterns sweeping through his body built up a picture of the awesome scene below. Like a great wound through which the Sun's life was ebbing into space, the vortex was now thousands of miles deep. From one edge a long tongue of flame was reaching out to form a half-completed bridge, defying the gales sweeping vertically past it. In a few hours, if it survived, it might span the abyss and divide the spot in twain. The fragments would drift apart, the fires of the photosphere would overwhelm them,

103

and soon the great globe would be unblemished again.

The Sun was still receding, and gradually into his slow, dim consciousness came the understanding that he could never return. The eruption that had hurled him into space had not given him sufficient velocity to escape forever, but a second giant force was beginning to exert its power. All his life he had been subjected to the fierce bombardment of solar radiation, pouring upon him from all directions. It was doing so no longer. The Sun now lay far beneath, and the force of its radiation was driving him out into space like a mighty wind. The great cloud of ions that was his body, more tenuous than air, was falling swiftly into the outer darkness.

Now the Sun was a globe of fire shrinking far behind, and the great spot no more than a black stain near the centre of its disc. Ahead lay darkness, utterly unrelieved, for his senses were far too coarse ever to detect the feeble light of the stars or the pale gleam of the circling planets. The only source of light he could ever know was dwindling from him. In a desperate effort to conserve his energy, he drew his body together into a tight, spherical cloud. Now he was almost as dense as air, but the electrostatic repulsion between his billions of constituent ions was too great for further concentration. When at last his strength weakened, they would disperse into space and no trace of his existence would remain.

He never felt the increasing gravitational pull from far ahead, and was unconscious of his changing speed. But presently the first faint intimations of the approaching magnetic field reached his consciousness and stirred it into sluggish life. He strained his senses out into the darkness, but to a creature whose home was the photosphere of the Sun the light of all other bodies was billions of times too faint even to be glimpsed, and the steadily strengthening field through which he was falling was an enigma beyond the comprehension of his rudimentary mind.

The tenuous outer fringes of the atmosphere checked his speed, and he fell slowly towards the invisible planet. Twice he felt a strange, tearing wrench as he passed through the ionosphere; then, no faster than a falling snowflake, he was drifting down through the cold, dense gas of the lower air. The descent took many hours and his strength was waning when he came to rest on a surface hard beyond anything he had ever imagined.

The waters of the Atlantic were bathed with brilliant sunlight, but to him the darkness was absolute save for the faint gleam of the infinitely distant Sun. For aeons he lay, incapable of movement, while the fires of consciousness burned lower within him and the last remnants of his energy ebbed away into the inconceivable cold.

It was long before he noticed the strange new radiation pulsing far off in the darkness – radiation of a kind he had never experienced before. Sluggishly he turned his mind towards it, considering what it might be and whence it came. It was closer than he had thought, for its movement was clearly visible and now it was climbing into the sky, approaching the Sun itself. But this was no second sun, for the strange illumination was waxing and waning, and only for a fraction of a cycle was it shining full upon him.

Nearer and nearer came that enigmatic glare; and as the throbbing rhythm of its brilliance grew fiercer he became aware of a strange, tearing resonance that seemed to shake the whole of his being. Now it was beating down upon him like a flail, tearing into his vitals and loosening his last hold on life itself. He had lost all control over the outer regions of his compressed but still enormous body.

The end came swiftly. The intolerable radiance was directly overhead, no longer pulsing but pouring down upon him in one continuous flood. Then there was neither pain nor wonder, nor the dull longing for the great golden world he had lost for ever ...

From the streamlined fairing beneath the great flying-wing, the long pencil of the radar beam was sweeping the Atlantic to the horizon's edge. Spinning in synchronism on the Plan Position Indicator, the faintly visible line of the time-base built up a picture of all that lay beneath. At the moment the screen was empty, for the coast of Ireland was more than three hundred miles away. Apart from an occasional brilliant blue spot – which was all that the greatest surface vessel became from fifty thousand feet – nothing would be visible until, in three hours' time, the eastern seaboard of America began to drift into the picture.

The navigator, checking his position continually by the North Atlantic radio lattice, seldom had any need for this part of the liner's radar. But to the passengers, the big skiatron indicator on the promenade deck was a source of constant interest, especially when the weather was bad and there was nothing to be seen below but the undulating hills and valleys of the cloud ceiling. There was still something magical, even in this age, about a radar landfall. No matter how often one had seen it before, it was fascinating to watch the pattern of the coastline forming on the screen, to pick out the harbours and the shipping and, presently, the hills and rivers and lakes of the land beneath.

To Edward Lindsey, returning from a week's leave in Europe, the Plan Position Indicator had a double interest. Fifteen years ago, as a young Coastal Command radio observer in the War of Liberation, he had spent long and tiring hours over these same waters, peering into a primitive forerunner of the great five-foot screen before him. He smiled wryly as his mind went back to those days. What would he have thought then, he wondered, if he could have seen himself as he was now, a prosperous accountant, travelling in comfort ten miles above the Atlantic at almost the velocity of sound? He thought also of the rest of S for Sugar's crew, and wondered what had happened to them in the intervening years.

105

At the edge of the scan, just crossing the three-hundred-mile range circle, a faint patch of light was beginning to drift into the picture. That was strange: there was no land there, for the Azores were further to the south. Besides, this seemed too ill-defined to be an island. The only thing it could possibly be was a storm-cloud heavy with rain.

Lindsey walked to the nearest window and looked out. The weather was extraordinarily fine. Far below, the waters of the Atlantic were crawling eastward towards Europe; even down to the horizon the sky was blue and cloudless.

He went back to the P.P.I. The echo was certainly a very curious one, approximately oval and as far as he could judge about ten miles long, although it was still too far away for accurate measurement. Lindsey did some rapid mental arithmetic. In twenty-five minutes it should be almost underneath them, for it was neatly bisected by the bright line that represented the aircraft's heading. Track? Course? Lord, how quickly one forgot that sort of thing! But it didn't matter; the wind could make little difference at the speed they were travelling. He would come back and have a look at it then, unless the gang in the bar got hold of him again.

Twenty minutes later he was even more puzzled. The tiny blue oval of light gleaming on the dark face of the screen was now only fifty miles away. If it were indeed a cloud, it was the strangest one he had ever seen. But the scale of the picture was still too small for him to make out any details.

The main controls of the indicator were safely locked away beneath the notice which read: PASSENGERS ARE REQUESTED NOT TO PLACE EMPTY GLASSES ON THE SKIATRON. However, one control had been left for the use of all comers. A massive three-position switch – guaranteed unbreakable – enabled anyone to select the tube's three diffrent ranges: three hundred, fifty, and ten miles. Normally the three-hundred-mile picture was used, but the more restricted fifty-mile scan gave much greater detail and was excellent for sightseeing overland. The ten-mile range was quite useless and no one knew why it was there.

Lindsey turned the switch to 50, and the picture seemed to explode. The mysterious echo, which had been nearing the screen's centre, now lay at its edge once more, enlarged six-fold. Lindsey waited until the afterglow of the old picture had died away; then he leaned over and carefully examined the new.

The echo almost filled the gap between the forty- and fifty-mile range circles, and now that he could see it clearly its strangeness almost took his breath away. From its centre radiated a curious network of filaments, while at its heart glowed a bright area perhaps two miles in length. It could only be fancy – yet he could have sworn that the central spot was pulsing very slowly.

Almost unable to believe his eyes, Lindsey stared into the screen. He watched in hypnotized fascination until the oval mist was less than forty miles away; then he ran to the nearest telephone and called for one of the ship's radio officers. While he was waiting, he went again to the observation port and looked out at the ocean beneath. He could see for at least a hundred miles – but there was absolutely nothing there but the blue Atlantic and the open sky.

It was a long walk from the control room to the promenade deck, and when Sub-Lieutenant Armstrong arrived, concealing his annoyance beneath a mask of polite but not obsequious service, the object was less than twenty miles away. Lindsey pointed to the skiatron.

'Look!' he said simply.

Sub-Lieutenant Armstrong looked. For a moment there was silence. Then came a curious, half-strangled ejaculation and he jumped back as if he had been stung. He leaned forward again and rubbed at the screen with his sleeve as if trying to remove something that shouldn't be there. Stopping himself in time, he grinned foolishly at Lindsey. Then he went to the observation window.

'There's nothing there. I've looked,' said Lindsey.

After the initial shock, Armstrong moved with commendable speed. He ran back to the skiatron, unlocked the controls with his master key, and made a series of swift adjustments. At once the time-base began to whirl round at a greatly increased speed, giving a more continuous picture than before.

It was much clearer now. The bright nucleus *was* pulsating, and faint knots of light were moving slowly outward along the radiating filaments. As he stared, fascinated, Lindsey suddenly remembered a glimpse he had once of an amoeba under the microscope. Apparently the same thought had occurred to the Sub-Lieutenant.

'It – it looks alive!' he whispered incredulously.

'I know,' said Lindsey. 'What do you think it is?'

The other hesitated for a while. 'I remember reading once that Appleton or someone had detected patches of ionization low down in the atmosphere. That's the only thing it can be.'

'But its structure! How do you explain that?'

The other shrugged his shoulders. 'I can't,' he said bluntly.

It was vertically beneath them now, disappearing into the blind area at the centre of the screen. While they were waiting for it to emerge again they had another look at the ocean below. It was uncanny: there was still absolutely nothing to be seen. But the radar could not lie. Something *must* be there –

It was fading fast when it reappeared a minute later, fading as if the full power of the radar transmitter had destroyed its cohesion. For the filaments were breaking up, and even as they watched the ten-mile-long

107

oval began to disintegrate. There was something awe-inspiring about the sight, and for some unfathomable reason Lindsey felt a surge of pity, as though he were witnessing the death of some gigantic beast. He shook his head angrily, but he could not get the thought out of his mind.

Twenty miles away, the last traces of ionization were dispersing to the winds. Soon eye and radar screen alike saw only the unbroken waters of the Atlantic rolling endlessly eastwards as if no power could ever disturb them.

And across the screen of the great indicator, two men stared speechlessly at one another, each afraid to guess what lay in the other's mind.

The Lost Machine

JOHN WYNDHAM

'FATHER, HERE, QUICKLY,' Joan's voice called down the long corridor. Dr Falkner, who was writing, checked himself in mid-sentence at the sound of his daughter's urgency.

'Father,' she called again.

'Coming,' he shouted as he hastily levered himself out of his easy chair. 'This way,' he added for the benefit of his two companions.

Joan was standing at the open door of the laboratory.

'It's gone,' she said.

'What do you mean?' he inquired brusquely as he brushed past her into the room. 'Run away?'

'No, not that,' Joan's dark curls fell forward as her head shook. 'Look there.'

He followed the line of her pointing finger to the corner of the room.

A pool of liquid metal was seeping into a widening circle. In the middle there rose an elongated, silvery mound which seemed to melt and run even as he looked. Speechlessly he watched the central mass flow out into the surrounding fluid, pushing the edges gradually further and further across the floor.

Then the mound was gone – nothing lay before him but a shapeless spread of glittering silver like a miniature lake of mercury.

For some moments the doctor seemed unable to speak. At length he recovered himself sufficiently to ask hoarsely:

'That – that was it?'

Joan nodded.

'It was recognizable when I first saw it,' she said.

Angrily he turned upon her.

'How did it happen? Who did it?' he demanded.

'I don't know,' the girl answered, her voice trembling a little as she spoke. 'As soon as I got back to the house I came in here just to see that it was all right. It wasn't in the usual corner and as I looked around I caught sight of it over here – melting. I shouted for you as soon as I realized what was happening.'

One of the doctor's companions stepped from the background.

'This,' he inquired, 'is – was the machine you were telling us about?'

109

There was a touch of a sneer in his voice as he put the question and indicated the quivering liquid with the toe of one shoe.

'Yes,' the doctor admitted slowly. 'That was it.'

'And, therefore, you can offer no proof of the talk you were handing out to us?' added the other man.

'We've got film records,' Joan began tentatively. 'They're pretty good . . .'

The second man brushed her words aside.

'Oh yes,' he said sarcastically. 'I've seen pictures of New York as it's going to look in a couple of hundred years, but that don't mean that anyone went there to take 'em. There's a whole lot of things that can be done with movies,' he insinuated.

Joan flushed, but kept silent. The doctor paid no attention. His brief flash of anger had subsided to leave him gazing at the remains before him.

'Who can have done it?' he repeated half to himself.

His daughter hesitated for a moment before she suggested:

'I think – I think it must have done it itself.'

'An accident? – I wonder,' murmured the doctor.

'No – no, not quite that,' she amended. 'I think it was – lonely,' the last word came out with a defiant rush.

There was a pause.

'Well, can you beat that?' said one of the others at last. 'Lonely – a lonely machine: that's a good one. And I suppose you're trying to feed us that it committed suicide, Miss? Well, it wouldn't surprise me any; nothing would, after the story your father gave us.'

He turned on his heel and added to his companion:

'Come on. I guess someone'll be turnin' this place into a sanatorium soon – we'd better not be here when it happens.'

With a laugh the two went out, leaving father and daughter to stare helplessly at the residue of a vanished machine.

At length Joan sighed and moved away. As she raised her eyes, she became aware of a pile of paper on the corner of a bench. She did not remember how it came to be there and crossed with idle curiosity to examine it.

The doctor was aroused from his reverie by the note of excitement in her voice.

'Look, here, Father,' she called sharply.

'What's that?' he asked, catching sight of the wad of sheets in her hand.

As he came closer he could see that the top one was covered with strange characters.

'What on earth . . .?' he began.

Joan's voice was curt with his stupidity.

'Don't you see?' she cried. 'It's written this for us.'

The doctor brightened for a moment; then the expression of gloom returned to his face.

'But how can we . . .?'

'The thing wasn't a fool – it must have learned enough of our language to put a key in somewhere to all this weird stuff, even if it couldn't write the whole thing in English. Look, this might be it, it looks even queerer than the rest.'

Several weeks of hard work followed for Joan in her efforts to decipher the curious document, but she held on with painstaking labour until she was able to lay the complete text before her father. That evening he picked up the pile of typed sheets and read steadily, without interruption, to the end . . .

Arrival

As we slowed to the end of our journey, Banuff began to show signs of excitement.

'Look,' he called to me. 'The third planet,* at last.'

I crossed to stand beside him and together we gazed down upon a stranger scene than any other fourth planet eyes have ever seen.

Though we were still high above the surface, there was plenty to cause us astonishment.

In place of our own homely red vegetation, we beheld a brilliant green. The whole land seemed to be covered with it. Anywhere it clung and thrived as though it needed no water. On the fourth planet, which the third planet men called Mars, the vegetation grows only in or around the canals, but here we could not even see any canals. The only sign of irrigation was one bright streak of water in the distance, twisting senselessly over the countryside – a symbolic warning of the incredible world we had reached.

Here and there our attention was attracted by outcroppings of various strange rocks amid all this green. Great masses of stone which sent up plumes of black smoke.

'The internal fires must be very near the surface of this world,' Banuff said, looking doubtfully at the rising vapours.

'See in how many places the smoke breaks out. I should doubt whether it has been possible for animal life to evolve on such a planet. It is possible yet that the ground may be too hot for us – or rather for me.'

There was a regret in his tone. The manner in which he voiced the last sentence stirred my sympathy. There are so many disadvantages in human construction which do not occur in us machines, and I knew that he was eager to obtain first-hand knowledge of the third planet.

For a long time we gazed in silent speculation at this queer, green world. At last Banuff broke the silence.

'I think we'll risk a landing there, Zat,' he said, indicating a smooth open space.

* The earth.

111

'You don't think it might be liquid,' I suggested, 'it looks curiously level.'

'No,' he replied, 'I fancy it's a kind of close vegetation. Anyway, we can risk it.'

A touch on the lever sent the machine sinking rapidly towards a green rectangle, so regular as to suggest the work of sentient creatures. On one of its sides lay a large stone outcrop, riddled with holes and smoking from the top like the rest, while on the other three sides, thick vegetation rose high and swayed in the wind.

'An atmosphere which can cause such commotion must be very dense,' commented Banuff.

'That rock is peculiarly regular,' I said, 'and the smoking points are evenly spaced. Do you suppose . . .?'

The slight jar of our landing interrupted me.

'Get ready, Zat,' Banuff ordered.

I was ready. I opened the inner door and stepped into the airlock. Banuff would have to remain inside until I could find out whether it was possible for him to adjust. Men may have more power of originality than we, and they do possess a greater degree of adaptability than any other form of life, but their limitations are, nevertheless, severe. It might require a deal of ponderous apparatus to enable Banuff to withstand the conditions, but for me, a machine, adaptation was simple.

The density of the atmosphere made no difference save slightly to slow my movements. The temperature, within very wide limits, had no effect upon me.

'The gravity will be stronger,' Banuff had warned me, 'this is a much larger planet than ours.'

It had been easy to prepare for that by the addition of a fourth pair of legs.

Now, as I walked out of the airlock, I was glad of them; the pull of the planet was immense.

After a moment or so of minor adjustment, I passed around our machine to the window where Banuff stood, and held up the instruments for him to see. As he read the air-pressure meter, the gravity indicator and the gas proportion scale, he shook his head. He might slowly adapt himself partway to the conditions, but an immediate venture was out of the question.

It had been agreed between us that in such an event I should perform the exploration and specimen collecting while he examined the neighbourhood from the machine.

He waved his arm as a signal and, in response, I set off at a good pace for the surrounding green and brown growths. I looked back as I reached them to see our silvery craft floating slowly up into the air.

A second later, there came a stunning explosion; a wave of sound so strong in this thick atmosphere that it almost shattered my receiving diaphragm.

The cause of the disaster must always remain a mystery: I only know that when I looked up, the vessel was nowhere to be seen – only a rain of metal parts dropping to earth all about me.

Cries of alarm came from the large stone outcrop and simultaneously human figures appeared at the lowest of its many openings.

They began to run towards the wreck, but my speed was far greater than theirs. They can have made but half the distance while I completed it. As I flashed across, I could see them falter and stop with ludicrous expressions of dismay on their faces.

'Lord, did you see that?' cried one of them.

'What the devil was it?' called another.

'Looked like a coffin on legs,' somebody said, 'Moving some, too.'

FLIGHT

Banuff lay in a ring of scattered débris.

Gently I raised him on my fore-rods. A very little examination showed that it was useless to attempt any assistance: he was too badly broken. He managed to smile faintly at me and then slid into unconsciousness.

I was sorry. Though Banuff was not of my own kind, yet he was of my own world and on the long trip I had grown to know him well. These humans are so fragile. Some little thing here or there breaks – they stop working and then, in a short time, they are decomposing. Had he been a machine, like myself, I could have mended him, replaced the broken parts and made him as good as new, but with these animal structures one is almost helpless.

I became aware, while I gazed at him, that the crowd of men and women had drawn closer and I began to suffer for the first time from what has been my most severe disability on the third planet – I could not communicate with them.

Their thoughts were understandable, for my sensitive plate was tuned to receive human mental waves, but I could not make myself understood. My language was unintelligible to them, and their minds, either from lack of development or some other cause, were unreceptive of my thought-radiations.

As they approached, huddled into a group, I made an astonishing discovery – they were afraid of me.

Men afraid of a machine.

It was incomprehensible. Why should they be afraid? Surely man and machine are natural complements: they assist one another. For a moment I thought I must have misread their minds – it was possible that thoughts registered differently on this planet, but it was a possibility I soon dismissed.

There were only two reasons for this apprehension. The one, that they had never seen a machine or, the other, that third planet machines had pursued a line of development inimical to them.

I turned to show Banuff lying inert on my fore-rods. Then, slowly, so as not to alarm them, I approached. I laid him down softly on the ground near by and retired a short distance. Experience has taught me that men like their own broken forms to be dealt with by their own kind. Some stepped forward to examine him, the rest held their ground, their eyes fixed upon me.

Banuff's dark colouring appeared to excite them not a little. Their own skins were pallid from lack of ultra-violet rays in their dense atmosphere.

'Dead?' asked one.

'Quite dead,' another one nodded. 'Curious-looking fellow,' he continued. 'Can't place him ethnologically at all. Just look at the frontal formation of the skull – very odd. And the size of his ears too, huge: the whole head is abnormally large.'

'Never mind him now,' one of the group broke in, 'he'll keep. That's the thing that puzzles me,' he went on, looking in my direction. 'What the devil do you suppose it is?'

They all turned wondering faces towards me. I stood motionless and waited while they summed me up.

'About six feet long,' ran the thoughts of one of them. 'Two feet broad and two deep. White metal, might be – (his thought conveyed nothing to me). Four legs to a side, fixed about half way up – jointed rather like a crab's, so are the arm-like things in front: but all metal. Wonder what the array of instruments and lenses on this end are? Anyhow, whatever kind of power it uses, it seems to have run down now . . .'

Hesitatingly he began to advance.

I tried a word of encouragement.

The whole group froze rigid.

'Did you hear that?' somebody whispered. 'It – it spoke.'

'Loudspeaker,' replied the one who had been making an inventory of me. Suddenly his expression brightened.

'I've got it,' he cried. 'Remote control – a telephone and television machine worked by remote control.'

So these people did know something of machinery, after all. He was far wrong in his guess, but in my relief I took a step forward.

An explosion roared: something thudded on my body case and whirred away. I saw that one of the men was pointing a hollow rod at me and I knew that he was about to make another explosion.

The first had done no injury but another might crack one of my lenses.

I turned and made top speed for the high, green vegetation. Two or three more bursts roared behind, but nothing touched me. The weapon was very primitive and grossly inaccurate.

Disappointment

For a day and a night I continued on among the hard stemmed growths.

For the first time since my making, I was completely out of touch with human control, and my existence seemed meaningless. The humans have a curious force they call ambition. It drives them, and, through them, it drives us. This force which keeps them active, we lack. Perhaps, in time, we machines will acquire it. Something of the kind – self-preservation which is allied to it – must have made me leave the man with the explosive tube and taken me into the strange country. But it was not enough to give me an objective. I seemed to go on because – well, because my machinery was constructed to go on.

On the way I made some odd discoveries.

Every now and then my path would be crossed by a band of hard matter, serving no useful purpose which I could then understand. Once, too, I found two unending rods of iron fixed horizontally to the ground and stretching away into the distance on either side. At first I thought they might be a method of guarding the land beyond, but they presented no obstacle.

Also, I found that the frequent outcroppings of stone were not natural, but laboriously constructed. Obviously this primitive race, with insufficient caves to hold its growing numbers, had been driven to construct artificial caves. The puzzling smoke arose from their method of heating these dwellings with naked fire – so wasteful a system of generating heat that no flame has been seen on the fourth planet, save in an accident, for thousands of years.

It was during the second day that I saw my first machine on this planet.

It stood at the side of one of the hard strips of land which had caused me so much wonder. The glitter of light upon its bright parts caught my lenses as I came through the bushes. My delight knew no bounds – at last I had found a being of my own kind. In my excitement I gave a call to attract its attention.

There was a flurry of movement round the far side and a human figure raised its head to look at me.

I was able to tell she was a woman despite the strange coverings that the third planet humans put upon themselves. She stared at me, her eyes widening in surprise while I could feel the shock in her mind. A spanner dropped from her hand and then, in a flash, she was into the machine, slamming the door behind her. There came a frantic whirring as she pressed a knob, but it produced no other result.

Slowly I continued to advance and as I came, the agitation in her mind increased. I had no wish to alarm her – it would have been more peaceful had her thought waves ceased to bombard me – but I was determined to know this machine.

As I drew clear of the bushes, I obtained a full view of the thing for the first time and disappointment hit me like a blow. *The thing had wheels.* Not just necessary parts of its internal arrangements, but wheels actually in contact with the ground. In a flash the explanation of all these hard streaks came to me. Unbelievable though it may seem, this could only follow a track specially built for it.

Later I found this was more or less true of all third planet land machines, but my first discouragement was painful. The primitive barbarity of the thing saddened me more than any discovery I had yet made.

Forlornly, and with little hope, I spoke to it.

There was no answer.

It stood there dumbly inert upon its foolish wheels as though it were a part of the ground itself.

Walking closer, I began to examine with growing disgust its crude internal arrangements. Incredibly, I found that its only means of propulsion was by a series of jerks from frequent explosions. Moreover, it was so ludicrously unorganized that both driving engine and brakes could be applied at the same time.

Sadly, as I gazed at the ponderous parts within, I began to feel that I was indeed alone. Until this encounter, my hope of discovering an intelligent machine had not really died. But now I knew that such a thing could not exist in the same world with this monster.

One of my fore-rods brushed against a part of it with a rasping sound and there came a startled cry of alarm from within. I looked up to the glass front where the woman's face peered affrightedly. Her mind was in such a state of confusion that it was difficult to know her wants clearly.

She hoped that I would go away – no, she wished the car would start and carry her away – she wondered whether I were an animal, whether I even really existed. In a jumble of emotions she was afraid and at the same time was angry with herself for being afraid. At last I managed to grasp that the machine was *unable* to run. I turned to find the trouble.

As I laboured with the thing's horrible vitals, it became clear to me why men, such as I had met, showed fear of me. No wonder they feared machines when their own mechanisms were as inefficient and futile as this. What reliance or trust could they place in a machine so erratic – so helpless that it could not even temporarily repair itself? It was not under its own control and only partially under theirs. Third planet men's attitude became understandable – commendable – if all their machines were as uncertain as this.

The alarm in the woman's mind yielded to amazement as she leaned forward and watched me work. She seemed to think me unreal, a kind of hallucination:

'I must be dreaming,' she told herself. 'That thing can't really be mending my car for me. It's impossible; some kind of horrid nightmare . . .'

There came a flash of panic at the thought of madness, but her mind soon rebalanced.

'I just don't understand it,' she said firmly and then, as though that settled it, proceeded to wait with a growing calm.

At last I had finished. As I wiped the things coarse, but necessary oil from my fore-rods, I signalled her to push again on the black knob. The whirr this time was succeeded by a roar – never would I have believed that a machine could be so inefficient.

116

Through the pandemonium I received an impression of gratitude on my thought plate. Mingling traces of nervousness remained, but first stood gratitude.

Then she was gone. Down the hard strip I watched the disgusting machine dwindle away to a speck.

Then I turned back to the bushes and went slowly on my way. Sadly I thought of the far away, red fourth planet and knew that my fate was sealed. I could not build a means of return. I was lost – the only one of my kind upon this primitive world.

THE BEASTS

They came upon me as I crossed one of the smooth, green spaces so frequent on this world.

My thought-cells were puzzling over my condition. On the fourth planet I had felt interest or disinterest, inclination or the lack of it, but little more. Now I had discovered reactions in myself which, had they lain in a human being, I should have called emotions. I was, for instance, lonely: I wanted the company of my own kind. Moreover, I had begun to experience excitement or, more particularly, apathy.

An apathetic machine!

I was considering whether this state was a development from the instinct of self-preservation, or whether it might not be due to the action of surrounding matter on my chemical cells, when I heard them coming.

First there was a drumming in my diaphragm, swelling gradually to a thunderous beat which shook the ground. Then I turned to see them charging down upon me.

Enormous beasts, extinct on my planet a million years, covered with hair and bearing spikes on their heads. Four-footed survivals of savagery battering across the land in unreasoning ferocity.

Only one course was possible since my escape was cut off by the windings of one of the imbecile-built canals. I folded my legs beneath me, crossed my fore-rods protectingly over my lenses and diaphragms, and waited.

They slowed as they drew closer. Suspiciously they came up to me and snuffled around. One of them gave a rap to my side with his spiked head, another pawed my case with a hoofed foot. I let them continue: they did not seem to offer any immediate danger. Such primitive animals, I thought, would be incapable of sustaining interest and soon move off elsewhere.

But they did not. Snuffling and rooting continued all around me. At last I determined to try an experimental waving of my fore-rods. The result was alarming. They plunged and milled around, made strange bellowing noises and stamped their hooves, but they did not go away. Neither did they attack, though they snorted and pawed the more energetically.

In the distance I heard a man's voice; his thought reached me faintly.

'What the 'ell's worritin' them damn cattle, Bill?' he called.

'Dunno,' came the reply of another. 'Let's go an' 'ave a look.'

The beasts gave way at the approach of the man and I could hear some of them thudding slowly away, though I did not, as yet, care to risk uncovering my lenses.

The men's voices drew quite near.

''Strewth,' said the first, ''ow did that get 'ere, Bill?'

'Search me,' answered the other. 'Wasn't 'ere 'arf an hour ago – that I'll swear. What is it, any'ow?'

''Anged if I know. 'Ere, give us a 'and and we'll turn it over.'

At this moment it seemed wise to make a movement; my balancers might be slow in adjusting to an inverted position.

There was a gasp then:

'Bill,' came an agitated whisper, 'did you see that rod there at the end? It moved, blessed if it didn't.'

'Go on,' scoffed the other. ''Ow could a thing like that move? You'll be sayin' next that it . . .'

I unfolded my legs and turned to face them.

For a moment both stood rooted, horror on their faces, then, with one accord, they turned and fled towards a group of their buildings in the distance. I followed them slowly: it seemed as good a direction as any other.

The buildings, not all of stone, were arranged so as almost to enclose a square. As the men disappeared through an opening in one side, I could hear their voices raised in warning and others demanding the reason for their excitement. I turned the corner in time to face a gaggling group of ten or twelve. Abruptly it broke as they ran to dark openings in search of safety. All, save one.

I halted and looked at this remaining one. He stared back, swaying a little as he stood, his eyes blinking in a vague uncertainty.

'What is it?' he exclaimed at last with a strange explosiveness, but as though talking to himself.

He was a sorely puzzled man. I found his mental processes difficult to follow. They were jumbled and erratic, hopping from this mind picture to that in uncontrolled jerks. But he was unafraid of me and I was glad of it. The first third planet man I had met who was not terror-ridden. Nevertheless, he seemed to doubt my reality.

'You fellowsh shee the shame s'I do?' he called deafeningly.

Muffled voices all around assured him that this was so.

'Thash all right, then,' he observed with relief, and took a step forward.

I advanced slowly not to alarm him and we met in the middle of the yard. Laying a rough hand on my body-case he seemed to steady himself, then he patted me once or twice.

'Goo' ol' dog,' he observed seriously. 'Goo' ol' feller. Come 'long, then.'

Looking over his shoulder to see that I followed and making strange whistling noises the while, he led the way to a building made of the hard, brown vegetable matter. At openings all about us scared faces watched our progress with incredulous amazement.

He opened the door and waved an uncertain hand in the direction of a pile of dried stalks which lay within.

'Goo' ol' dog,' he repeated. 'Lie down. There'sh a goo' dog.'

In spite of the fact that I, a machine, was being mistaken for a primitive animal, I obeyed the suggestion – after all, he, at least, was not afraid.

He had a little difficulty with the door fastening as he went out.

THE CIRCUS

There followed one of those dark periods of quiet. The animal origin of human beings puts them under the disability of requiring frequent periods of recuperation and, since they cannot use the infra-red rays for sight, as we do, their rests take place at times when they are unable to see.

With the return of sunlight came a commotion outside the door. Expostulations were being levelled at one named Tom – he who had led me here the previous day.

'You ain't really goin' to let it out?' one voice was asking nervously.

''Course I am. Why not?' Tom replied.

'The thing don't look right to me. I wouldn't touch it,' said another.

'Scared, that's what you are,' Tom suggested.

'P'raps I am – p'raps you'd've been scared last night if you 'adn't been so far gone.'

'Well, it didn't do nothin' to me when I'd had a few,' argued Tom, 'so why should it now?'

His words were confident enough, but I could feel a trepidation in his mind.

'It's your own funeral,' said the other. 'Don't say afterwards that I didn't warn you.'

I could hear the rest of them retire to what they considered a safe distance. Tom approached, making a show of courage with his words.

'Of course I'm goin' to let it out. What's more, I'm takin' it to a place I know of – it ought to be worth a bit.'

'You'll never . . .'

'Oh, won't I?'

He rattled open the door and addressed me in a fierce voice which masked a threatening panic.

'Come on,' he ordered, 'out of it.'

He almost turned to run as he saw me rise, but managed to master the impulse with an effort. Outwardly calm, he led the way to one of those machines which use the hard tracks, opened a rear door and pointed inside.

'In you get,' he said.

I doubt if ever a man was more relieved and surprised than he, when I did so.

With a grin of triumph he turned around, gave a mocking sweep with his cap to the rest, and climbed into the front seat.

My last sight as we roared away was of a crowd of open-mouthed men.

The sun was high when we reached our destination. The limitations of the machine were such that we had been delayed more than once to replenish fuel and water before we stopped, at last, in front of large gates set in a wooden fence.

Over the top could be seen the upper parts of pieces of white cloth tightly stretched over poles and decorated by further pieces of coloured cloth flapping in the wind. I had by this time given up the attempt to guess the purposes of third planet constructions, such incredible things managed to exist on this primitive world that it was simpler to wait and find out.

From behind the fence a rhythmical braying noise persisted, then there came the sound of a man's voice shouting above the din:

'What do you want – main entrance is round the other side.'

'Where's the boss?' called Tom. 'I got something for him.'

The doors opened to allow us to enter.

'Over there in his office,' said the man, jerking a thumb over his shoulder.

As we approached I could see that the third planet mania for wheels had led them even to mount the 'office' thus.

Tom entered and reappeared shortly, accompanied by another man.

'There it is,' he said, pointing to me, 'and there ain't another like it nowhere. The only all-metal animal in the world – how'll that look on the posters?'

The other regarded me with no enthusiasm in his eyes and a deal of disbelief in his mind.

'That long box thing?' he inquired.

'Sure, "that box thing". Here, you,' he added to me, 'get out of it.'

Both retreated a step as I advanced, the new man looked apprehensively at my fore-rods.

'You're sure it's safe?' he asked nervously.

'Safe?' said Tom. ' 'Course it's safe.'

To prove it he came across and patted my case.

'I'm offering you the biggest noise in the show business. It's worth ten times what I'm asking for it – I tell you, there ain't another one in the world.'

'Well, I ain't heard of another,' admitted the showman grudgingly. 'Where'd you get it?'

'Made it,' said Tom blandly. 'Spare time.'

The man continued to regard me with little enthusiasm.

'Can it do anything?' he asked at last.

'Can it—?' began Tom indignantly. 'Here you,' he added, 'fetch that lump of wood.'

120

When I brought it, the other looked a trifle less doubtful.

'What's inside it?' he demanded.

'Secrets,' said Tom shortly.

'Well, it's got to stop bein' a secret before I buy it. What sort of a fool do you take me for? Let's have a look at the thing's innards.'

'No,' said Tom, sending a nervous look sideways at me. 'Either you take it or leave it.'

'Ho, so that's your little game, is it? I'm to be the sucker who buys the thing and then finds the kid inside, workin' it. It wouldn't surprise me to find that the police'd like to know about this.'

'There ain't no kid inside,' denied Tom, 'it's just – just secret works. That's what it is.'

'I'll believe you when I see.'

Tom waited a moment before he answered.

'All right,' he said desperately, 'we'll get the blasted lid off of it . . . Here, hey, come back, you.'

The last was a shout to me but I gave it no notice. It was one thing to observe the curious ways of these humans, but it was quite a different matter to let them pry into my machinery. The clumsiness of such as Tom was capable of damaging my arrangements seriously.

'Stop it,' bawled Tom, behind me.

A man in my path landed a futile blow on my body case as I swept him aside. Before me was the biggest of all the cloth-covered erections.

'Here,' I thought, 'there will be plenty of room to hide.'

I was wrong. Inside, in a circular space, stood a line of four-footed animals. They were unlike the others I had met, in that they had no spikes on their heads and were of a much slender build, but they were just as primitive. All around, in tier upon tier of rings, sat hundreds of human beings.

Just a glimpse, I had, and then the animals saw me. They bolted in all directions and shouts of terror arose from the crowd.

I don't remember clearly what happened to me, but somewhere and somehow in the confusion which followed I found Tom in the act of starting his car. His first glance at me was one of pure alarm, then he seemed to think better of it.

'Get in,' he snapped, 'we've got to get clear of this somehow – and quick.'

Although I could make far better speed than that preposterous machine, it seemed better to accompany him than to wander aimlessly.

The Crash

Sadly, that night I gazed up at the red, fourth planet.

There rolled a world which I could understand, but here, all around me, was chaos, incredible unreasoning madness.

With me, in the machine, sat three friends of Tom's whom he had picked

121

up at the last town, and Tom himself who was steering the contraption. I shut my plate off from their thoughts and considered the day I had spent.

Once he was assured that we were free from pursuit, Tom had said to himself:

'Well, I guess that deserves a drink.'

Then he stopped on a part of the hard strip which was bordered by a row of artificial caves.

Continually, as the day wore on, he led me past gaping crowds into places where every man held a glass of coloured liquid. Strange liquids they were, although men do not value water on the third planet. And each time he proudly showed me to his friends in these places, he came to believe more firmly that he had created me.

Towards sunset something seemed to go seriously wrong with his machinery. He leaned heavily upon me for support and his voice became as uncertain as his thoughts were jumbled.

'Anybody comin' my way?' he had inquired at last and at that invitation the other three men had joined us.

The machine seemed to have become as queer as the men. In the morning it had held a straight line, but now it swayed from side to side, sometimes as though it would leave the track. Each time it just avoided the edge, all four men would break off their continuous wailing sounds to laugh senselessly and loudly.

It was while I struggled to find some meaning in all this madness that the disaster occurred.

Another machine appeared ahead. Its lights showed its approach and ours must have been as plain. Then an astounding thing happened. Instead of avoiding one another as would two intelligent machines, the two lumbering masses charged blindly together. Truly this was an insane world.

There came a rending smash. Our machine toppled over on its side. The other left the hard strip, struck one of the growths at the side of the road and burst into naked flames.

None of the four men seemed more than a little dazed. As one of them scrambled free, he pointed to the blaze.

'Thash good bonfire,' he said. 'Jolly good bonfire. Wonder if anybody'sh inshide?'

They all reeled over to examine the wreck while I, forgotten, waited for the next imbecility to occur on this nightmare world.

'It'sh a girl,' said Tom's voice.

One of the others nodded solemnly.

'I think you're right,' he agreed with difficult dignity.

After an interval, there came the girl's voice.

'But what shall I do? I'm miles from home.'

'S'all righ',' said Tom. 'Quite all righ'. You come along with me. Nishe fellow I am.'

I could read the intention behind his words – so could the girl.

There was the sound of a scuffle.

'No, you don't my beauty. No runnin' away. Dangeroush for li'l girlsh – 'lone in the dark.'

She started to scream, but a hand quickly stifled the sound.

I caught the upsurge of terror in her mind and at that moment I knew her. The girl whose machine I had mended – who had been grateful.

In a flash I was among them. Three of the men stared back in alarm, but not Tom. He was contemptuous of me because I had obeyed him. He lifted a heavy boot to send it crashing at my lens. Human movement is slow: before his leg had completed the back swing, I had caught it and whirled him away. The rest started futilely to close in on me.

I picked the girl up in my fore-rods and raced away into the darkness out of their sight.

DISCOURAGEMENT

At first she was bewildered and not a little frightened, though our first meeting must have shown that I intended no harm.

Gently I placed her on top of my case-work and, holding her there with my fore-rods, set off in the direction of her journey. She was hurt, blood was pouring down her right arm.

We made the best speed my eight legs could take us. I was afraid lest from lack of blood her mind might go blank and fail to direct me. At length it did. Her mental vibrations had been growing fainter and fainter until they ceased altogether. But she had been thinking ahead of us, picturing the way we should go, and I had read her mind.

At last, confronted by a closed door she had shown me, I pushed it down and held her out on my fore-rods to her father.

'Joan . . .?' he said, and for the moment seemed unsurprised at me – the only third planet man who ever was. Not until he had dressed his daughter's wounds and roused her to consciousness did he even look at me again.

There is little more. They have been kind, those two. They have tried to comprehend, though they cannot. He once removed a piece of my casing – I allowed him to do so, for he was intelligent – but he did not understand. I could feel him mentally trying to classify my structure among electrically operated devices – the highest form of power known to him, but still too primitive.

This whole world is too primitive. It does not even know the metal of which I am made. I am a freak . . . a curiosity outside comprehension.

These men long to know how I was built; I can read in their minds that they want to copy me. There is hope for them: some day, perhaps, they will have real machines of their own. . . . But not through my help will they build them, nothing of me shall go to the making of them.

I know what it is to be an intelligent machine in a world of madness . . .

The doctor looked up as he turned the last page.

'And so,' he said, 'it dissolved itself with my acids.'

He walked slowly over to the window and gazed up to Mars, swimming serenely among a myriad stars.

'I wonder,' he murmured, 'I wonder.'

He handed the typewritten sheets back to his daughter.

'Joan, my dear, I think it would be wisest to burn them. We have no desire to be certified.'

Joan nodded.

'As you prefer, Father,' she agreed.

The papers curled, flared and blackened on the coals – but Joan kept a copy.

'—And He Built a Crooked House—'

ROBERT A. HEINLEIN

AMERICANS ARE CONSIDERED crazy anywhere in the world.

They will usually concede a basis for the accusation but point to California as the focus of the infection. Californians stoutly maintain that their bad reputation is derived solely from the acts of the inhabitants of Los Angeles County. Angelenos will, when pressed, admit the charge but explain hastily, 'It's Hollywood. It's not our fault – we didn't ask for it; Hollywood just grew.'

The people in Hollywood don't care; they glory in it. If you are interested, they will drive you up Laurel Canyon ' – where we keep the violent cases.' The Canyonites – the brown-legged women, the trunks-clad men constantly busy building and rebuilding their slap-happy unfinished houses – regard with faint contempt the dull creatures who live down in the flats, and treasure in their hearts the secret knowledge that they, and only they, know how to live.

Lookout Mountain Avenue is the name of a side canyon which twists up from Laurel Canyon. The other Canyonites don't like to have it mentioned; after all, one must draw the line somewhere!

High up on Lookout Mountain at number 8775, across the street from the Hermit – the original Hermit of Hollywood – lived Quintus Teal, graduate architect.

Even the architecture of southern California is different. Hot dogs are sold from a structure built like and designated 'The Pup.' Ice cream cones come from a giant stucco ice cream cone, and neon proclaims 'Get the Chili Bowl Habit!' from the roofs of buildings which are indisputably chili bowls. Gasoline, oil, and free road maps are dispensed beneath the wings of tri-motored transport planes, while the certified rest rooms, inspected hourly for your comfort, are located in the cabin of the plane itself. These things may surprise, or amuse, the tourist, but the local residents, who walk bareheaded in the famous California noonday sun, take them as a matter of course.

Quintus Teal regarded the efforts of his colleagues in architecture as faint-hearted, fumbling, and timid.

'What is a house?' Teal demanded of his friend, Homer Bailey.

125

'Well –' Bailey admitted cautiously, 'speaking in broad terms, I've always regarded a house as a gadget to keep off the rain.'

'Nuts! You're as bad as the rest of them.'

'I didn't say the definition was complete –'

'Complete! It isn't even in the right direction. From that point of view we might just as well be squatting in caves. But I don't blame you,' Teal went on magnanimously, 'you're no worse than the lugs you find practising architecture. Even the Moderns – all they've done is to abandon the Wedding Cake School in favour of the Service Station School, chucked away the gingerbread and slapped on some chromium, but at heart they are as conservative and traditional as a county courthouse. Neutra! Schindler! What have those bums got? What's Frank Lloyd Wright got that I haven't got?'

'Commissions,' his friend answered succinctly.

'Huh? Wha' d'ju say?' Teal stumbled slightly in his flow of words, did a slight double take, and recovered himself. 'Commissions. Correct. And why? Because I don't think of a house as an upholstered cave; I think of it as a machine for living, a vital process, a live dynamic thing, changing with the mood of the dweller – not a dead, static, oversized coffin. Why should we be held down by the frozen concepts of our ancestors? Any fool with a little smattering of descriptive geometry can design a house in the ordinary way. Is the static geometry of Euclid the only mathematics? Are we to completely disregard the Picard-Vessiot theory? How about modular systems? – to say nothing of the rich suggestions of stereochemistry. Isn't there a place in architecture for transformation, for homomorphology, for actional structures?'

'Blessed if I know,' answered Bailey. 'You might just as well be talking about the fourth dimension for all it means to me.'

'And why not? Why should we limit ourselves to the – Say!' He interrupted himself and stared into distances. 'Homer, I think you've really got something. After all, why not? Think of the infinite richness of articulation and relationship in four dimensions. What a house, what a house –' He stood quite still, his pale bulging eyes blinking thoughtfully.

Bailey reached up and shook his arm. 'Snap out of it. What the hell are you talking about, four dimensions? Time is the fourth dimension; you can't drive nails into *that*.'

Teal shrugged him off. 'Sure. Sure. Time is *a* fourth dimension, but I'm thinking about a fourth spatial dimension, like length, breadth and thickness. For economy of materials and convenience of arrangement you couldn't beat it. To say nothing of the saving of ground space – you could put an eight-room house on the land now occupied by a one-room house. Like a tesseract –'

'What's a tesseract?'

'Didn't you go to school? A tesseract is a hypercube, a square figure with

126

four dimensions to it, like a cube has three, and a square has two. Here, I'll show you.' Teal dashed out into the kitchen of his apartment and returned with a box of toothpicks which he spilled on the table between them, brushing glasses and a nearly empty Holland gin bottle carelessly aside. 'I'll need some plasticine. I had some around here last week.' He burrowed into a drawer of the littered desk which crowded one corner of his dining room and emerged with a lump of oily sculptor's clay. 'Here's some.'

'What are you going to do?'

'I'll show you.' Teal rapidly pinched off small masses of the clay and rolled them into pea-sized balls. He stuck toothpicks into four of these and hooked them together into a square. 'There! That's a square.'

'Obviously.'

'Another one like it, four more toothpicks, and we make a cube.' The toothpicks were now arranged in the framework of a square box, a cube, with the pellets of clay holding the corners together. 'Now we make another cube just like the first one, and the two of them will be two sides of the tesseract.'

Bailey started to help him roll the little balls of clay for the second cube, but became diverted by the sensuous feel of the docile clay and started working and shaping it with his fingers.

'Look,' he said, holding up his effort, a tiny figurine, 'Gypsy Rose Lee.'

'Looks more like Gargantua; she ought to sue you. Now pay attention. You open up one corner of the first cube, interlock the second cube at one corner, and then close the corner. Then take eight more toothpicks and join the bottom of the first cube to the bottom of the second, on a slant, and the top of the first to the top of the second, the same way.' This he did rapidly, while he talked.

'What's that supposed to be?' Bailey demanded suspiciously.

'That's a tesseract, eight cubes forming the sides of a hypercube in four dimensions.'

'It looks more like a cat's cradle to me. You've only go two cubes there anyhow. Where are the other six?'

'Use your imagination, man. Consider the top of the first cube in relation to the top of the second; that's cube number three. Then the two bottom squares, then the front faces of each cube, the back faces, the right hand, the left hand – eight cubes.' He pointed them out.

'Yeah, I see 'em. But they still aren't cubes; they're whatchamucallems – prisms. They are not square, they slant.'

'That's just the way you look at it, in perspective. If you drew a picture of a cube on a piece of paper, the side squares would be slaunchwise, wouldn't they? That's perspective. When you look at a four-dimensional figure in three dimensions, naturally it looks crooked. But those are all cubes just the same.'

'Maybe they are to you, brother, but they still look crooked to me.'

Teal ignored the objections and went on. 'Now consider this as the framework of an eight-room house; there's one room on the ground floor – that's for service, utilities, and garage. There are six rooms opening off it on the next floor, living room, dining room, bath, bedrooms, and so forth. And up at the top, completely enclosed and with windows on four sides, is your study. There! How do you like it?'

'Seems to me you have the bathtub hanging out of the living room ceiling. Those rooms are interlaced like an octopus.'

'Only in perspective, only in perspective. Here, I'll do it another way so you can see it.' This time Teal made a cube of toothpicks, then made a second of halves of toothpicks, and set it exactly in the centre of the first by attaching the corners of the small cube to the large cube by short lengths of toothpick. 'Now – the big cube is your ground floor, the little cube inside is your study on the top floor. The six cubes joining them are the living rooms See?'

Bailey studied the figure, then shook his head. 'I still don't see but two cubes, a big one and a little one. Those other six things, they look like pyramids this time instead of prisms, but they still aren't cubes.'

'Certainly, certainly, you are seeing them in different perspective. Can't you see that?'

'Well, maybe. But that room on the inside, there. It's completely surrounded by the thingamujigs. I thought you said it had windows on four sides.'

'It has – it just looks like it was surrounded. That's the grand feature about a tesseract house, complete outside exposure for every room, yet every wall serves two rooms and an eight-room house requires only a one-room foundation. It's revolutionary.'

'That's putting it mildly. You're crazy, bud; you can't build a house like that. That inside room is on the inside, and there she stays.'

Teal looked at his friend in controlled exasperation. 'It's guys like you that keep architecture in its infancy. How many square sides has a cube?'

'Six.'

'How many of them are inside?'

'Why, none of 'em. They're all on the outside.'

'All right. Now listen – a tesseract has eight cubical sides, *all on the outside*. Now watch me. I'm going to open up this tesseract like you can open up a cubical pasteboard box, until it's flat. That way you'll be able to see all eight of the cubes.' Working very rapidly, he constructed four cubes, piling one on top of the other in an unsteady tower. He then built out four more cubes from the four exposed faces of the second cube in the pile. The structure swayed a little under the loose coupling of the clay pellets, but it stood, eight cubes in an inverted cross, a double cross, as the four additional cubes stuck out in four directions. 'Do you see it now? It rests on the ground floor room, the next six cubes are the living rooms, and there is your study, up at the top.'

Bailey regarded it with more approval than he had the other figures. 'At least I can understand it. You say that is a tesseract, too?'

'That is a tesseract unfolded in three dimensions. To put it back together you tuck the top cube onto the bottom cube, fold those side cubes in till they meet the top cube and there you are. You do all this folding through a fourth dimension of course; you don't distort any of the cubes, or fold them into each other.'

Bailey studied the wobbly framework further. 'Look here,' he said at last, 'why don't you forget about folding this thing up through a fourth dimension – you can't anyway – and build a house like this?'

'What do you mean, I can't? It's a simple mathematical problem – '

'Take it easy, son. It may be simple in mathematics, but you could never get your plans approved for construction. There isn't any fourth dimension; forget it. But this kind of a house – it might have some advantages.'

Checked, Teal studied the model. 'Hm-m-m – Maybe you got something. We could have the same number of rooms, and we'd save the same amount of ground space. Yet, and we would set that middle cross-shaped floor northeast, southwest, and so forth, so that every room would get sunlight all day long. That central axis lends itself nicely to central heating. We'll put the dining room on the northeast and the kitchen on the southeast, with big view windows in every room. O.K., Homer, I'll do it! Where do you want it built?'

'Wait a minute! Wait a minute! I didn't say you were going to build it for me – '

'Of course I am. Who else? Your wife wants a new house; this is it.'

'But Mrs Bailey wants a Georgian house – '

'Just an idea she has. Women don't know what they want – '

'Mrs Bailey does.'

'Just some idea an out-of-date architect has put in her head. She drives a 1941 car, doesn't she? She wears the very latest styles – why should she live in an eighteenth-century house? This house will be even later than a 1941 model; it's years in the future. She'll be the talk of the town.'

'Well – I'll have to talk to her.'

'Nothing of the sort. We'll surprise her with it. Have another drink.'

'Anyhow, we can't do anything about it now. Mrs Bailey and I are driving up to Bakersfield tomorrow. The company's bringing in a couple of wells tomorrow.'

'Nonsense. That's just the opportunity we want. It will be a surprise for her when you get back. You can just write me a cheque right now, and your worries are over.'

'I oughtn't to do anything like this without consulting her. She won't like it.'

'Say, who wears the pants in your family anyhow?'

The cheque was signed about halfway down the second bottle.

Things are done fast in southern California. Ordinary houses there are usually built in a month's time. Under Teal's impassioned heckling the tesseract house climbed dizzily skyward in days rather than weeks, and its cross-shaped second storey came jutting out at the four corners of the world. He had some trouble at first with the inspectors over these four projecting rooms but by using strong girders and folding money he had been able to convince them of the soundness of his engineering.

By arrangement, Teal drove up in front of the Bailey residence the morning after their return to town. He improvised on his two-tone horn. Bailey stuck his head out the front door. 'Why don't you use the bell?'

'Too slow,' answered Teal cheerfully. 'I'm a man of action. Is Mrs Bailey ready? Ah, there you are, Mrs Bailey! Welcome home, welcome home. Jump in, we've got a surprise for you!'

'You know Teal, my dear,' Bailey put in uncomfortably.

Mrs Bailey sniffed. 'I know him. We'll go in our own car, Homer.'

'Certainly, my dear.'

'Good idea,' Teal agreed; ''sgot more power than mine; we'll get there faster. I'll drive, I know the way.' He took the keys from Bailey, slid into the driver's seat, and had the engine started before Mrs Bailey could rally her forces.

'Never have to worry about my driving,' he assured Mrs Bailey, turning his head as he did so, while he shot the powerful car down the avenue and swung onto Sunset Boulevard, 'it's a matter of power and control, a dynamic process, just my meat – I've never had a serious accident.'

'You won't have but one,' she said bitingly. 'Will you *please* keep your eyes on the traffic?'

He attempted to explain to her that a traffic situation was a matter, not of eyesight, but intuitive integration of courses, speeds, and probabilities, but Bailey cut him short. 'Where is the house, Quintus?'

'House?' asked Mrs Bailey suspiciously. 'What's this about a house, Homer? Have you been up to something without telling me?'

Teal cut in with his best diplomatic manner. 'It certainly is a house, Mrs Bailey. And what a house! It's a surprise for you from a devoted husband. Just wait till you see it – '

'I shall,' she agreed grimly. 'What style is it?'

'This house sets a new style. It's later than television, newer than next week. It must be seen to be appreciated. By the way,' he went on rapidly, heading off any retort, 'did you folks feel the earthquake last night?'

'Earthquake? What earthquake? Homer, was there an earthquake?'

'Just a little one,' Teal continued, 'about two A.M. If I hadn't been awake, I wouldn't have noticed it.'

Mrs Bailey shuddered. 'Oh, this awful country! Do you hear that, Homer? We might have been killed in our beds and never have known it. Why did I ever let you persuade me to leave Iowa?'

'But my dear,' he protested hopelessly, 'you wanted to come out to California; you didn't like Des Moines.'

130

'We needn't go into that,' she said firmly. 'You are a man; you should anticipate such things. Earthquakes!'

'That's one thing you needn't fear in your new home, Mrs Bailey,' Teal told her. 'It's absolutely earthquake-proof; every part is in perfect dynamic balance with every other part.'

'Well, I hope so. Where is this house?'

'Just around this bend. There's the sign now.' A large arrow sign, of the sort favoured by real estate promoters, proclaimed in letters that were large and bright even for southern California:

THE HOUSE OF THE FUTURE!!!

COLOSSAL – AMAZING – REVOLUTIONARY

SEE HOW YOUR GRANDCHILDREN WILL LIVE!

Q. TEAL, ARCHITECT

'Of course that will be taken down,' he added hastily, noting her expression, 'as soon as you take possession.' He slued around the corner and brought the car to a squealing halt in front of the House of the Future. '*Voilà!*' He watched their faces for response.

Bailey stared unbelievingly, Mrs Bailey in open dislike. They saw a simple cubical mass, possessing doors and windows, but no other architectural features, save that it was decorated in intricate mathematical designs. 'Teal,' Bailey asked slowly, 'what have you been up to?'

Teal turned from their faces to the house. Gone was the crazy tower with its jutting second-storey rooms. No trace remained of the seven rooms above ground floor level. Nothing remained but the single room that rested on the foundations. 'Great jumping cats!' he yelled, 'I've been robbed!'

He broke into a run.

But it did him no good. Front or back, the story was the same; the other seven rooms had disappeared, vanished completely. Bailey caught up with him, and took his arm. 'Explain yourself. What is this about being robbed? How come you built anything like this – it's not according to agreement.'

'But I didn't. I built just what we had planned to build, an eight-room house in the form of a developed tesseract. I've been sabotaged; that's what it is! Jealousy! The other architects in town didn't dare let me finish this job; they knew they'd be washed up if I did.'

'When were you last here?'

'Yesterday afternoon.'

'Everything all right then?'

'Yes. The gardeners were just finishing up.'

Bailey glanced around at the faultlessly manicured landscaping. 'I don't see how seven rooms could have been dismantled and carted away from here in a single night without wrecking this garden.'

Teal looked around, too. 'It doesn't look it. I don't understand it.'

Mrs Bailey joined them. 'Well? Well? Am I to be left to amuse myself? We might as well look it over as long as we are here, though I'm warning you, Homer, I'm not going to like it.'

'We might as well,' agreed Teal, and drew a key from his pocket with which he let them in the front door. 'We may pick up some clues.'

The entrance hall was in perfect order, the sliding screens that separated it from the garage space were back, permitting them to see the entire compartment. 'This looks all right,' observed Bailey. 'Let's go up on the roof and try to figure out what happened. Where's the staircase? Have they stolen that, too?'

'Oh no,' Teal denied, 'look – ' He pressed a button below the light switch; a panel in the ceiling fell away and a light, graceful flight of stairs swung noiselessly down. Its strength members were the frosty silver of duralumin, its treads and risers transparent plastic. Teal wriggled like a boy who had successfully performed a card trick, while Mrs Bailey thawed perceptibly.

It was beautiful.

'Pretty slick,' Bailey admitted. 'Howsomever it doesn't seem to go any place – '

'Oh, that – ' Teal followed his gaze. 'The cover lifts up as you approach the top. Open stairwells are anachronisms. Come on.' As predicted, the lid of the staircase got out of their way as they climbed the flight and permitted them to debouch at the top, but not, as they had expected, on the roof of the single room. They found themselves standing in the middle one of the five rooms which constituted the second floor of the original structure.

For the first time on record Teal had nothing to say. Bailey echoed him, chewing on his cigar. Everything was in perfect order. Before them, through open doorway and translucent partition, lay the kitchen, a chef's dream of up-to-the-minute domestic engineering, monel metal, continuous counter space, concealed lighting, functional arrangement. On the left the formal, yet gracious and hospitable dining room awaited guests, its furniture in parade-ground alignment.

Teal knew before he turned his head that the drawing room and lounge would be found in equally substantial and impossible existence.

'Well, I must admit this *is* charming,' Mrs Bailey approved, 'and the kitchen is just *too* quaint for words – though I would never have guessed from the exterior that this house had so much room upstairs. Of course *some* changes will have to be made. That secretary now – if we moved it over *here* and put the settle over *there* – '

'Stow it, Matilda,' Bailey cut in brusquely. 'Wha'd' yuh make of it, Teal?'

'Why, Homer Bailey! The very id – '

'Stow it, I said. Well, Teal?'

132

The architect shuffled his rambling body. 'I'm afraid to say. Let's go on up.'

'How?'

'Like this.' He touched another button; a mate, in deeper colours, to the fairy bridge that had let them up from below offered them access to the next floor. They climbed it, Mrs Bailey expostulating in the rear, and found themselves in the master bedroom. Its shades were drawn, as had been those on the level below, but the mellow lighting came on automatically. Teal at once activated the switch which controlled still another flight of stairs, and they hurried up into the top-floor study.

'Look, Teal,' suggested Bailey when he had caught his breath, 'can we get to the roof above this room? Then we could look around.'

'Sure, it's an observatory platform.' They climbed a fourth flight of stairs, but when the cover at the top lifted to let them reach the level above, they found themselves, not on the roof, but *standing in the ground floor room where they had entered the house.*

Mr Bailey turned a sickly grey. 'Angels in heaven,' he cried, 'this place is haunted. We're getting out of here.' Grabbing his wife he threw open the front door and plunged out.

Teal was too much preoccupied to bother with their departure. There was an answer to all this, an answer that he did not believe. But he was forced to break off considering it because of hoarse shouts from somewhere above him. He lowered the staircase and rushed upstairs. Bailey was in the central room leaning over Mrs Bailey, who had fainted. Teal took in the situation, went to the bar built into the lounge, and poured three fingers of brandy, which he returned with and handed to Bailey. 'Here – this'll fix her up.'

Bailey drank it.

'That was for Mrs Bailey,' said Teal.

'Don't quibble,' snapped Bailey. 'Get her another.' Teal took the precaution of taking one himself before returning with a dose earmarked for his client's wife. He found her just opening her eyes.

'Here, Mrs Bailey,' he soothed, 'this will make you feel better.'

'I never touch spirits,' she protested, and gulped it.

'Now tell me what happened,' suggested Teal. 'I thought you two had left.'

'But we did – we walked out the front door and found ourselves up here, in the lounge.'

'The hell you say! Hm-m-m – wait a minute.' Teal went into the lounge. There he found that the big view window at the end of the room was open. He peered cautiously through it. He stared, not out at the California countryside, but into the ground floor room – or a reasonable facsimile thereof. He said nothing, but went back to the stairwell which he had left open and looked down it. The ground-floor room was still in place.

Somehow, it managed to be in two different places at once, on different levels.

He came back into the central room and seated himself opposite Bailey in a deep, low chair, and sighted him past his upthrust bony knees. 'Homer,' he said impressively, 'do you know what has happened?'

'No, I don't – but if I don't find out pretty soon, something is going to happen and pretty drastic, too!'

'Homer, this is a vindication of my theories. This house is a real tesseract.'

'What's he talking about, Homer?'

'Wait, Matilda – now Teal, that's ridiculous. You've pulled some hanky-panky here and I won't have it – scaring Mrs Bailey half to death, and making me nervous. All I want is to get out of here, with no more of your trapdoors and silly practical jokes.'

'Speak for yourself, Homer,' Mrs Bailey interrupted, 'I was *not* frightened; I was just took all over queer for a moment. It's my heart; all of my people are delicate and highstrung. Now about this tessy thing – explain yourself, Mr Teal. Speak up.'

He told her as well as he could in the face of numerous interruptions the theory back of the house. 'Now as I see it, Mrs Bailey,' he concluded, 'this house, while perfectly stable in three dimensions, was not stable in four dimensions. I had built a house in the shape of an unfolded tesseract; something happened to it, some jar or side thrust, and it collapsed into its normal shape – it folded up.' He snapped his fingers suddenly. 'I've got it! The earthquake!'

'Earthquake?'

'Yes, yes, the little shake we had last night. From a four-dimensional standpoint this house was like a plane balanced on edge. One little push and it fell over, collapsed along its natural joints into a stable four-dimensional figure.'

'I thought you boasted about how safe this house was.'

'It *is* safe – three-dimensionally.'

'I don't call a house safe,' commented Bailey edgily, 'that collapses at the first little tremor.'

'But look around you, man!' Teal protested. 'Nothing has been disturbed, not a piece of glassware cracked. Rotation through a fourth dimension can't affect a three-dimensional figure any more than you can shake letters off a printed page. If you had been sleeping in here last night, you would never have awakened.'

'That's just what I'm afraid of. Incidentally, has your great genius figured out any way for us to get out of this booby trap?'

'Huh? Oh, yes, you and Mrs Bailey started to leave and landed back up here, didn't you? But I'm sure there is no real difficulty – we came in, we can go out. I'll try it.' He was up and hurrying downstairs before he had finished talking. He flung open the front door, stepped through, and found himself staring at his companions, down the length of the second-floor lounge. 'Well, there does seem to be some slight problem,' he admitted blandly. 'A mere technicality, though – we can always go out a window.' He jerked aside the long drapes that covered the deep French windows set in one side wall of the lounge. He stopped suddenly.

'Hm-m-m,' he said, 'this is interesting – very.'

'What is?' asked Bailey, joining him.

'This.' This window stared directly into the dining room, instead of looking outdoors. Bailey stepped back to the corner where the lounge and the dining room joined the central room at ninety degrees.

'But that can't be,' he protested, 'that window is maybe fifteen, twenty feet from the dining room.'

'Not in a tesseract,' corrected Teal. 'Watch.' He opened the window and stepped through, talking back over his shoulder as he did so.

From the point of view of the Baileys he simply disappeared.

But not from his own viewpoint. It took him some seconds to catch his breath. Then he cautiously disentangled himself from the rosebush to which he had become almost irrevocably wedded, making a mental note the while never again to order landscaping which involved plants with thorns, and looked around him.

He was outside the house. The massive bulk of the ground floor room thrust up beside him. Apparently he had fallen off the roof.

He dashed around the corner of the house, flung open the front door and hurried up the stairs. 'Homer!' he called out, 'Mrs Bailey! I've found a way out!'

Bailey looked annoyed rather than pleased to see him. 'What happened to you?'

'I fell out. I've been outside the house. You can do it just as easily – just step through those French windows. Mind the rosebush, though – we may have to build another stairway.'

'How did you get back in?'

'Through the front door.'

'Then we shall leave the same way. Come, my dear.' Bailey set his hat firmly on his head and marched down the stairs, his wife on his arm.

Teal met them in the lounge. 'I could have told you that wouldn't work,' he announced. 'Now here's what we have to do: As I see it, in a four-dimensional figure a three-dimensional man has two choices every time he crosses a line of juncture, like a wall or a threshold. Ordinarily he will make a ninety-degree turn through the fourth dimension, only he doesn't feel it with his three dimensions. Look.' He stepped through the very window that he had fallen out of a moment before. Stepped through and arrived in the dining room, where he stood, still talking.

'I watched where I was going and arrived where I intended to.' He stepped back into the lounge. 'The time before I didn't watch and I moved on through normal space and fell out of the house. It must be a matter of subconscious orientation.'

'I'd hate to depend on subconscious orientation when I step out for the morning paper.'

'You won't have to; it'll become automatic. Now to get out of the house this time – Mrs Bailey, if you will stand here with your back to the window, and jump backward, I'm pretty sure you will land in the garden.'

Mrs Bailey's face expressed her opinion of Teal and his ideas. 'Homer Bailey,' she said shrilly, 'are you going to stand there and let him suggest such –'

'But Mrs Bailey,' Teal attempted to explain, 'we can tie a rope on you and lower you down eas –'

'Forget it, Teal,' Bailey cut him off brusquely. 'We'll have to find a better way than that. Neither Mrs Bailey nor I are fitted for jumping.'

Teal was temporarily nonplussed; there ensued a short silence. Bailey broke it with, 'Did you hear that, Teal?'

'Hear what?'

'Someone talking off in the distance. D'you s'pose there could be someone else in the house, playing tricks on us, maybe?'

'Oh, not a chance. I've got the only key.'

'But I'm sure of it,' Mrs Bailey confirmed. 'I've heard them ever since we came in. Voices. Homer, I can't stand much more of this. Do something.'

'Now, now, Mrs Bailey,' Teal soothed, 'don't get upset. There can't be anyone else in the house, but I'll explore and make sure. Homer, you stay here with Mrs Bailey and keep an eye on the rooms on this floor.' He passed from the lounge into the ground-floor room and from there to the kitchen and on into the bedroom. This led him back to the lounge by a straight-line route, that is to say, by going straight ahead on the entire trip he returned to the place from which he started.

'Nobody around,' he reported. 'I opened all of the doors and windows as I went – all except this one.' He stepped to the window opposite the one through which he had recently fallen and thrust back the drapes.

He saw a man with his back towards him, four rooms away. Teal snatched open the French window and dived through it, shouting, 'There he goes now! Stop thief!'

The figure evidently heard him; it fled precipitately. Teal pursued, his gangling limbs stirred to unanimous activity, through drawing room, kitchen, dining room, lounge – room and room, yet in spite of Teal's best efforts he could not seem to cut down the four-room lead that the interloper had started with.

He saw the pursued jump awkwardly but actively over the low sill of a French window and in so doing knock off his hat. When he came up to the point where his quarry had lost his headgear, he stopped and picked it up, glad of an excuse to stop and catch his breath. He was back in the lounge.

136

'I guess he got away from me,' he admitted. 'Anyhow, here's his hat. Maybe we can identify him.'

Bailey took the hat, looked at it, then snorted, and slapped it on Teal's head. It fitted perfectly. Teal looked puzzled, took the hat off, and examined it. On the sweat band were the initials 'Q.T.' It was his own.

Slowly comprehension filtered through Teal's features. He went back to the French window and gazed down the series of rooms through which he had pursued the mysterious stranger. They saw him wave his arms semaphore fashion. 'What are you doing?' asked Bailey.

'Come see.' The two joined him and followed his stare with their own. Four rooms away they saw the backs of three figures, two male and one female. The taller, thinner of the men was waving his arms in a silly fashion.

Mrs Bailey screamed and fainted again.

Some minutes later, when Mrs Bailey had been resuscitated and somewhat composed, Bailey and Teal took stock. 'Teal,' said Bailey, 'I won't waste any time blaming you; recriminations are useless and I'm sure you didn't plan for this to happen, but I suppose you realize we are in a pretty serious predicament. How are we going to get out of here? It looks now as if we would stay until we starve; every room leads into another room.'

'Oh, it's not that bad. I got out once, you know.'

'Yes, but you can't repeat it – you tried.'

'Anyhow we haven't tried all the rooms. There's still the study.'

'Oh, yes, the study. We went through there when we first came in, and didn't stop. Is it your idea that we might get out through its windows?'

'Don't get your hopes up. Mathematically, it ought to look into the four side rooms on this floor. Still we never opened the blinds; maybe we ought to look.'

''Twon't do any harm anyhow. Dear, I think you had best just stay here and rest –'

'Be left alone in this horrible place? I should say not!' Mrs Bailey was up off the couch where she had been recuperating even as she spoke.

They went upstairs. 'This is the inside room, isn't it, Teal?' Bailey inquired as they passed through the master bedroom and climbed on up towards the study. 'I mean it was the little cube, in your diagram that was in the middle of the big cube, and completely surrounded.'

'That's right,' agreed Teal. 'Well, let's have a look. I figure this window ought to give into the kitchen.' He grasped the cords of Venetian blinds and pulled them.

It did not. Waves of vertigo shook them. Involuntarily they fell to the floor and grasped helplessly at the pattern on the rug to keep from falling. 'Close it! Close it!' moaned Bailey.

Mastering in part a primitive atavistic fear, Teal worked his way back to the window and managed to release the screen. The window had looked *down* instead of *out*, down from a terrifying height.

Mrs Bailey had fainted again.

Teal went back after more brandy while Bailey chafed her wrists. When she had recovered, Teal went cautiously to the window and raised the screen a crack. Bracing his knees, he studied the scene. He turned to Bailey. 'Come look at this, Homer. See if you recognize it.'

'You stay away from there, Homer Bailey!'

'Now Matilda, I'll be careful.' Bailey joined him and peered out.

'See up there? That's the Chrysler Building, sure as shooting. And there's the East River, and Brooklyn.' They gazed straight down the sheer face of an enormously tall building. More than a thousand feet away a toy city, very much alive, was spread out before them. 'As near as I can figure it out, we are looking down the side of the Empire State Building from a point just above its tower.'

'What is it? A mirage?'

'I don't think so – it's too perfect. I think space is folded over through the fourth dimension here and we are looking past the fold.'

'You mean we aren't really seeing it?'

'No, we're seeing it all right. I don't know what would happen if we climbed out this window, but I for one don't want to try. But what a view! Oh boy, what a view! Let's try the other windows.'

They approached the next window more cautiously, and it was well that they did, for it was even more disconcerting, more reason-shaking, than the one looking down the gasping height of the skyscraper. It was a simple seascape, open ocean and blue sky – but the ocean was where the sky should have been, and contrariwise. This time they were somewhat braced for it, but they both felt seasickness about to overcome them at the sight of waves rolling overhead; they lowered the blind quickly without giving Mrs Bailey a chance to be disturbed by it.

Teal looked at the third window. 'Game to try it, Homer?'

'Hrrumph – well, we won't be satisfied if we don't. Take it easy.' Teal lifted the blind a few inches. He saw nothing, and raised it a little more – still nothing. Slowly he raised it until the window was fully exposed. They gazed out at – nothing.

Nothing, nothing at all. What colour is nothing? Don't be silly! What shape is it? Shape is an attribute of *something*. It had neither depth nor form. It had not even blackness. It was *nothing*.

Bailey chewed at his cigar. 'Teal, what do you make of that?'

Teal's insouciance was shaken for the first time. 'I don't know, Homer, I don't rightly know – but I think that window ought to be walled up.' He stared at the lowered blind for a moment. 'I think maybe we looked at a place where space *isn't*. We looked around a fourth-dimensional corner and there wasn't anything there.' He rubbed his eyes. 'I've got a headache.'

They waited for a while before tackling the fourth window. Like an unopened letter, it might *not* contain bad news. The doubt left hope. Finally the suspense stretched too thin and Bailey pulled the cord himself, in the face of his wife's protests.

It was not so bad. A landscape stretched away from them, right side up, and on such a level that the study appeared to be a ground-floor room. But it was distinctly unfriendly.

A hot, hot sun beat down from lemon-coloured sky. The flat ground seemed burned a sterile, bleached brown and incapable of supporting life. Life there was, strange stunted trees that lifted knotted, twisted arms to the sky. Little clumps of spiky leaves grew on the outer extremities of these misshapen growths.

'Heavenly day,' breathed Bailey, 'where is that?'

Teal shook his head, his eyes troubled. 'It beats me.'

'It doesn't look like anything on Earth. It looks more like another planet — Mars, maybe.'

'I wouldn't know. But, do you know, Homer, it might be worse than that, worse than another planet, I mean.'

'Huh? What's that you say?'

'It might be clear out of our space entirely. I'm not sure that that is our Sun at all. It seems too bright.'

Mrs Bailey had somewhat timidly joined them and now gazed out at the outré scene. 'Homer,' she said in a subdued voice, 'those hideous trees — they frighten me.'

He patted her hand.

Teal fumbled with the window catch.

'What are you doing?' Bailey demanded.

'I thought if I stuck my head out the window I might be able to look around and tell a bit more.'

'Well — all right,' Bailey grudged, 'but be careful.'

'I will.' He opened the window a crack and sniffed. 'The air is all right, at least.' He threw it open wide.

His attention was diverted before he could carry out his plan. An uneasy tremor, like the first intimation of nausea, shivered the entire building for a long second, and was gone.

'Earthquake!' They all said it at once. Mrs Bailey flung her arms around her husband's neck.

Teal gulped and recovered himself, saying:

'It's all right, Mrs Bailey. This house is perfectly safe. You know you can expect settling tremors after a shock like last night.' He had just settled his features into an expression of reassurance when the second shock came. This one was no mild shimmy but the real seasick roll.

In every Californian, native born or grafted, there is a deep-rooted primitive reflex. An earthquake fills him with soul-shaking claustrophobia which impels him blindly to *get outdoors!* Model boy scouts will push aged grandmothers aside to obey it. It is a matter of record that Teal and Bailey landed on top of Mrs Bailey. Therefore, she must have jumped through the window first. The order of precedence cannot be attributed to chivalry; it must be assumed that she was in readier position to spring.

They pulled themselves together, collected their wits a little, and rubbed sand from their eyes. Their first sensations were relief at feeling the solid sand of the desert land under them. Then Bailey noticed something that brought them to their feet and checked Mrs Bailey from bursting into the speech that she had ready.

'Where's the house?'

It was gone. There was no sign of it at all. They stood in the centre of flat desolation, the landscape they had seen from the window. But, aside from the tortured, twisted trees there was nothing to be seen but the yellow sky and the luminary overhead, whose furnacelike glare was already almost insufferable.

Bailey looked slowly around, then turned to the architect. 'Well, Teal?' His voice was ominous.

Teal shrugged helplessly. 'I wish I knew. I wish I could even be sure that we were on Earth.'

'Well, we can't stand here. It's sure death if we do. Which direction?'

'Any, I guess. Let's keep a bearing on the Sun.'

They had trudged on for an undetermined distance when Mrs Bailey demanded a rest. They stopped. Teal said in an aside to Bailey, 'Any ideas?'

'No . . . no, none. Say, do you hear anything?'

Teal listened. 'Maybe – unless it's my imagination.'

'Sounds like an automobile. Say, it *is* an automobile!'

They came to the highway in less than another hundred yards. The automobile, when it arrived, proved to be an elderly, puffing light truck, driven by a rancher. He crunched to a stop at their hail. 'We're stranded. Can you help us out?'

'Sure. Pile in.'

'Where are you headed?'

'Los Angeles.'

'Los Angeles? Say, where is this place?'

'Well, you're right in the middle of the Joshua-Tree National Forest.'

The return was as dispiriting as the Retreat from Moscow. Mr and Mrs Bailey sat up in front with the driver while Teal bumped along in the body of the truck, and tried to protect his head from the Sun. Bailey subsidized the friendly rancher to detour to the tesseract house, not because they wanted to see it again, but in order to pick up their car.

At last the rancher turned the corner that brought them back to where they had started. But the house was no longer there.

There was not even the ground floor room. It had vanished. The Baileys, interested in spite of themselves, poked around the foundations with Teal.

'Got any answers for this one, Teal?' asked Bailey.

'It must be that on that last shock it simply fell through into another section of space. I can see now that I should have anchored it at the foundations.'

'That's not all you should have done.'

'Well, I don't see that there is anything to get downhearted about. The house was insured, and we've learned an amazing lot. There are possibilities, man, possibilities! Why, right now I've got a great new revolutionary idea for a house –'

Teal ducked in time. He was always a man of action.

The Third Expedition

RAY BRADBURY

THE SHIP CAME DOWN from space. It came from the stars, and the black velocities, and the shining movements, and the silent gulfs of space. It was a new ship; it had fire in its body and men in its metal cells, and it moved with a clean silence, fiery and warm. In it were seventeen men, including a captain. The crowd at the Ohio field had shouted and waved their hands up into the sunlight, and the rocket had bloomed out great flowers of heat and colour and run away into space on the *third* voyage to Mars!

Now it was decelerating with metal efficiency in the upper Martian atmospheres. It was still a thing of beauty and strength. It had moved in the midnight waters of space like a pale sea leviathan; it had passed the ancient moon and thrown itself onward into one nothingness following another. The men within it had been battered, thrown about, sickened, made well again, each in his turn. One man had died, but now the remaining sixteen, with their eyes clear in their heads and their faces pressed to the thick glass ports, watched Mars swing up under them.

'Mars!' cried Navigator Lustig.

'Good old Mars!' said Samuel Hinkston, archaeologist.

'Well,' said Captain John Black.

The rocket landed on a lawn of green grass. Outside, upon this lawn, stood an iron deer. Farther up on the green stood a tall brown Victorian house, quiet in the sunlight, all covered with scrolls and rococo, its windows made of blue and pink and yellow and green coloured glass. Upon the porch were hairy geraniums and an old swing which was hooked into the porch ceiling and which now swung back and forth, back and forth, in a little breeze. At the summit of the house was a cupola with diamond leaded-glass windows and a dunce-cap roof! Through the front window you could see a piece of music titled 'Beautiful Ohio' sitting on the music-rest.

Around the rocket in four directions spread the little town, green and motionless in the Martian spring. There were white houses and red brick ones, and tall elm-trees blowing in the wind, and tall maples and horse-chestnuts. And church steeples with golden bells silent in them.

The rocket men looked out and saw this. Then they looked at one another and then they looked out again. They held to each other's elbows, suddenly unable to breathe, it seemed. Their faces grew pale.

'I'll be damned,' whispered Lustig, rubbing his face with his numb fingers. 'I'll be damned.'

'It just can't be,' said Samuel Hinkston.

'Lord,' said Captain John Blake.

There was a call from the chemist. 'Sir, the atmosphere is thin for breathing. But there's enough oxygen. It's safe.'

'Then we'll go out,' said Lustig.

'Hold on,' said Captain John Black. 'How do we know what this is?'

'It's a small town with thin but breathable air in it, sir.'

'And it's a small town the like of Earth towns,' said Hinkston, the archaeologist. 'Incredible. It can't be, but it *is*.'

Captain John Black looked at him idly. 'Do you think that the civilizations of two planets can progress at the same rate and evolve in the same way, Hinkston?'

'I wouldn't have thought so, sir.'

Captain Black stood by the port. 'Look out there. The geraniums. A specialized plant. That specific variety has only been known on Earth for fifty years. Think of the thousands of years it takes to evolve plants. Then tell me if it is logical that the Martians should have: one, leaded-glass windows ; two, cupolas; three, porch swings; four, an instrument that looks like a piano and probably *is* a piano; and five, if you look closely through this telescopic lens here, is it logical that a Martian composer would have published a piece of music titled, strangely enough, "Beautiful Ohio"? All of which means that we have an Ohio River on Mars!'

'Captain Williams, of course!' cried Hinkston.

'What?'

'Captain Williams and his crew of three men! Or Nathaniel York and his partner. That would explain it!'

'That would explain absolutely nothing. As far as we've been able to figure, the York expedition exploded the day it reached Mars, killing York and his partner. As for Williams and his three men, their ship exploded the second day after their arrival. At least the pulsations from their radios ceased at that time, so we figure that if the men were alive after that they'd have contacted us. And anyway, the York expedition was only a year ago, while Captain Williams and his men landed here some time during last August. Theorizing that they are still alive, could they, even with the help of a brilliant Martian race, have built such a town as this and *aged* it in so short a time? Look at that town out there; why, it's been standing here for the last seventy years. Look at the wood on the porch newel; look at the trees, a century old, all of them! No, this isn't York's work or Williams's. It's something else. I don't like it. And

I'm not leaving the ship until I know what it is.'

'For that matter,' said Lustig, nodding, 'Williams and his men, as well as York, landed on the *opposite* side of Mars. We were very careful to land on *this* side.'

'An excellent point. Just in case a hostile local tribe of Martians killed off York and Williams, we have instructions to land in a farther region, to forestall a recurrence of such a disaster. So here we are, as far as we know, in a land that Williams and York never saw.'

'Damn it,' said Hinkston, 'I want to get out into this town, sir, with your permission. It may be there *are* similar thought patterns, civilization graphs on every planet in our sun system. We may be on the threshold of the greatest psychological and metaphysical discovery of our age!'

'I'm willing to wait a moment,' said Captain John Black.

'It may be, sir, that we're looking upon a phenomenon that, for the first time, would absolutely prove the existence of God, sir.'

'There are many people who are of good faith without such proof, Mr Hinkston.'

'I'm one myself, sir. But certainly a town like this could not occur without divine intervention. The *detail*. It fills me with such feelings that I don't know whether to laugh or cry.'

'Do neither, then, until we know what we're up against.'

'Up against?' Lustig broke in. 'Against nothing, Captain. It's a good, quiet green town, a lot like the old-fashioned one I was born in. I like the looks of it.'

'When were you born, Lustig?'

'Nineteen-fifty, sir.'

'And you, Hinkston?'

'Nineteen fifty-five, sir. Grinnell, Iowa. And this looks like home to me.'

'Hinkston, Lustig, I could be either of your fathers. I'm just eighty years old. Born in 1920 Illinois, and through the grace of God and a science that, in the last fifty years, knows how to make *some* old men young again, here I am on Mars, not any more tired than the rest of you, but infinitely more suspicious. This town out here looks very peaceful and cool, and so much like Green Bluff, Illinois, that it frightens me. Its too *much* like Green Bluff.' He turned to the radio-man. 'Radio Earth. Tell them we've landed. That's all. Tell them we'll radio a full report tomorrow.'

'Yes, sir.'

Captain Black looked out the rocket port with his face that should have been the face of a man of eighty but seemed like the face of a man in his fortieth years. 'Tell you what we'll do, Lustig; you and I and Hinkston'll look the town over. The other men'll stay aboard. If anything happens they can get the hell out. A loss of three men's better than a whole ship. If something bad happens, our crew can warn the next rocket. That's Captain Wilder's rocket, I think, due to be ready to take off next Christmas. If there's something hostile about Mars we certainly want the next rocket to be well armed.'

'So are we. We've got a regular arsenal with us.'

'Tell the men to stand by the guns, then. Come on, Lustig, Hinkston.'

The three men walked together down through the levels of the ship.

It was a beautiful spring day. A robin sat on a blossoming apple-tree and sang continuously. Showers of petal snow sifted down when the wind touched the green branches, and the blossom scent drifted upon the air. Somewhere in the town someone was playing the piano, and the music came and went, came and went, softly, drowsily. The song was 'Beautiful Dreamer.' Somewhere else a phonograph, scratchy and faded, was hissing out a record of 'Roamin' through the Gloamin', sung by Harry Lauder.

The three men stood outside the ship. They sucked and gasped at the thin, thin air and moved slowly so as not to tire themselves.

Now the phonograph record being played was:

'Oh, give me a June night,
The moonlight and you ...'

Lustig began to tremble. Samuel Hinkston did likewise.

The sky was serene and quiet, and somewhere a stream of water ran through the cool caverns and tree shadings of a ravine. Somewhere a horse and wagon trotted and rolled by, bumping.

'Sir,' said Samuel Hinkston, 'it must be, it *has* to be, that rocket travel to Mars began in the years before the first World War!'

'No.'

'How else can you explain these houses, the iron deer, the pianos, the music?' Hinkston took the captain's elbow persuasively and looked into the captain's face. 'Say that there were people in the year 1905 who hated war and got together with some scientists in secret and built a rocket and came out here to Mars — —'

'No, no, Hinkston.'

'Why not? The world was a different world in 1905; they could have kept it a secret much more easily.'

'But a complex thing like a rocket; no, you couldn't keep it secret.'

'And they came up here to live, and naturally the houses they built were similar to Earth houses because they brought the culture with them.'

'And they've lived here all these years?' said the captain.

145

'In peace and quiet, yes. Maybe they made a few trips, enough to bring enough people here for one small town, and then stopped for fear of being discovered. That's why this town seems so old-fashioned. I don't see a thing, myself, older than the year 1927, do you? Or maybe, sir, rocket travel is older than we think. Perhaps it started in some part of the world centuries ago and was kept secret by the small number of men who came to Mars with only occasional visits to Earth over the centuries.'

'You make it sound almost reasonable.'

'It has to be. We've the proof here before us; all we have to do is find some people and verify it.'

Their boots were deadened of all sound in the thick green grass. It smelled from a fresh mowing. In spite of himself, Captain John Black felt a great peace come over him. It had been thirty years since he had been in a small town, and the buzzing of spring bees on the air lulled and quieted him, and the fresh look of things was a balm to the soul.

They set foot upon the porch. Hollow echoes sounded from under the boards as they walked to the screen door. Inside they could see a bead curtain hung across the hall entry, and a crystal chandelier and a Maxfield Parrish painting framed on one wall over a comfortable Morris chair. The house smelled old, and of the attic, and infinitely comfortable. You could hear the tinkle of ice in a lemonade pitcher. In a distant kitchen, because of the heat of the day, someone was preparing a cold lunch. Someone was humming under her breath, high and sweet.

Captain John Black rang the bell.

Footsteps, dainty and thin, came along the hall, and a kind-faced lady of some forty years, dressed in the sort of dress you might expect in the year 1909, peered out at them.

'Can I help you?' she asked.

'Beg your pardon,' said Captain Black uncertainly. 'But we're looking for – that is, could you help us – – ' He stopped. She looked out at him with dark, wondering eyes.

'If you're selling something – – ' she began.

'No, wait!' he cried. 'What town is this?'

She looked him up and down. 'What do you mean, what town is it? How could you be in a town and not know the name?'

The captain looked as if he wanted to go sit under a shady apple tree. 'We're strangers here. We want to know how this town got here and how you got here.'

'Are you census-takers?'

'No.'

'Everyone knows,' she said, 'this town was built in 1868. Is this a game?'

'No, not a game!' cried the captain. 'We're from Earth.'

146

'Out of the *ground*, do you mean?' she wondered.

'No, we came from the third planet, Earth, in a ship. And we've landed here on the fourth planet, Mars – – '

'This,' explained the woman, as if she were addressing a child, 'is Green Bluff, Illinois, on the continent of America, surrounded by the Atlantic and Pacific oceans, on a place called the world, or, sometimes, the Earth. Go away now. Good-bye.'

She trotted down the hall, running her fingers through the beaded curtains.

The three men looked at one another.

'Let's knock the screen door in,' said Lustig.

'We can't do that. This is private property. Good God!'

They went to sit down on the porch step.

'Did it ever strike you, Hinkston, that perhaps we got ourselves somehow, in some way, off track, and by accident came back and landed on Earth?'

'How could we have done that?'

'I don't know, I don't know. Oh God, let me think!'

Hinkston said, 'But we checked every mile of the way. Our chronometers said so many miles. We went past the Moon and out into space, and here we are. I'm *positive* we're on Mars.'

Lustig said, 'But suppose, by accident, in space, in time, we got lost in the dimensions and landed on an Earth that is thirty or forty years ago.'

'Oh, go away, Lustig!'

Lustig went to the door, rang the bell, and called into the cool dim rooms: 'What year is this?'

'Nineteen twenty-six, of course,' said the lady, sitting in a rocking-chair, taking a sip of her lemonade.

'Did you hear that?' Lustig turned wildly to the others. 'Nineteen twenty-six! We *have* gone back in time! This *is* Earth!'

Lustig sat down, and the three men let the wonder and terror of the thought afflict them. Their hands stirred fitfully on their knees. The captain said, 'I didn't ask for a thing like this. It scares the hell out of me. How can a thing like this happen? I wish we'd brought Einstein with us.'

'Will anyone in this town believe us?' said Hinkston. 'Are we playing with something dangerous? Time, I mean. Shouldn't we just take off and go home?'

'No. Not until we try another house.'

They walked three houses down to a little white cottage under an oak-tree. 'I like to be as logical as I can be,' said the captain. 'And I don't believe we've put our finger on it yet. Suppose, Hinkston, as you originally suggested, that rocket travel occurred years ago? And when the Earth people lived here a number of years they began to get homesick for

Earth. First a mild neurosis about it, then a full-fledged psychosis. Then threatened insanity. What would you do as a psychiatrist if faced with such a problem?'

Hinkston thought. 'Well, I think I'd arrange the civilization on Mars so it resembled Earth more and more each day. If there was any way of reproducing every plant, every road, and every lake, and even an ocean, I'd do so. Then by some vast crowd hypnosis I'd convince everyone in a town this size that this really was Earth, not Mars at all.'

'Good enough, Hinkston. I think we're on the right track now. That woman in that house there just *thinks* she's living on Earth. It protects her sanity. She and all the others in this town are the patients of the greatest experiment in migration and hypnosis you will ever lay eyes on in your life.'

'That's *it*, sir!' cried Lustig.

'Right!' said Hinkston.

'Well.' The captain sighed. 'Now we've got somewhere. I feel better. It's all a bit more logical. That talk about time and going back and forth and travelling through time turns my stomach upside down. But *this* way – – ' The captain smiled. 'Well, well, it looks as if we'll be fairly popular here.'

'Or will we?' said Lustig. 'After all, like the Pilgrims, these people came here to escape Earth. Maybe they won't be too happy to see us. Maybe they'll try to drive us out or kill us.'

'We have superior weapons. This next house now. Up we go.'

But they had hardly crossed the lawn when Lustig stopped and looked off across the town, down the quiet, dreaming afternoon street. 'Sir,' he said.

'What is it, Lustig?'

'Oh, sir, *sir*, what I see – – ' said Lustig, and he began to cry. His fingers came up, twisting and shaking, and his face was all wonder and joy and incredulity. He sounded as if at any moment he might go quite insane with happiness. He looked down the street and began to run, stumbling awkwardly, falling, picking himself up, and running on. 'Look, look!'

'Don't let him get away!' The captain broke into a run.

Now Lustig was running swiftly, shouting. He turned into a yard half-way down the shady street and leaped up upon the porch of a large green house with an iron rooster on the roof.

He was beating at the door, hollering and crying, when Hinkston and the captain ran up behind him. They were all gasping and wheezing, exhausted from their run in the thin air. 'Grandma! Grandpa!' cried Lustig.

Two old people stood in the doorway.

'David!' their voices piped, and they rushed out to embrace and pat

148

him on the back and move around him. 'David, oh, David, it's been so many years! How you've grown, boy; how big you are, boy! Oh, David boy, how are you?'

'Grandma, Grandpa!' sobbed David Lustig. 'You look fine, fine!' He held them, turned them, kissed them, hugged them, cried on them, held them out again, blinking at the little old people. The sun was in the sky, the wind blew, the grass was green, the screen door stood wide.

'Come in, boy, come in. There's iced tea for you, fresh; lots of it!'

'I've got friends here.' Lustig turned and waved at the captain and Hinkston frantically, laughing. 'Captain, come on up.'

'Howdy,' said the old people. 'Come in. Any friends of David's are our friends too. Don't stand there!'

In the living-room of the old house it was cool, and a grandfather clock ticked high and long and bronzed in one corner. There were soft pillows on large couches and walls filled with books and a rug cut in a thick rose pattern, and iced tea in the hand, sweating, and cool on the thirsty tongue.

'Here's to our health.' Grandma tipped her glass to her porcelain teeth.

'How long you been here, Grandma?' said Lustig.

'Ever since we died,' she said tartly.

'Ever since you what?' Captain John Black set down his glass.

'Oh yes.' Lustig nodded. 'They've been dead thirty years.'

'And you sit there calmly!' shouted the captain.

'Tush.' The old woman winked glitteringly. 'Who are you to question what happens? Here we are. What's life, anyway? Who does what for why and where? All we know is here we are, alive again, and no questions asked. A second chance.' She toddled over and held out her thin wrist. 'Feel.' The captain felt. 'Solid, ain't it?' she asked. He nodded. 'Well, then,' she said triumphantly, 'why go around questioning?'

'Well,' said the captain, 'it's simply that we never thought we'd find a thing like this on Mars.'

'And now you've found it. I dare say there's lots on every planet that'll show you God's infinite ways.'

'Is this heaven?' asked Hinkston.

'Nonsense, no. It's a world and we get a second chance. Nobody told us why. But then nobody told us why we were on Earth, either. That other Earth, I mean. The one you came from. How do we know there wasn't *another* before *that* one?'

'A good question,' said the captain.

Lustig kept smiling at his grandparents. 'Gosh, it's good to see you. Gosh, it's good.'

The captain stood up and slapped his hand on his leg in a casual fashion. 'We've got to be going. Thank you for the drinks.'

'You'll be back, of course,' said the old people. 'For supper tonight?'

'We'll try to make it, thanks. There's so much to be done. My men are waiting for me back at the rocket and – – '

He stopped. He looked towards the door, startled.

Far away in the sunlight there was a sound of voices, a shouting and a great hello.

'What's that?' asked Hinkston.

'We'll soon find out.' And Captain John Black was out of the front door abruptly, running across the green lawn into the street of the Martian town.

He stood looking at the rocket. The ports were open and his crew was streaming out, waving their hands. A crowd of people had gathered, and in and through and among these people the members of the crew were hurrying, talking, laughing, shaking hands. People did little dances. People swarmed. The rocket lay empty and abandoned.

A brass band exploded in the sunlight, flinging off a gay tune from upraised tubas and trumpets. There was a bang of drums and a shrill of fifes. Little girls with golden hair jumped up and down. Little boys shouted, 'Hooray!' Fat men passed around ten-cent cigars. The town mayor made a speech. Then each member of the crew, with a mother on one arm, a father or sister on the other, was spirited off down the street into little cottages or big mansions.

'Stop!' cried Captain Black.

The doors slammed shut.

The heat rose in the clear spring sky, and all was silent. The brass band banged off around a corner, leaving the rocket to shine and dazzle alone in the sunlight.

'Abandoned!' said the captain. 'They abandoned the ship, they did! I'll have their skins, by God! They had orders!'

'Sir,' said Lustig, 'don't be too hard on them. Those were all old relatives and friends.'

'That's no excuse!'

'Think how they felt, Captain, seeing familiar faces outside the ship!'

'They had their orders, damn it!'

'But how would you have felt, Captain?'

'I would have obeyed orders – – ' The captain's mouth remained open.

Striding along the sidewalk under the Martian sun, tall, smiling, eyes amazingly clear and blue, came a young man of some twenty-six years. 'John!' the man called out, and broke into a trot.

'What?' Captain John Black swayed.

'John, you old son of a bitch!'

The man ran up and gripped his hand and slapped him on the back.

'It's you,' said Captain Black.

'Of course, who'd you *think* it was?'

'Edward!' The captain appealed now to Lustig and Hinkston, holding the stranger's hand. 'This is my brother Edward. Ed, meet my men, Lustig, Hinkston! My brother!'

They tugged at each other's hands and arms and then finally embraced. 'Ed!' 'John, you bum, you!' 'You're looking fine, Ed; but, Ed, what *is* this? You haven't changed over the years. You died, I remember, when you were twenty-six and I was nineteen. Good God! so many years ago, and here you are and, Lord, what goes on?'

'Mom's waiting,' said Edward Black, grinning.

'Mom?'

'And Dad too.'

'Dad?' The captain almost fell as if he had been hit by a mighty weapon. He walked stiffly and without coordination. 'Mom and Dad alive? Where?'

'At the old house on Oak Knoll Avenue.'

'The old house.' The captain stared in delighted amaze. 'Did you hear that, Lustig, Hinkston?'

Hinkston was gone. He had seen his own house down the street and was running for it. Lustig was laughing. 'You see, Captain, what happened to everyone on the rocket? They couldn't help themselves.'

'Yes. Yes.' The captain shut his eyes. 'When I open my eyes you'll be gone.' He blinked. 'You're still there. God, Ed, but you look *fine!*'

'Come on; lunch's waiting. I told Mom.'

Lustig said, 'Sir, I'll be with my grandfolks if you need me.'

'What? Oh, fine, Lustig. Later, then.'

Edward seized his arm and marched him. 'There's the house. Remember it?'

'Hell! Bet I can beat you to the front porch!'

They ran. The trees roared over Captain Black's head; the earth roared under his feet. He saw the golden figure of Edward Black pull ahead of him in the amazing dream of reality. He saw the house rush forward, the screen door swing wide.

'Beat you!' cried Edward.

'I'm an old man,' panted the captain, 'and you're still young. But then, you *always* beat me, I remember!'

In the doorway, Mom, pink, plump, and bright. Behind her, pepper-grey, Dad, his pipe in his hand.

'Mom, Dad!'

He ran up the steps like a child to meet them.

It was a fine long afternoon. They finished a late lunch and they sat in the parlour and he told them all about his rocket and they nodded and smiled upon him and Mother was just the same and Dad bit the end off a cigar and lighted it thoughtfully in his old fashion. There was a big turkey dinner at night and time flowing on. When the drumsticks were sucked clean and lay brittle upon the plates, the captain leaned back and exhaled his deep satisfaction. Night was in all the trees and colouring the sky, and the lamps were halos of pink light in the gentle house. From all the other houses down the street came sounds of music, pianos playing, doors slamming.

Mom put a record on the victrola, and she and Captain John Black had a dance. She was wearing the same perfume he remembered from the summer when she and Dad had been killed in the train accident. She was very real in his arms as they danced lightly to the music. 'It's not every day,' she said, 'you get a second chance to live.'

'I'll wake in the morning,' said the captain. 'And I'll be in my rocket, in space, and all this will be gone.'

'No, don't think that,' she cried softly. 'Don't question. God's good to us. Let's be happy.'

'Sorry, Mom.'

The record ended in a circular hissing.

'You're tired, Son.' Dad pointed with his pipe. 'Your old bedroom's waiting for you, brass bed and all.'

'But I should report my men in.'

'Why?'

'Why? Well, I don't know. No reason, I guess. No, none at all. They're all eating or in bed. A good night's sleep won't hurt them.'

'Good night, Son.' Mom kissed his cheek. 'It's good to have you home.'

'It's good to be home.'

He left the land of cigar-smoke and perfume and books and gentle light and ascended the stairs, talking, talking with Edward. Edward pushed a door open, and there was the yellow brass bed and the old semaphore banners from college and a very musty racoon coat which he stroked with muted affection. 'It's too much,' said the captain. 'I'm numb and I'm tired. Too much has happened today. I feel as if I'd been out in a pounding rain for forty-eight hours without an umbrella or a coat. I'm soaked to the skin with emotion.'

Edward slapped wide the snowy linens and flounced the pillows. He slid the window up and let the night-blooming jasmine float in. There was moonlight and the sound of distant dancing and whispering.

'So this is Mars,' said the captain, undressing.

'This is it.' Edward undressed in idle, leisurely moves, drawing his shirt off over his head, revealing golden shoulders and the good muscular neck.

The lights were out; they were in bed, side by side, as in the days how many decades ago? The captain lolled and was nourished by the scent of jasmine pushing the lace curtains out upon the dark air of the room. Among the trees, upon a lawn, someone had cranked up a portable phonograph and now it was playing softly, 'Always'.

The thought of Marilyn came to his mind.

'Is Marilyn here?'

His brother, lying straight out in the moonlight from the window, waited and then said, 'Yes. She's out of town. But she'll be here in the morning.'

The captain shut his eyes. 'I want to see Marilyn very much.'

The room was square and quiet except for their breathing.

'Good night, Ed.'

A pause. 'Good night, John.'

He lay peacefully, letting his thoughts float. For the first time the stress of the day was moved aside; he could think logically now. It had all been emotion. The bands playing, the familiar faces. But now . . .

How? he wondered. How was all this made? And why? For what purpose? Out of the goodness of some divine intervention? Was God, then, really that thoughtful of his children? How and why and what for?

He considered the various theories advanced in the first heat of the afternoon by Hinkston and Lustig. He let all kinds of new theories drop in lazy pebbles down through his mind, turning, throwing out dull flashes of light. Mom. Dad. Edward. Mars. Earth. Mars. Martians.

Who had lived here a thousand years ago on Mars? Martians? Or had this always been the way it was today?

Martians. He repeated the word idly, inwardly.

He laughed out loud almost. He had the most ridiculous theory quite suddenly. It gave him a kind of chill. It was really nothing to consider, of course. Highly improbable. Silly. Forget it. Ridiculous.

But, he thought, just *suppose* . . . Just suppose, now, that there were Martians living on Mars and they saw our ship coming and saw us inside our ship and hated us. Suppose, now, just for the hell of it, that they wanted to destroy us, as invaders, as unwanted ones, and they wanted to do it in a very clever way, so that we would be taken off guard. Well, what would the best weapon be that a Martian could use against Earth Men with atomic weapons?

The answer was interesting. Telepathy, hypnosis, memory, and imagination.

Suppose all of these houses aren't real at all, this bed not real, but only figments of my own imagination, given substance by telepathy and hypnosis through the Martians, thought Captain John Black. Suppose these houses are really some *other* shape, a Martian shape, but, by playing on my desires and wants, these Martians have made this seem like my old home town, my old house, to lull me out of my suspicions. What better way to fool a man, using his own mother and father as bait?

And this town, so old, from the year 1926, long before any of my men were born. From a year when I was six years old and there *were* records of Harry Lauder, and Maxfield Parrish paintings *still* hanging, and bead

153

curtains, and 'Beautiful Ohio', and turn-of-the-century architecture. What if the Martians took the memories of a town *exclusively* from *my* mind? They say childhood memories are the clearest. And after they built the town from *my* mind, they postulated it with the most-loved people from all the minds of the people on the rocket!

And suppose those two people in the next room, asleep, are not my mother and father at all. But two Martians, incredibly brilliant, with the ability to keep me under this dreaming hypnosis all of the time.

And that brass band today? What a startlingly wonderful plan it would be! First, fool Lustig, then Hinkston, then gather a crowd; and all the men in the rocket, seeing mothers, aunts, uncles, sweethearts, dead ten, twenty years ago, naturally, disregarding orders, rush out and abandon ship. What more natural? What more unsuspecting? What more simple? A man doesn't ask too many questions when his mother is suddenly brought back to life; he's much too happy. And here we all are tonight, in various houses, in various beds, with no weapons to protect us, and the rocket lies in the moonlight, empty. And wouldn't it be horrible and terrifying to discover that all of this was part of some great clever plan by the Martians to divide and conquer us, and kill us? Sometime during the night, perhaps, my brother here on this bed will change form, melt, shift, and become another thing, a terrible thing, a Martian. It would be very simple for him just to turn over in bed and put a knife into my heart. And in all those other houses down the street, a dozen other brothers or fathers suddenly melting away and taking knives and doing things to the unsuspecting, sleeping men of Earth....

His hands were shaking under the covers. His body was cold. Suddenly it was not a theory. Suddenly he was very afraid.

He lifted himself in bed and listened. The night was very quiet. The music had stopped. The wind had died. His brother lay sleeping beside him.

Carefully he lifted the covers, rolled them back. He slipped from bed and was walking softly across the room when his brother's voice said, 'Where are you going?'

'What?'

His brother's voice was quite cold. 'I said, where do you think you're going?'

'For a drink of water.'

'But you're not thirsty.'

'Yes, yes, I am.'

'No, you're not.'

Captain John Black broke and ran across the room. He screamed. He screamed twice.

He never reached the door.

In the morning the brass band played a mournful dirge. From every house in the street came little solemn processions bearing long boxes, and along the sun-filled street, weeping, came the grandmas and mothers and sisters and brothers and uncles and fathers, walking to the churchyard, where there were new holes freshly dug and new tombstones installed. Sixteen holes in all, and sixteen tombstones.

The mayor made a little sad speech, his face sometimes looking like the mayor, sometimes looking like something else.

Mother and Father Black were there, with Brother Edward, and they cried, their faces melting now from a familiar face into something else.

Grandpa and Grandma Lustig were there, weeping, their faces shifting like wax, shimmering as all things shimmer on a hot day.

The coffins were lowered. Someone murmured about 'the unexpected and sudden deaths of sixteen fine men during the night – – '

Earth pounded down on the coffin lids.

The brass band, playing 'Columbia, the Gem of the Ocean', marched and slammed back into town, and everyone took the day off.

The Day Before The Revolution

URSULA K. LE GUIN

THE SPEAKER'S VOICE was loud as empty beer-trucks in a stone street, and the people at the meeting were jammed up close, cobblestones, that great voice booming over them. Taviri was somewhere on the other side of the hall. She had to get to him. She wormed and pushed her way among the dark-clothed, close-packed people. She did not hear the words, nor see the faces, only the booming, and the bodies pressed one behind the other. She could not see Taviri, she was too short. A broad black-vested belly and chest loomed up blocking her way. She must get through to Taviri. Sweating, she jabbed fiercely with her fist. It was like hitting stones, he did not move at all, but the huge lungs let out right over her head in a prodigious noise, a bellow. She cowered. Then she understood that the bellow had not been at her. Others were shouting. The speaker had said something, something fine about taxes or shadows. Thrilled, she joined the shouting – 'Yes! Yes!' – and shoving on, came out easily into the open expanse of the Regimental Drill Field in Parheo. Overhead the evening sky lay deep and colourless, and all around her nodded the tall weeds with dry, white, close-floreted heads. She had never known what they were called. The flowers nodded above her head, swaying in the wind that always blew across the fields in the dusk. She ran among them, and they whipped lithe aside and stood up again swaying, silent. Taviri stood among the tall weeds in his good suit, the dark grey one that made him look like a professor or a play-actor, harshly elegant. He did not look happy, but he was laughing, and saying something to her. The sound of his voice made her cry, and she reached out to catch hold of his hand, but she did not stop, quite. She could not stop. 'Oh, Taviri,' she said, 'it's just on there!' The queer sweet smell of the white weeds was heavy as she went on. There were thorns, tangles underfoot, there were slopes, pits. She feared to fall ... she stopped.

Sun, bright morning-glare, straight in the eyes, relentless. She had forgotten to pull the blind last night. She turned her back on the sun, but the right side wasn't comfortable. No use. Day. She sighed twice, sat up, got her legs over the edge of the bed, and sat hunched in her nightdress looking down at her feet.

156

The toes, compressed by a lifetime of cheap shoes, were almost square where they touched each other, and bulged out above in corns; the nails were discoloured and shapeless. Between the knob-like ankle bones ran fine, dry wrinkles. The brief little plain at the base of the toes had kept its delicacy, but the skin was the colour of mud, and knotted veins crossed the instep. Disgusting. Sad, depressing. Mean. Pitiful. She tried on all the words, and they all fit, like hideous little hats. Hideous: yes, that one too. To look at oneself and find it hideous, what a job! But then, when she hadn't been hideous, had she sat around and stared at herself like this? Not much! A proper body's not an object, not an implement, not a belonging to be admired, it's just you, yourself. Only when it's no longer you, but yours, a thing owned, do you worry about it – Is it in good shape? Will it do? Will it last?

'Who cares?' said Laia fiercely, and stood up.

It made her giddy to stand up suddenly. She had to put out her hand to the bedtable, for she dreaded falling. At that she thought of reaching out to Taviri, in the dream.

What had he said? She could not remember. She was not sure if she had even touched his hand. She frowned, trying to force memory. It had been so long since she had dreamed about Taviri; and now not even to remember what he had said!

It was gone, it was gone. She stood there hunched in her nightdress, frowning, one hand on the bedtable. How long was it since she had thought of him – let alone dreamed of him – even thought of him, as 'Taviri'? How long since she had said his name?

Asieo said. When Asieo and I were in prison in the North. Before I met Asieo. Asieo's theory of reciprocity. Oh yes, she talked about him, talked about him too much no doubt, maundered, dragged him in. But as 'Asieo', the last name, the public man. The private man was gone, utterly gone. There were so few left who had even known him. They had all used to be in jail. One laughed about it on those days, all the friends in all the jails. But they weren't even there, these days. They were in the prison cemeteries. Or in the common graves.

'Oh, oh my dear,' Laia said out loud, and she sank down on to the bed again because she could not stand up under the remembrance of those first weeks in the Fort, in the cell, those first weeks of the nine years in the Fort in Drio, in the cell, those first weeks after they told her that Asieo had been killed in the fighting in Capitol Square and had been buried with the Fourteen Hundred in the lime-ditches behind Oring Gate. In the cell. Her hands fell into the old position on her lap, the left clenched and locked inside the grip of the right, the right thumb working back and forth a little pressing and rubbing on the knuckle of the left first finger. Hours, days, night. She had thought of them all, each one, each one of the fourteen hundred, how they lay, how the quicklime worked on the flesh,

157

how the bones touched in the burning dark. Who touched him? How did the slender bones of the hand lie now? Hours, years.

'Taviri, I have never forgotten you!' she whispered, and the stupidity of it brought her back to morning-light and the rumpled bed. Of course she hadn't forgotten him. These things go without saying between husband and wife. There were her ugly old feet flat on the floor again, just as before. She had gone in a circle. She stood up with a grunt of effort and disapproval, and went to the closet for her dressing gown.

The young people went about the halls of the House in becoming immodesty, but she was too old for that. She didn't want to spoil some young man's breakfast with the sight of her. Besides, they had grown up in the principle of freedom of dress and sex and all the rest, and she hadn't. All she had done was invent it. It's not the same.

Like speaking of Asieo as 'my husband'. They winced. The word she should use as a good Odonian, of course, was 'partner'. But why the hell did she have to be a good Odonian?

She shuffled down the hall to the bathrooms. Mairo was there, washing her hair in a lavatory. Laia looked at the long, sleek, wet hank with admiration. She got out of the House so seldom now that she didn't know when she had last seen a respectably shaven scalp, but still the sight of a full head of hair gave her pleasure, vigorous pleasure. How many times had she been jeered at, *Longhair, Longhair*, had her hair pulled by policemen or young toughs, had her hair shaved off down to the scalp by a grinning soldier at each new prison? And then had grown it all over again, through the fuzz, to the frizz, to the curls, to the mane... In the old days. For God's love, couldn't she think of anything today but the old days?

Dressed, her bed made, she went down to commons. It was a good breakfast, but she had never got her appetite back since the damned stroke. She drank two cups of herb tea, but couldn't finish the piece of fruit she had taken. How she had craved fruit as a child, badly enough to steal it; and in the Fort – oh for God's love stop it! She smiled and replied to the greetings and friendly inquiries of the other breakfasters and big Aevi who was serving the counter this morning. It was he who had tempted her with the peach, 'Look at this, I've been saving it for you,' and how could she refuse? Anyway she had always loved fruit, and never got enough; once when she was six or seven she had stolen a piece off a vendor's cart in River Street. But it was hard to eat when everyone was talking so excitedly. There was news from Thu, real news. She was inclined to discount it at first, being wary of enthusiasms, but after she had read the article in the paper, and read between the lines of it, she thought, with a strange kind of certainty, deep but cold, Why, this is it; it has come. And in Thu, not here. Thu will break before this country does; the Revolution will first prevail there. As if that mattered! There will be no more nations. And yet it did matter somehow, it made her a little cold and sad – envious, in fact. Of all the infinite stupidities. She did not join the talk much, and soon got up to go back to her room, feeling sorry for herself. She could not share their excitement. She was out of it, really out of it. It's not easy, she said to herself in justification, laboriously climbing the stairs, to accept being out of it when you've been in it, in the centre of it, for fifty years. Oh for God's love. Whining!

She got the stairs and the self-pity behind her, entering her room. It was a good room, and it was good to be by herself. It was a great relief. Even if it wasn't strictly fair. Some of the kids in the attics were living five to a room no bigger than this. There were always more people wanting to live in an Odonian House than could be properly acccommodated. She had this big room all to herself because she was an old woman who had had a stroke. And maybe because she was Odo. If she hadn't been Odo, but merely the old woman with a stroke, would she have had it? Very likely. After all who the hell wanted to room with a drooling old woman? But it was hard to be sure. Favouritism, elitism, leader-worship, they crept back and cropped out everywhere. But she had never hoped to see them eradicated in her lifetime, in one generation; only Time works the great changes. Meanwhile this was a nice, large sunny room, proper for a drooling old woman who had started a world revolution.

Her secretary would be coming in an hour to help her dispatch the day's work. She shuffled over to the desk, a beautiful, big piece, a present from the Nio Cabinet-makers' Syndicate because somebody had heard her remark once that the only piece of furniture she had ever really longed for was a desk with drawers and enough room on top ... damn, the top was practically covered with papers with notes clipped to them, mostly in Noi's small clear handwriting: Urgent. – Northern Provinces. – Consult w/R.T.?

Her own handwriting had never been the same since Asieo's death. It was odd, when you thought about it. After all, within five years after his death she had written the whole *Analogy*. And there were those letters, which the tall guard with the watery grey eyes, what was his name, never mind, had smuggled out of the Fort for her for two years. *The Prison Letters* they called them now, there were a dozen different editions of them. All that stuff, the letters which people kept telling her were so full of 'spiritual strength' – which probably meant she had been lying herself blue in the face when she wrote them, trying to keep her spirits up – and the *Analogy* which was certainly the solidest intellectual work she had ever done, all of that had been written in the Fort in Drio, in the cell, after Asieo's death. One had to do something, and in the Fort they let one have paper and pens ... But it had all been written in the hasty, scribbling hand which she had never felt was hers, not her own like the round, black scrollings of the manuscript of *Society Without Government*, forty-five years old. Taviri had taken not only her body's and her heart's desire to the quick-lime

159

with him, but even her good clear handwriting.

But he had left her the revolution.

How brave of you to go on, to work, to write, in prison, after such a defeat for the Movement, after your partner's death, people had used to say. Damn fools. What else had there been to do? Bravery, courage – what was courage? She had never figured it out. Not fearing, some said. Fearing yet going on, others said. But what could one do but go on? Had one any real choice, ever?

To die was merely to go on in another direction.

If you wanted to come home you had to keep going on, that was what she meant when she wrote, 'True journey is return,' but it had never been more than an intuition, and she was farther than ever now from being able to rationalize it. She bent down, too suddenly, so that she grunted a little at the creak in her bones, and began to root in a bottom drawer of the desk. Her hand came to an age-softened folder and drew it out, recognizing it by touch before sight confirmed: the manuscript of *Syndical Organization in Revolutionary Transition*. He had printed the title on the folder and written his name under it, Taviri Odo Asieo, IX 741. There was an elegant handwriting, every letter well-formed, bold, and fluent. But he had preferred to use a voiceprinter. The manuscript was all in voiceprint, and high quality too, hesitancies adjusted and idiosyncrasies of speech normalized. You couldn't see there how he had said 'o' deep in his throat as they did on the North Coast. There was nothing of him there but his mind. She had nothing of him at all except his name written on the folder. She hadn't kept his letters, it was sentimental to keep letters. Besides, she never kept anything. She couldn't think of anything that she had ever owned for more than a few years, except this ramshackle old body, of course, and she was stuck with that...

Dualizing again. 'She' and 'it'. Age and illness made one dualist, made one escapist; the mind insisted, *It's not me, it's not me.* But it was. Maybe the mystics could detach mind from body, she had always rather wistfully envied them the chance, without hope of emulating them. Escape had never been her game. She had sought for freedom here, now, body and soul.

First self-pity, then self-praise, and here she still sat, for God's love, holding Asieo's name in her hand, why? Didn't she know his name without looking it up? What was wrong with her? She raised the folder to her lips and kissed the handwritten name firmly and squarely, replaced the folder in the back of the bottom drawer, shut the drawer, and straightened up in the chair. Her right hand tingled. She scratched it, and then shook it in the air, spitefully. It had never quite got over the stroke. Neither had her right leg, or right eye, or the right corner of her mouth. They were sluggish, inept, they tingled. They made her feel like a robot with a short circuit.

And time was getting on, Noi would be coming, what had she been doing ever since breakfast?

She got up so hastily that she lurched, and grabbed at the chair-back to make sure she did not fall. She went down the hall to the bathroom and looked in the big mirror there. Her grey knot was loose and droopy, she hadn't done it up well before breakfast. She struggled with it a while. It was hard to keep her arms up in the air. Amai, running in to piss, stopped and said, 'Let me do it!' and knotted it up tight and neat in no time, with her round, strong, pretty fingers, smiling and silent. Amai was twenty, less than a third of Laia's age. Her parents had both been members of the Movement, one killed in the insurrection of '60, the other still recruiting in the South Provinces. Amai had grown up in Odonian Houses, born to the Revolution, a true daughter of anarchy. And so quiet and free and beautiful a child, enough to make you cry when you thought: this is what we worked for, this is what we meant, this is it, here she is, alive, the kindly, lovely future.

Laia Osaieo Odo's right eye wept several little tears, as she stood between the lavatories and the latrines having her hair done up by the daughter she had not borne; but her left eye, the strong one, did not weep, nor did it know what the right eye did.

She thanked Amai and hurried back to her room. She had noticed, in the mirror, a stain on her collar. Peach juice, probably. Damned old dribbler. She didn't want Noi to come in and find her with drool on her collar.

As the clean shirt went on over her head, she thought, What's so special about Noi?

She fastened the collar-frogs with her left hand, slowly.

Noi was thirty or so, a slight, muscular fellow with a soft voice and alert dark eyes. That's what was special about Noi. It was that simple. Good old sex. She had never been drawn to a fair man or a fat one, or the tall fellows with big biceps, never, not even when she was fourteen and fell in love with every passing fart. Dark, spare, and fiery, that was the recipe. Taviri, of course. This boy wasn't a patch on Taviri for brains, nor even for looks, but there it was: She didn't want him to see her with dribble on her collar and her hair coming undone.

Her thin, grey hair.

Noi came in, just pausing in the open doorway – my God, she hadn't even shut the door while changing her shirt! – She looked at him and saw herself. The old woman.

You could brush your hair and change your shirt, or you could wear last week's shirt and last night's braids, or you could put on cloth of gold and dust your shaven scalp with diamond powder. None of it would make the slightest difference. The old woman would look a little less, or a little

161

more, grotesque.

One keeps oneself neat out of mere decency, mere sanity, awareness of other people.

And finally even that goes, and one dribbles unashamed.

'Good morning,' the young man said in his gentle voice.

'Hello, Noi.'

No, by God, it was *not* out of mere decency. Decency be damned. Because the man she had loved, and to whom her age would not have mattered – because he was dead, must she pretend she had no sex? Must she suppress the truth, like a damned puritan authoritarian? Even six months ago, before the stroke, she had made men look at her and like to look at her; and now, though she could give no pleasure, by God she could please herself.

When she was six years old, and Papa's friend Gadeo used to come by to talk politics with Papa after dinner, she would put on the gold-coloured necklace that Mama had found on a trash-heap and brought home for her. It was so short that it always got hidden under her collar where nobody could see it. She liked it that way. She knew she had it on. She sat on the doorstep and listened to them talk, and knew that she looked nice for Gadeo. He was dark, with white teeth that flashed. Sometimes he called her 'pretty Laia.' 'There's my pretty Laia!' Sixty-six years ago.

'What? My head's dull. I had a terrible night.' It was true. She had slept even less than usual.

'I was asking if you'd seen the papers this morning.'

She nodded.

'Pleased about Soinehe?'

Soinehe was the province in Thu which had declared its secession from the Thuvian State last night.

He was pleased about it. His white teeth flashed in his dark, alert face. Pretty Laia.

'Yes. And apprehensive.'

'I know. But it's the real thing, this time. It's the beginning of the end of the Government in Thu. They haven't even tried to order troops into Soinehe, you know. It would merely provoke the soldiers into rebellion sooner, and they know it.'

She agreed with him. She herself had felt that certainty. But she could not share his delight. After a lifetime of living on hope because there is nothing but hope, one loses the taste for victory. A real sense of triumph must be preceded by real despair. She had unlearned despair a long time ago. There were no more triumphs. One went on.

'Shall we do those letters today?'

'All right. Which letters?'

'To the people in the North,' he said without impatience.

'In the North?'

'Parheo, Oaidun.'

She had been born in Parheo, the dirty city on the dirty river. She had not come here to the capital till she was twenty-two and ready to bring the Revolution. Though in those days, before she and the others had thought it through, it had been a very green and puerile revolution. Strikes for better wages, representation for women. Votes and wages – Power and Money, for the love of God! Well, one does learn a little, after all, in fifty years.

But then one must forget it all.

'Start with Oaidun,' she said, sitting down in the armchair. Noi was at the desk ready to work. He read out excerpts from the letters she was to answer. She tried to pay attention, and succeeded well enough that she dictated one whole letter and started on another. 'Remember that at this stage your brotherhood is vulnerable to the threat of ... no, to the danger ... to ...' She groped till Noi suggested, 'The danger of leader-worship,'

'All right. And that nothing is so soon corrupted by power-seeking as altruism. No. And that nothing corrupts altruism – no. Oh for God's love you know what I'm trying to say, Noi, you write it. They know it too, it's just the same old stuff, why can't they read my books!'

'Touch,' Noi said gently, smiling, citing one of the central Odonian themes.

'All right, but I'm tired of being touched. If you'll write the letter I'll sign it, but I can't be bothered with it this morning.' He was looking at her with a little question or concern. She said, irritable, 'There is something else I have to do!'

When Noi had gone she sat down at the desk and moved the papers about, pretending to be doing something, because she had been startled, frightened, by the words she had said. She had nothing else to do. She never had had anything else to do. This was her work: her lifework. The speaking tours and the meetings and the streets were out of reach for her now, but she could still write, and that was her work. And anyhow if she had had anything else to do, Noi would have known it; he kept her schedule, and tactfully reminded her of things, like the visit from the foreign students this afternoon.

Oh, damn. She liked the young, and there was always something to learn from a foreigner, but she was tired of new faces, and tired of being on view. She learned from them, but they didn't learn from her; they had learnt all she had to teach long ago, from her books, from the Movement. They just came to look, as if she were the Great Tower in Rodarred, or the Canyon of the Tulaevea. A phenomenon, a monument. They were awed, adoring. She snarled at them: Think your own thoughts! – That's not anarchism, that's mere obscurantism. – You don't think liberty and discipline are incompatible, do you? – They accepted their tonguelashing meekly as children, gratefully, as if she were some kind of All-Mother, the idol of the Big Sheltering Womb. She! She who had mined the shipyards at Seissero, and had cursed Premier Inoilte to his face in front of a crowd of seven thousand, telling him he would have cut off his own balls and had them bronzed and sold as souvenirs, if he thought there were any profit in it – she who had screeched, and sworn, and kicked policemen, and spat at priests, and pissed in public on the big brass plaque in Capitol Square that said HERE WAS FOUNDED THE SOVEREIGN NATION STATE OF A-10 ETC ETC, pssssssss to all that! And now she was everybody's grandmama, the dear old lady, the sweet old monument, come worship at the womb. The fire's out, boys, it's safe to come up close.

'No, I won't,' Laia said out loud. 'I will not.' She was not self-conscious about talking to herself, because she always had talked to herself. 'Laia's invisible audience,' Taviri had used to say, as she went through the room muttering. 'You needn't come, I won't be here,' she told the invisible audience now. She had just decided what it was she had to do. She had to go out. To go into the streets.

It was inconsiderate to disappoint the foreign students. It was erratic, typically senile. It was un-Odonian. Pssssss to all that. What was the good working for freedom all your life and ending up without any freedom at all? She would go out for a walk.

'What is an anarchist? One who, choosing, accepts the responsibility of choice.'

On the way downstairs she decided, scowling, to stay and see the foreign students. But then she would go out.

They were very young students, very earnest: doe-eyed, shaggy, charming creatures from the Western Hemisphere, Benbili and the Kingdom of Mand, the girls in white trousers, the boys in long kilts, warlike and archaic. They spoke of their hopes. 'We in Mand are so very far from the Revolution that maybe we are near it,' said one of the girls, wistful and smiling: 'The Circle of Life!' and she showed the extremes meeting, in the circle of her slender, dark-skinned fingers. Amai and Aevi served them white wine and brown bread, the hospitality of the House. But the visitors, unpresumptuous, all rose to take their leave after barely half an hour. 'No, no, no,' Laia said, 'stay here, talk with Aevi and Amai. It's just that I get stiff sitting down, you see, I have to change about. It has been so good to meet you, will you come back to see me, my little brothers and sisters, soon?' For her heart went out to them, and theirs to her, and she exchanged kisses all round, laughing, delighted by their dark young cheeks, the affectionate eyes, the scented hair, before she shuffled off. She was really a little tired, but to go up and take a nap would be a defeat. She had wanted to go out. She would go out. She had not been alone outdoors since – when? since winter! before the stroke. No wonder she was getting morbid. It had been a regular jail sentence. Outside, the streets, that's where she lived.

She went quietly out of the side door of the House, past the vegetable patch, to the street. The narrow strip of sour city dirt had been beautifully gardened and was producing a fine crop of beans and *ceea*, but Laia's eyes for farming was unenlightened. Of course it had been clear that anarchist communities, even in the time of transition, must work towards optimal self-support, but how that was to be managed in the way of actual dirt and plants wasn't her business. There were farmers and agronomists for that. Her job was the streets, the noisy, stinking streets of stone, where she had grown up and lived all her life, except for the fifteen years in prison.

She looked up fondly at the façade of the House. That it had been built as a bank gave peculiar satisfaction to its present occupants. They kept their sacks of meal in the bomb-proof money-vault, and aged their cider in kegs in safe deposit boxes. Over the fussy columns that faced the street, carved letters still read, 'NATIONAL INVESTORS AND GRAIN FACTORS BANKING ASSOCIATION.' The Movement was not strong on names. They had no flag. Slogans came and went as the need did. There was always the Circle of Life to scratch on walls and pavements where Authority would have to see it. But when it came to names they were indifferent, accepting and ignoring whatever they got called, afraid of being pinned down and penned in, unafraid of being absurd. So this best known and second oldest of all the cooperative Houses had no name except The Bank.

It faced on a wide and quiet street, but only a block away began the Temeba, an open market, once famous as a centre for black market psychogenics and teratogenics, now reduced to vegetables, secondhand clothes, and miserable sideshows. Its crapulous vitality, was gone, leaving only half-paralysed alcoholics, addicts, cripples, hucksters, and fifth-rate whores, pawnshops, gambling dens, fortune-tellers, body sculptors, and cheap hotels. Laia turned to the Temeba as water seeks its level.

She had never feared or despised the city. It was her country. There would not be slums like this, if the Revolution prevailed. But there would be misery. There would always be misery, waste, cruelty. She had never pretended to be changing the human condition, to be Mama taking tragedy away from the children so they won't hurt themselves. Anything but. So long as people were free to choose, if they chose to drink flybane and live in sewers, it was their business. Just so long as it wasn't the business of Business, the source of profit and the means to power for other people. She had felt all that before she knew anything; before she wrote the first pamphlet, before she left Parheo, before she knew what 'capital' meant, before she'd been farther than River Street where she played rolltaggie kneeling on scabby knees on the pavement with the other

165

six-year-olds. She had known it: that she, and the other kids, and her parents, and their parents, and the drunks and whores and all of River Street, was at the bottom of something – was the foundation, the reality, the source.

But will you drag civilization down into the mud? cried the shocked decent people, later on, and she had tried for years to explain to them that if all you had was mud, then if you were God you made it into human beings, and if you were human you tried to make it into houses where human beings could live. But nobody who thought he was better than mud would understand. Now, water seeking its level, mud to mud, Laia shuffled through the foul, noisy street, and all the ugly weakness of her old age was at home. The sleepy whores, their lacquered hair-arrangements dilapidated and askew, the one-eyed woman wearily yelling her vegetables to sell, the halfwit beggar slapping flies, these were her countrywomen. They looked like her, they were all sad, disgusting, mean, pitiful, hideous. They were her sisters, her own people.

She did not feel very well. It had been a long time since she had walked so far, four or five blocks, by herself, in the noise and push and stinking summer heat of the streets. She had wanted to get to Koly Park, the triangle of scruffy grass at the end of the Temeba, and sit there for a while with the other old men and women who always sat there, to see what it was like to sit there and be old; but it was too far. If she didn't turn back now, she might get a dizzy spell, and she had a dread of falling down, falling down and having to lie there and look up at the people come to stare at the old woman in a fit. She turned and started home, frowning with effort and self-disgust. She could feel her face very red, and a swimming feeling came and went in her ears. It got a bit much, she was really afraid she might keel over. She saw a doorstep in the shade and made for it, let herself down cautiously, sat, sighed.

Nearby was a fruit-seller, sitting silent behind his dusty, withered stock. People went by. Nobody bought from him. Nobody looked at her. Odo, who was Odo? Famous revolutionary, author of *Community. The Analogy*, etc. etc. She, who was she? An old woman with grey hair and a red face sitting on a dirty doorstep in a slum, muttering to herself.

True? Was that she? Certainly it was what anybody passing her saw. But was it she, herself, any more than the famous revoutionary, etc., was? No. It was not. But who was she, then?

The one who loved Taviri.

Yes. True enough. But not enough. That was gone; he had been dead so long.

'Who am I?' Laia muttered to her invisible audience, and they knew the answer and told it to her with one voice. She was the little girl with scabby knees, sitting on the doorstep staring down through the dirty golden haze of River Street in the heat of late summer, the six-year-old, the sixteen-year-old, the fierce cross, dream-ridden girl, untouched, untouchable. She was herself. Indeed she had been the tireless worker and thinker, but a bloodclot in a vein had taken that woman away from her. Indeed she had been the lover, the swimmer in the midst of life, but Taviri, dying, had taken that woman away with him. There was nothing left, really, but the foundations. She had come home; she had never left home. 'True voyage is return.' Dust and mud and a doorstep in the slums. And beyond, at the far end of the street, the field full of tall dry weeds blowing in the wind as night came.

'Laia! What are you doing here? Are you all right?'

One of the people from the House, of course, a nice woman, a bit fanatical and always talking. Laia could not remember her name though she had known her for years. She let herself be taken home, the woman talking all the way. In the big cool commonroom (once occupied by tellers counting money behind polished counters supervised by armed gaurds) Laia sat down in a chair. She was unable just as yet to face climbing the stairs, though she would have liked to be alone. The woman kept on talking, and other excited people came in. It appeared that a demonstration was being planned. Events in Thu were moving so fast that the mood here had caught fire, and something must be done. Day after tomorrow, no, tomorrow, there was to be a march, a big one, from Old Town to Capitol Square – the old route. 'Another Ninth Month Uprising,' said a young man, fiery and laughing, glancing at Laia. He had not even been born at the time of the Ninth Month Uprising, it was all history to him. Now he wanted to make some history of his own. The room had filled up. A general meeting would be held here, tomorrow, at eight in the morning. 'You must talk, Laia.'

'Tomorrow? Oh, I won't be here tomorrow,' she said brusquely. Whoever had asked her smiled, another one laughed, though Amai glanced round at her with a puzzled look. They went on talking and shouting. The Revolution. What on earth had made her say that? What a thing to say on the eve of the Revolution, even if it was true.

She waited her time, managed to get up and, for all her clumsiness, to slip away unnoticed among the people busy with their planning and excitement. She got to the hall, to the stairs, and began to climb them one by one. 'The general strike,' a voice, two voices, ten voices were saying in the room below, behind her. 'The general strike,' Laia muttered, resting for a moment on the landing. Above, ahead, in her room, what awaited her? The private stroke. That was mildly funny. She started up the second flight of stairs, one by one, one leg at a time, like a small child. She was dizzy, but she was no longer afraid to fall. On ahead, on there, dry white flowers nodded and whispered in the open fields of evening. Seventy-two years and she had never had time to learn what they were called.

The Insect Tapes
MICHAEL SCOTT ROHAN

A Fly, that up and down himself doth shove ...

(Wordsworth)

BUZZ BUZZ BUZZ WONDER why he does! Here I am all alone in the *Argosy*, and who is me but a honey-bee? I do beg your pardon, but I'm the one with the Insect Tapes. The oxygen plants are being done the dirty by the Colorado beetle which has also buggered the potatoes, and a moth is fluttering around in my head; it blundered in through my ear, attracted by the light of my last, my very last bright idea. If only I'd had the flower tapes on the *Argosy*, if only someone else had had the stinking lousy Insect Tapes –

But the thing I really dread
When I've just got out of bed

– sing the entertainment tapes which are not at all like the Insect Tapes –

Is to find that there's a Spider in the bath!

EEEEE! If only there *was*! I have a bath – though the *Drosophila* flies have clogged the showerhead, they shall not conquer – I have, as I said before the insects, a bath. Somewhere. Somewhere in the spiders, that is, *among* the spiders, also the death's-head hawk moths, stick insects and dungbeetles that have made their home in the bathroom. It is blacker than black with them. I even blocked off the gravity and had them all over the ceiling, but some just scuttled down the walls and my bath would not remain in the bath. I had to keep getting up and putting it back and finally my jury-rigged cancelling switch went BLOOEY! and the insects and the bath – not the bath itself but its essential constituent, the water – fell on me oh they did oh boy didn't they. Have you ever – no you have not. If you had six hundred-odd – very odd – spiders and sundry insects fall on naked cringing you, 't'would be *you* telling *me* this tale. *You* would have been the one with the Insect Tapes.

Oh, we can't do without them, can we – can they? Can all those canned colonists frozen in the hold, can they do without their flutterbysies and buzzingly beesies and so forth? No. I'd like to wake them, wake them, let the ants crawl up *their* noses, let *them* bathe in beetles, let the termites gnaw those sterile suspension tanks they snore in. Read in the Library what the book-lice chew not. Read how back when there was all that life on Earth insects was a natural enemy and us all overrunning if it were not for the nice sweet lovely SINGING birds. I do not have the bird tapes. The *Odysseus*, Joey on the *Odysseus*, he has them. Birds sing at least, even if they foul up the statues and say 'Pieces of Eight!' in your ear all the time like in the old movie the termites ate. Insects do not sing.

> *– from the store there shrills*
> *the cricket's song, in warmth increasing ever –*

Crickets do not sing, they creak like the door mechanisms full of squashed bug. I would like to take the guy that said crickets sing to *Il Trovatore* in a version for crickets. *I* have an aversion for crickets. You will find *them* on number 5 deck, where my gymnasium is. I try to pretend it's just my muscles creaking but it's no good. I did a backward roll and gooshed two hundred of them. Somebody – anybody? – want to buy the Insect Tapes? Buyer collects, from the tarantula house that used to be Main Growth Control. You turn left at the cockroaches – Filipino roaches six inches long – knock three times and ask for archy. Step on the weevils in the carpet in passing, dodge the clouds of sandflies in the elevator and there you are and more fool you.

More fool me, to have bolted just because tarantulas kept popping out at me. Have *you* ever seen a tarantula pop? It freezes the soul, does a popping tarantula. Wouldn't *you* have bolted if you'd expected pretty little ladybirds and got poisonous perambulating pin-cushions? While somewhere in there the Growth Elements are still hiccupping away to themselves churning out seventy of everything in two sexes, no waiting, come and get 'em while they're hot! Some disaffected bookworms have chomped half the circuitry out of the controls which are now as dead as the bookworms, and the Tapes totter blindly about, occasionally stopping to churn out another insect assortment. When they randomly light on track 84400(b) I will have fleas ... Still, perhaps they will like the Witchiti grubs better than myself. They cannot like the Witchiti grubs *less* than myself. The Library, in between stinkbugs and fireflies, informs me that the Australian aborigines considered Witchiti a delicacy. I'm convinced this was a bad joke played on explorers – The Abos' Revenge! My God, Holmes, how diabolically clever! They're like sausages with a viable metabolism. I was a vegetarian, you see, my Growth Elements set to turn out fruit trees and pretty flowers, miles and miles of edible and aesthetic vegetation of all kinds. But now the Control is out of, the flies feast on my sugar beets and all's hell. The controls I thought I could fix, taking the tarantulas in my stride – squidge! heeheehee – but now my right hand will be swollen for a week, from them and the Kongo ants in the emergency rations. They are INCHES long. Now the Growth won't stop, the Insect Tapes have the Hellstrom Hiccups and repeat for ever and ever, bugs without end, amen.

The mosquitoes and sandflies drain me of blood, the tsetses will no doubt put me to sleep before the sexton beetles come for me, however. How can one drive a stake through all the little bastards' hearts? Each night they rise from their weeny coffins, wrap their Insect Capes about their shoulders and rush forth to suck the blood of innocent maidens and failing that they find me. I wish they'd club together and *get* some innocent maidens – I could use them too. I might even stake them to it – but isn't that my problem?

Yes, Sir, it all started with insects. The right kind – you can hardly see them. They call them the San José Scale – sounds like something you weigh your peyote in. Actually – says the library – they are *Diaspididae, Aspidiotus perniciosus*. Very *perniciosus* they are, too. They made my lovely grove of fruit trees on number 2 deck look as if it had dandruff. You can hardly see them as individuals, but en masse they coat your trees like ashes to ashes, dust to dust, if the whisky don't get you the *Diaspididae* must. So I ask the Library, the then gleaming, quiet, bugless Library what to do.

'Ah,' it says in wise paternal tones. 'No doubt some plant on your Tapes had some Scale eggs on it and they got scanned with it. When you reproduced the plant the eggs came too. *Hunc illae lacrimae.*'

'So what do I do, my mentor?' say I.

'Fight fire with fire. Ref. 331117(a). The Ladybird, or Ladybug (vern.), natural predator of diverse species of insects such as greenfly, San José Scale, etc. Comes in pleasing range of colours, especially shades of red, and various intriguing polkadot patterns. Unleash the Ladybird,' intones the Library from deep in its files, 'and your problems are over.' Indeed, I got ladybirds eventually, and they managed to eat most of the Scale before the locusts ate all the fruit trees. This leaves me with a food problem. From somewhere I remember reading some line in a poem about –

– locust flesh steeped in a pitcher –

My brain, my then still sane un-mothulated non-hymenopteral brain, set to work. An old poem, egad. What was a pitcher? A fragment of my now, alas!, extinct thesaurus referred me to ' – phora; bottle; jug – ' and there the termites had truncated it about the same time they clogged the Library. Aha! says I – 'pitcher' is liquid, else things could not be steeped in it. The references bear me out – bear me out gently, ye burying beetles, when I am fly-blown and maggot-bait! Locust-flesh steeped in *pitcher*, eh? So I drowned a couple of them in synthoskotch. The result was hallucinogenic, I thought my guts were leaving me and going home to Momma, leaving me here tangled up in the endless, ceaseless, peaceless repeating of the damnable Insect Tapes!

> *Dune-bug, moon-bug, was that a June-bug?*
> *Beating on my temples,*
> *Trying to get in,*
> *Will it wake the neighbours with all this din?*

There's a wasps' nest on the main control board and it's bollixed the settings. There's caddis-fly in the water supply. Cocoons hang from the astrocompass, blowflies and wasps drown the clear buzzing of the engines. Touch-sensitive controls – the merest brush of a dragonfly's wings would set them off. It does. I always rush and switch the lifesystems back on but the wasps defeat me. The motors have been slowed to a crawl, we progress as fast as a fly flies. I tell the *cantharides* to get out and push, but they ignore me.

Beep! What insect makes *that* sound? The fleas have at last sprung forth from the Tapes and are even now biting my eardrums. Beep! They're doing it again – have not the mosquitoes declared my blood supply a closed shop? Beep! The shipcom it is, but it will not be me they are calling, it must be the insects they want.

'It's for you!' I shout, but they are lazy buzzers and will not answer it. I have to do everything here, so I goosh a horsefly and press the control, ending the sorrows of a silverfish. A minutes fuzz, during which interval I do a dance with an inquisitive scorpion, then more fuzz appears on the screen. It is the hair of my friend Joey, face agleam.

'*Odysseus* callin', hiya, hi-de-ho! Caught you up, has I, you leaf-eatin' bastard? Why you slow down? How's tricks?'

My story spills forth like maggots from my last peach. He listens – and laughs! Laughs at my sorrows! Where is the brotherhood of spacemen, I wail.

'Listen, my little honky pal,' he says when he stops giggling, 'what you need is some *birds*!'

'Yes yes pretty birds you've got the Bird Tapes – can you duplicate me a set over the shipcom pretty please?' He frowns.

'Not at this range, whitey. Love to play a set on you, but the signal wouldn't be that precise. Pick up interference, distortion, you get blur, you get blurred birds and man could *that* be heavy shit! No way.' My wails and gibberings start the very ichneumons from within their caterpillars.

171

'But you doan' need Bird Tapes!' he bawls. All is suddenly very quiet.

'Man,' I say at last, 'you come over here and say that . . .' He shakes his head furiously.

'No, spook, I mean you got 'em already. In the Insect Tapes. No, doan' scream. Didn' that last RNA shot *take*, man? Insects can't exist in isolation – could anythin'? You shoulda seen that, dope – you got spiders first and they're not insects – they're *predators* on insects. Neither is half the stuff I see crawling over the wall behind you insects. What you got in these Tapes is a complete miniature temporary-type ecology to keep the insect stock goin' on the colony world until the proper ecology gets set up. Same with my birds – I got bugs and all kinda things on the tapes.'

'Then why don't *I* get any birds?'

'Could be your Growth Control – it was set for plants and mebbe ladybugs, right? Now *they're* small and simple – minimum settin'. Seedlin's and itsy bugs, man, that's nuthin'! But a bird now – big and complicated. On minimum settin' you get maybe an egg, but what use is that? All you gotta do is adjust the settin', no matter if you turn it off – and you can dodge the spiders long enough to turn one control! Run off, little pal, for I am now overtakin' you and movin' out of range – run off – 'the picture fades', – and get lotsa birds, goin' CHEEP!' Fuzz fades into fuzz; he is gone, his hair melting into the static it resembles. I am gone also so fast I leave the sound of my own gibbering behind.

The Taped insects are like piped music, they get in your ears and up your nose. But I am as one possessed and win through to the Control, where I tap-dance with tarantulas.

> *Tip-toe*
> *Through-the-tulips,*
> *On-the-spiders –*

A second to adjust the control and out pops a hummingbird which the tarantulas fall on with cries of joy, as on all the other sixty-nine. At least this gets them off me but I object to providing the bastards with *haute cuisine*. Still I persevere, and birds are upon me, around me, above me, below me, they would be beside me as well only I am beside myself with glee for the *Argosy*'s an aviary and the Ouroboros Tapes have bitten their own tails. In a spacecraft there is no chance of achieving a balanced ecology. The bugs are doomed.

You would never believe what birds are necessary to an insect-oriented ecology. I could list 'em all, but I won't. I am now the best shot in the spacefleet and none of your goddam *clay* pigeons neither. There is something with a moustache that is apparently a night-jar and swallows and swifts that whizz dementedly about. Also there are other birds that eat my new fruit trees nearly as well as the Scale and the locusts, even if they do it more politely. Still, I am saner now and birds are easier to wipe out. What remains untermited of my plant tapes supplies me well enough, and I supplement that with the six thousand eggs I have deep-frozen. If I get desperate enough to eat meat there's everything from pheasant to *coq au vin*, since some dumb cluck raided my wine cellar and drank himself to death. No, it could be – it has been ! – worse. I think I am free of all the bugs and all the birds at last.

Or am I? A swish of flight in long-deserted corridors; a far-distant cry, bleak and eerie, echoes across the chill stillness of the suspension tanks in which the colonists lie, the icy waste of frozen bodies. A glimmer of white wings in the cool depths of the engine room. I think I have identified it now, this big ghostly white bird. How it could be part of an insect ecology I cannot imagine. I must get rid of it. I am out of ammunition, but have cobbled together a crude steel-spring crossbow which should cope with any albatross. This could be a hell of a voyage.

Carrier

ROBERT SHECKLEY

EDWARD ECKS AWOKE, yawned, and stretched. He squinted at the sunlight pouring in through the open east wall of his one-room apartment, and ordered his clothes to come to him.

They didn't obey! He wiped sleep from his eyes and ordered again. But the closet door remained stubbornly shut, and not a garment stirred.

Thoroughly alarmed, Ecks swung out of bed and walked over to the closet. He began to phrase the mental command again, but stopped himself. He must not become panicky. If the clothes didn't obey, it was because he was still half asleep.

Deliberately he turned and walked to the east wall. He had rolled it up during the night and now he stood, bare toes gripping the edge, where the floor met the outside wall of the building, looking out at the city.

It was early. The milkmen were out, soaring up to the terraces to deposit their milk. A man in full evening dress passed, flying like a wounded bird. Drunk, Ecks decided, noting how uncertain the man's levitation sense was. The man banked, narrowly missing a building, dodged a milkman, misjudged the ground and fell the last two feet. Miraculously he held his balance, shook his head and continued on foot.

Ecks grinned, watching him weave down the street. That was the safest place for him. No one ever used the streets, except the Normals, or psis who *wanted* to walk for some reason. But levitating in his condition, he might get clipped by a teleported bale, or break his neck against a building.

A newsboy floated past the window, goggles dangling from his hip pocket. The boy caught his breath and shot up, straight and true, to a twentieth-floor penthouse.

Ecks craned his neck to watch the boy land his paper on the sunny terrace and sweep on. A penthouse, Ecks thought. That was the life. He lived on the third floor of an ancient building – so old that it still had stairway and elevator. But once he had finished his courses at Mycrowski University – once he had his degree – –

There was no time for dreaming. Mr Ollen didn't like him to be late; and his job at Mr Ollen's store enabled him to attend the University.

Ecks walked back, opened the closet and dressed. Then, thoroughly calm, he ordered the bed to make itself.

A blanket half-lifted, wavered, and fell back on the bed. He ordered again, angrily. The sheets sluggishly straightened, the blankets slowly crawled into place. The pillow wouldn't move.

On the fifth order the pillow dragged itself to the head of the bed. It had taken him almost five minutes to make the bed – a task he usually finished in seconds.

A shocking realization struck him, and his knees buckled; he sat down on the edge of the bed. He wasn't even able to handle simple motor-response teleportation.

And that, he knew, was how people discovered they had The Disease.

But why? How had it begun? He didn't have any unexplained tensions, any vital, unresolved problems. At twenty-six life was just beginning for him. His studies at the University were going well. His general psi rating was in the upper tenth, and his sensitivity rating approached the all-time high set by The Sleeper.

Why should it happen to him? Why should he catch the only disease left on Earth.

'I'll be damned, I don't feel sick,' he said out loud, wiping perspiration from his face. Quickly he commanded the wall to close, just to see if it would. And it did! He turned on a faucet by mental command, levitated a glass, filled it and brought it to him, without spilling a drop.

'Temporary blockage,' he told himself. 'A fluke.' Perhaps he had been studying too hard. More social life, that was what he needed.

He sent the glass back to the sink, watching the sunlight glint from it as it swooped through the air.

'I'm as good as I ever was,' he said.

The glass dropped to the floor, shattering.

'Just a little shaky,' he reassured himself. Of course, he should go to Psi-Health for an examination. If there is any impairment of your psi abilities, don't wait. Don't infect others. Get an examination.

Well, should he? Yes, he probably should.

But the Psi-Health agents were a jumpy bunch. If he showed his face they'd probably isolate him. Give him a few years of solitary rehabilitation, just to play safe.

That would be the end of him. Highly extroverted, Ecks knew himself well enough to realize that he could never stand solitary. His psi abilities would be completely wrecked that way.

Nuts, he said, and walked to the wall. Opening it, he looked out on the three storey drop, steeled himself, and jumped.

For a horrible moment, he thought he had forgotten even the basic skill of levitation. Then he caught it, and soared toward Mr Ollen's store. Weaving slightly, like a wounded bird.

Psi-Health Headquarters on the eighty-second floor of the Aerinon

Building hummed with activity. Messengers levitated in and out of the great windows, flying across the room to drop their reports on the Receiving desk. Other reports were teleped in, recorded by Psi-Grade Three telepathic-sensitive office girls. Samples were teleported through the windows, recorded, and shuttled downstairs by Grade Two Polters. A skinny Grade Four psi girl collected the typed reports and levitated them across the room in a steady stream to the file clerks.

Three messengers swept in through a single window, laughing, barely clearing the jambs, and shot across the room. One, misjudging his arc, intercepted the path of reports.

'Why don't you look where you're going?' the Grade Four girl asked angrily. Her bridge of papers was scattered across the floor. She levitated them again.

'Sorry, honey,' the messenger said, grinning and handing his report to the receiving desk. He winked at her, looped over the white stream, and shot out the window.

'Some nerve,' the girl murmured, watching him streak into the sky. Without her attention, the papers began to scatter again.

The end-product of all the activity was funnelled to the orderly black desk of Senior Health Officer Paul Marrin.

'Anything wrong, chief?' Marrin looked up and nodded to his assistant, Joe Leffert. Silently he handed him five file cards.

They were breakdown reports. Leffert scanned the first one rapidly.

'June Martinelli, waitress, Silver Cow, 4543 Broadway. Subject: Loss of psi ability. Observations: Discoordination of psi motor functions. Diagnosis: Acute loss of confidence. Infectious. Recommended: Quarantine, indefinite period.'

The other reports were about the same.

'Quite a few,' Leffert said, his tone perfectly even.

Another pile of cards was dropped on the black desk. Marrin leafed through them rapidly, his face impassive. The impassivity was mental as well. Not a thought leaked out of his rigidly held mind.

'Six more.' He turned to a large map behind his desk and pinpointed the new locations. They formed an irregular pattern across almost a third of New York.

Leffert didn't have to speak. Even undirected, his teleped thought was strong enough for Marrin to catch.

Epidemic!

'Keep that to yourself,' Marrin said in his normal low voice. He walked slowly back to his desk, considering the implications of eleven cases in a single day, when their average was one a week.

'Get me the full reports on these people,' Marrin said, handing Leffert the file cards. 'I want a list of everyone they've been in contact with over the past two weeks. And keep quiet about it.' Leffert hurried away.

Marrin thought for a moment, then teleped Krandall, chief of The Sleeper project. Normally, teleped messages were handled through a series of telepathic-sensitive girls; there were just too many minds for most people to make contact easily, without auxiliary guidance. But Marrin's psi abilities were of unusual strength. Also, he was strongly attuned to Krandall, having worked with him for many years.

'What's up?' Krandall asked, and the accompanying identity-image had the full, indescribable flavour of the man.

Quickly Marrin outlined the situation.

'I want you to find out if it's a random scattering, or if we've got a carrier to deal with,' Marrin finished.

'That'll cost you a supper,' Krandall teleped. From the peripheral thoughts, Marrin knew that he was sitting on a pier at Stag Harbour, fishing. 'A supper at The Eagles.'

'Fine. I'll have all the data. Is five-thirty all right?'

'Please, my boy! Make it six-thirty. A man of my – ah – dimensions – shouldn't levitate too rapidly.' The accompanying visual was of an overstuffed sausage.

'At six-thirty, then.' They broke contact. Marrin sat back and arranged the papers on his desk into still neater piles. At the moment he wished he were a health officer in some earlier age, with a nice fat germ to hunt down.

The source of The Disease was more subtle.

Diagnosis: Acute Loss of Confidence. Try putting that under your microscope.

He thought momentarily about the waitress, the first case on the files. Perhaps she had been stacking plates on a shelf. A doubt planted in her mind hours before, minutes before, blossomed. The plates fell. And a girl was seriously sick, horribly infected with mankind's last disease. *Loss of motor-coordination.* So she had to go into solitary, in order not to infect anyone else. For how long? A day, a year. A life.

But in the meantime, perhaps some of the customers had caught it from her. And spread it to their wives . . .

He sat upright and teleped his wife. Her answering thought was quick and warm.

'Hello, Paul!'

He told her he would be working late.

'All right,' she said, but her accompanying thoughts were confused with a strong desire to know why, and the knowledge that she couldn't ask.

'Nothing serious,' he said in reply to the unspoken question, and regretted it instantly. Lies, untruths, half-truths – even little white lies – didn't telep well. Nevertheless, he didn't retract it.

'All right Paul,' his wife said, and they broke contact.

Five o'clock, and the office staff put away their papers and headed for the windows, flying to their homes in Westchester, Long Island and New Jersey.

'Here's the stuff, chief,' Leffert said, flying up the desk with a thick briefcase. 'Anything else?'

'I'd like you to stand by,' Marrin said, taking the briefcase. 'Telep a few more agents, also.'

'Right. Do you think something might break?'

'I don't know. Better get some supper.' Leffert nodded. His eyes grew blank, and Marrin knew he was teleping his wife in Greenwich, telling her he wouldn't be home tonight.

Leffert left, and Marrin was left alone in the room, staring at the sunset. Out of the west window he could see the great red disc of the sun, and flitting across it were the black silhouettes of commuters, levitating home.

Marrin felt very much alone. Just him and a probable epidemic.

At exactly six-twenty, Marrin picked up the briefcase and levitated to The Eagles.

The Eagles restaurant was two thousand feet above New York, suspended on the backs of 200 men. The men were Grade One Psi labourers, government-tested for load capacity. As Marrin approached, he saw them under the base of the building. The restaurant floated above them, easily supported by their enormous psi strength.

Marrin landed on the main guest desk and was greeted by the head waiter.

'How's everything, Mr Marrin?' the waiter asked, leading him to a terrace.

'Fine,' Marrin said, as he always did.

'You should try our other place some time, Mr Marrin. If you're ever near Miami, there's an Eagles there. Same high-quality food.'

And high-quality prices, Marrin thought, ordering a martini. The owner of the Eagles was making a fortune. Airborne restaurants were common now, but Eagles had been the first and was still the most popular. The owner didn't even have to pay a New York property tax; when he wasn't open, he parked his restaurant in a pasture in Pennsylvania.

The terraces were starting to fill up when Krandall arrived out of wind and perspiring.

'My God,' he gasped, sitting down. 'Why aren't there any more airplanes? Bucked a head wind all the way in. Scotch on the rocks.'

The waiter hurried away.

'Why do you have your emergencies on my day off?' Krandall asked, teleping the question. 'Long distance flights are for the strong young apes. I am a mental worker. How is your wife?'

'The same,' Marrin said. His face, schooled for years into a health officer's blank mask, refused to smile now. He ordered his dinner, and handed Krandall the briefcase.

'Hmmm.' Krandall bent over the pages, scanning them rapidly. His broad, good-natured face grew abstract as he memorized the information.

178

Marrin looked across the terrace while Krandall absorbed the data. The sun was almost gone, and most of the land was in shadow. Beneath him, the lights of New York were winking on in the shaded areas. Above, the stars snapped on.

Krandall ignored his soup, flipping the pages quickly. Before the soup was cold, he was through.

'That's that,' he said. 'What shall we talk about?' Krandall was the finest psi calculator in the business. He had to be to head the important Sleeper project. Like all calculators, he let his unconscious do the work. Once the data was committed, he ignored it. Unconsciously, the information was assimilated, examined, compared, synthesized. In a few minutes or hours he could have an answer. Krandall's great talent was compensated for in other ways, though. He couldn't pass a newsboy's test for levitation, and teleportation or telekinetic manifestations were almost out of the question for him.

'Is there anything new with The Sleeper?' Marrin asked.

'Still sleeping. Some of the boys cooked up a subconscious-infiltration technique. They're trying that in a few days.'

'Do you think it will work?'

Krandall laughed. 'I give them a one-point-one probability. That's high, compared with some of the stuff they've tried.'

Krandall's brook trout was served, teleported fresh from the stream. Marrin's steak followed.

'Do you think anything will work?' Marrin asked.

'No.' Krandall's face was serious as he looked at the lean, impassive health officer, 'I don't believe the Sleeper will ever awaken.'

Marrin frowned. The Sleeper was one of Psi's most important projects, and its least successful. It had started about thirty years ago.

Psi had been standard, but still unpredicable. It had come a long way in two hundred years from Rhine's halting experiments in extra-sensory perception, but it still had a long way to go.

Mycrowski took a lot of the wild-talent aspect from psi. Classified as an extreme sensitive with genius-level psi abilities, Mycrowski was the outstanding man of his age.

With men like Krandall, Myers, Blacenck, and others, Mycrowski led the telekinesis projects, explored projection techniques, theorized on instantaneous transfer in teleportation, and examined the possibilities of new, undiscovered psi abilities.

In his spare time he worked on his own pet ideas, and founded the School for Parapsychological Research, later changed to Mycrowski University.

What *really* happened to him was argued for years. One day, Krandall and Blacenck found him lying on a couch with a bare whisper of pulse to show that he was alive. They were unable to revive him.

Mycrowski had always believed that the mind was a separate and distinct

179

entity from the body. It was believed that he had discovered a separation-projection technique for the mind.

But the mind never returned.

Others argued that his mind had simply snapped from too much strain, leaving him in a catatonic state. In any case, periodic attempts were made to awaken him, without success. Krandall, Myers, and a few others had kept the project alive, but in a few years they had all the help they needed. The rare quality of Mycrowski's genius was recognized.

The tomb where the living body of Mycrowski, The Sleeper, vegetated, became a tourists' shrine.

'Haven't *you* any idea what he was looking for?' Marrin asked.

'I don't think he did himself,' Krandall said, starting his cherry jubilee. 'Oddest damned man in the world. Didn't like to talk about anything until he could throw it in your face as done. None of us had any reason to think anything was going to happen. We were sure that the stars were right around the corner and immortality was following that.' He shook his head. 'Ah, youth, youth.'

Over the coffee Krandall looked up, pursed his lips and frowned. The assimilated data had synthesized. His conscious mind had the answer in a manner once called intuitive, until psi research pinned down the hidden factor as subconscious reasoning.

'You know, Marrin, you've definitely got a growing epidemic on your hands. There's no random scattering of cases.'

Marrin felt his chest contract. He teleped the question tightly. 'Is there a carrier?'

'There is.' Mentally, Krandall checked the names on his list. His subconscious had correlated the frequency factors, tabulated probabilities and sent up a 'hunch.' 'His name is Edward Ecks. He is a student, living at 141 Fourth Avenue.'

Marrin teleped Leffert immediately and told him to pick up Ecks.

'Hold it,' Krandall said. 'I don't believe you'll find him there. Here's a probability-course of his movements.' He teleped the information to Leffert.

'Try his apartment first,' Marrin told Leffert. 'If he's not there, try the next probability. I'll meet you downtown, in case we have to hunt him.' He broke contact and turned to Krandall. 'For the extent of the emergency you'll work with me?' It was hardly a question.

'Of course,' Krandall said. 'Health has top priority, and The Sleeper isn't going to be doing much moving. But I doubt if you'll have much trouble picking up Ecks. He should be completely crippled by this time.'

Upon landing, Ecks lost his balance and fell heavily to his knees. He got up at once, brushed himself off, and started walking. A sloppy levitation, he told himself. So even that was going!

The crumbling streets of the lower New York slums were scattered with

Normals, people who had never mastered the basic psi power. The mass of land-borne people was a sight never seen in the more respectable uptown areas. Ecks moved into the crowd, feeling safer.

He discovered, suddenly, that he was hungry. He went into a luncheonette, sat down at the empty counter and ordered a hamburger. The cook had one all ready. Expertly he teleported it to a plate and, without watching, made the plate loop in the air and drop lightly in front of Ecks.

Ecks cursed the man's casual ability and reached for the ketchup. He expected the bottle to slide towards him, but it didn't. He looked at it for a moment, blankly, then stretched his arm. He'd have to watch his step, making a mistake like that.

Ecks was beginning to discover what it was like to be a cripple.

Finished, he held out his hand, palm up, expecting the change in his pocket to come. But of course, it didn't. He cursed silently. He was so used to it – it didn't seem possible that he could have lost all his faculties at once.

But he had, he knew. His unconscious had decided, and no amount of surface assurance would help.

The cook was looking at him oddly, so he reached quickly in his pocket, found the change, and paid. He tried to smile at the cook, then hurried out the door.

'Queer guy,' the cook thought. He dismissed it, but down deep in his mind an appraisal was going on. Inability to command a bottle . . . Inability to command coins . . .

Ecks walked down the crowded, grimy streets. His legs began to ache. He had never walked so much in his life. Around him were mixed groups of Normals and psis. The Normals walked naturally, as they had all their lives. The psis were awkward, unaccustomed to long stretches on foot. With relief they soared into their natural element, the air. People landed and took off, and the air was filled with teleported objects.

Looking back, Ecks saw a well-dressed man drop out of the air and stop one of the walking psis. He talked to him for a moment, then moved on.

A health-agent! Ecks knew he had been traced.

He twisted around a corner and started to run.

The street lights became fewer as Ecks moved on, pushing his aching legs. He tried to levitate, but couldn't get off the ground.

In panic he tried to telep his friends. Useless. His telepathic sense had no power.

The shock broke over him like an ocean wave, and he stumbled against a lamp post and hung on. The full realization came.

In a word where men flew, he was landbound.

In a word of telepathic contact, he was reduced to clumsy words at face-to-face distance.

In a world where artificial light was unnecessary, he could see only when his eyes were stimulated.

Crippled. Blind, deaf, and dumb.

He walked on, into narrower streets, dingy, damp alleys. His numbed mind started working again. He had one advantage. His blunted mind no longer broadcast a strong identity-pattern. That would make him more difficult to find.

What he needed, he decided, was a sanctuary. Some place where he wouldn't infect anyone, and where the health officers couldn't find him. Perhaps he could find a Normal boarding house. He could stay there and study, find out what was wrong with him; treat himself. And he wouldn't be alone. Normals were better than no people at all.

He came to the end of an alley, where the streets branched off. Automatically he pushed out his location sense, to find out what was ahead.

Useless. It was paralysed, as dead as the rest of him. But the right-hand turn seemed the safest. He started for it.

'Don't!'

Ecks whirled, alarmed at the spoken word. A girl had come out of a doorway. She ran to him.

'They're waiting for me?' Ecks asked, his heart pounding like a triphammer.

'The health officers. They figured you'd take the right turn. Something about your right-hand tropism, I couldn't hear it all. Take the street on your left.'

Ecks looked at her closely. At first he thought she was about fifteen years old, but he revised his estimate to twenty. She was small, slender with large dark eyes in a bony face.

'Why are you helping me?' he asked.

'My uncle told me to,' the girl said. 'Hurry!'

There was no time to argue. Ecks walked in the alley, following the girl. She ran ahead, and Ecks had trouble keeping up with her.

She was a Normal, to judge by her sure stride. But how had she overheard the health-officer's conversation? Almost certainly they had teleped on a tight beam.

Her uncle, perhaps?

The alley opened into a courtyard. Ecks raced in, and stopped. From the tops of the buildings men floated down. They dropped quickly, surrounding him.

The health officers!

He looked around, but the girl had darted back into the alley. The way was blocked for him. He backed against a building, wondering how he could have been so stupid. Of course! This was how they liked to take people. Quietly, so no one else would become infected.

That damned girl! He tightened his aching legs, to run for it...

Just as Krandall predicted, Marrin thought. 'Take his arms and legs.'

Hovering fifty feet in the air, he supervised the operation.

Without pity, he watched. The agents moved in cautiously. They didn't want to use the force of their minds against him if they could help him.

After all, the man was a cripple.

They had almost reached him, when – –

Ecks started to fade. Marrin dropped closer, unable to believe his eyes. Ecks was dissolving into the wall, becoming a part of it, disappearing.

Then he was gone.

'Look for a door!' Marrin teleped. 'Examine the pavement!'

While his agents were looking, Marrin considered what he had seen. After the initial surprise, he didn't doubt it. The search for a door was an excuse for his agents. If they thought the man had disappeared through a hidden door, good. It wouldn't help their confidence – their sanity – to believe what had actually happened.

The cripple, Ecks, merging with the wall.

Marrin ordered a search of the building. But there wasn't a trace of Ecks' thought pattern. He was gone, as though he had never been.

But how, Marrin asked himself. Did someone help him? Who?

Who would help a carrier?

The first thing Ecks saw when he returned to consciousness was the cracked, stained plaster wall in front of him. He stared at it for a long time, watching dust motes floating in the sunlight, across the bed's torn brown blanket.

The bed! Ecks sat up and looked around. He was in a dingy little room. Long cracks ran across the ceiling. Aside from the bed, the only other piece of furniture was a plain wooden chair, set hear the half-open door.

But what was he doing here? He remembered the events of last night; it must have been last night, he decided. The blank wall, the health officers. He must have been rescued. But how?

'How do you feel?' A girl's voice asked from the door. Ecks turned, and recognized the pale, sensitive face. It was the girl who had warned him last night.

'I feel all right,' Ecks said. 'How did I get here?'

'My uncle brought you,' the girl said, coming into the room. 'You must be hungry.'

'Not especially,' Ecks said.

'You should eat,' she told him. 'My uncle tells me that dematerialization is quite a strain on the nervous system. That's how he rescued you from the psis, you know.' She paused. 'I can give you some very nice broth.'

'He *dematerialized* me?' Ecks asked.

'He can do things like that,' the girl said serenely. 'The power came to him afterwards.' She walked over and opened the window. 'Shall I get the broth?'

Ecks frowned at her. The situation was becoming unreal, at a time when he needed his fullest grasp on reality. This girl seemed to consider it perfectly normal to have an uncle with the power of dematerialization – although psi science had never discovered it.

'Shall I get the broth?' she asked again.

'No,' Ecks said. He wondered what the repeated emphasis on food might mean. There was nothing in the girl's face to tell him. She was handsome enough, even in a cheap, unbecoming dress. She had unusually dark eyes, and an unusually calm expression. Or lack of expression, really.

He filed his suspicions for the moment, and asked. 'Is your uncle a psi?'

'No,' the girl said. 'My uncle doesn't hold with psi powers. His strength is spiritual.'

'I see,' Ecks said, and he thought he had the answer. Throughout history, people had preferred to believe that their natural psi gifts were the product of demon intervention. Strange powers were the devil's gift until psi regularized and formuralized them. And even in this day there were gullible Normals, people who preferred to believe that their occasional flashes of supernormal power were spirit-guided. Evidently the uncle fell into this category.

'Has your uncle been able to do this sort of thing long?' Ecks asked.

'Only for about five years,' she said. 'Only since he died.'

'Perfectly correct,' a voice said. Ecks looked around quickly. The voice seemed to come from behind his shoulder.

'Don't look for me,' the voice said. 'All that there is of me in this room is a voice. I am the spirit of Cari's Uncle John.'

Ecks had a quick moment of panic before he realized the trick. It was a teleped voice, of course; cleverly focused and masked to give the effect of speech. A teleped voice meant only one thing; this was a psi passing himself off as a spirit.

'Mr Ecks,' the voice said, cleverly simulating the effects of spoken words, 'I have rescued you by the intervention of my powers. You are a crippled psi, a carrier. Capture and isolation are, I believe, distasteful to you. Is that not true?'

'Perfectly,' Ecks said. He probed with his blunted senses for the source of the voice. The imitation was perfect; not a single image leaked, to show the telepathic-human source.

'You feel, perhaps, a certain gratitude towards me?' the voice asked.

Ecks looked at the girl. Her face was still expressionless. 'Of course I do,' he said.

'I know your desires,' Uncle John told him. 'You wish sanctuary for a sufficient time to restore your powers. And you shall have it, Edward Ecks. You shall have it.'

'I'm very grateful,' Ecks said. His mind was working quickly, trying to decide upon a course of action. Was he expected to keep up the pretence of believing in this spirit? Surely the teleping psi knew that no university-trained person was going to accept something like that. On the other hand, he might be dealing with a neurotic, playing spirit for his own reasons. He decided to play along. After all, he wasn't interested in the man's pretensions. What mattered was the sanctuary.

'You would not, I am certain, object to doing me a small favour,' Uncle John said.

'What do you want me to do?' Ecks asked, immediately on his guard.

'I sense your thought,' the voice said. 'You think there may be danger involved. I assure you, such is not the case. Although I am not omnipotent, I have certain powers unknown to you – or to psi science. Accept that fact. Surely your rescue proves it. And accept that I have your best interests at heart.'

'When do I find out about this errand?' Ecks asked.

'When the time is right. For now, goodbye, Edward Ecks.' The voice was gone.

Ecks sat down in the chair. He had had two possible explanations before; that the 'uncle' was a psychotic, or a psi. Now he had another.

What if the uncle was a mutant psi? The next evolution in the procession. What then?

Cari left and returned with a bowl of soup.

'What was your uncle like?' Ecks asked the girl. 'What sort of man was he – when he was alive?'

'Oh, he was a very nice man,' she said, holding the steaming soup carefully. 'He was a shoemaker. He raised me when my father died.'

'Did he ever show any signs of psi power? Or supernatural power?'

'No,' Cari said. 'He led a quiet life. It was only after he died – – '

Ecks looked at the girl with pity. She was the saddest part of the whole thing. The psi had undoubtedly read her mind, found the dead uncle – and the gullibility. And used her as his pawn. A cruel game.

'Please eat the soup,' she said. He reached for it automatically, glancing at her face. Then he pulled back his hand.

'You eat it,' he said. The first tinge of colour came into her cheeks.

With an apology, she started on the soup, spilling some in her eagerness.

The sailboat heeled sharply, and Marrin let out a foot of mainsail to steady it. His wife, seated on the bow, waved to him, enjoying the plunging motion.

Below, he could see a bank of thunderheads, a storm in the making.

'Let's have our picnic on those clouds over there,' Myra said, pointing to a wispy cirrus formation, bright and sunny above the thunderheads. Marrin changed course. Myra lay back on the bow, her feet propped against the mast.

Marrin was holding the entire weight of the boat himself, but he scarcely noticed it. The light rig weighed less than two hundred pounds, sail and all. His and Myra's combined weight added about two hundred and sixty pounds more, but Marrin's tested levitation capacity was over two tons.

And the wind did most of the work. All the operator of the boat did was to supply enough power to keep it in the air. The wind drove it, a twisting white feather.

Marrin couldn't get his mind off the carrier. How in hell had Ecks disappeared? Dematerialization – impossible! And yet there it was.

Ecks, into the wall. And gone, without a thought-trace.

'Stop thinking,' Myra said. 'Your doctor told you not to think about anything but me today.' He knew that his thoughts hadn't leaked; nor had his face changed. But Myra was sensitive to his moods. He didn't have to grimace for her to know he was happy, or cry to demonstrate sadness.

Marrin brought the light, flat boat to a stop in the clouds, and, heading into the wind, dropped the sail. They spread their picnic on the bow of the boat. Marrin did most of the levitation, although Myra was trying ... gallantly.

As she had been trying for seven years, since her partial infection by a carrier. Although her psi faculties never left her completely, they were spasmodic.

Another reason for hunting down Ecks.

The sandwiches Myra made were very like herself; small and decorative. And tasty, Marrin thought, teleping the thought.

'Beast,' Myra said out loud. The warm sun beat down on them, and Marrin felt wonderfully lazy. The two of them stretched out on the deck of the boat, Marrin holding it up by reflex. He was more relaxed than he had been in weeks.

'*Marrin!*'

Marrin started, awakened out of near-sleep by the teleped voice.

'Look, I'm awfully sorry, boy.' It was Krandall, embarrassed and apologetic.

'I hate breaking in on your day, but I've got a lead, and a pretty damned good one. Evidently someone doesn't like our carrier. I've just been told where he'll be in about four hours. Of course, it may be a crank, but I knew you'd want to know – – '

'I'm coming,' Marrin said. 'We can't afford to pass up anything.' He broke contact and turned to his wife. 'I'm terribly sorry, dear.'

She smiled, and her eyes were clear with understanding. She hadn't been included in Krandall's tight-beam message, but she knew what it meant.

'Can you take it down yourself?' Marrin asked.

'Of course. Good hunting.' Marrin kissed her and jumped off the boat. He watched for a few seconds, to see that she had it under control; then he teleped the rental service.

'My wife's bringing it in,' he told them. 'I wish you'd keep an eye on her.'

They promised. Now, even if she went out of control there'd be no danger.

Marrin hurled himself down. He was so busy calculating the rate of disease increase that he barely saw the danger in time.

It flashed past him, then turned, twenty feet away, and came again. Marrin reached out for it mentally, but the telekineticized knife broke free. He barely deflected it, grappled, and had it in his hand. Quickly he tried to trace the wielder, but he was gone without a trace.

Not quite without a trace. Marrin was able to catch the tail end of an identity thought, the hardest kind to control. He puzzled over it, trying to place the image. Then he had it.

Ecks!

Ecks, the cripple, Blind Ecks, the carrier, who vanished into walls. And who, evidently, could polter a dagger.

Or had someone do it for him.

Grimly, with the growing awareness that it was turning into a personal affair, Marrin levitated into the Psi-Health Offices.

In the darkened room, Edward Ecks lay on the tattered brown blanket. His eyes were lightly closed, his body passive. Little muscles in his legs jumped. He willed them to relax.

'Relaxation is one of the keys to psi power. Complete relaxation calls forth confidence; fears disappear, tensions evaporate. Relaxation is vital to psi.' Ecks told himself this, breathing deeply.

Don't think about the disease. There is no disease. There is only rest, and relaxation.

The leg muscles slackened. Ecks concentrated on his heart, ordering it to pump more easily. He sent orders to his lungs, to breathe deeply and slowly.

Uncle John? He hadn't heard from him for almost two days now. But he mustn't think of him. Not now. An unexplained factor, Uncle John would be resolved in time. The awareness of deception, Ecks told himself, is the first step in finding out what the deception is.

And what about the pale, hungry, attractive niece? Don't think about her, either.

The unsettling memories sponged away as his breathing deepened. Next, the eyes. It was hard to relax the eyes. After-images danced across his retina. Sunlight. Darkness, a building, a disappearance.

No. Don't think.

'My eyes are so heavy,' he told himself. 'My eyes are made of lead. They want to sink – to sink – – '

Then his eye-muscles relaxed. His thoughts seemed calm, but just under the surface was a crazy welter of images and impressions.

A cripple, through dim streets. A ghost that wasn't. A hungry niece. Hungry for what? A turmoil of sense-impressions, flashes of red and purple, memories of classes in Mycrowski University, tele-wrestling at the

Palladium, a date at Skytop.

All had to be smoothed down. 'Relaxation is the first step towards reintegration.' Ecks told himself that everything was blue. All thoughts were swallowed in a vast blue abyss.

Slowly, he succeeded in calming his mind. A deep peace started to seep into him, slowly, soothingly – –

'*Edward Ecks.*'

'Yes?' Ecks opened his eyes at once; the relaxation had been that superficial. He looked around and realized that it was the uncle's voice.

'Take this.' A small sphere darted into the room, and came to rest in front of Ecks. He picked it up and examined it. The sphere seemed to be made of some shiny, solid plastic.

'What is it?' he asked.

'You will place this sphere inside the Cordeer Building,' the voice of Uncle John told him, ignoring the question. 'Leave it on a desk, behind a door, in an ashtray, anywhere. Then return directly here.'

'What will the sphere do?' Ecks asked.

'That is not your concern,' the voice told him. 'The sphere is the apex of a psychic triangle of forces which you do not understand. Suffice it to say that it will harm no one and will greatly aid me.'

'Every officer in the city is looking for me,' Ecks said. 'I'll be picked up if I go back to the main part of the city.'

'You have forgotten my powers, Ecks. You will be safe, if you keep to the route I map out for you.'

Ecks hesitated. He wanted to know more about the uncle, and his game. Above all, why was he masquerading as a spirit?

Or was he?

After all, what would a spirit have to do with Earth? The classic yarns of demons seeking temporal power were just so much muggy anthropomorphizing.

'Will I be left alone after I get back?' Ecks wanted to know.

'You have my word. Do this to my satisfaction and you will receive all the sanctuary you need. Now go. Cari has the route drawn up for you. She is waiting at the door.'

The voice was gone. Even with his blunted senses, Ecks could feel the withdrawn contact.

With the sphere in his hand, he walked to the door. Cari was waiting.

'Here are the instructions,' she said.

Ecks looked at her sharply. He wished he had some psi-abilities left. He would have given a good deal to know what was going on behind that quiet, pretty face. Psis never bothered to read faces; the affective aura surrounding every individual was a far better indicator.

If one had normal psi-sensitivity to read it.

'Have you eaten?' he asked.

'Oh, yes,' she said, following him outside. The sunlight was momentarily blinding, after two days in the little room. Ecks blinked and looked around automatically. There was no one in sight.

They walked in silence for a while, following Uncle John's instructions. Ecks glanced right and left, pitifully aware of his vulnerability, on the lookout for detection. The instructions laid out a devious, meaningless pattern for Ecks to walk; doubling back on streets, circling others. They approached West Broadway, moving out of the slums into psi territory.

'Has your uncle ever told you what he wishes to do?' Ecks asked.

'No,' Cari said. They walked in silence for a while longer. Ecks tried not to look at the sky, out of which he expected the psi officers to fall, like avenging angels.

'Sometimes I'm afraid of Uncle John,' Cari volunteered, after a few moments. 'He's so strange, sometimes.'

Ecks nodded absently. Then he thought about the girl's position. Actually, she was worse off than he was. He knew the score. She was being used for some unknown purpose. She might well be in danger, although he didn't know why that should concern him.

'Look,' he said, 'If anything happens, do you know the Angler's Bar on Sixth and Bleeker?'

'No, but I could find it.'

'Meet me there, if anything goes wrong.'

'All right,' she said. 'Thank you.'

Ecks smiled wryly. How idiotic of him to offer her protection! When he couldn't even protect himself. At least, he told himself, it was an understandable urge. Even if he didn't quite understand it himself.

They walked several more blocks. Then the girl looked at Ecks nervously.

'There's one thing I don't understand,' she said.

'What's that?'

'Well,' she began, 'I sometimes can see things that are going to be. I never know when, but just sometimes I have a picture of something. Then in a little while it happens.'

'That's interesting,' Ecks said. 'You're probably an undeveloped clairvoyant. You should go to Mycrowski University. They're always looking for people like you.'

'So far, everything I've seen has turned out right,' she said.

'That's a nice record,' Ecks told her. He wondered what the girl was driving at. Did she want praise? She couldn't be naive enough to believe that she was the only person in the world with latent clairvoyance.

'So far my uncle has been right in everything he's said, too,' she told him.

'Very commendable,' Ecks said acidly. He was in no mood for a family panegyric. They were approaching Fourteenth Street, and the air was thick with psis. A few people were walking – but very few.

The Cordeer Building was three blocks ahead.

'What I'm wondering is,' she said, 'If I see something happening one way, and my uncle sees it happening the other way, which of us will be right?'

'What do you mean?' Ecks said, taking her arm as they crossed a street filled with jagged rocks.

'My uncle said you'd be safe,' she said, 'and I just don't understand.'

'What?' He stopped.

'I think they're going to try to capture you.'

'When?'

'Now,' she said. Ecks stared at her, then stiffened. He didn't need psi power to know that the trap was sprung.

The health men weren't being gentle this time. Telekinetic force jerked him off his feet. He looked for Cari, but the girl was gone. Then his head was forced painfully down, his hands and feet seized.

Physically, not a hand had touched him yet.

Ecks fought wildly, in blind panic. *Capture* seemed to touch off some ultimate instability in his personality. He tried desperately to snap the telekinetic bonds.

He almost did. Power came. He freed an arm and managed to throw himself into the air. Frantically he tried for height.

He was smashed to the pavement.

Again he tried, a supreme effort – –

And passed out.

His last conscious thought was a realization that he had been tricked. The uncle – he determined to kill him, if the opportunity ever presented itself.

And then there was blackness.

A meeting of World-Health was called at once. Marrin, in Psi headquarters in New York, opened the special channel. Chiefs in Rio, London, Paris, Canton, came into emergency circuit.

Marrin's tightly organized information was flashed around the world in less than a minute. At once he received a question.

'I would like to know,' the Health Chief from Barcelona asked, 'how this Ecks person escaped you *twice*.' The thought carried its inevitable identity pattern. The Barcelona chief's face was dimly apparent; long, sad, moustached. Not his true face, of course. Identity patterns were always idealized in the manner the particular mind viewed itself. Actually, the Barcelonan might be short, fat, and clean shaven.

'The second escape was in broad daylight, was it not?' the Berlin chief asked, and the other chiefs glimpsed his broad, powerful, idealized face.

'It was,' Marrin replied. 'I cannot explain it.' Marrin was seated at his black desk in Psi-Health. Around him hummed the normal activity of the day. He was unaware of it.

'Here is the complete sequence.' It took longer to telep the scene-by-scene breakdown of the attempted rescue.

After the attack by the poltered dagger, Marrin had assembled his men around the point where Krandall's informant said Ecks would appear.

'This informant. Who – –'

'Later. Let him complete the sequence.'

Fifty agents covered the area. Ecks appeared on time, and in the indicated place. He was restrained with little difficulty, at first. Fighting, he showed a slight surge of latent strength; then he collapsed.

At that moment his energy potential took an explosive, exponential jump. Ecks vanished.

With Marrin's permission, his recollection of the moment was broken down and scrutinized more closely. The picture remained clear. One moment Ecks was there, the next, he was gone.

The images were slowed to one a half second. In this running there was a blur of energy around Ecks just before he vanished. The energy was on so high a band that it was almost indetectable.

There was no known explanation for it.

The impressions of the particpating agents, as recorded by Marrin, were combed, with no positive result.

'Would the Health-Chief from New York care to give his theories?'

'Since Ecks is a cripple,' Marrin said, 'I can only assume that someone is helping him.'

'There is another possibility,' the Warsaw Chief said. His idealized identity came though with the thought; slim, white-haired, gay. 'Ecks may have stumbled on some undiscovered form of psi power.'

'That would appear to be beyond the realm of probability,' the sad-eyed Barcelonan teleped.

'Not at all. Consider the emergence of the original psi faculties. They began as wild talents. Couldn't the next mutation begin in a wild talent stage?'

'There are tremendous implications in that,' the London Chief said. 'But if so, why hasn't Ecks utilized it to greater advantage?'

'He is probably unaware of it. But he has an inherent protection system, perhaps, which shunts him out of danger at stress moments.' 'I don't know,' Marrin said dubiously. 'It is a possibility, of course. We are well aware that there are many untouched secrets of the mind. Still . . .'

'An argument against *your* theory,' the Warsaw Chief broke in, teleping directly to Marrin, 'is the fact that anyone helping Ecks would necessarily have this extra-psi power. They would have to, to effect an almost instantaneous disappearance. If they did have it, wouldn't they have more of a plan – less randomness – –'

'Or seeming randomness,' the Londoner said. 'It could be a test of strength. By dangling Ecks in front of Marrin, such a group could determine a good deal about his capabilities and, by extrapolation, the capabilities of all psis. The repeated inability to capture Ecks would be meaningful.'

'It's a possibility,' Marrin said cautiously. Academically, he found the discussion interesting. But it didn't seem to be serving any practical good.

'What about Krandall's informant?' the Barcelonan teleped. 'Has he been questioned?'

'He has never been found,' Marrin said. 'The sender was able to block all identity-thoughts and he left no trace to follow.'

'What do you plan to do?'

'First,' Marrin said, 'to alert you. That is the purpose of the meeting, since the carrier might well get out of New York. Also, the disease rate here has passed the minimum epidemic level. It can be expected to spread, even though I'm closing the city.' He paused and wiped his forehead.

'Second, I'm going to trace Ecks myself, working on a new set of probability locations supplied by Krandall. Working alone, I'll be able to avoid all thought haze and deflection. It's just possible one may do what many cannot.'

Marrin discussed it with them for half an hour longer, then broke contact. He sat for a few moments, moodily sorting papers. Then he shrugged off his mood of despair and went to see Krandall.

Krandall was in his office at the tomb of The Sleeper. He grunted hello when Marrin levitated in and motioned him to a chair.

'I'd like to see those probability locations,' Marrin said.

'Right,' Krandall said. The end-product was quite simple: a list of streets and times. But to get that information, Krandall had correlated the total amount of data available. The locations of Ecks' disappearances, his reappearances, his psychological index, plus the added correlates of suitable hiding spots in the city where a cripple could stay undetected.

'I think you stand a pretty good chance of finding him,' Krandall said. 'Of course, holding him is something else again.'

'I know,' Marrin said, 'I've come to a decision about that.' He looked away from Krandall. 'I'm going to have to kill Ecks.'

'I know,' Krandall said.

'What?'

'You can't risk having him loose any more. Your infection rate is still rising.'

'That's right. The policy of the Health Board is to quarantine diseased persons. But this is a matter of public safety.'

'You don't have to justify it to me,' Krandall said.

'What do you mean?' Marrin got halfway to his feet, then sat down again and shook his head. 'You're right. Evidently Ecks can't be captured. We'll see if he can be killed.'

'Good hunting,' Krandall said. 'I hope you have better luck on *your* project.'

'The Sleeper?'

'The latest attempt flopped. Not a stir out of him.'

Marrin frowned. That was bad news. If they ever needed Mycrowski's intellect, it was now. Mycrowski was the man to resolve these events into a related whole.

'Would you like to see him?' Krandall asked.

Marrin glanced at the probability list and saw that the first time-street fix was almost an hour off. He nodded, and followed Krandall. They went down a dim corridor to an elevator, and then through another corridor.

'You haven't ever been here, have you?' Krandall asked, at the end of the corridor.

'No. But I helped draw up plans for the remodelling ten years ago.'

Krandall unlocked and opened the last door.

In the brightly lighted room. The Sleeper rested. Tubes ran into his arms, carrying the nutriest solutions that kept him alive. The bed he lay on slowly massaged The Sleeper's flabby muscles. The Sleeper's face was blank and expressionless, as it had been for thirty years. The face of a dead man, still living.

'That's enough,' Marrin said. 'I'm depressed enough.'

They went back upstairs.

'Those streets I gave you are in the slums,' Krandall said. 'Watch your step. Asociality is still present in such places.'

'I'm feeling pretty asocial myself,' Marrin said, and left.

He levitated to the fringe of the slums, and dropped to the street. His sensitive, trained mind was keyed for stimulation. He walked, sorting impressions as he went, searching for the dull, almost obliterated throb of the carrier's mind. Marrin's web extended for blocks, sifting, feeling, sorting.

If Ecks was alive and conscious he would find him.

And kill him.

'You fool! You incompetent! You imbecile!' The disembodied voice roared at Ecks.

Blurrily, Ecks realized that he was back in Cari's house, in the slums.

'I gave you a course to follow,' Uncle John screamed, his voice bouncing against the walls. 'You took the wrong turn!'

'I did not,' Ecks said, getting to his feet. He wondered vaguely how long he had been unconscious.

'Don't contradict me! You did. And you must do it again!'

'Just a minute,' Ecks said evenly. 'I don't know what your game is, but I followed your instructions to the letter. I turned down every street you wrote down.'

'You didn't!'

'Stop this farce!' Ecks shouted back. 'Who in hell are you?'

'Get out!' Uncle John roared. 'Get out – or I'll kill you.'

'Be reasonable,' Ecks said. 'Just tell me what you want. Tell me what I'm supposed to do. Explain it. I don't work well in a mystery.'

'Get out,' the voice said ominously.

'I can't,' Ecks said in despair. 'Why don't you drop this spirit pose and tell me what it is you want? I'm a normal person. Health officers are everywhere. They will kill me too. I must first regain my abilities. But I can't — — '

'Are you going?' the voice asked.

Ecks didn't answer.

Invisible hands were at Ecks' throat. He jerked back. The grip tightened. Force battered him against the wall, chopping down at him. Ecks rolled, trying to escape the merciless beating. The air was alive with energy, hurling itself at him, crushing him, smothering him.

Marrin sensed the increase in energy output at once. He traced it, got a fix and levitated towards the location, sifting through the energy manifestations for some identity pattern.

Ecks!

Marrin crashed through a flimsy wooden door, and stopped. He saw Ecks' crumpled body.

Berserk force was alive in the room, undirected now. Suddenly, Marrin found himself fighting for his life. Shielding, he smashed against the telekinetic power that surged around him.

A chair was swept up and thrown at him. He deflected it, and was struck from behind by a pitcher. A bed tried to crush him against the wall. Avoiding it, he was struck in the back by a poltered table. A lamp shattered on the wall above his head, spraying him with fragments. A broom caught him behind the knees.

Marrin shielded and located the psi power source.

In the basement of the building.

He sent a tremendous wave rippling across it, poltering chairs and tables with it. The attack stopped abruptly. The place was a shambles of broken furniture.

Marrin looked around, Ecks was gone again. He searched for his identity pattern, but couldn't locate it.

The man in the cellar?

Also gone. But a trace was left behind!

Marrin went through a window, following the trace thought. Trained for this work, he held contact with the attenuated, stifled thought as its owner shot into the city. He followed it through a twisting maze of buildings, and out into open air.

One part of his mind was still able to probe for Ecks. No luck.

But he had Ecks' accomplice, if he could hold him.

He shortened the distance by fractions. Ecks' helper – and attacker – shot out of the city, heading West.

Marrin followed.

'A glass of beer, please,' Ecks said, trying hard to catch his breath. It had been a long run. Luckily the bartender was a Normal, and a phlegmatic one at that. He moved stolidly to the tap.

Ecks saw Cari at the end of the bar, leaning against the wall. Thank God she had remembered. He paid for his beer and carried it to where she was.

'What happened?' she asked, looking at his bruised face.

'Your nice uncle tried to kill me,' Ecks said wryly. 'A health-officer came bursting in, and I let them fight it out.' Ecks had slipped out the door during the fight. He had counted on the insensitivity of his thought pattern to conceal him. Crippled, he was hardly able to broadcast an identity thought. For once, the loss of telepathic power was an asset.

Cari shook her head sadly. 'I just don't understand it,' she said. 'You may not believe this, but Uncle John was always a good man. He was the most harmless person I ever knew. I just don't understand – –'

'Simple,' Ecks said. 'Try to understand this. That was not Uncle John. Some highly developed psi has been masquerading as him.'

'But why?' she asked.

'I don't know,' Ecks said. 'He saves me, tries to get me captured again, then tries to kill me. It doesn't make sense.'

'What now?' she asked.

Ecks finished his beer. 'Now, the end,' he said.

'Isn't there some place we can go?' she sked. 'Some place we can hide?'

'I don't know of any,' Ecks said. 'You'd better go on your own. I'm a risky person to be with.'

'I'd rather not,' Cari said.

'Why not?' Ecks wanted to know.

She looked away. 'I'd just rather not.'

Even without telepathy, Ecks had an intimation of what she meant. Mentally, he cursed. He didn't like the idea of having the responsibility of her. Psi-Health must be getting desperate. They wouldn't pull any punches this time, and she might get hurt.

'Go away,' he said firmly.

'No!'

'Well, come on,' he said. 'We'll just have to get by as well as we can. The only thing I can think of is getting out of the city. I should have done that at first, instead of playing spirit.' Now it was undoubtedly too late. The psi officers would be checking everyone on foot.

'Can you use that clairvoyance of yours?' he asked. 'Is there anything you can see?'

'No,' she said sadly. 'The future's a blank to me.'

That was how Ecks saw it, too.

Marrin sensed that he had greater inherent strength than the man he was pursuing. He detected the signs of weakening and pushed harder.

The fugitive was visible now, a mile ahead of him doubling back towards the city. As he got closer, Marrin threw his telekinetic strength, pulling the man down.

He clung doggedly. The man was slowing, fighting spasmodically. Marrin overhauled him, brought him down and pinned him to the ground. Coming down himself, he probed for an identity thought.

And found one.

Krandall!

For a moment all he could do was stare.

'Did you get Ecks?' Krandall teleped. The exertion had drained the big man of everything. He lay, face down, fighting for breath.

'No. You were his backer all along. Is that right?'

Krandall's thought was affirmative.

'How could you! What were you thinking of? You know what the disease means!'

'I'll explain later,' Krandall panted.

'Now!'

'No time. You have to find Ecks.'

'I know that,' Marrin said. 'But why did you help him?'

'I didn't,' the fat man said. 'Not really. I tried to kill him. *You* must kill him.' He dragged himself to his feet. 'He's a far greater menace than you think. Believe me, Marrin. Ecks must be killed!'

'Why did you rescue him?' Marrin asked.

'In order to put him back into danger,' Krandall gasped. 'I couldn't let you capture and isolate him. He must be killed.'

'Go on,' Marrin said.

'Not now,' Krandall said. 'I poltered the dagger at you, to make you consider Ecks a personal menace. I had to goad you to the point where you would kill him.'

'*What is he?*'

'Not now! Get him!'

'Another thing,' Marrin said. 'You couldn't handle that amount of telekinetic power. Who was doing it?'

'The girl,' Krandall said, swaying on his feet. 'The girl Cari. I was posing as her uncle's spirit. She's in back of it all. You must kill her, too.' He wiped his streaming face.

'I'm sorry I had to play it this way, Paul. You'll hear the whole story at the right time. Just take my word for it now.'

Krandall tightened his hands into fists and shook them at Marrin.

'You must kill those two! Before they kill everything you stand for!'

The teleped thought had the ring of truth. Marrin took to the air again, contacting his agents. Briefly he gave his instructions.

'Kill both of them,' he said. 'And pick up Krandall and hold him.'

Ecks turned down streets at random, hoping the lack of plan would confuse the psis. Every shadow seemed to have a meaning of its own. He waited for the mental bolt that would drop him.

Why had the uncle tried to kill him? Impossible to answer. Why was he so seemingly important? Another unanswerable question. And the girl?

Ecks watched her out of the corner of his eye. Cari walked silently beside him. Her face had some colour now, and some animation. She seemed almost gay; perhaps freedom from the uncle was the reason for that. What other reason could there be?

Because she was with him?

The air was thick with the usual day's traffic. A load of ore was being brought in, tons of it, expertly shepherded by a dozen workers. Other cargoes were being flown in from Southern ports; fruit and vegetables from Brazil, meat from Argentina.

And psi officers. Ecks wasn't especially surprised. The city was being watched too thoroughly for a fly to escape, much less a crippled man.

The psi officers dropped down, forming a tight mental linkage.

'All right,' Ecks called. 'The hell with it, I give up.' He decided that it was time he bowed to the inevitable. He had the girl to consider also. The psis were probably tired of playing; this time, if he tried to escape, they might play for keeps.

A bolt of energy sheered him off his feet.

'I said I give up!' he shouted. Beside him, Cari fell also. Energy swept over them, twisting them across the courtyard, increasing, building.

'Stop it!' Ecks shouted. 'You'll hurt – – ' He had time – an infinitesimal fraction of a second – to realize fully his own feeling about the girl. He couldn't let anything happen to her. Ecks didn't have to consider how or why; the feeling was there.

A sad, bitter sensation of love.

Ecks tried to get to his feet. The linked mental energy smashed him down again. Stones and rocks were poltered at him.

Ecks realized that he wasn't going to be allowed to surrender. They were going to kill him.

And Cari.

At first, it seemed as though it were a dream. He had become used to the possibility of death in the last few days. He tried to shield, aware of his nakedness, tried to cover Cari. She doubled up as a poltered rock caught her in the stomach. Rocks hummed around them.

Seeing Cari struck, Ecks could have burst with rage. He struggled to his feet and swayed two steps forward, hands outstretched.

He was knocked down again. A section of wall started to collapse, pushed by psi force. He tried to drag Cari out of the way. Too late. The wall fell – –

In that moment Ecks bridged the gap. His tortured, over-strained mind performed the energy leap into the new potential. In that instant, contact and comprehension flooded his mind.

The wall thundered down. But Ecks and Cari weren't under it.

'*Marrin!*'

Dully, the psi chief raised his head. He was back at his desk in Psi-Health. Again it had happened.

'*Marrin!*'

'Who is it?' the psi chief asked.

'Ecks.'

Nothing could surprise him now. That Ecks was capable of tight-beam telepathy just didn't matter.

'What do you want?' he asked.

'I want to meet you. Name a place.'

'Wherever you wish,' Marrin said, with the calmness of despair. Then curiosity overcame him. 'How are you able to telep?'

'All psis can telep,' Ecks said mockingly.

'Where did you go?' Marrin asked. He tried to get a location on the message. But Ecks was easily managing the tight beam, allowing only the direct message to go through.

'I want a little quiet,' Ecks said. 'So I'm in the tomb of The Sleeper. Would you care to meet me there?'

'Coming,' Marrin said, and broke contact. 'Leffert,' he said aloud.

'Yes, Chief?' his assistant said, coming over.

'I want you to take over until I get back. If I get back.'

'What *is* Ecks?' Leffert asked.

'I don't know,' Marrin said. 'I don't know what powers he has. I don't know why Krandall wanted to kill him, but I concur in the judgment.'

'Could we bomb the tomb?' Leffert asked.

'There's nothing faster than thought,' Marrin answered. 'Ecks has discovered some form of near-instantaneous transportation. He could be away before the bombs were dropped.' He paused. 'There is a way, but I'm not going to say any more. He might be listening in on this conversation.'

'Impossible!' Leffert said. 'This is direct-talk. He couldn't – – '

'He couldn't escape,' Marrin reminded him wearily. 'We're through underestimating Mr Ecks. Hereafter, consider him capable of anything.'

'Right,' Leffert said dubiously.

'Have you got the latest figures on the contagion rate?' Marrin asked, walking to the window.

'They're way past epidemic. And the disease has jumped as far as the Rockies.'

'It can't be checked now,' Marrin said. 'We've been pushed off the cliff – on the wrong side. In a year we'll be lucky if there are a thousand psis left in the world.' He tightened his hands into fists. 'For that alone I could cut Ecks into little pieces.'

He levitated out the window.

The first thing Marrin saw when he entered The Sleeper's chamber was Mycrowski himself, still unconscious. Ecks and the girl were standing beside him.

Marrin walked forward.

'I'd like you to meet Cari,' Ecks said, smiling.

Marrin ignored the dazed-looking girl. 'I'd like an explanation,' he said.

'Of course,' Ecks said. 'Would you like to know what I am, to begin with?'

'Yes,' Marrin said.

'I am the stage after psi. The para-psi.'

'I see. And this came – – '

'When you tried to kill Cari.'

'We'd better start somewhere else,' Marrin said. He decided to hear the explanation first before taking the final step. 'Why have you removed the nutrient pipes from The Sleeper?'

'Because Mycrowski won't need them any more,' Ecks said. He turned to The Sleeper, and the room suddenly hummed with energy.

'*Good work, Ecks.*' For a moment Marrin thought it was the girl who had teleped. Then he realized that it was Mycrowski!

'He won't be fully conscious for a while,' Ecks said. 'Let me start at the beginning. As you know, thirty years ago Mycrowski was searching for the extra-psi powers. He split mind and body to find them. Then, having the knowledge, he was unable to get back in his body. It required a leap into a higher energy level to do that and, without a nervous system at his command, he couldn't gather that power. No ordinary psi could help him, either. To attain the new level, all normal channels must be blocked and redirected, and a terrific strain is placed on the whole nervous system.

'That is, essentially, the same method by which the first true psis got their power.'

Marrin looked puzzled for a moment, then asked. 'Then you're not a mutation?'

'Mutations have nothing to do with this. Let me go on. Mycrowski couldn't bridge the gap unaided. He had to have a para-psi bridge the gap for him. That's where I come in.'

'It is also where *you* come in,' Mycrowski, conscious now, teleped to Marrin. 'And the girl, and Krandall. I was in telepathic contact with Krandall. Together we chose Ecks for the experiment. It couldn't be Krandall himself, because his nervous system was not suitable. Ecks was picked for his temperament and sensitivity. And, I might add, for his selfishness and suggestibility. Everything was predicted, including Cari's role.'

Marrin listened coldly. Let them explain. He had an answer of his own. A final one.

'First, the rechannelling. Ecks' psi senses were blocked. Then he was put in a position of stress; incipient capture and isolation, both repugnant to his nature. When he failed to bridge the gap, Krandall rescued him, with my help. With Krandall posing as Cari's Uncle John we threatened his life, increasing the stress.'

'So that's what Krandall meant,' Marrin said.

'Yes. Krandall told you that you had to kill Ecks. That was true. You had to try. He told you that the girl was the key to the whole thing. And that was true also. Because when Ecks' life and the girl's were threatened, it was the greatest stress we could bring to bear. He bridged the gap to the higher potential. Comprehension followed immediately.'

'And he gave you back your body,' Marrin added.

'And he gave me back my body,' Mycrowski agreed.

Marrin knew what he had to do, and he thanked God for the foresight of Psi-Health. Nevertheless, he delayed for a moment.

'Then if I understand correctly, all this – the infection of Ecks, his miraculous rescues, all the deviousness you used, was designed to create a force great enough to get you back in your body?'

'That's a part of it,' Mycrowski said. 'Another part is the creation, in Ecks, of another para-psi.'

'Very well,' Marrin said. 'It will interest you to know that Psi-Health has always considered, as one possibility, the return of The Sleeper – insane. Against that eventuality, this room is wired for atomic explosion. All four walls, ceiling, and roof are keyed to me. Atomic explosions are not instantaneous, I realize.' He smiled humourlessly, 'But then, I doubt if para-psi transit is, either.'

'My thought-processes are as fast as yours. I am going to explode this place.'

'You health men *are* a suspicious lot,' Mycrowski said. 'But why on earth would you want to do a thing like that?' Marrin noticed that he seemed genuinely surprised.

'*Why?* Do you realize what you have done? You have regained your body. But the disease is uncontrollable now. Psi science and all it stands for is destroyed, because of your selfishness.' Mentally, Marrin reached for the key.

'Wait!' Ecks said. 'Evidently you don't understand. There'll be a temporary disturbance, true. But it won't affect everyone at once. Diseased persons can be trained.'

'Trained? To what?'

'Para-psi, of course,' Ecks said. 'A complete rechannelling is necessary to reach the next para-psychological step. The disease is the initial point. The present level of psi is unstable, anyhow. If I didn't set it off, someone else would in a few years.'

'It'll be easier when we get a few more people to bridge the gap,'

Mycrowski said. 'As in the first development of psi, the rest is relatively easy after the initial gain has been made.'

Marrin shook his head. 'How can I believe you?'

'How? *Look!*' ·

Telepathy transmits delicate shades of meaning quite lost in spoken language. A 'true' statement, teleped, reveals immediately how 'true' the sender believes it to be. There are an infinite number of gradations to the 'truth.'

As Ecks had, Marrin read Mycrowski's belief in the para-psi—read it clear down to the subconscious level. An unimaginably 'true' truth! There was no possible argument.

Suddenly Cari smiled. She had had one of her flash premonitions – a pleasant one.

'Help me up,' Mycrowski said to Marrin, 'Let me outline my training programme.' Marrin walked over to help him.

Then Ecks grinned. He had just read Cari's premonition.

Descending

THOMAS M.DISCH

CATSUP, MUSTARD, pickle relish, mayonnaise, two kinds of salad dressing, bacon grease, and a lemon. Oh, yes, two trays of ice cubes. In the cupboard it wasn't much better: jars and boxes of spice, flour, sugar, salt – and a box of raisins!

An empty box of raisins.

Not even any coffee. Not even tea, which he hated. Nothing in the mailbox but a bill from Underwood's: *Unless we receive the arrears on your account ...*

$4.75 in change jingled in his coat pocket – the plunder of the Chianti bottle he had promised himself never to break open. He was spared the unpleasantness of having to sell his books. They had all been sold. The letter to Graham had gone out a week ago. If his brother intended to send something this time, it would have come by now.

– I should be desperate, he thought. Perhaps I am.

He might have looked in the *Times*. But, no, that was too depressing – applying for jobs at $50 a week and being turned down. Not that he blamed them; he wouldn't have hired himself, himself. He had been a grasshopper for years. The ants were on to his tricks.

He shaved without soap and brushed his shoes to a high polish. He whitened the sepulchre of his unwashed torso with a fresh, starched shirt and chose his sombrest tie from the rack. He began to feel excited and expressed it, characteristically, by appearing statuesquely, icily calm.

Descending the stairway to the first floor, he encountered Mrs Beale, who was pretending to sweep the well-swept floor of the entrance.

'Good afternoon – or I s'pose it's good morning for you, eh?'

'Good afternoon, Mrs Beale.'

'Your letter come?'

'Not yet.'

'The first of the month isn't far off.'

'Yes, indeed, Mrs Beale.'

At the subway station he considered a moment before answering the attendant: One token or two? Two, he decided. After all, he had no choice but to return to his apartment. The first of the month was still a long way off.

– If Jean Valjean had had a charge account, he would have never gone to prison.

Having thus cheered himself, he settled down to enjoy the ads in the subway car. *Smoke. Try. Eat. Give. See. Drink. Use. Buy.* He thought of Alice with her mushrooms: Eat me.

At 34th Street he got off and entered Underwood's Department Store directly from the train platform. On the main floor he stopped at the cigar stand and bought a carton of cigarettes.

'Cash or charge?'

'Charge.' He handed the clerk the laminated plastic card. The charge was rung up.

Fancy Groceries was on 5. He made his selection judiciously. A jar of instant and a two-pound can of drip-ground coffee, a large tin of corned beef, packed soups and boxes of pancake mix and condensed milk. Jam, peanut butter, and honey. Six cans of tuna fish. Then he indulged himself in perishables: English cookies, an Edam cheese, a small frozen pheasant – even fruitcake. He never ate so well as when he was broke. He couldn't afford to.

'$14.87.'

This time after ringing up his charge, the clerk checked the number on his card against her list of closed or doubtful accounts. She smiled apologetically and handed the card back.

'Sorry, but we have to check.'

'I understand.'

The bag of groceries weighed a good twenty pounds. Carrying it with the exquisite casualness of a burglar passing before a policeman with his loot, he took the escalator to the bookshop on 8. His choice of books was determined by the same principle as his choice of groceries. First, the staples: two Victorian novels he had never read, *Vanity Fair* and *Middlemarch*; the Sayers' translation of Dante, and a two-volume anthology of German plays none of which he had read and few he had even heard of. Then the perishables: a sensational novel that had reached the best-seller list via the Supreme Court, and two mysteries.

He had begun to feel giddy with self-indulgence. He reached into his jacket pocket for a coin.

– Heads a new suit; tails the Sky Room.

Tails.

The Sky Room on 15 was empty of all but a few women chatting over coffee and cakes. He was able to get a seat by a window. He ordered from the *à la carte* side of the menu and finished his meal with espresso and baklava. He handed the waitress his credit card and tipped her fifty cents.

Dawdling over his second cup of coffee, he began *Vanity Fair*. Rather to

203

his surprise, he found himself enjoying it. The waitress returned with his card and a receipt for the meal.

Since the Sky Room was on the top floor of Underwood's, there was only one escalator to take now – Descending. Riding down, he continued to read *Vanity Fair*. He could read anywhere – in restaurants, on subways, even walking down the street. At each landing he made his way from the foot of one escalator to the head of the next without lifting his eyes from the book. When he came to the Bargain Basement, he would be only a few steps from the subway turnstile.

He was halfway through chapter VI (on page 55, to be exact) when he began to feel something amiss.

– How long does this damn thing take to reach the basement?

He stopped at the next landing, but there was no sign to indicate on what floor he was nor any door by which he might re-enter the store. Deducing from this that he was between floors, he took the escalator down one more flight only to find the same perplexing absence of landmarks.

There was, however, a water fountain, and he stooped to take a drink.

– I must have gone to a sub-basement. But this was not too likely after all. Escalators were seldom provided for janitors and stockboys.

He waited on the landing watching the steps of the escalator slowly descend towards him and, at the end of their journey, telescope in upon themselves and disappear. He waited a long while, and no one else came down the moving steps.

– Perhaps the store was closed.

Having no wristwatch and having rather lost track of the time, he had no way of knowing. At last, he reasoned that he had become so engrossed in the Thackeray novel that he had simply stopped on one of the upper landings – say, on 8 – to finish a chapter and had read on to page 55 without realizing that he was making no progress on the escalators.

When he read, he could forget everything else.

He must, therefore, still be somewhere above the main floor. The absence of exits, though disconcerting, could be explained by some quirk in the floor plan. The absence of signs was merely a carelessness on the part of the management.

He tucked *Vanity Fair* into his shopping-bag and stepped on to the grilled lip of the down-going escalator – not, it must be admitted, without a certain degree of reluctance. At each landing, he marked his progress by a number spoken aloud. By *eight* he was uneasy; by *fifteen* he was desperate.

It was, of course, possible that he had to descend two flights of stairs for every floor of the department store. With this possibility in mind, he counted off fifteen more landings.

– No.

Dazedly, and as though to deny the reality of this seemingly interminable stairwell, he continued his descent. When he stopped again at the forty-fifth landing, he was trembling. He was afraid.

He rested the shopping-bag on the bare concrete floor of the landing, realizing that his arm had gone quite sore from supporting the twenty pounds and more of groceries and books. He discounted the enticing possibility that 'it was all a dream', for the dream-world is the reality of the dreamer, to which he could not weakly surrender, no more than he could surrender to the realities of life. Besides, he was not dreaming; of that he was quite sure.

He checked his pulse. It was fast – say, eighty a minute. He rode down two more flights, counting his pulse. Eighty almost exactly. Two flights took only one minute.

He could read approximately one page a minute, a little less on an escalator. Suppose he had spent one hour on the escalators while he had read: sixty minutes – one hundred and twenty floors. Plus forty-seven that he had counted. One hundred and sixty-seven. The Sky Room was on 15.

$$167 - 15 = 152.$$

He was in the one-hundred-and-fifty-second sub-basement. That was impossible.

The appropriate response to an impossible situation was to deal with it as though it were commonplace – like Alice in Wonderland. Ergo, he would return to Underwood's the same way he had (apparently) left it. He would walk up one hundred and fifty-two flights of down-going escalators. Taking the steps three at a time and running, it was almost like going up a regular staircase. But after ascending the second escalator in this manner he found himself already out of breath.

There was no hurry. He would not allow himself to be overtaken by panic.

No.

He picked up the bag of groceries and books he had left on that landing, waiting for his breath to return, and darted up a third and fourth flight. While he rested on the landing, he tried to count the steps between floors, but his count differed depending on whether he counted with the current or against it, down or up. The average was roughly eighteen steps, and the steps appeared to be eight or nine inches deep. Each flight was, therefore, about twelve feet.

It was one-third of a mile, as the plumb drops, to Underwood's main floor.

Dashing up the ninth escalator, the bag of groceries broke open at the bottom, where the thawing pheasant had dampened the paper. Groceries and books tumbled on to the steps, some rolling of their own accord to the landing below, others being transported there by the moving stairs and forming a neat little pile. Only the jam jar had been broken.

He stacked the groceries in the corner of the landing, except for the half-thawed pheasant, which he stuffed into his coat pocket, anticipating that his ascent would take him well past his dinner hour.

Physical exertion had dulled his finer feelings – to be precise, his capacity for fear. Like a cross-country runner in his last laps, he thought single-mindedly of the task at hand and made no effort to understand what he had in any case already decided was not to be understood. He mounted one flight, rested, mounted and rested again. Each mount was wearier; each rest longer. He stopped counting the landings after the twenty-eighth, and some time after that – how long he had no idea – his legs gave out and he collapsed to the concrete floor of the landing. His calves were hard aching knots of muscle; his thighs quivered erratically. He tried to do knee-bends and fell backwards.

Despite his recent dinner (assuming that it had been recent), he was hungry, and he devoured the entire pheasant, completely thawed now, without being able to tell if it were raw or had been pre-cooked.

– This is what it's like to be a cannibal, he thought as he fell asleep.

Sleeping, he dreamt he was falling down a bottomless pit. Waking, he discovered nothing had changed, except the dull ache in his legs, which had become a sharp pain.

Overhead, a single strip of fluorescent lighting snaked down the stairwell. The mechanical purr of the escalators seemed to have heightened to the roar of a Niagara, and their rate of descent seemed to have increased proportionately.

Fever, he decided. He stood up stiffly and flexed some of the soreness from his muscles.

Halfway up the third escalator, his legs gave way under him. He attempted the climb again and succeeded. He collapsed again on the next flight. Lying on the landing where the escalator had deposited him, he realized that his hunger had returned. He also needed to have water – and to let it.

The latter necessity he could easily – and without false modesty – satisfy. Also he remembered the water fountain he had drunk from yesterday, and he found another three floors below.

– It's so much easier going down.

His groceries were down there. To go after them now, he would erase whatever progress he had made in his ascent. Perhaps Underwood's main floor was only a few more flights up. Or a hundred. There was no way to know.

Because he was hungry and because he was tired and because the futility of mounting endless flights of descending escalators was, as he now considered it, a labour of Sisyphus, he returned, descended, gave in.

At first, he allowed the escalator to take him along at its own mild pace, but he soon grew impatient of this. He found that the exercise of running down the steps three at a time was not so exhausting as running *up*. It was refreshing, almost. And, by swimming with the current instead of against it, his progress, if such it can be called, was appreciable. In only minutes he was back at his cache of groceries.

After eating half the fruitcake and a little cheese, he fashioned his coat into a sort of sling for the groceries, knotting the sleeves together and buttoning it closed. With one hand at the collar and the other about the hem, he could carry all his food with him.

He looked up the descending staircase with a scornful smile, for he had decided with the wisdom of failure to abandon *that* venture. If the stairs wished to take him down, then down, giddily, he would go.

Then down he did go, down dizzily, down, down and always, it seemed, faster, spinning about lightly on his heels at each landing so that there was hardly any break in the wild speed of his descent. He whooped and haloo'd and laughed to hear his whooping echo in the narrow, low-vaulted corridors, following him as though they could not keep up his pace.

Down, ever deeper down.

Twice he slipped at the landings and once he missed his footing in mid-leap on the escalator, hurtled forward, letting go of the sling of groceries, and falling, hands stretched out to cushion him, on to the steps, which imperturbably, continued their descent.

He must have been unconscious then, for he woke up in a pile of groceries with a split cheek and a splitting headache. The telescoping steps of the escalator gently grazed his heels.

He knew then his first moment of terror – a premonition that there was no *end* to his descent, but this feeling gave way quickly to a laughing fit.

'I'm going to hell!' he shouted, though he could not drown with his voice the steady purr of the escalators. 'This is the way to hell. Abandon hope all ye who enter here.'

– If only I were, he reflected.

– If that were the case, it would make sense. Not quite orthodox sense, but some sense, a little.

Sanity, however, was so integral to his character that neither hysteria nor horror could long have their way with him. He gathered up his groceries again, relieved to find that only the jar of instant coffee had been broken this time, for which he could conceive no use – under the present circumstances. And he would allow himself, for the sake of sanity, to conceive of no other circumstances than those.

He began a more deliberate descent. He returned to *Vanity Fair*, reading it as he paced down the down-going steps. He did not let himself consider the extent of the abyss into which he was plunging, and the vicarious excitements of the novel helped him keep his thoughts from his own situation. At page 235, he lunched (that is, he took his second meal of the day) on the remainder of the cheese and fruitcake; at 523 he rested and dined on the English cookies dipped in peanut butter.

  – Perhaps I had better ration my food.

If he could regard his absurd dilemma merely as a struggle for survival, another chapter in his own Robinson Crusoe story, he might get to the bottom of this mechanized vortex alive and sane. He thought proudly that many people in his position could not have adjusted, would have gone mad.

Of course, he *was* descending ...

But he was still sane. He had chosen his course and now he was following it.

There was no night in the stairwell, and scarcely any shadows. He slept when his legs could no longer bear his weight and his eyes were tearful from reading. Sleeping, he dreamt that he was continuing his descent on the escalators. Waking, his hand resting on the rubber railing that moved along at the same rate as the steps, he discovered this to be the case.

Somnambulistically, he had ridden the escalators further down into this mild, interminable hell, leaving behind his bundle of food and even the still-unread Thackeray novel.

Stumbling up the escalators, he began, for the first time, to cry. Without the novel, there was nothing to *think* of but this, this ...

  – How far? How long did I sleep?

His legs, which had only been slightly wearied by his descent, gave out twenty flights up. His spirit gave out soon after. Again he turned around, allowed himself to be swept up by the current – or, more exactly, swept down.

The escalator seemed to be travelling more rapidly, the pitch of the steps to be more pronounced. But he no longer trusted the evidence of his senses.

  – I am, perhaps, insane – or sick from hunger. Yet I would have run out of food eventually. This will bring the crisis to a head. Optimism, that's the spirit!

Continuing his descent, he occupied himself with closer analysis of his environment, not undertaken with any hope of bettering his condition but only for lack of other diversions. The walls and ceilings were hard, smooth, and off-white. The escalator steps were a dull nickel colour, the treads being somewhat shinier, the crevices darker. Did that mean that the treads were polished from use? Or were they designed in that fashion? The treads were half an inch wide and spaced apart from each other by the same width. They projected slightly over the edge of each step, resembling somewhat the head of a barber's shears. Whenever he stopped at a landing, his attention would become fixed on the illusory 'disappearance' of the steps, as they sank flush to the floor and slid, tread in groove, into the grilled baseplate.

Less and less would he run, or even walk, down the stairs, content merely to ride his chosen step from top to bottom of each flight and, at the landing, step (left foot, right, and left again) on to the escalator that would transport him to the floor below. The stairwell now had tunnelled, by his calculations, miles beneath the department store – so many miles that he began to congratulate himself upon his unsought adventure, wondering if he had established some sort of record. Just so, a criminal will stand in awe of his own baseness and be most proud of his vilest crime, which he believes unparalleled.

In the days that followed, when his only nourishment was the water from the fountains provided at every tenth landing, he thought frequently of food, preparing imaginary meals from the store of groceries he had left behind, savouring the ideal sweetness of the honey, the richness of the soup which he would prepare by soaking the powder in the emptied cookie-tin, licking the film of gelatine lining the opened can of corned beef. When he thought of the six cans of tuna fish, his anxiety became intolerable, for he had (would have had) no way to open them. Merely to stamp on them would not be enough. What, then? He turned the question over and over in his head, like a squirrel spinning the wheel in its cage, to no avail.

Then a curious thing happened. He quickened again the speed of his descent, faster now than when first he had done this, eagerly, headlong, absolutely heedless. The several landings seemed to flash by like a montage of Flight, each scarcely perceived before the next was before him. A demonic, pointless race – and why? He was running, so he thought, towards his store of groceries, either believing that they had been left *below* or thinking that he was running *up*. Clearly, he was delirious.

It did not last. His weakened body could not maintain the frantic pace, and he woke from his delirium confused and utterly spent. Now began another, more rational delirium, a madness fired by logic. Lying on the landing, rubbing a torn muscle in his ankle, he speculated on the nature, origin and purpose of the escalators. Reasoned thought was of no more use to him, however, than unreasoning action. Ingenuity was helpless to solve a riddle that had no answer, which was its own reason, self-contained and whole. He – not the escalators – needed an answer.

Perhaps his most interesting theory was the notion that these escalators were a kind of exercise wheel, like those found in a squirrel cage, from which, because it was a closed system, there could be no escape. This theory required some minor alterations in his conception of the physical universe, which had always appeared highly Euclidean to him before, a universe in which his descent seemingly along a plumb-line was, in fact, describing a loop. This theory cheered him, for he might hope, coming full circle, to return to his store of groceries again, if not to Underwood's. Perhaps in his abstracted state he had passed one or the other already several times without observing.

There was another, and related, theory concerning the measures taken by Underwood's Credit Department against delinquent accounts. This was mere paranoia.

– Theories! I don't need theories. I must get on with it.

So, favouring his good leg, he continued his descent, although his speculations did not immediately cease. They became, if anything, more metaphysical. They became vague. Eventually, he could regard the escalators as being entirely matter of fact, requiring no more explanation than, by their sheer existence, they offered him.

He discovered that he was losing weight. Being so long without food (by the evidence of his beard, he estimated that more than a week had gone by), this was only to be expected. Yet, there was another possibility that he could not exclude: that he was approaching the centre of the earth where, as he understood, all things were weightless.

– Now *that*, he thought, is something worth striving for.

He had discovered a goal. On the other hand, he was dying, a process he did not give all the attention it deserved. Unwilling to admit this eventuality, and yet not so foolish as to admit any other, he side-stepped the issue by pretending to hope.

– Maybe someone will rescue me, he hoped.

But his hope was as mechanical as the escalators he rode – and tended, in much the same way, to sink.

Waking and sleeping were no longer distinct states of which he could say: 'Now I am sleeping,' or 'Now I am awake.' Sometimes he would discover himself descending and be unable to tell whether he had been woken from sleep or roused from inattention.

He hallucinated.

A woman, loaded with packages from Underwood's and wearing a trim, pillbox-style hat, came down the escalator towards him, turned around on the landing, high heels clicking smartly, and rode away without even nodding to him.

More and more, when he awoke or was roused from his stupor, he found himself, instead of hurrying to his goal, lying on a landing, weak, dazed, and beyond hunger. Then, he would crawl to the down-going escalator and pull himself on to one of the steps, which he would ride to the bottom, sprawled head foremost, hands and shoulders braced against the treads to keep from skittering bumpily down.

– At the bottom, he thought, at the bottom ... I will ... when I get there ...

From the bottom, which he conceived of as the centre of the earth, there would be literally nowhere to go but up. Probably by another chain of escalators, ascending escalators, but preferably by an elevator. It was important to believe in a bottom.

Thought was becoming as difficult, as demanding and painful, as once his struggle to ascend had been. His perceptions were fuzzy. He did not know what was real and what imaginary. He thought he was eating and discovered he was gnawing at his hands.

He thought he had come to the bottom. It was a large, high-ceilinged room. Signs pointed to another escalator: *Ascending*. But there was a chain across it and a small typed announcement.

'Out of order. Please bear with us while the escalators are being repaired. Thank-you. The Management.'

He laughed weakly.

He devised a way to open the tuna-fish cans. He would slip the can sideways beneath the projecting treads of the escalator, just at the point where the steps were sinking flush to the floor. Either the escalator would split the can open or the can would jam the escalator. Perhaps if one escalator were jammed the whole chain of them would stop. He should have thought of that before, but he was, nevertheless, quite pleased to have thought of it at all.

– I might have escaped.

His body seemed to weigh so little now. He must have come hundreds of miles. Thousands.

Again, he descended.

Then he was lying at the foot of the escalator. His head rested on the cold metal of the baseplate and he was looking at his hand, the fingers of which were pressed into the creviced grille. One after another, in perfect order, the steps of the escalator slipped into these crevices, tread in groove, rasping at his fingertips, occasionally tearing away a sliver of his flesh.

That was the last thing he remembered.

Abreaction

THEODORE STURGEON

I SAT AT THE CONTROLS of the big D-8 bulldozer, and I tried to remember. The airfield shoulder, built on a saltflat, stretched around me. On to the west was a clumb of buildings – the gas station and grease rack. Near it was the skeletal silhouette of a temporary weather observation post with its spinning, velocimeter and vane and windsock. Everything seemed normal, but there was something *else*. . . .

I could remember people, beautiful people in shining, floating garments. I remembered them as if I had seen them just a minute ago, and yet at a distance; but the memories were of faces close – close. One face – a golden girl; eyes and skin and hair three different shades of gold.

I shook my head so violently that it hurt. I was a bulldozer operator. I was – what was I supposed to be doing? I looked around me, saw the gravel spread behind me, the bare earth ahead; knew, then, that I was spreading gravel with the machine. But I seemed to – to – Look, without the physical fact of the half-done job around me, I wouldn't have known why I was there at all!

I knew where I had seen that girl, those people. I thought I knew . . . but the thought was just where I couldn't reach it. My mind put out searching tendrils for that knowledge of place, that was so certainly there, and the knowledge receded so that the tendrils stretched out thin and cracked with the effort, and my head ached from it.

A big trailer-type bottom-dump truck came hurtling and howling over the shoulder towards me, the huge fenderless driving wheels throwing clots of mud high in the air. The driver was a Puerto-Rican, a hefty middle-aged fellow. I knew him well. Well – didn't I? He threw out one arm, palm up, signalling 'Where do you want it?' I pointed vaguely to the right, to the advancing edge of the spread gravel. He spun his steering wheel with one hand, put the other on the trip-lever on his steering column, keeping his eyes on my face. As he struck the edge of the gravel fill with his wheels I dropped my hand; he punched the lever and the bottom of the trailer opened up, streaming gravel out in a windrow thirty feet long and a foot deep – twelve cubic yards of it, delivered at full speed. The driver waved and headed off, the straightgut exhaust of his high-speed Diesel snorting and snarling as the rough ground bounced the

212

man's foot on the accelerator.

I waved back at the Puerto-Rican – what was his name? I knew him, didn't I? He knew me, the way he waved as he left. His name – was it Paco? Cruz? Eulalio? Damn it, no, and I knew it as well as I knew my own –

But I didn't know my own name!

Oh hell, oh hell, I'm crazy. I'm scared. I'm scared crazy. What had happened to my head? ... Everything whirled around me and without effort I remembered about the people in the shining clothes and as my mind closed on it, it evaporated again and there was nothing there.

Once when I was a kid in school I fell off the parallel bars and knocked myself out, and when I came to it was like this. I could see everything and feel and smell and taste everything, but I couldn't remember anything. Not for a minute. I would ask what had happened, and they would tell me, and five minutes later I'd ask again. They asked me my address so they could take me home, and I couldn't remember it. They got the address from the school files and took me home, and my feet found the way in and up the four flights of stairs to our apartment – I didn't remember which way to go but my feet did. I went in and tried to tell my mother what was the matter with me and I couldn't remember, and she put me to bed and I woke four hours later perfectly all right again.

In a minute, there on the bulldozer, I didn't get over being scared but I began to get used to it, so I could think a little. I tried to remember everything at first, but that was too hard, so I tried to find something I could remember. I sat there and let my mind go quite blank. Right away there was something about a bottom-dump truck and some gravel. It was there, clear enough, but I didn't know where it fit nor how far back. I looked around me and there was the windrow of gravel waiting to be spread. Then that was what the truck was for; and – had it just been there, or had I been waiting there for long, for ever so long, waiting to remember that I must spread it?

Then I saw that I could remember ideas, but not events. Events were there, yes, but not in order. No continuity. A year ago – a second ago – same thing. Nothing clear, nothing very real, all mixed up. Ideas were there whatever, and continuity didn't matter. That I could remember an idea, that I could know that windrow of gravel meant that gravel must be spread; *that* was an idea, a condition of things which I could recognize. The truck's coming and going and dumping, that was an event. I knew it had happened because the gravel was there, but I didn't know when, or if anything had happened in between.

I looked at the controls and frowned. Could I remember what to do with them? This lever and that pedal – what did they mean to me? Nothing, and nothing again. ...

I mustn't think about that. I don't have to think about that. I must think about *what* I must do and not how I must do it. I've got to spread the stone. Here there is spread stone and there there is none, and at the edge of the spread stone is the windrow of gravel. So, watching it, seeing how it lay, I let my hands and feet remember about the levers and pedals. They throttled up, raised the blade off the ground, shifted into third gear, swung the three-ton mouldboard and its twelve-foot cutting edge into the windrow. The blade loaded and gravel ran off the ends in two even rolls, and my right hand flicked to and away from me on the blade-control, knowing how to raise it enough to let the gravel run out evenly underneath the cutting edge, not too high so that it would make a bobble in the fill for the tracks to teeter on when they reached it – for a bulldozer builds the road it walks on, and if the road is rough the machine see-saws forward and the blade cuts and fills to make waves which, when the tracks reach them, makes the machine see-saw and cut waves, which, when the tracks reach them ... anyway, my hands knew what to do, and my feet; and they did it all the time when I could only see what was to be done, and could not understand the events of doing it.

This won't do, I thought desperately. I'm all right, I guess, because I can do my work. It's all laid out in front of me, and I know what has to be done and my hands and feet know how to do it; but suppose somebody comes and speaks to me or tells me to go somewhere else. I who can't even remember my own name. My hands and my feet have more sense than my head.

So I thought that I had to inventory everything I could trust, everything I knew positively. What were the things I knew?

The machine was there and true, and the gravel, and the bottom-dump that brought it. My being there was a real thing. You have to start everything with the belief that you yourself exist.

The job, the work, they were true things.

Where was I?

I must be where I should be, where I belonged, for the bottom-dump driver knew me, knew I was there, and the fact that it was unfinished. 'Airfield' was like a corollary to me, with the runway and the windsock its supporting axioms, and I had no need to think further. The people in the shining garments, and the girl –

But there was nothing about them here. Nothing at all.

To spread stone was a thing I had to do. But was that all? It wasn't just spreading stone. I had to spread it to – to –

Not to help finish the airfield. It wasn't that. It was something else, something –

Oh. Oh! I had to spread stone to *get* somewhere.

I didn't want to go anywhere, except maybe to a place where I could think again, where I could know what was happening to me, where I could reach out with my mind and grasp those important things, like my name, and the name of the bottom-dump driver, Paco, or Cruz, or Eulalio or maybe even Emanualo von Hachmann de la Vega, or whatever. But being able to think straight again and know all these important things was arriving at a *state* of consciousness, not at a *place*. I knew, I knew, somehow I knew truly that to arrive at that state I had to arrive at a point.

Suddenly, overwhelmingly, I had a flash of knowledge about the point – not what it was, but how it was, and I screamed and hurt my throat and fell blindly back in the seat of the tractor trying to push away *how* it was.

My abdomen kneaded itself with the horror of it. I put my hands on my face and my hands and face were wet with sweat and tears. Afraid? Have you ever been afraid to die, seeing Death looking right at you; closer than that; have you seen Death turn away from you because He knows you must follow Him? Have you seen that and been afraid?

Well, this was worse. For this I'd hug Death to me, for He alone could spare me what would happen to me when I reached the place I was going to.

So I wouldn't spread stone.

I wouldn't do anything that would bring me closer to reaching the place where that thing would happen to me. *Had happened* to me.... I wouldn't do it. That was an important thing.

There was one other important thing. I must not go on like this, not knowing my name, and what the name of the bottom-dump driver was, and where this airfield and this base were, and all those things.

These two things were the most important things in the world. In *this* world.... THIS world....

This world, this world – *other* world....

There was a desert all around me.

Ha! So the airfield wasn't real, and the bottom-dump wasn't real, and the anemometer and the grease racks weren't real. Ha! (Why worry about the driver's name if he wasn't real?)

The bulldozer was real, though. I was sitting on it. The six big cylinders were ticking over, and the master-clutch lever was twitching rhythmically as if its lower end was buried in something that breathed. Otherwise – just desert, and some hills over there, and a sun which was too orange.

Think, now, think. This desert means something important. I wasn't surprised at being in the desert. That was important. This place in the desert was near something, near an awful something that would hurt me.

I looked all around me, I couldn't see it, but it was there, the something that would hurt so. I wouldn't go through that again –

Again.

Again – that was an important thing. I wouldn't spread stone and reach that place. I wouldn't go through that which had happened to me even if I stayed crazy like I was for the rest of eternity. Let them put me away and tie me up and shake their head over me and walk away and leave me, and put bars on the window to slice the light of the crooked moon into black and silver bars on the floor of my cell. I didn't care about all that. I could face the ache of wanting to know about my name and the name of the driver of the bottom-dump (he was a Puerto-Rican, so his name must be Villamil or Roberto, not Bucyrus-Erie or Caterpillar Thirteen Thousand) and the people in the shining clothes; I *was* facing all that, and I knew how it hurt, but I would not go through that place again and be hurt so much more. Not again. Not again.

Again. Again again again. What is the again-ness of everything? Everything I am doing I am doing again. I could remember that feeling from before – years ago it used to happen to me every once in a while. You've never been to a certain village before, we'll say, and you come up over the crown of the hill on your bicycle and see the way the church is and the houses, and the turn of that crooked cobblestoned street, the shape and tone of the very flower-stems. You know that if you were asked, you could say how many pickets were in the white gate in the blue-and-white fence in the little house third from the corner. All the scientists nod and smile and say you did see it for the second time – a twentieth of a second after the first glimpse; and that the impact of familiarity was built up in the next twentieth of a second. And you nod and smile too and say well, whaddaye know. But you *know* you've seen that place before, no matter what they say.

That's the way I knew it, sitting there on my machine in the desert and not surprised, and having that feeling of again-ness; because I was remembering the last time the bottom-dump came to me there on the airfield shoulder, trailing a plume of blue smoke from the exhaust stack, bouncing and barking as it hurtled towards me. It meant nothing at first, remembering, that it came, nor that it came, nor that it was the same driver, the Puerto-Rican; and of course he was carrying the same sized load of the same material. All trips of the bottom-dump were pretty much the same. But there was one thing I remembered – *now* I remembered –

There was a grade-stake driven into the fill, to guide the depth of the gravel, and *it was no nearer to me than it had ever been.* So that hadn't been the same bottom-dump, back another time. It was the *same time,* all over again! The last time was wiped out. It was on a kind of escalator and it carried me up until I reached the place where I realized about what I had to go through, and screamed. And then I was snatched back and put on the bottom again, at the place where the Puerto-Rican driver Senor

What's-his-name dumped the gravel and went away again.

And this desert, now. This desert was a sort of landing at the side of the escalator, where I might fall sometimes instead of going all the way to the bottom where the truck came. I had been here before, and I was here again. I had been at the unfinished air base again and again. And there was the other place, with the shining people, and the girl with all those kinds of gold. That was the same place with the crooked moon.

I covered my eyes with my hands and tried to think. The clacking Diesel annoyed me, suddenly, and I got up and reached under the hood and pulled the compression release. Gases chattered out of the ports, and a bubble of silence formed around me, swelling, the last little sounds scampering away from me in all directions, leaving me quiet.

There was a soft thump in the sand beside the machine. It was one of the shining people, the old one, whose forehead was so broad and whose hair was fine, fine like a cobweb. I knew him. I knew his name, too, though I couldn't think of it at the moment.

He dismounted from his flying-chair and came to me.

'Hello,' I said. I took my shirt from the seat beside me and hung it on my shoulder. 'Come on up.'

He smiled and put up his hand. I took it and helped him climb up over the cat. His hands were very strong. He stepped over me and sat down.

'How do you feel?' Sometimes he spoke aloud, and sometimes he didn't, but I always understood him.

'I feel – mixed up.'

'Yes, of course,' he said kindly. 'Go on. Ask me about it.' I looked at him. 'Do I – *always* ask you about it?'

'Every time.'

'Oh.' I looked all around, at the desert, at the hills, at the dozer, at the sun which was too orange. 'Where am I?'

'On Earth,' he said; only the word he used for Earth meant Earth only to him. It meant *his* earth.

'I know that,' I said. 'I mean, where am I really? Am I on that air base, or am I here?'

'Oh, you are here,' he said.

Somehow I was vastly relieved to hear it. 'Maybe you'd better tell me all about it again.'

'You said "again",' he said, and put his hand on my arm. 'You're beginning to realize.... Good lad. Good. All right. I'll tell you once more.

'You came here a long time ago. You followed a road with your big noisy machine, and came roaring down out of the desert to the city. The people had never seen a noisy machine before, and they clustered around the gate to see you come. They stood aside to let you pass, and wondered, and you swung the machine and crushed six of them against the gateposts.'

'I *did*?' I cried. Then I said. 'I did. Oh, I did.'

He smiled at me again. 'Shh. Don't. It was a long time ago. Shall I go on?

'We couldn't stop you. We have no weapons. We could do nothing in the face of that monster you were driving. You ranged up and down the streets, smashing the fronts of buildings, running people down, and laughing. We had to wait until you got off the machine, and then we overpowered you. You were totally mad. It was,' he added thoughtfully, 'a very interesting study.'

'Why did I do it?' I whispered. 'How could I do such things to –*you*?'

'You had been hurt. Dreadfully hurt. You had come here, arriving somewhere near this spot. You were crazed by what you had endured. Later, we followed the tracks of your machine back. We found where you had driven it aimlessly over the desert, and where, once, you had left the machine and lived in a cave, probably for weeks. You ate desert grasses and the eight-legged crabs. You killed everything you could, through some strange, warped revenge motivation.

'You were crazed with thirst and revenge, and you were very thin, and your face was covered with hair, of all extraordinary things, though analysis showed that you had a constant desire for a hairless face. After treatment you became almost rational. But your time-sense was almost totally destroyed. And you had two almost unbreakable psychological blocks – your memory of how you came here, and your sense of identity.

'We did what we could for you, but you were unhappy. The moons had an odd effect on you. We have two, one well inside the other in its orbit, but both with the same period. Without instruments they appear to be an eclipse when they are full. The sight of what you called that crooked moon undid a lot of our work. And then you would get the attacks of an overwhelming emotion you term "remorse", which appeared to be something like cruelty and something like love and included a partial negation of the will to survive ... and you could not understand why we would not punish you. Punish you – when you were sick!'

'Yes,' I said. 'I – remember most of it now. You gave me everything I could want. You even gave me – gave me –'

'Oh – that. Yes. You had some deep-seated convictions about love, and marriage. We felt you would be happier –'

'I was, and then I wasn't. I – I wanted –'

'I know, I know,' he said soothingly. 'You wanted your name again, and somehow you wanted your own earth.'

I clenched my fists until my forearms hurt. 'I should be satisfied,' I cried. 'I should be. You are all so kind, and she – and she – she's been –' I shook my head angrily. 'I must be crazy.'

218

'You generally ask me,' he said smiling, 'at this point, how you came here.'

'I do?'

'You do. I'll repeat it. You see, there are irregularities in the fabric of space. No – not space, exactly. We have a word for it – ' (he spoke it) '– which means, literally, "space which is time which is psyche". It is a condition of space which by its nature creates time and thought and matter. Your world, relative to ours, is in the infinitely great, or in the infinitely small, or perhaps in the infinitely distant, either in space or in time – it does not matter, for they are all the same thing in their ultimate extensions ... but to go on:

'While you were at your work, you ran your machine into a point of tension in this fabric – a freak, completely improbable position in – ' (he spoke the word again) ' – in which your universe and ours were tangential. You – went through.'

I tensed as he said it.

'Yes, that was the thing. It caused you inconceivable agony. It drove you mad. It filled you full of vengeance and fear. Well, we – cured you of everything but the single fear of going through that agony again, and the peculiar melancholy involving the loss of your ego – your desire to know your own name. Since we failed there – ' he shrugged ' – we have been doing the only thing left to us. We are trying to send you back.'

'Why? Why bother?'

'You are not content here. Our whole social system, our entire philosophy, is based on the contentment of the individual. So we must do what we can ... in addition, you have given us a tremendous amount of research material in psychology and in theoretical cosmogony. We are grateful. We want you to have what you want. Your fear is great. Your desire is greater. And to help you achieve your desire, we have put you on this course of abreaction.'

'Abreaction?'

He nodded. 'The psychological re-enactment, or retracing, of everything you have done since you came here, in an effort to return you to the entrance-point in exactly the same frame of mind as that in which you came through it. We cannot find that point. It has something to do with your particular psychic matrix. But if the point is still here, and if, by hypnosis, we can cause you to do exactly what you did when you first came through – why, then, you'll go back.'

'Will it be – dangerous?'

'Yes,' he said, unhesitatingly. 'Even if the point of tangency is still here, where you emerged, it may not be at the same point on your earth. Don't forget – you have been here for eleven of your years. ... And then there's the agony – bad enough if you do go through, infinitely worse if you do not, for you may drift in – in *somewhere* forever, quite conscious, and with no possibility of release.

'You know all this, and yet you still want us to try. . . .' He sighed. 'We admire you deeply, and wonder too; for you are the bravest man we have ever known. We wonder most particularly at your culture, which can produce such an incredible regard for the ego. . . . Shall we try again?'

I looked at the sun which was too orange, and at the hills, and at his broad, quiet, beautiful face. If I could have spoken my name then, I think I should have stayed. If I could have seen *her* just at that moment, I think I should have waited a little longer, at least.

'Yes,' I said. 'Let's try it again.'

I was so afraid that I wouldn't remember my name or the name of Gracias de Nada, or something, the fellow who drove the bottom-dump. I couldn't remember how to run the machine; but my hands remembered, and my feet.

Now I sat and looked at the windrow; and then I pulled back the throttle and raised the blade. I swung into the windrow, and the gravel loaded clean on to the blade and cleanly ran off in two even rolls at the sides. When I sensed that the gravel was all off the blade. I stopped, shifted into high reverse, pulled the left steering clutch to me, let in the master clutch, stamped the left brake. . . .

That was the thing, then. Back-blading that roll out – the long small windrow of gravel that had run off the ends of my blade. As I backed over it, the machine straddling it, I dropped the blade on to it and floated it, so that it smoothed out the roll. Then it was that I looked back – force of habit, for a bulldozer that size can do real damage backing into power-poles or buildings – and I saw the muzzy bit of fill.

It was a patch of spread gravel that seemed whirling, blurred at the edges. Look into the sun and then suddenly at the floor. There will be a muzzy patch there whirling and swirling like that. I thought something funny had happened to my eyes. But I didn't stop the machine, and then suddenly I was in it.

Again.

It built up slowly, the agony. It built up in a way that promised more and then carefully fulfilled the promise, and made of the peak of pain a further promise. There was no sense of strain, for everything was poised and counter-balanced and nothing would break. All of the inner force was as strong as all the outer forces, and all of me was the point of equilibrium.

Don't try to think about it. Don't try to imagine for a second. A second of that, unbalanced, would crush you to cosmic dust. There were years of it for me; years and years. . . . I was in an unused stockpile of years, somewhere in a hyperspace, and the weight of them all was on me and in me, consecutively, concurrently.

I woke up very slowly. I hurt all over, and that was an excruciating pleasure, because the pain was only physical.

I began to forget right away.

A company doctor came in and peeped at me. I said, 'Hi.'

'Well, well,' he said, beaming. 'So the flying catskinner is with us again.'

'What flying catskinner? What happened? Where am I?'

'You're in the dispensary. You, my boy, were working your bulldozer out on the fill and all of a sudden took it into your head to be a flying kaydet at the same time. That's what they say, anyhow. I do know that there wasn't a mark around the machine where it lay – not for sixty feet. You sure didn't drive it over there.'

'What are you talking about?'

'That, son, I wouldn't know. But I went and looked myself. There lay the Cat, all broken up, and you beside it with your lungs all full of your own ribs. Deadest looking man I ever saw get better.'

'I don't get it. Did anybody see this happen? Are you trying to –'

'Only one claims to have seen it was a Puerto-Rican bottom-dump driver. Doesn't speak any English, but he swears on every saint in the calendar that he looked back after dumping a load and saw you and twenty tons of bulldozer *forty feet in the air*, and then it was coming down!'

I stared. 'Who was the man?'

'Heavy-set fellow. About forty-five. Strong as a rhino and seemed sane.'

'I know him,' I said. 'A good man.' Suddenly, then, happily: 'Doc – you know what his name is?'

'No. Didn't ask. Some flowery Spanish moniker, I guess.'

'No, it isn't,' I said. 'His name is Kirkpatrick. Alonzo Padin de Kirkpatrick.'

He laughed. 'The Irish are a wonderful people. Go to sleep. You've been unconscious for nearly three weeks.'

'I've been unconscious for eleven years,' I said, and felt foolish as hell because I hadn't meant to say anything like that and couldn't imagine what put it into my head.

Vault of the Beast

A.E. VAN VOGT

THE CREATURE CREPT. It whimpered from fear and pain, a thin, slobbering sound horrible to hear. Shapeless, formless thing yet changing shape and form with every jerky movement.

It crept along the corridor of the space freighter, fighting the terrible urge of its elements to take the shape of its surroundings. A grey blob of disintegrating stuff, it crept, it cascaded, it rolled, flowed, dissolved, every movement an agony of struggle against the abnormal need to become a stable shape.

Any shape! The hard, chilled-blue metal wall of the Earth-bound freighter, the thick, rubbery floor. The floor was easy to fight. It wasn't like the metal that pulled and pulled. It would be easy to become metal for all eternity.

But something prevented. An implanted purpose. A purpose that drummed from electron to electron, vibrated from atom to atom with an unvarying intensity that was like a special pain: *Find the greatest mathematical mind in the Solar System, and bring it to the vault of the Martian ultimate metal. The Great One must be freed! The prime number time lock must be opened!*

That was the purpose that hummed with unrelenting agony through its elements. That was the thought that had been seared into its fundamental consciousness by the great and evil minds that had created it.

There was movement at the far end of the corridor. A door opened. Footsteps sounded. A man whistling to himself. With a metallic hiss, almost a sigh, the creature dissolved, looking momentarily like diluted mercury. Then it turned brown like the floor. It became the floor, a slightly thicker stretch of dark-brown rubber spread out for yards.

It was ecstasy just to lie there, to be flat and to have shape, and to be so nearly dead that there was no pain. Death was so sweet, so utterly desirable. And life such an unbearable torment of agony, such a throbbing, piercing nightmare of anguished convulsion. If only the life that was approaching would pass swiftly. If the life stopped, it would pull it into shape. Life could do that. Life was stronger than metal, stronger than anything. The approaching life meant torture, struggle, pain.

The creature tensed its now flat, grotesque body – the body that could develop muscles of steel – and waited in terror for the death struggle.

Spacecraftsman Parelli whistled happily as he strode along the gleaming corridor that led from the engine room. He had just received a wireless from the hospital. His wife was doing well, and it was a boy. Eight pounds, the radiogram had said. He suppressed a desire to whoop and dance. A boy. Life sure was good.

Pain came to the thing on the floor. Primeval pain that sucked through its elements like acid burning, burning. The brown floor shuddered in every atom as Parelli strode over it. The aching urge to pull towards him, to take his shape. The thing fought its horrible desire, fought with anguish and shivering dread, more consciously now that it could think with Parelli's brain. A ripple of floor rolled after the man.

Fighting didn't help. The ripple grew into a blob that momentarily seemed to become a human head. Grey, hellish nightmare of demoniac shape. The creature hissed metallically in terror, then collapsed palpitating, slobbering with fear and pain and hate as Parelli strode on rapidly – too rapidly for its creeping pace.

The thin, horrible sound died; the thing dissolved into brown floor, and lay quiescent yet quivering in every atom from its unquenchable, uncontrollable urge to live – live in spite of pain, in spite of abysmal terror and primordial longing for stable shape. To live and fulfil the purpose of its lusting and malignant creators.

Thirty feet up the corridor, Parelli stopped. He jerked his mind from its thoughts of child and wife. He spun on his heels, and stared uncertainly along the passageway from the engine room.

'Now, what the devil was that?' he pondered aloud.

A sound – a queer, faint yet unmistakably horrid sound was echoing and re-echoing through his consciousness. A shiver ran the length of his spine. That sound – that devilish sound.

He stood there, a tall, magnificently muscled man, stripped to the waist, sweating from the heat generated by the rockets that were decelerating the craft after its meteoric flight from Mars. Shuddering, he clenched his fists, and walked slowly back the way he had come.

The creature throbbed with the pull of him, a gnawing, writhing, tormenting struggle that pierced into the deeps of every restless, agitated cell, stabbing agonizingly along the alien nervous system; and then became terrifyingly aware of the inevitable, the irresistible need to take the shape of the life.

Parelli stopped uncertainly. The floor moved under him, a visible wave that reared brown and horrible before his incredulous eyes and grew into a bulbous, slobbering, hissing mass. A venomous demon head reared on twisted, half-human shoulders. Gnarled hands on apelike, malformed

223

arms clawed at his face with insensate rage – and changed even as they tore at him.

'Good God!' Parelli bellowed.

The hands, the arms that clutched him grew more normal, more human, brown, muscular. The face assumed familiar lines, sprouted a nose, eyes, a red gash of mouth. The body was suddenly his own, trousers and all, sweat and all.

' – God!' his image echoed; and pawed at him with letching fingers and an impossible strength.

Gasping, Parelli fought free, then launched one crushing blow straight into the distorted face. A drooling scream of agony came from the thing. It turned and ran, dissolving as it ran, fighting dissolution, uttering strange half-human cries.

And, struggling against horror, Parelli chased it, his knees weak and trembling from sheer funk and incredulity. His arm reached out, and plucked at the disintegrating trousers. A piece came away in his hand, a cold, slimy, writhing lump like wet clay.

The feel of it was too much. His gorge rising in disgust, he faltered in his stride. He heard the pilot shouting ahead:

'What's the matter?'

Parelli saw the open door of the storeroom. With a gasp, he dived in, came out a moment later, wild-eyed, an ato-gun in his fingers. He saw the pilot, standing with staring, horrid brown eyes, white face and rigid body, facing one of the great windows.

'There it is!' the man cried.

A grey blob was dissolving into the edge of the glass, becoming glass. Parelli rushed forward, ato-gun poised. A ripple went through the glass, darkening it; and then, briefly, he caught a glimpse of a blob emerging on the other side of the glass into the cold of space.

The officer stood gaping beside him; the two of them watched the grey, shapeless mass creep out of sight along the side of the rushing freight liner.

Parelli sprang to life. 'I got a piece of it!' he gasped. 'Flung it down on the floor of the storeroom.'

It was Lieutenant Morton who found it. A tiny section of floor reared up, and then grew amazingly large as it tried to expand into human shape. Parelli with distorted, crazy eyes scooped it up in a shovel. It hissed; it nearly became a part of the metal shovel, but couldn't because Parelli was so close. Changing, fighting for shape, it slobbered and hissed as Parelli staggered with it behind his superior officer. He was laughing hysterically. 'I touched it,' he kept saying. 'I touched it.'

A large blister of metal on the outside of the space freighter stirred into sluggish life, as the ship tore into the Earth's atmosphere. The metal walls of the freighter grew red, then white-hot, but the creature, unaffected, continued its slow transformation into grey mass. Vague thought came to the thing, realization that it was time to act.

Suddenly, it was floating free of the ship, falling slowly, heavily, as if somehow the gravitation of Earth had no serious effect upon it. A minute distortion in its electrons started it falling faster, as in some alien way it suddenly became more allergic to gravity.

The Earth was green below; and in the dim distance a gorgeous and tremendous city of spires and massive buildings glittered in the sinking Sun. The thing slowed, and drifted like a falling leaf in a breeze towards the still-distant Earth. It landed in an arroyo beside a bridge at the outskirts of the city.

A man walked over the bridge with quick, nervous steps. He would have been amazed, if he had looked back, to see a replica of himself climb from the ditch to the road, and start walking briskly after him.

Find the – greatest mathematician!

It was an hour later; and the pain of that throbbing thought was a dull, continuous ache in the creature's brain, as it walked along the crowded street. There were other pains, too. The pain of fighting the pull of the pushing, hurrying mass of humanity that swarmed by with unseeing eyes. But it was easier to think, easier to hold form now that it had the brain and body of a man.

Find – mathematician!

'Why?' asked the man's brain of the thing; and the whole body shook with startled shock at such heretical questioning. The brown eyes darted in fright from side to side, as if expecting instant and terrible doom. The face dissolved a little in that brief moment of mental chaos, became successively the man with the hooked nose who swung by, the tanned face of the tall woman who was looking into the shop window, the –

With a second gasp, the creature pulled its mind back from fear, and fought to readjust its face to that of the smooth-shaven young man who sauntered idly in from a side street. The young man glanced at him, looked away, then glanced back again startled. The creature echoed the thought in the man's brain: 'Who the devil is that? Where have I seen that fellow before?'

Half a dozen women in a group approached. The creature shrank aside as they passed, its face twisted with the agony of the urge to become woman. Its brown suit turned just the faintest shade of blue, the colour of the nearest dress, as it momentarily lost control of its outer atoms. Its mind hummed with the chatter of clothes and 'My dear, didn't she look dreadful in that awful hat?'

There was a solid cluster of giant buildings ahead. The thing shook its human head consciously. So many buildings meant metal; and the forces that held metal together would pull and pull at its human shape. The

225

creature comprehended the reason for this with the understanding of the slight man in a dark suit who wandered by dully. The slight man was a clerk; the thing caught his thought. He was thinking enviously of his boss who was Jim Brender, of the financial firm of J.P. Brender & Co.

The overtones of that thought struck along the vibrating elements of the creature. It turned abruptly and followed Lawrence Pearson, bookkeeper. If people ever paid attention to other people on the street, they would have been amazed after a moment to see two Lawrence Pearsons proceeding down the street, one some fifty feet behind the other. The second Lawrence Pearson had learned from the mind of the first that Jim Brender was a Harvard graduate in mathematics, finance and political economy, the latest of a long line of financial geniuses, thirty years old, and the head of the tremendously wealthy J.P. Brender & Co. Jim Brender had just married the most beautiful girl in the world; and this was the reason for Lawrence Pearson's discontent with life.

'Here I'm thirty, too,' his thoughts echoed in the creature's mind, 'and I've got nothing. He's got everything – everything while all I've got to look forward to is the same old boarding-house till the end of time.'

It was getting dark as the two crossed the river. The creature quickened its pace, striding forward with aggressive alertness that Lawrence Pearson in the flesh could never have managed. Some glimmering of its terrible purpose communicated itself in that last instant to the victim. The slight man turned; and let out a faint squawk as those steel-muscled fingers jerked at his throat, a single, fearful snap.

The creature's brain went black with dizziness as the brain of Lawrence Pearson crashed into the night of death. Gasping, whimpering, fighting dissolution, it finally gained control of itself. With one sweeping movement, it caught the dead body and flung it over the cement railing. There was a splash below, then a sound of gurgling water.

The thing that was now Lawrence Pearson walked on hurriedly, then more slowly till it came to a large, rambling brick house. It looked anxiously at the number, suddenly uncertain if it had remembered rightly. Hesitantly, it opened the door.

A streamer of yellow light splashed out, and laughter vibrated in the thing's sensitive ears. There was the same hum of many thoughts and many brains, as there had been in the street. The creature fought against the inflow of thought that threatened to crowd out the mind of Lawrence Pearson. A little dazed by the struggle, it found itself in a large, bright hall, which looked through a door into a room where a dozen people were sitting around a dining table.

'Oh, it's you, Mr Pearson,' said the landlady from the head of the table. She was a sharp-nosed, thin-mouthed woman at whom the creature stared with brief intentness. From her mind, a thought had come. She had a son who was a mathematics teacher in a high school. The creature shrugged. In one penetrating glance, the truth throbbed along the intricate atomic structure of its body. This woman's son was as much of an intellectual lightweight as his mother.

'You're just in time,' she said incuriously. 'Sarah, bring Mr Pearson's plate.'

'Thank you, but I'm not feeling hungry,' the creature replied; and its human brain vibrated to the first silent, ironic laughter that it had ever known. 'I think I'll just lie down.'

All night long it lay on the bed of Lawrence Pearson, bright-eyed, alert, becoming more and more aware of itself. It thought:

'I'm a machine, without a brain of my own. I use the brains of other people, but somehow my creators made it possible for me to be more than just an echo. I use people's brains to carry out my purpose.'

It pondered about those creators, and felt a surge of panic sweeping along its alien system, darkening its human mind. There was a vague physiological memory of pain unutterable, and of tearing chemical action that was frightening.

The creature rose at dawn, and walked the streets till half past nine. At that hour, it approached the imposing marble entrance of J.P. Brender & Co. Inside, it sank down in the comfortable chair initialed L.P.; and began painstakingly to work at the books Lawrence Pearson had put away the night before.

At ten o'clock, a tall young man in a dark suit entered the arched hallway and walked briskly through the row after row of offices. He smiled with easy confidence to every side. The thing did not need the chorus of 'Good morning, Mr Brender' to know that his prey had arrived.

Terrible in its slow-won self-confidence, it rose with a lithe, graceful movement that would have been impossible to the real Lawrence Pearson, and walked briskly to the washroom. A moment later, the very image of Jim Brender emerged from the door and walked with easy confidence to the door of the private office which Jim Brender had entered a few minutes before.

The thing knocked and walked in – and simultaneously became aware of three things: The first was that it had found the mind after which it had been sent. The second was that its image mind was incapable of imitating the finer subtleties of the razor-sharp brain of the young man who was staring up from dark-grey eyes that were a little startled. And the third was the large metal bas-relief that hung on the wall.

With a shock that almost brought chaos, it felt the overpowering tug of that metal. And in one flash it knew that this was ultimate metal, product of the fine craft of the ancient Martians, whose metal cities, loaded with treasures of furniture, art and machinery were slowly being dug up by enterprising human beings from the sands under which they had been buried for thirty or fifty million years.

The ultimate metal! The metal that no heat would even warm, that no diamond or other cutting device could scratch, never duplicated by human beings, as mysterious as the *ieis* force which the Martians made from apparent nothingness.

All these thoughts crowded the creature's brain, as it explored the memory cells of Jim Brender. With an effort that was a special pain, the thing wrenched its mind from the metal, and fastened its eyes on Jim Brender. It caught the full flood of the wonder in his mind, as he stood up.

'Good lord,' said Jim Brender, 'who are you?'

'My name's Jim Brender,' said the thing, conscious of grim amusement, conscious, too, that it was progress for it to be able to feel such an emotion.

The real Jim Brender had recovered himself. 'Sit down, sit down,' he said heartily. 'This is the most amazing coincidence I've ever seen.'

He went over to the mirror that made one panel of the left wall. He stared, first at himself, then at the creature. 'Amazing,' he said. 'Absolutely amazing.'

'Mr Brender,' said the creature, 'I saw your picture in the paper, and I thought our astounding resemblance would make you listen, where otherwise you might pay no attention. I have recently returned from Mars, and I am here to persuade you to come back to Mars with me.'

'That,' said Jim Brender, 'is impossible.'

'Wait,' the creature said, 'until I have told you why. Have you ever heard of the Tower of the Beast?'

'The Tower of the Beast!' Jim Brender repeated slowly. He went around his desk and pushed a button.

A voice from an ornamental box said: 'Yes, Mr Brender?'

'Dave, get me all the data on the Tower of the Beast and the legendary city of Li in which it is supposed to exist.'

'Don't need to look it up,' came the crisp reply. 'Most Martian histories refer to it as the beast that fell from the sky when Mars was young – some terrible warning connected with it – the beast was unconscious when found – said to be the result of its falling out of sub-space. Martians read its mind; and were so horrified by its subconscious intentions they tried to kill it, but couldn't. So they built a huge vault, about fifteen hundred feet in diameter and a mile high – and the beast, apparently of these dimensions, was locked in. Several attempts have been made to find the city of Li, but without success. Generally believed to be a myth. That's all, Jim.'

'Thank you!' Jim Brender clicked off the connection, and turned to his visitor. 'Well?'

'It is not a myth. I know where the Tower of the Beast is; and I also know that the beast is still alive.'

'Now, see here,' said Brender good-humouredly, 'I'm intrigued by your resemblance to me; and as a matter of fact I'd like Pamela – my wife – to see you. How about coming over to dinner? But don't, for Heaven's sake, expect me to believe such a story. The beast, if there is such a thing, fell from the sky when Mars was young. There are some authorities who maintain that the Martian race died out a hundred million years ago, though twenty-five million is the conservative estimate. The only things remaining of their civilization are their constructions of ultimate metal. Fortunately, towards the end they built almost everything from that indestructible metal.'

'Let me tell you about the Tower of the Beast,' said the thing quietly. 'It is a tower of gigantic size, but only a hundred feet or so projected above the sand when I saw it. The whole top is a door, and that door is geared to a time lock, which in turn has been integrated along a line of ieis to the ultimate prime number.'

Jim Brender stared; and the thing caught his startled thought, the first uncertainty, and the beginning of belief.

'Ultimate prime number!' Brender ejaculated. 'What do you mean?' He caught himself. 'I know of course that a prime number is a number divisible only by itself and by one.'

He snatched at a book from the little wall library beside his desk, and rippled through it. 'The largest known prime is – ah, here it is – is 230584300921393951. Some others, according to this authority, are 77843839397, 182521213001, and 78875943472201.'

He frowned. 'That makes the whole thing ridiculous. The ultimate prime would be an indefinite number.' He smiled at the thing. 'If there is a beast, and it is locked up in a vault of ultimate metal, the door of which is geared to a time lock, integrated along a line of ieis to the ultimate prime number – then the beast is caught. Nothing in the world can free it.'

'To the contrary,' said the creature. 'I have been assured by the beast that it is within the scope of human mathematics to solve the problem, but that what is required is a born mathematical mind, equipped with all the mathematical training that Earth science can afford. You are that man.'

'You expect me to release this evil creature – even if I could perform this miracle of mathematics.'

'Evil nothing!' snapped the thing. 'That ridiculous fear of the unknown which made the Martians imprison it has resulted in a very grave wrong. The beast is a scientist from another space, accidentally caught in one of his experiments. I say "his" when of course I do not know whether this race has a sexual differentiation.'

'You actually talked with the beast?'

'It communicated with me by mental telepathy.'

'It has been proven that thoughts cannot penetrate ultimate metal.'

'What do humans know about telepathy? They cannot even communicate with each other except under special conditions.' The creature spoke contemptuously.

'That's right. And if your story is true, then this is a matter for the Council.'

'This is a matter for two men, you and I. Have you forgotten that the vault of the beast is the central tower of the great city of Li – billions of dollars' worth of treasure in furniture, art and machinery? The beast demands release from its prison before it will permit anyone to mine that treasure. You can release it. We can share the treasure.'

'Let me ask you a question,' said Jim Brender. 'What is your real name?'

'P-Pierce Lawrence!' the creature stammered. For the moment, it could think of no greater variation of the name of its first victim than reversing the two words, with a slight change on 'Pearson.' Its thoughts darkened with confusion as the voice of Brender pounded:

'On what ship did you come from Mars?'

'O-on *F4961*,' the thing stammered chaotically, fury adding to the confused state of its mind. It fought for control, felt itself slipping, suddenly felt the pull of the ultimate metal that made up the bas-relief on the wall, and knew by that tug that it was dangerously near dissolution.

'That would be a freighter,' said Jim Brender. He pressed a button. 'Carltons, find out if the *F4961* had a passenger or person aboard, named Pierce Lawrence. How long will it take?'

'About a minute, sir.'

'You see,' said Jim Brender, leaning back, 'this is mere formality. If you were on that ship, then I shall be compelled to give serious attention to your statements. You can understand, of course, that I could not possibly go into a thing like this blindly. I – '

The buzzer rang. 'Yes?' said Jim Brender.

'Only the crew of two was on the *F4961* when it landed yesterday. No such person as Pierce Lawrence was aboard.'

'Thank you.' Jim Brender stood up. He said coldly, 'Good-bye, Mr Lawrence. I cannot imagine what you hoped to gain by this ridiculous story. However it has been most intriguing, and the problem you presented was very ingenious indeed – '

The buzzer was ringing. 'What is it?'

'Mr Gorson to see you sir.'

'Very well, send him right in.'

The thing had greater control of its brain now, and it saw in Brender's mind that Gorson was a financial magnate, whose business ranked with the Brender firm. It saw other things, too; things that made it walk out of the private office, out of the building, and wait patiently until Mr Gorson emerged from the imposing entrance. A few minutes later, there were two Mr Gorsons walking down the street.

Mr Gorson was a vigorous man in his early fifties. He had lived a clean, active life; and the hard memories of many climates and several planets were stored away in his brain. The thing caught the alertness of this man on its sensitive elements, and followed him warily, respectfully, not quite decided whether it would act.

It thought: 'I've come a long way from the primitive life that couldn't hold its shape. My creators, in designing me, gave to me powers of learning, developing. It is easier to fight dissolution, easier to be human. In handling this man, I must remember that my strength is invincible when properly used.'

With minute care, it explored in the mind of its intended victim the exact route of his walk to his office. There was the entrance to a large building clearly etched on his mind. Then a long, marble corridor, into an automatic elevator up to the eighth floor, along a short corridor with two doors. One door led to the private entrance of the man's private office. The other to a storeroom used by the janitor. Gorson had looked into the place on various occasions; and there was in his mind, among other things, the memory of a large chest –

The thing waited in the storeroom till the unsuspecting Gorson was past the door. The door creaked. Gorson turned, his eyes widening. He didn't have a chance. A fist of solid steel smashed his face to a pulp, knocking the bones back into his brain.

This time, the creature did not make the mistake of keeping its mind tuned to that of its victim. It caught him viciously as he fell, forcing its steel fist back to a semblance of human flesh. With furious speed, it stuffed the bulky and athletic form into the large chest, and clamped the lid down tight.

Alertly, it emerged from the storeroom, entered the private office of Mr Gorson, and sat down before the gleaming desk of oak. The man who responded to the pressing of a button saw John Gorson sitting there, and heard John Gorson say:

'Crispins, I want you to start selling these stocks through the secret channels right away. Sell until I tell you to stop, even if you think it's crazy. I have information of something big on.'

Crispins glanced down the row after row of stock names; and his eyes grew wider and wider. 'Good lord, man!' he gasped finally, with that familiarity which is the right of a trusted adviser, 'these are all the gilt-edged stocks. Your whole fortune can't swing a deal like this.'

'I told you I'm not in this alone.'

'But it's against the law to break the market,' the man protested.

'Crispins, you heard what I said. I'm leaving the office. Don't try to get in touch with me. I'll call you.'

The thing that was John Gorson stood up, paying no attention to the bewildered thoughts that flowed from Crispins. It went out of the door by which it had entered. As it emerged from the building, it was thinking: 'All I've got to do is kill half a dozen financial giants, start their stocks selling, and then – '

By one o'clock it was over. The exchange didn't close till three, but at one o'clock, the news was flashed on the New York tickers. In London, where it was getting dark, the papers brought out an extra. In Hankow and Shanghai, a dazzling new day was breaking as the newsboys ran along the streets in the shadows of skyscrapers, and shouted that J.P. Brender & Co. had assigned; and that there was to be an investigation –

'We are facing,' said the chairman of the investigation committee, in his opening address the following morning, 'one of the most astounding coincidences in all history. An ancient and respected firm, with world-wide affiliations and branches, with investments in more than a thousand companies of every description, is struck bankrupt by an unexpected crash in every stock in which the firm was interested. It will require months to take evidence on the responsibility for the short-selling which brought about this disaster. In the meantime, I see no reason, regrettable as the action must be to all the old friends of the late J.P. Brender, and of his son, why the demands of the creditors should not be met, and the properties, liquidated through auction sales and such other methods as may be deemed proper and legal – '

'Really, I don't blame her,' said the first woman, as they wandered through the spacious rooms of the Brenders' Chinese palace. 'I have no doubt she does love Jim Brender, but no one could seriously expect her to remain married to him *now*. She's a woman of the world, and its utterly impossible to expect her to live with a man who's going to be a mere pilot or space hand or something on a Martian spaceship – '

Commander Hughes of Interplanetary Spaceways entered the office of his employer truculently. He was a small man, but extremely wiry; and the thing that was Louis Dyer gazed at him tensely, conscious of the force and power of this man.

Hughes began: 'You have my report on this Brender case?'

The thing twirled the moustache of Louis Dyer nervously; then picked up a small folder, and read out aloud:

'Dangerous for psychological reasons ... to employ Brender.... So many blows in succession. Loss of wealth, position and wife.... No normal man could remain normal under ... circumstances. Take him into office ... befriend him ... give him a sinecure, or position where his undoubted great ability ... but not on a spaceship, where the utmost

232

hardiness, both mental, moral, spiritual and physical is required – '

Hughes interrupted: 'Those are exactly the points which I am stressing. I knew you would see what I meant, Louis.'

'Of course, I see,' said the creature, smiling in grim amusement, for it was feeling very superior these days. 'Your thoughts, your ideas, your code and your methods are stamped irrevocably on your brain and' – it added hastily – 'you have never left me in doubts as to where you stand. However, in this case, I must insist. Jim Brender will not take an ordinary position offered by his friends. And it is ridiculous to ask him to subordinate himself to men to whom he is in every way superior. He has commanded his own space yacht; he knows more about the mathematical end of the work than our whole staff put together; and that is no reflection on our staff. He knows the hardships connected with space flying, and believes that it is exactly what he needs. I, therefore, command you, for the first time in our long association, Peter, to put him on space freighter *F4961* in the place of Spacecraftsman Parelli who collapsed into a nervous breakdown after that curious affair with the creature from space, as Lieutenant Morton described it – By the way, did you find the ... er ... sample of that creature yet?'

'No, sir, it vanished the day you came in to look at it. We've searched the place high and low – queerest stuff you ever saw. Goes through glass as easy as light; you'd think it was some form of light-stuff – scares me, too. A pure sympodial development – actually more adaptable to environment than anything hitherto discovered; and that's putting it mildly. I tell you, sir – But see here, you can't steer me off the Brender case like that.'

'Peter, I don't understand your attitude. This is the first time I've interfered with your end of the work and – '

'I'll resign,' groaned that sorely beset man.

The thing stifled a smile. 'Peter, you've built up the staff of Spaceways. It's your child, your creation; you can't give it up, you know you can't – '

The words hissed softly into alarm; for into Hughes' brain had flashed the first real intention of resigning. Just hearing of his accomplishments and the story of his beloved job brought such a rush of memories, such a realization of how tremendous an outrage was this threatened interference. In one mental leap, the creature saw what this man's resignation would mean: The discontent of the men; the swift perception of the situation by Jim Brender; and his refusal to accept the job. There was only one way out – that Brender would get to the ship without finding out what had happened. Once on it, he must carry through with one trip to Mars; and that was all that was needed.

The thing pondered the possibility of imitating Hughes' body; then agonizingly realized that it was hopeless. Both Louis Dyer and Hughes must be around until the last minute.

233

'But, Peter, listen!' the creature began chaotically. Then it said, 'Damn!' for it was very human in its mentality; and the realization that Hughes took its words as a sign of weakness was maddening. Uncertainty descended like a black cloud over its brain.

'I'll tell Brender when he arrives in five minutes how I feel about all this!' Hughes snapped; and the creature knew that the worst had happened. 'If you forbid me to tell him, then I resign. I – Good God, man, your face!'

Confusion and horror came to the creature simultaneously. It knew abruptly that its face had dissolved before the threatened ruins of its plans. It fought for control, leaped to its feet, seeing the incredible danger. The large office just beyond the frosted glass door – Hughes' first outcry would bring help –

With a half sob, it sought to force its arm into an imitation of a metal fist, but there was no metal in the room to pull it into shape. There was only the solid maple desk. With a harsh cry, the creature leaped completely over the desk, and sought to bury a pointed shaft of stick into Hughes' throat.

Hughes cursed in amazement, and caught at the stick with furious strength. There was sudden commotion in the outer office, raised voices, running feet –

It was quite accidental the way it happened. The surface cars swayed to a stop, drawing up side by side as the red light blinked on ahead. Jim Brender glanced at the next car.

A girl and a man sat in the rear of the long, shiny, streamlined affair, and the girl was desperately striving to crouch down out of his sight, striving with equal desperation not to be too obvious in her intention. Realizing that she was seen, she smiled brilliantly, and leaned out of the window.

'Hello, Jim, how's everything?'

'Hello, Pamela!' Jim Brender's fingers tightened on the steering wheel till the knuckles showed white, as he tried to keep his voice steady. He couldn't help adding: 'When does the divorce become final?'

'I get my papers tomorrow,' she said, 'but I suppose you won't get yours till you return from your first trip. Leaving today, aren't you?'

'In about fifteen minutes.' He hesitated. 'When is the wedding?'

The rather plump, white-faced man who had not participated in the conversation so far, leaned forward.

'Next week,' he said. He put his fingers possessively over Pamela's hand. 'I wanted it tomorrow but Pamela wouldn't – er, good-bye.'

His last words were hastily spoken, as the traffic lights switched, and the cars rolls on, separating at the first corner.

The rest of the drive to the spaceport was a blur. He hadn't expected

234

the wedding to take place so soon. Hadn't, when he came right down to it, expected it to take place at all. Like a fool, he had hoped blindly –

Not that it was Pamela's fault. Her training, her very life made this the only possible course of action for her. But – *one week!* The spaceship would be one fourth of the long trip to Mars –

He parked his car. As he paused beside the runway that led to the open door of *F4961* – a huge globe of shining metal, three hundred feet in diameter – he saw a man running towards him. Then he recognized Hughes.

The thing that was Hughes approached, fighting for calmness. The whole world was a flame of cross-pulling forces. It shrank from the thoughts of the people milling about in the office it had just left. Everything had gone wrong. It had never intended to do what it now had to do. It had intended to spend most of the trip to Mars as a blister of metal on the outer shield of the ship. With an effort, it controlled its funk, its terror, its brain.

'We're leaving right away,' it said.

Brender looked amazed. 'But that means I'll have to figure out a new orbit under the most difficult – '

'Exactly,' the creature interrupted. 'I've been hearing a lot about your marvellous mathematical ability. It's time the words were proved by deeds.'

Jim Brender shrugged. 'I have no objection. But how is it that you're coming along?'

'I always go with a new man.'

It sounded reasonable. Brender climbed the runway, closely followed by Hughes. The powerful pull of the metal was the first real pain the creature had known for days. For a long month, it would now have to fight the metal, fight to retain the shape of Hughes – and carry on a thousand duties at the same time.

That first stabbing pain tore along its elements, and smashed the confidence that days of being human had built up. And then, as it followed Brender through the door, it heard a shout behind it. It looked back hastily. People were streaming out of several doors, running towards the ship.

Brender was several yards along the corridor. With a hiss that was almost a sob, the creature leaped inside, and pulled the lever that clicked the great door shut.

There was an emergency lever that controlled the antigravity plates. With one jerk, the creature pulled the heavy lever hard over. There was a sensation of lightness and a sense of falling.

Through the great plate window, the creature caught a flashing glimpse of the field below, swarming with people. White faces turning upward, arms waving. Then the scene grew remote, as a thunder of rockets vibrated through the ship.

'I hope,' said Brender, as Hughes entered the control room, 'you wanted me to start the rockets.'

'Yes,' the thing replied, and felt brief panic at the chaos in its brain, the tendency of its tongue to blur. 'I'm leaving the mathematical end entirely in your hands.'

It didn't dare stay so near the heavy metal engines, even with Brender's body there to help it keep its human shape. Hurriedly, it started up the corridor. The best place would be the insulated bedroom –

Abruptly, it stopped in its headlong walk, teetered for an instant on tiptoes. From the control room it had just left, a thought was trickling – a thought from Brender's brain. The creature almost dissolved in terror as it realized that Brender was sitting at the radio, answering an insistent call from Earth –

It burst into the control room, and braked to a halt, its eyes widening with humanlike dismay. Brender whirled from before the radio with a single twisting step. In his fingers, he held a revolver. In his mind, the creature read a dawning comprehension of the whole truth. Brender cried:

'You're the ... thing that came to my office, and talked about prime numbers and the vault of the beast.'

He took a step to one side to cover an open doorway that led down another corridor. The movement brought the telescreen into the vision of the creature. In the screen was the image of the real Hughes. Simultaneously, Hughes saw the thing.

'Brender,' he bellowed, 'it's the monster that Morton and Parelli saw on their trip from Mars. It doesn't react to heat or any chemicals, but we never tried bullets. Shoot, you fool!'

It was too much, there was too much metal, too much confusion. With a whimpering cry, the creature dissolved. The pull of the metal twisted it horribly into thick half-metal; the struggle to be human left it a malignant structure of bulbous head, with one eye half gone, and two snakelike arms attached to the half metal of the body.

Instinctively, it fought closer to Brender, letting the pull of his body make it more human. The half metal became fleshlike stuff that sought to return to its human shape.

'Listen, Brender!' Hughes' voice came urgently. 'The fuel vats in the engine room are made of ultimate metal. One of them is empty. We caught a part of this thing once before, and it couldn't get out of the small jar of ultimate metal. If you could drive it into the vat while its lost control of itself, as it seems to do very easily –'

'I'll see what lead can do!' Brender rapped in a brittle voice.

Bang! The half-human creature screamed from its half-formed slit of mouth, and retreated, its legs dissolving into grey dough.

'It hurts, doesn't it?' Brender ground out. 'Get over into the engine room, you damned thing, into the vat!'

'Go on, go on!' Hughes was screaming from the telescreen.

Brender fired again. The creature made a horrible slobbering sound, and retreated once more. But it was bigger again, more human; and in one caricature hand a caricature of Brender's revolver was growing.

It raised the unfinished, unformed gun. There was an explosion, and a shriek from the thing. The revolver fell, a shapeless, tattered blob, to the floor. The little grey mass of it scrambled frantically towards the parent body, and attached itself like some monstrous canker to the right foot.

And then, for the first time, the mighty and evil brains that had created the thing, sought to dominate their robot. Furious, yet conscious that the game must be carefully played, the Controller forced the terrified and utterly beaten thing to its will. Scream after agonized scream rent the air, as the change was forced upon the unstable elements. In an instant, the thing stood in the shape of Brender, but instead of a revolver, there grew from one browned, powerful hand a pencil of shining metal. Mirror bright, it glittered in every facet like some incredible gem.

The metal glowed ever so faintly, an unearthly radiance. And where the radio had been, and the screen with Hughes' face on it, there was a gaping hole. Desperately, Brender pumped bullets into the body before him, but though the shape trembled it stared at him now, unaffected. The shining weapon swung towards him.

'When you are quite finished,' it said, 'perhaps we can talk.'

It spoke so mildly that Brender, tensing to meet death, lowered his gun in amazement. The thing went on:

'Do not be alarmed. This which you hear and see is a robot, designed by us to cope with your space and number world. Several of us are working here under the most difficult conditions to maintain this connection, so I must be brief.

'We exist in a time world immeasurably more slow than your own. By a system of synchronization, we have geared a number of these spaces in such fashion that, though one of our days is millions of your years, we can communicate. Our purpose is to free our colleague, Kalorn, from the Martian vault. Kalorn was caught accidentally in a time warp of his own making and precipitated onto the planet you know as Mars. The Martians, needlessly fearing his great size, constructed a most diabolical prison, and we need your knowledge of the mathematics peculiar to your space and number world – and to it alone – in order to free him.'

The calm voice continued, earnest but not offensively so, insistent but friendly. He regretted that their robot had killed human beings. In greater detail, he explained that every space was constructed on a different numbers system, some all negative, some all positive, some a mixture of the two, the whole an infinite variety, and every mathematic interwoven into the very fabric of the space it ruled.

Ieis force was not really mysterious. It was simply a flow from one space to another, the result of a difference in potential. This flow, however, was one of the universal forces, which only one other force could affect, the one he had used a few minutes before. Ultimate metal was *actually* ultimate.

In their space they had a similar metal, built up from negative atoms. He could see from Brender's mind that the Martians had known nothing about minus numbers, so that they must have built it up from ordinary atoms. It could be done that way, too, though not so easily. He finished:

'The problem narrows down to this: Your mathematic must tell us how, with our universal force, we can short-circuit the ultimate prime number – that is, factor it – so that the door will open any time. You may ask how a prime can be factored when it is divisible only by itself and by one. That problem is, for your system, solvable only by your mathematic. Will you do it?'

Brender realized with a start that he was still holding his revolver. He tossed it aside. His nerves were calm as he said:

'Everything you have said sounds reasonable and honest. If you were desirous of making trouble, it would be the simplest thing in the world to send as many of your kind as you wished. Of course, the whole affair must be placed before the Council – '

'Then it is hopeless – the Council could not possible accede – '

'And you expect me to do what you do not believe the highest governmental authority in the System would do?' Brender exclaimed.

'It is inherent in the nature of a democracy that it cannot gamble with the lives of its citizens. We have such a government here; and its members have already informed us that, in a similar condition, they would not consider releasing an unknown beast upon their people. Individuals, however, can gamble where governments must not. You have agreed that our argument is logical. What system do men follow if not that of logic?'

The Controller, through its robot, watched Brender's thoughts alertly. It saw doubt and uncertainty, opposed by a very human desire to help, based upon the logical conviction that it was safe. Probing his mind, it saw swiftly that it was unwise, in dealing with men, to trust too much to logic. It pressed on:

'To an individual we can offer – everything. In a minute, with your permission, we shall transfer this ship to Mars; not in thirty days, but in thirty seconds. The knowledge of how this is done will remain with you. Arrived at Mars, you will find yourself the only living person who knows the whereabouts of the ancient city of Li, of which the vault of the beast is the central tower. In this city will be found literally billions of dollars' worth of treasure made of ultimate metal; and according to the laws of Earth, fifty per cent will be yours. Your fortune re-established you will be able to return to Earth this very day, and reclaim your former wife, and your position. Poor silly child, she loves you still, but the iron conventions and training of her youth leave her no alternative. If she were older, she would have the character to defy those conventions. You must save her from herself. Will you do it?'

Brender was as white as a sheet, his hands clenching and unclenching. Malevolently, the thing watched the flaming thought sweeping through his brain – the memory of a pudgy white hand closing over Pamela's fingers, watched the reaction of Brender to its words, those words that expressed exactly what he had always thought. Brender looked up with tortured eyes.

'Yes,' he said, 'I'll do what I can.'

A bleak range of mountains fell away into a valley of reddish grey sand. The thin winds of Mars blew a mist of sand against the building.

Such a building! At a distance, it looked merely big. A bare hundred feet projected above the desert, a hundred feet of length and *fifteen hundred feet of diameter*. Literally thousands of feet must extend beneath the restless ocean of sand to make the perfect balance of form, the graceful flow, the fairy-like beauty, which the long-dead Martians demanded of all their constructions, however massive. Brender felt suddenly small and insignificant as the rockets of his spacesuit pounded him along a few feet above the sand towards the incredible building.

At close range the ugliness of sheer size was miraculously lost in the wealth of the decoration. Columns and pilasters assembled in groups and clusters, broke up the façades, gathered and dispersed again restlessly. The flat surfaces of wall and roof melted into a wealth of ornaments and imitation stucco work, vanished and broke into a play of light and shade.

The creature floated beside Brender; and its Controller said: 'I see that you have been giving considerable thought to the problem, but this robot seems incapable of following abstract thoughts, so I have no means of knowing the course of your speculations. I see however that you seem to be satisfied.'

'I think I've got the answer,' said Brender, 'but first I wish to see the time lock. Let's climb.'

They rose into the sky, dipping over the lip of the building. Brender saw a vast flat expanse; and in the centre – He caught his breath!

The meagre light from the distant sun of Mars shone down on a structure located at what seemed the exact centre of the great door. The structure was about fifty feet high, and seemed nothing less than a series of quadrants coming together at the centre, which was a metal arrow pointing straight up.

The arrow head was not solid metal. Rather it was as if the metal had divided in two parts, then curved together again. But not quite together. About a foot separated the two sections of metal. But that foot was bridged by a vague, thin, green flame of ieis force.

'The time lock!' Brender nodded. 'I thought it would be something like that, though I expected it would be bigger, more substantial.'

'Do not be deceived by its fragile appearance,' answered the thing. 'Theoretically, the strength of ultimate metal is infinite; and the ieis force can only be affected by the universal I have mentioned. Exactly what the effect will be, it is impossible to say as it involves the temporary derangement of the whole number system upon which that particular area of space is built. But now tell us what to do.'

'Very well.' Brender eased himself onto a bank of sand, and cut off his antigravity plates. He lay on his back, and stared thoughtfully into the blue-black sky. For the time being all doubts, worries and fears were gone from him, forced out by sheer will power. He began to explain:

'The Martian mathematic, like that of Euclid and Pythagoras, was based on endless magnitude. Minus numbers were beyond their philosophy. On Earth, however, beginning with Descartes, an analytical mathematic was evolved. Magnitude and perceivable dimensions were replaced by that of variable relation-values between positions in space.

'For the Martians, there was only one number between 1 and 3. Actually, the totality of such numbers is an infinite aggregate. And with the introduction of the idea of the square root of minus one – or i – and the complex numbers, mathematics definitely ceased to be a simple thing of magnitude, perceivable in pictures. Only the intellectual step from the infinitely small quantity to the lower limit of every possible finite magnitude brought out the conception of a variable number which oscillated beneath any assignable number that was not zero.

'The prime number, being a conception of pure magnitude, had no reality in *real* mathematics, but in this case was rigidly bound up with the reality of the ieis force. The Martians knew ieis as a pale-green flow about a foot in length and developing say a thousand horsepower. (It was actually 12.171 inches and 1021.23 horsepower, but that was unimportant.) The power produced never varied, the length never varied, from year end to year end, for tens of thousands of years. The Martians took the length as their basis of measurement, and called it one "el"; they took the power as their basis of power and called it one "rb". And because of the absolute invariability of the flow they knew it was eternal.

'They knew furthermore that nothing could be eternal without being prime; their whole mathematic was based on numbers which could be factored, that is, disintegrated, destroyed, rendered less than they had been; and numbers which could not be factored, disintegrated or divided into smaller groups.

'Any number which could be factored was incapable of being infinite. Contrariwise, the infinite number must be prime.

'Therefore, they built a lock and integrated it along a line of ieis, to operate when the ieis ceased to flow – which would be at the end of Time, provided it was not interfered with. To prevent interference, they buried the motivating mechanism of the flow in ultimate metal, which could not be destroyed or corroded in any way. According to their mathematic, that settled it.'

'But you have the answer,' said the voice of the thing eagerly.

'Simply this: The Martians set a value on the flow of one "rb." If you interfere with that flow to no matter what small degree, you no longer have an "rb." You have something less. The flow, which is a universal, becomes automatically less than a universal, less than infinite. The prime number ceases to be prime. Let us suppose that you interfere with it to the extent of *infinity minus one*. You will then have a number divisible by two. As a matter of fact, the number, like most large numbers, will immediately break into thousands of pieces, i.e., it will be divisible by tens of thousands of smaller numbers. If the present time falls anywhere near one of those breaks, the door would open then. In other words, the door will open immediately if you can so interfere with the flow that one of the factors occurs in immediate time.'

'That is very clear,' said the Controller with satisfaction and the image of Brender was smiling triumphantly. 'We shall now use this robot to manufacture a universal; and Kalorn shall be free very shortly.' He laughed aloud. 'The poor robot is protesting violently at the thought of being destroyed, but after all it is only a machine, and not a very good one at that. Besides, it is interfering with my proper reception of your thoughts. Listen to it scream, as I twist it into shape.'

The cold-blooded words chilled Brender, pulled him from the heights of his abstract thought. Because of the prolonged intensity of his thinking, he saw with sharp clarity something that had escaped him before.

'Just a minute,' he said. 'How is it that the robot, introduced from your world, is living at the same time rate as I am, whereas Kalorn continues to live at your time rate?'

'A very good question.' The face of the robot was twisted into a triumphant sneer, as the Controller continued. 'Because, my dear Brender, you have been duped. It is true that Kalorn is living in our time rate, but that was due to a shortcoming in our machine. The machine which Kalorn built, while large enough to transport him, was not large enough in its adaptive mechanism to adapt him to each new space as he entered it. With the result that he was transported but not adapted. It was possible of course for us, his helpers, to transport such a small thing as the robot, though we have no more idea of the machine's construction

241

than you have.

'In short, we can use what there is of the machine, but the secret of its construction is locked in the insides of our own particular ultimate metal, and in the brain of Kalorn. Its invention by Kalorn was one of those accidents which, by the law of averages, will not be repeated in millions of our years. Now that you have provided us with the method of bringing Kalorn back, we shall be able to build innumerable interspace machines. Our purpose is to control all spaces, all worlds – particularly those which are inhabited. We intend to be absolute rulers of the entire Universe.'

The ironic voice ended; and Brender lay in his prone position the prey of horror. The horror was twofold, partly due to the Controller's monstrous plan, and partly due to the thought that was pulsing in his brain. He groaned, as he realized that warning thought must be ticking away on the automatic receiving brain of the robot. 'Wait,' his thought was saying, 'That adds a new factor. Time –'

There was a scream from the creature as it was forcibly dissolved. The scream choked to a sob, then silence. An intricate machine of shining metal lay there on that great grey-brown expanse of sand and ultimate metal.

The metal glowed; and then the machine was floating in the air. It rose to the top of the arrow, and settled over the green flame of ieis.

Brender jerked on his antigravity screen, and leaped to his feet. The violent action carried him some hundred feet into the air. His rockets sputtered into staccato fire, and he clamped his teeth against the pain of acceleration.

Below him, the great door began to turn, to unscrew, faster and faster, till it was like a flywheel. Sand flew in all directions in a miniature storm.

At top acceleration, Brender darted to one side.

Just in time. First, the robot machine was flung off that tremendous wheel by sheer centrifugal power. Then the door came off, and, spinning now at an incredible rate, hurtled straight into the air, and vanished into space.

A puff of black dust came floating up out of the blackness of the vault. Suppressing his horror, yet perspiring from awful relief, he rocketed to where the robot had fallen into the sand.

Instead of glistening metal, a time-dulled piece of junk lay there. The dull metal flowed sluggishly and assumed a quasi-human shape. The flesh remained grey and in little rolls as if it were ready to fall apart from old age. The thing tried to stand up on wrinkled, horrible legs, but finally lay still. Its lips moved, mumbled:

'I caught your warning thought, but I didn't let them know. Now, Kalorn is dead. They realized the truth as it was happening. End of Time came –'

It faltered into silence; and Brender went on: 'Yes, end of Time came when the flow became momentarily less than eternal – came at the factor point which occurred a few minutes ago.'

'I was ... only partly ... within its ... influence, Kalorn all the way. ... Even if they're lucky ... will be years before ... they invent another machine ... and one of their years is billions ... of yours. ... I didn't tell them. ... I caught your thought ... and kept it ... from them –'

'But why did you do it? Why?'

'Because they were hurting me. They were going to destroy me. Because ... I liked ... being human. I was ... somebody!'

The flesh dissolved. It flowed slowly into a pool of lavalike grey. The lava crinkled, split into dry, brittle pieces. Brender touched one of the pieces. It crumbled into a fine powder of grey dust. He gazed out across that grim, deserted valley of sand, and said aloud, pityingly:

'Poor Frankenstein.'

He turned towards the distant spaceship, towards the swift trip to Earth. As he climbed out of the ship a few minutes later, one of the first persons he saw was Pamela.

She flew into his arms. 'Oh, Jim, Jim,' she sobbed. 'What a fool I've been. When I heard what had happened, and realized you were in danger, I – Oh, Jim!'

Later, he would tell her about their new fortune.

Eurema's Dam

R.A. LAFFERTY

HE WAS ABOUT THE LAST of them.

What? The last of the great individualists? The last of the true creative geniuses of the century? The last of the sheer precursors?

No. No. He was the last of the dolts.

Kids were being born smarter all the time when he came along, and they would be so forevermore. He was about the last dumb kid ever born.

Even his mother had to admit that Albert was a slow child. What else can you call a boy who doesn't begin to talk till he is four years old, who won't learn to handle a spoon till he is six, who can't operate a doorknob till he is eight? What else can you say about one who put his shoes on the wrong feet and walked in pain? And who had to be told to close his mouth after yawning?

Some things would always be beyond him – like whether it was the big hand or the little hand of the clock that told the hours. But this wasn't something serious. He never did care what time it was.

When, about the middle of his ninth year, Albert made a breakthrough at telling his right hand from his left he did it by the most ridiculous set of mnemonics ever put together. It had to do with the way dogs turn around before lying down, the direction of whirlpools and whirlwinds, the side a cow is milked from and a horse is mounted from, the direction of twist of oak and sycamore leaves, the maze patterns of rock moss and tree moss, the cleavage of limestone, the direction of a hawk's wheeling, a shrike's hunting, and a snake's coiling (remembering that the Mountain Boomer is an exception), the lay of cedar fronds and balsam fronds, the twist of a hole dug by a skunk and by a badger (remembering pungently that skunks sometimes use old badger holes). Well, Albert finally learned to remember which was right and which was left, but an observant boy would have learned his right hand from his left without all that nonsense.

Albert never learned to write a readable hand. To get by in school he cheated. From a bicycle speedometer, a midget motor, tiny eccentric cams, and batteries stolen from his grandfather's hearing aid Albert made a machine to write for him. It was small as a doodlebug and fitted onto pen or pencil so that Albert could conceal it with his fingers. It

244

formed the letters beautifully as Albert had set the cams to follow a copybook model. He triggered the different letters with keys no bigger than whiskers. Sure it was crooked, but what else can you do when you're too dumb to learn how to write passably?

Albert couldn't figure at all. He had to make another machine to figure for him. It was a palm-of-the-hand thing that would add and subtract and multiply and divide. The next year when he was in the ninth grade they gave him algebra, and he had to devise a flipper to go on the end of his gadget to work quadratic and simultaneous equations. If it weren't for such cheating Albert wouldn't have gotten any marks at all in school.

He had another difficulty when he came to his fifteenth year. People, that is an understatement. There should be a stronger word than 'difficulty' for it. He was afraid of girls.

What to do?

'I will build me a machine that is not afraid of girls,' Albert said. He set to work on it. He had it nearly finished when a thought came to him: 'But *no* machine is afraid of girls. How will this help me?'

His logic was at fault and analogy broke down. He did what he always did. He cheated.

He took the programming rollers from an old player piano in the attic, found a gear case that would serve, used magnetized sheets instead of perforated music rolls, fed a copy of Wormwood's *Logic* into the matrix, and he had a logic machine that would answer questions.

'What's the matter with me that I'm afraid of girls?' Albert asked his logic machine.

'Nothing the matter with you,' the logic machine told him. 'It's logical to be afraid of girls. They seem pretty spooky to me too.'

'But what can I do about it?'

'Wait for time and circumstance. They sure are slow. Unless you want to cheat – '

'Yes, yes, what then?'

'Build a machine that looks just like you, Albert, and talks just like you. Only make it smarter than you are, and not bashful. And, ah, Albert, there's a special thing you'd better put into it in case things go wrong. I'll whisper it to you. It's dangerous.'

So Albert made Little Danny, a dummy who looked like him and talked like him, only he was smarter and not bashful. He filled Little Danny with quips from *Mad* magazine and from *Quip*, and then they were set.

Albert and Little Danny went to call on Alice.

'Why, he's wonderful!' Alice said. 'Why can't you be like that, Albert? Aren't you wonderful, Little Danny? Why do you have to be so stupid, Albert, when Little Danny is so wonderful?'

245

'I, uh, uh, I don't know,' Albert said, 'uh, uh, uh.'

'He sounds like a fish with the hiccups,' Little Danny said.

'You do, Albert, really you do!' Alice screamed. 'Why can't you say smart things like Little Danny does, Albert? Why are you so stupid?'

This wasn't working out very well, but Albert kept with it. He programmed Little Danny to play the ukulele and to sing. He wished that he could programme himself to do it. Alice loved everything about Little Danny, but she paid no attention to Albert. And one day Albert had had enough.

'Wha- wha- what do we need with this dummy?' Albert asked. 'I just made him to am- to amu- to make you laugh. Let's go off and leave him.'

'Go off with you, Albert?' Alice asked. 'But you're so stupid. I tell you what. Let's you and me go off and leave Albert, Little Danny. We can have more fun without him.'

'Who needs him?' Little Danny asked. 'Get lost, Buster.'

Albert walked away from them. He was glad that he'd taken his logic machine's advice as to the special thing to be built into Little Danny. He walked fifty steps. A hundred. 'Far enough,' Albert said, and he pushed a button in his pocket.

Nobody but Albert and his logic machine ever did know what that explosion was. Tiny wheels out of Little Danny and small pieces of Alice rained down a little later, but there weren't enough fragments for anyone to identify.

Albert had learned one lesson from his logic machine: never make anything that you can't unmake.

Well, Albert finally grew to be a man, in years at least. He would always have something about him of a very awkward teenager. And yet he fought his own war against those who were teenagers in years, and defeated them completely. There was enmity between them forever. He hadn't been a very well-adjusted adolescent, and he hated the memory of it. And nobody ever mistook him for an adjusted man.

Albert was too awkward to earn a living at an honest trade. He was reduced to peddling his little tricks and contrivances to shysters and promoters. But he did back into a sort of fame, and he did become burdened with wealth.

He was too stupid to handle his own monetary affairs, but he built an actuary machine to do his investing and became rich by accident; he built the damned thing too good and he regretted it.

Albert became one of that furtive group that has saddled us with all the things in our history. There was that Punic who couldn't learn the rich variety of hieroglyphic characters and who devised the crippled short alphabet for wan-wits. There was the nameless Arab who couldn't count beyond ten and who set up the ten-number system for babies and idiots. There was the double-Dutchman with his movable type who drove fine copy out of the world. Albert was of their miserable company.

Albert himself wasn't much good at anything. But he had in himself a low knack for making machines that were good at everything.

His machines did a few things. You remember that anciently there was smog in the cities. Oh, it could be drawn out of the air easily enough. All it took was a tickler. Albert made a tickler machine. He would set it fresh every morning. It would clear the air in a circle three hundred yards around his hovel and gather a little over a ton of residue every twenty-four hours. This residue was rich in large polysyllabic molecules which one of his chemical machines could use.

'Why can't you clear all the air?' the people asked him.

'This is as much of the stuff as Clarence Deoxyribonucleiconibus needs every day,' Albert said. That was the name of this particular chemical machine.

'But we die from the smog,' the people told him. 'Have mercy on us.'

'Oh, all right,' Albert said. He turned it over to one of his reduplicating machines to make as many copies as were necessary.

You remember that once there was a teen-ager problem? You remember when those little buggers used to be mean? Albert got enough of them. There was something ungainly about them that reminded him too much of himself. He made a teen-ager of his own. It was rough. To the others it looked like one of themselves, the ring in the left ear, the dangling side-locks, the brass knucks and the long knife, the guitar pluck to jab in the eye. But it was incomparably rougher than the human teen-agers. It terrorized all in the neighbourhood and made them behave, and dress like real people. There was one thing about the teen-age machine that Albert made. It was made of such polarized metal and glass that it was invisible except to teen-ager eyes.

'Why is your neighbourhood different?' the people asked him. 'Why are there such good and polite teen-agers in your neighbourhood and such mean ones everywhere else? It's as though something had spooked all those right around here.'

'Oh, I thought I was the only one who didn't like the regular kind,' Albert said.

'Oh no, no,' the people said. 'If there is anything at all you can do about it – '

So Albert turned his mostly invisible teen-ager machine over to one of his reduplicating machines to make as many copies as were necessary, and set up one in every neighbourhood. From that day to this the teen-agers have all been good and polite and a little bit frightened. But there is no evidence of what keeps them that way except an occasional eye

247

dangling from the jab of an invisible guitar pluck.

So the two most pressing problems of the latter part of the twentieth century were solved, but accidentally and to the credit of no one.

As the years went by, Albert felt his inferiority most when in the presence of his own machines, particularly those in the form of men. Albert just hadn't their urbanity or sparkle or wit. He was a clod beside them, and they made him feel it.

Why not? One of Albert's devices sat in the President's Cabinet. One of them was on the High Council of World-Watchers that kept the peace everywhere. One of them presided at Riches Unlimited, that private-public-international instrument that guaranteed reasonable riches to everyone in the world. One of them was the guiding hand in the Health and Longevity Foundation that provided those things to everyone. Why should not such splendid and successful machines look down on their shabby uncle who had made them?

'I'm rich by a curious twist,' Albert said to himself one day, 'and honoured through a mistake of circumstance. But there isn't a man or a machine in the world who is really my friend. A book here tells how to make friends, but I can't do it that way. I'll make one my own way.'

So Albert set out to make a friend.

He made Poor Charles, a machine as stupid and awkward and inept as himself. 'Now I will have a companion,' Albert said, but it didn't work. Add two zeroes together and you still have zero. Poor Charles was too much like Albert to be good for anything.

Poor Charles! Unable to think, he made a – (*but wait a mole-skin-gloved minute here, Colonel, this isn't going to work at all*) – he made a machi – (*but isn't this the same blamed thing all over again?*) – he made a machine to think for him and to –

Hold it, hold it! That's enough. Poor Charles was the only machine that Albert ever made that was dumb enough to do a thing like that.

Well, whatever it was, the machine that Poor Charles made was in control of the situation and of Poor Charles when Albert came onto them accidentally. The machine's machine, the device that Poor Charles had constructed to think for him, was lecturing Poor Charles in a humiliating way.

'Only the inept and the deficient will invent,' that damned machine's machine was droning. 'The Greeks in their high period did not invent. They used neither adjunct power nor instrumentation. They used, as intelligent men or machines will always use, slaves. They did not descend to gadgets. They, who did the difficult with ease, did not seek the easier way.

'But the incompetent will invent. The insufficient will invent. The depraved will invent. And knaves will invent.'

Albert, in a seldom fit of anger, killed them both. But he knew that the machine of his machine had spoken the truth.

Albert was very much cast down. A more intelligent man would have had a hunch as to what was wrong. Albert had only a hunch that he was not very good at hunches and would never be. Seeing no way out, he fabricated a machine and named it Hunchy.

In most ways this was the worst machine he ever made. In building it he tried to express something of his unease for the future. It was an awkward thing in mind and mechanism, a misfit.

His more intelligent machines gathered around and hooted at him while he put it together.

'Boy! Are you lost!' they taunted. 'That thing is a primitive! To draw its power from the ambient! We talked you into throwing that away twenty years ago and setting up coded power for all of us.'

'Uh – someday there may be social disturbances and all centres of power and apparatuses seized,' Albert stammered. 'But Hunchy would be able to operate if the whole world were wiped smooth.'

'It isn't even tuned to our information matrix,' they jibed. 'It's worse than Poor Charles. The stupid thing practically starts from scratch.'

'Maybe there'll be a new kind of itch for it,' said Albert.

'It's not even housebroken!' the urbane machines shouted their indignation. 'Look at that! Some sort of primitive lubrication all over the floor.'

'Remembering my childhood, I sympathize,' Albert said.

'What's it good for?' they demanded.

'Ah – it gets hunches,' Albert mumbled.

'Duplication!' they shouted. 'That's all you're good for yourself, and not very good at that. We suggest an election to replace you as – pardon our laughter – head of these enterprises.'

'Boss, I got a hunch how we can block them there,' the unfinished Hunchy whispered.

'They're bluffing,' Albert whispered back. 'My first logic machine taught me never to make anything I can't unmake. I've got them there, and they know it. I wish I could think up things like that myself.'

'Maybe there will come an awkward time and I will be good for something,' Hunchy said.

Only once, and that rather late in life, did a sort of honesty flare up in Albert. He did one thing (and it was a dismal failure) on his own. That was the night in the year of the double millennium when Albert was presented with the Finnerty-Hochmann Trophy, the highest award that the intellectual world could give. Albert was certainly an odd choice for it, but it had been noticed that almost every basic invention for thirty years could be traced back to him or to the devices with which he had surrounded himself.

You know the trophy. Atop it was Eurema, the synthetic Greek goddess of invention, with arms spread as though she would take flight. Below this was a stylized brain cut away to show the convoluted cortex. And below this was the coat of arms of the Academicians: Ancient Scholar rampant (argent); the Anderson Analyzer sinister (gules); the Mondeman Space-Drive dexter (vair). It was a very fine work by Groben, his ninth period.

Albert had the speech composed for him by his speech-writing machine, but for some reason he did not use it. He went on his own, and that was disaster. He got to his feet when he was introduced, and he stuttered and spoke nonsense:

'Ah – only the sick oyster produces nacre,' he said, and they all gaped at him. What sort of beginning for a speech was that? 'Or do I have the wrong creature?' Albert asked weakly.

'Eurema does not look like that!' Albert gawked out and pointed suddenly at the trophy. 'No, no, that isn't her at all. Eurema walks backward and is blind. And her mother is a brainless hulk.'

Everybody was watching him with pained expression.

'Nothing rises without a leaven,' Albert tried to explain, 'but the yeast is itself a fungus and a disease. You be regularizers all, splendid and supreme. But you cannot live without the irregulars. You will die, and who will tell you that you are dead? When there are no longer any deprived or insufficient, *who will invent?* What will you do when there are none of us defectives left? Who will leaven your lump then?'

'Are you unwell?' the master of ceremonies asked him quietly. 'Should you not make an end of it? People will understand.'

'Of course I'm unwell. Always have been,' Albert said. 'What good would I be otherwise? You set the ideal that all should be healthy and well adjusted. No! No! Were we all well adjusted, we would ossify and die. The world is kept healthy only by some of the unhealthy minds lurking in it. The first implement made by man was not a scraper or celt or stone knife. It was a crutch, and it wasn't devised by a hale man.'

'Perhaps you should rest,' a functionary said in a low voice, for this sort of rambling nonsense talk had never been heard at an awards dinner before.

'Know you,' said Albert, 'that it is not the fine bulls and wonderful cattle who make the new paths. Only a crippled calf makes a new path. In everything that survives there must be an element of the incongruous. Hey, you know the woman who said, "My husband is incongruous, but I never liked Washington in the summertime."'

Everybody gazed at him in stupor.

'That's the first joke I ever made,' Albert said lamely. 'My joke-making machine makes them lots better than I do.' He paused and gaped, and gulped a big breath. 'Dolts!' he croaked out fiercely then. 'What will you do for dolts when the last of us is gone? How will you survive without us?'

Albert had finished. He gaped and forgot to close his mouth. They led him back to his seat. His publicity machine explained that Albert was tired from overwork, and then the thing passed around copies of the speech that Albert was supposed to have given.

It had been an unfortunate episode. How noisome it is that the innovators are never great men. And the great men are never good for anything but just being great men.

In that year a decree went forth from Caesar that a census of the whole country should be taken. The decree was from Cesare Panebianco, the President of the country; it was the decimal year proper for the census, and there was nothing unusual about the decree. Certain provisions, however, were made for taking a census of the drifters and decrepits who were usually missed, to examine them and to see why they were so. It was in the course of this that Albert was picked up. If any man ever looked like a drifter and a decrepit, it was Albert.

Albert was herded in with other derelicts, sat down at a table, and asked tortuous questions. As:

'What is your name?'

He almost muffed that one, but he rallied and answered, 'Albert.'

'What time is it by that clock?'

They had him there in his old weak spot. Which hand was which? He gaped and didn't answer.

'Can you read?'

'Not without my – ' Albert began. 'I don't have with me my – No, I can't read very well by myself.'

'Try.'

They gave him a paper to mark up with true and false questions. Albert marked them all true, believing that he would have half of them right. But they were all false. The regularized people are partial to falsehood. Then they gave him a supply-the-word test on proverbs.

'– – is the best policy' didn't mean a thing to him. He couldn't remember the names of the companies that he had his own policies with.

'A – – in time saves nine' contained more mathematics than Albert could handle. 'There appear to be six unknowns,' he told himself, 'and only one positive value, nine. The equation verb "saves" is a vague one. I cannot solve this equation. I am not even sure that it is an equation. If only I had with me my – '

But he hadn't any of his gadgets or machines with him. He was on his own. He left half a dozen more proverb fill-ins blank. Then he saw the chance to recoup. Nobody is so dumb as not to know one answer if

251

enough questions are asked.

'– – is the mother of invention,' it said.

'Stupidity,' Albert wrote in his weird ragged hand. Then he sat back in triumph. 'I know that Eurema and her mother,' he snickered. 'Man, how I do know them!'

But they marked him wrong on that one too. He had missed every answer to every test. They began to fix him a ticket to a progressive booby hatch where he might learn to do something with his hands, his head being hopeless.

A couple of Albert's urbane machines came down and got him out of it. They explained that, while he was a drifter and derelict, yet he was a rich drifter and derelict and that he was even a man of some note.

'He doesn't look it, but he really is – pardon our laughter – a man of some importance,' one of the fine machines explained. 'He has to be told to close his mouth after he has yawned, but for all that he is the winner of the Finnerty-Hochmann Award. We will be responsible for him.'

Albert was miserable as his fine machines took him out, especially when they asked that he walk three or four steps behind them and not seem to be with them. They gave him some pretty rough banter and turned him into a squirming worm of a man. Albert left them and went to a little hide-out he kept.

'I'll blow my crawfishing brains out,' he swore. 'The humiliation is more than I can bear. Can't do it myself, though. I'll have to have it done.'

He set to work building a device in his hide-out.

'What you doing, boss?' Hunchy asked him. 'I had a hunch you'd come here and start building something.'

'Building a machine to blow my pumpkin-picking brains out,' Albert shouted. 'I'm too yellow to do it myself.'

'Boss, I got a hunch there's something better to do. Let's have some fun.'

'Don't believe I know how to,' Albert said thoughtfully. 'I built a fun machine once to do it for me. He had a real revel till he flew apart, but he never seemed to do anything for me.'

'This fun will be for you and me. Consider the world spread out. What is it?'

'It's a world too fine for me to live in any longer,' Albert said. 'Everything and all the people are perfect, and all alike. They're at the top of the heap. They've won it all and arranged it all neatly. There's no place for a clutter-up like me in the world. So I get out.'

'Boss, I've got a hunch that you're seeing it wrong. You've got better eyes than that. Look again, real canny, at it. Now what do you see?'

'Hunchy, Hunchy, it that possible? Is that really what it is? I wonder why I never noticed it before. That's the way of it, though, now that I look closer.

'Six billion patsies waiting to be took! Six billion patsies without a defence of any kind! A couple of guys out for some fun, man, they could mow them down like fields of Albert-Improved Concho Wheat!'

'Boss, I've got a hunch this is what I was made for. The world sure has been getting stuffy. Let's tie into it and eat off the top layer. Man, we can cut a swath!'

'We'll inaugurate a new era!' Albert gloated. 'We'll call it the Turning of the Worm. We'll have fun, Hunchy. We'll gobble them up like goobers. How come I never saw it like that before? Six billion patsies!'

The twenty-first century began on this rather odd note.

Ghetto

POUL ANDERSON

THE MONORAIL SET THEM off at Kith Town, on the edge of the great city. Its blaze of light, red and gold and green looped between high slim towers, pulsed in the sky above them, but here it was dark and still, night had come. Kenri Shaun stood for a moment with the others, shifting awkwardly on his feet and wondering what to say. They knew he was going to resign, but the Kithman's rule of privacy kept the words from their lips.

'Well,' he said at last, 'I'll be seeing you around.'

'Oh, sure,' said Graf Kishna. 'We won't be leaving Earth again for months yet.'

After a pause, he added: 'We'll miss you when we do go. I – wish you'd change your mind, Kenri.'

'No,' said Kenri. 'I'm staying. But thanks.'

'Come see us,' invited Graf. 'We'll have to get a bunch together for a poker game sometime soon.'

'Sure. Sure I will.'

Graf's hand brushed Kenri's shoulder, one of the Kith gestures which said more than speech ever could. 'Goodnight,' he spoke aloud.

'Goodnight.'

Words murmured in the dimness. They stood there for an instant longer, half a dozen men in the loose blue doublets, baggy trousers, and soft shoes of the Kith in Town. There was a curious similarity about them, they were all of small and slender build, dark-complexioned, but it was the style of movement and the expression of face which stamped them most. They had looked on strangeness all their lives, out between the stars.

Then the group dissolved and each went his own way. Kenri started towards his father's place. There was a thin chill in the air, the northern pole was spinning into autumn, and Kenri hunched his shoulders and jammed his hands into his pockets.

The streets of the Town were narrow concrete strips, non-luminous, lit by old-style radiant globes. These threw a vague whiteness on lawns and trees and the little half-underground houses set far back from the roads. There weren't many people abroad: an elderly officer, grave in mantle

254

and hood; a young couple walking slowly, hand in hand; a group of children tumbling on the grass; small lithe forms filling the air with their laughter, filling themselves with the beauty and mystery which were Earth. They might have been born a hundred years ago, some of those children, and looked on worlds whose very suns were invisible here, but always the planet drew men home again. They might cross the Galaxy someday, but always they would return to murmurous forests and galloping seas, rain and wind and swift-footed clouds, through all space and time they would come back to their mother.

Most of the hemispheres Kenri passed were dark, tended only by machines while their families flitted somewhere beyond the sky. He passed the home of a friend, Jong Errifrans, and wondered when he would see him again. The *Golden Flyer* wasn't due in from Betelgeuse for another Earth century, and by then the *Fleetwing*, Kenri's own ship, might well be gone – *No, wait, I'm staying here. I'll be a very old man when Jong comes back, still young and merry, still with a guitar across his shoulders and laughter on his lips. I'll be an Earthling then.*

The town held only a few thousand houses, and most of its inhabitants were away at any given time. Only the *Fleetwing*, the *Flying Cloud*, the *High Barbaree*, the *Our Lady*, and the *Princess Karen* were at Sol now: their crews would add up to about 1200, counting the children. He whispered the lovely, archaic names, savouring them on his tongue. Kith Town, like Kith society, was changeless; it had to be. When you travelled near the speed of light and time shrank so that you could be gone a decade and come back to find a century flown on Earth – And here was home, where you were among your own kind and not a tommy who had to bow and wheedle the great merchants of Sol, here you could walk like a man. It wasn't true what they said on Earth, that tommies were rootless, without planet or history or loyalty. There was a deeper belongingness here than the feverish rise and warring and fall of Sol could ever know.

'– Good evening, Kenri Shaun.'

He stopped, jerked out of his reverie, and looked at the young woman. The pale light of a street globe spilled across her long dark hair and down her slim shape. 'Oh – ' He caught himself and bowed. 'Good evening to you, Theye Barinn. I haven't seen you in a long time, Two years, isn't it?'

'Not quite so long for me,' she said. 'The *High Barbaree* went clear to Vega last trip. We've been in orbit here about an Earth-month. The *Fleetwing* got in a couple of weeks ago, didn't she?'

Covering up, not daring to speak plainly. He knew she knew almost to the hour when the great spaceship had arrived from Sirius and taken her orbit about the home planet.

'Yes,' he said, 'but our astrogation computer was burned out and I had to stay aboard with some others and get it fixed.'

'I know,' she answered. 'I asked your parents why you weren't in

255

Town. Weren't you – impatient?'

'Yes,' he said, and a thinness edged his tone. He didn't speak of the fever that had burned in him, to get away, get downside, and go to Dorthy where she waited for him among the roses of Earth. 'Yes, of course, but the ship came first, and I was the best man for the job. My father sold my share of the cargo for me; I never liked business anyway.'

Small talk, he thought, biting back the words, chatter eating away the time he could be with Dorthy. But he couldn't quite break away, Theye was a friend. Once he had thought she might be more, but that was before he knew Dorthy.

'Things haven't changed much since we left,' she said. 'Not in twenty-five Earth-years. The Star Empire is still here, with its language and its genetic hierarchy – a little bigger, a little more hectic, a little closer to revolt or invasion and the end. I remember the Africans were much like this, a generation or two before they fell.'

'So they were,' said Kenri. 'So were others. So will still others be. But I've heard the Stars are clamping down on us.'

'Yes.' Her voice was a whisper. 'We have to buy badges now, at an outrageous price, and wear them everywhere outside the Town. It may get worse. I think it will.'

He saw that her mouth trembled a little under the strong curve of her nose, and the eyes turned up to his were suddenly filmed with a brightness of tears. 'Kenri – is it true what they're saying about you?'

'Is what true?' Despite himself, he snapped it out.

'That you're going to resign? Quit the Kith – become an ... Earthling?'

'I'll talk about it later.' It was a harshness in his throat. 'I haven't time now.'

'But Kenri –' She drew a long breath and pulled her hand back.

'Goodnight, Theye. I'll see you later. I have to hurry.'

He bowed and went on, quickly, not looking back. The lights and the shadows slid their bars across him as he walked.

Dorthy was waiting, and he would see her tonight. But just then he couldn't feel happy about it, somehow.

He felt like hell.

She had stood at the vision port, looking out into a dark that crawled with otherness, and the white light of the ship's walls had been cool in her hair. He came softly behind her and thought again what a wonder she was. Even a millennium ago, such tall slender blondes had been rare on Earth. If the human breeders of the Star Empire had done nothing else, they should be remembered with love for having created her kind.

She turned around quickly, sensing him with a keenness of perception he could not match. The silver-blue eyes were enormous on him, and her lips parted a little, half covered by one slim hand. He thought what a beautiful thing a woman's hand was.

'You startled me, Kenri Shaun.'

'I am sorry, Freelady,' he said contritely.

'It – ' She smiled with a hint of shakiness. 'It is nothing. I am too nervous – don't know interstellar space at all.'

'It can be ... unsettling, I suppose, if you aren't used to it, Freelady,' he said. 'I was born between the stars, myself.'

She shivered faintly under the thin blue tunic. 'It is too big,' she said. 'Too big and old and strange for us, Kenri Shaun. I thought travelling between the planets was something beyond human understanding, but this – ' Her hand touched his, and his fingers closed on it, almost against his own will. 'This is like nothing I ever imagined.'

'When you travel nearly at the speed of light,' he said, covering his shyness with pedantry, 'you can't expect conditions to be the same. Aberration displaces the stars, and Doppler effect changes the colour. That's all, Freelady.'

The ship hummed around them, as if talking to herself. Dorthy had once wondered what the vessel's robot brain thought – what it felt like to be a spaceship, forever a wanderer between foreign skies. He had told her the robot lacked consciousness, but the idea had haunted him since. Maybe only because it was Dorthy's idea.

'It's the time shrinking that frightens me most, perhaps,' she said. Her hand remained in his, the fingers tightening. He sensed the faint wild perfume she wore, it was a heady draught in his nostrils. 'You – I can't get over the fact that you were born a thousand years ago, Kenri Shaun. That you will still be travelling between the stars when I am down in dust.'

It was an obvious opening for a compliment, but his tongue was locked with awkwardness. He was a spacefarer, a Kith-man, a dirty slimy tommy, and she was Star-Free, unspecialized, genius, the finest flower of the Empire's genetic hierarchy. He said only: 'It is no paradox, Freelady. As the relative velocity approaches that of light, the measured time interval decreases, just as the mass increases; but only to a "stationary" observer. One set of measurements is as "real" as another. We're running with a tau factor of about 33 this trip, which means that it takes us some four months to go from Sirius to Sol; but to a watcher at either star, we'll take almost eleven years.' His mouth felt stiff, but he twisted it into a smile. 'That's not so long, Freelady. You'll have been gone, let's see, twice eleven plus a year in the Sirian System – twenty-four years. Your estates will still be there.'

'Doesn't it take an awful reaction mass?' she asked. A fine line appeared on the broad forehead as she frowned, trying to understand.

'No, Freelady. Or, rather, it does, but we don't have to expel matter as an interplanetary ship must. The field drive reacts directly against the mass of local stars – theoretically the entire universe – and converts our mercury "ballast" into kinetic energy for the rest of the ship. It acts equally on all mass, so we don't experience acceleration pressure and can approach light-speed in a few days. In fact, if we didn't rotate the ship, we'd be weightless. When we reach Sol, the agoratron will convert the energy back into mercury atoms and we'll again be stationary with respect to Earth.'

257

'I'm afraid I never was much good at physics,' she laughed. 'We leave that to Star-A and Norm-A types on Earth.'

The sense of rejection was strangling in him. Yes, he thought, brain work and muscle work are still just work. Let the inferiors sweat over it, Star-Frees need all their time just to be ornamental. *Her fingers had relaxed, and he drew his hand back to him.*

She looked pained, sensing his hurt, and reached impulsively out to touch his cheek. 'I'm sorry,' she said quietly. 'I didn't mean to ... I didn't mean what you think.'

'It is nothing, Freelady,' he said stiffly, to cover his bewilderment. That an aristocrat should apologize – !

'But it is much,' she said earnestly. 'I know how many people there are who don't like the Kith. You just don't fit into our society, you realize that. You've never really belonged on Earth.' A slow flush crept up her pale cheeks, and she looked down. Her lashes were long and smoky black. 'But I do know a little about people, Kenri Shaun. I know a superior type when I meet it. You could be a Star-Free yourself, except ... we might bore you.'

'Never that, Freelady,' he said thickly.

He had gone away from her with a singing in him. Three months, he thought gloriously, three ship-months yet before they came to Sol.

A hedge rustled dryly as he turned in at the Shaun gate. Overhead, a maple tree stirred, talking to the light wind, and fluttered a blood-coloured leaf down on him. *Early frost this year,* he thought. The weather-control system had never been rebuilt after the Mechanoclasts abolished it, and maybe they had been right there. He paused to inhale the smell of the wind. It was cool and damp, full of odours from mould and turned earth and ripened berries. It struck him suddenly that he had never been here during a winter. He had never seen the hills turn white and glittering, or known the immense hush of snow-fall.

Warm yellow light spilled out to make circles on the lawn. He put his hand on the doorplate, it scanned his pattern and the door opened for him. When he walked into the small, cluttered living room, crowded with half a dozen kids, he caught the lingering whiff of dinner and regretted being too late for it. He'd eaten on shipboard, but there was no cook in the Galaxy quite like his mother.

He saluted his parents as custom prescribed, and his father nodded gravely. His mother was less restrained, she hugged him and said how thin he had gotten. The kids said hello and went back to their books and games and chatter. They'd seen their older brother often enough, and were too young to realize what his decision of resignation meant.

'Come, Kenri, I will fix a sandwich for you at least – ' said his mother. 'It is good to have you back.'

'I haven't time,' he said. Helplessly: 'I'd like to, but – well – I have to go out again.'

She turned away. 'Theye Barinn was asking about you,' she said, elaborately casual. The *High Barbaree* got back an Earth-month ago.'

'Oh, yes,' he said. 'I met her on the street.'

'Theye is a nice girl,' said his mother. 'You ought to go call on her. It's not too late tonight.'

'Some other time,' he said.

'The *High Barbaree* is off to Tau Ceti in another two months,' said his mother. 'You won't have much chance to see Theye, unless – ' Her voice trailed off. *Unless you marry her. She's your sort, Kerri. She would belong well on the* Fleetwing. *She would give me strong grandchildren.*

'Some other time,' he repeated. He regretted the brusqueness in his tone, but he couldn't help it. Turning to his father: 'Dad, what's this about a new tax on us?'

Volden Shaun scowled. 'A damned imposition,' he said. 'May all their spacesuits spring leaks. We have to wear these badges now, and pay through the nose for them.'

'Can . . . can I borrow yours for tonight? I have to go into the city.'

Slowly, Volden met the eyes of his son. Then he sighed and got up. 'It's in my study,' he said. 'Come along and help me find it.'

They entered the little room together. It was filled with Volden's books – he read on every imaginable subject, like most Kithmen – and his carefully polished astrogation instruments and his mementos of other voyages. It all meant something. That intricately chased sword had been given him by an armourer on Procyon V, a many-armed monster who had been his friend. That stereograph was a view of the sharp hills on Isis, frozen gases like molten amber in the glow of mighty Osiris. That set of antlers was from a hunting trip on Loki, in the days of his youth. That light, leaping statuette had been a god on Dagon. Volden's close-cropped grey head bent over the desk, his hands fumbling among the papers.

'Do you really mean to go through with this resignation?' he asked quietly.

Kenri's face grew warm. 'Yes,' he said. 'I'm sorry, but – Yes.'

'I've seen others do it,' said Volden. 'They even prospered, most of them. But I don't think they were ever very happy.'

'I wonder,' said Kenri.

'The *Fleetwing*'s next trip will probably be clear to Rigel,' said Volden. 'We won't be back for more than a thousand years. There won't be any Star Empire here. Your very name will be forgotten.'

'I heard talk about that voyage.' Kenri's voice thickened a little. 'It's one reason I'm staying behind.'

Volden looked up, challengingly. 'What's so good about the Stars?' he asked. 'I've seen twelve hundred years of human history, good times and bad times. This is not one of the good times. And it's going to get worse.'

Kenri didn't answer.

259

'That girl is out of your class, son,' said Volden. 'She's a Star-Free. You're just a damn filthy tommy.'

'The prejudice against us isn't racial,' said Kenri, avoiding his father's gaze. 'It's cultural. A spaceman who goes terrestrial is ... all right by them.'

'So far,' said Volden. 'It's beginning to get racial already, though. We may all have to abandon Earth for a while.'

'I'll get into her class,' said Kenri. 'Give me that badge.'

Volden sighed. 'We'll have to overhaul the ship to raise our tau factor,' he said. 'You've got a good six months yet. We won't leave any sooner. I hope you'll change your mind.'

'I might,' said Kenri, and knew he lied in his teeth.

'Here it is.' Volden held out a small yellow loop of braided cords. 'Pin it on your jacket.' He took forth a heavy wallet. 'And here is a thousand decards of your money. You've got fifty thousand more in the bank, but don't let this get stolen.'

Kenri fastened the symbol on. It seemed to have weight, like a stone around his neck. He was saved from deeper humiliation by the automatic reaction of his mind. Fifty thousand decards ... what to buy? A spaceman necessarily invested in tangible and lasting property –

Then he remembered that he would be staying here. The money ought to have value during his lifetime, at least. And money had a way of greasing the skids of prejudice.

'I'll be back ... tomorrow, maybe,' he said. 'Thanks, Dad. Goodnight.'

Volden's gaunt face drew into tighter lines. His voice was toneless, but it caught just a little.

'Goodnight, son,' he said.

Kenri went out the door, into the darkness of Earth.

The first time, neither of them had been much impressed. Captain Seralpin had told Kenri: 'We've got us another passenger. She's over at Landfall, on Ishtar. Want to pick her up?'

'Let her stay there till we're ready to leave,' said Kenri. 'Why would she want to spend a month on Marduk?'

Seralpin shrugged: 'I don't know or care. But she'll pay for conveyance here. Take Boat Five,' he said.

Kenri had fuelled up the little interplanetary flitter and shot away from the Fleetwing, grumbling to himself. Ishtar was on the other side of Sirius at the moment, and even on an acceleration orbit it took days to get there. He spent the time studying Murinn's General Cosmology, a book he'd never gotten around to before though it was a good 2500 years old. There had been no basic advance in science since the fall of the African Empire, he reflected, and on Earth today the conviction was that all the important questions had been answered. After all, the universe was finite, so the scientific horizon must be too; after several hundred years during which research turned up no phenomenon not already predicted by theory, there would naturally be a loss of interest which ultimately became a dogma.

Kenri wasn't sure the dogma was right. He had seen too much of the cosmos to have any great faith in man's ability to understand it. There were problems in a hundred fields – physics, chemistry, biology, psychology, history, epistemology – to which the Nine Books gave no quantitative answer; but when he tried to tell an Earthling that, he got a blank look or a superior smile. . . . No, science was a social enterprise, it couldn't exist when the society didn't want it. But no civilization lasts forever. Someday there would again be a questioning.

Most of the Fleetwing's passengers were time-expired engineers or planters returning home. Few of the big ships had ever transported a Star aristocrat. When he came down to Landfall, in a spuming rain, and walked through the hot wet streets and onto the bowered verandah of the town's hotel, it was a shock to find that his cargo was a young and beautiful woman. He bowed to her, crossing arms on breast as prescribed, and felt the stiffness of embarrassment. He was the outsider, the inferior, the space tramp, and she was one of Earth's owners.

'I hope the boat will not be too uncomfortable for you, Freelady,' he mumbled, and hated himself for the obsequiousness of it. He should have said, you useless brainless bitch, my people keep Earth alive and you ought to be kneeling to me in thanks. But he bowed again instead, and helped her up the ladder into the cramped cabin.

'I'll make out,' she laughed. She was too young, he guessed, to have taken on the snotty manners of her class. The fog of Ishtar lay in cool drops in her hair, like small jewels. The blue eyes were not unfriendly as they rested on his sharp dark face.

He computed an orbit back to Marduk. 'It'll take us four-plus days, Freelady,' he said. 'I hope you aren't in too much of a hurry.'

'Oh, no,' she said. 'I just wanted to see that planet too, before leaving.' He thought of what it must be costing her, and felt a vague sense of outrage that anyone should throw good money around on mere tourism; but he only nodded.

They were in space before long. He emerged from his curtained bunk after a few hour's sleep to find her already up, leafing through Murinn. 'I don't understand a word of it,' she said. 'Does he ever use one syllable where six will do?'

'He cared a great deal for precision, Freelady,' said Kenri as he started breakfast. Impulsively, he added: 'I would have liked to know him.'

Her eyes wandered around the boat's library, shelf on shelf of microbooks and full-sized volumes. 'You people do a lot of reading, don't you?' she asked.

'Not too much else to do on a long voyage, Freelady,' he said. 'There are handicrafts, of course, and the preparation of goods for sale – things like that – but there's still plenty of time for reading.'

'I'm surprised you have such big crews,' she said. 'Surely you don't need that many people to man a ship.'

'No, Freelady,' he replied. 'A ship between the stars just about runs itself. But when we reach a planet, a lot of hands are needed.'

'There's company, too, I suppose,' she ventured. 'Wives and children and friends.'

'Yes, Freelady.' His voice grew cold. What business of hers was it?

'I like your Town,' she said. 'I used to go there often. It's so – quaint? Like a bit of the past, kept alive all these centuries.'

Sure, he wanted to say, sure, your sort come around to stare. You come around drunk, and peer into our homes, and when an old man goes by you remark what a funny little geezer he is, without even lowering your voices, and when you bargain with a shopkeeper and he tries to get a fair price it only proves to you that all tommies think of nothing but money. Oh, yes, we're very glad to have you visit us. 'Yes, Freelady.'

She looked hurt, and said little for many hours. After a while she went back into the space he had screened off for her, and he heard her playing a violin. It was a very old melody, older than man's starward wish, unbelievably old, and still it was young and tender and trustful, still it was everything which was good and dear in man. He couldn't quite track down the music, what was it – ? After a while, she stopped. He felt a desire to impress her. The Kith had their own tunes. He got out his guitar and strummed a few chords and let his mind wander.

Presently he began to sing.

He sensed her come quietly out and stand behind him, but pretended not to be aware of her. His voice lilted between the thrumming walls, and he looked out towards cold stars and the ruddy crest of Marduk.

He ended the song with a crash of strings and looked around and got up to bow.

'No . . . sit down,' she said. 'This isn't Earth. What was that song?'

'Jerry Clawson, Freelady,' he replied. 'It's ancient – in fact, I was singing a translation from the original English. It goes clear back to the early days of interplanetary travel.'

Star-Frees were supposed to be intellectuals as well as esthetes. He waited for her to say that somebody ought to collect Kith folk ballads in a book.

'I like it,' she said. 'I like it very much.'

He looked away. 'Thank you, Freelady,' he said. 'May I make bold to ask what you were playing earlier?'

'Oh . . . that's even older,' she said. 'A theme from the Kreutzer Sonata. *I'm awfully fond of it.' She smiled slowly. 'I think I would have liked to know Beethoven.'*

They met each other's eyes, then, and did not look away or speak for what seemed like a long time.

The Town ended as sharply as if cut off by a knife. It had been like that for 3000 years, a sanctuary from time; sometimes it stood alone on open windy moors, with no other work of man in sight except a few broken walls; sometimes it was altogether swallowed by a roaring monster of a city; sometimes, as now, it lay on the fringe of a great commune; but always it was the Town, changeless and inviolate.

No – not so. There had been days when war swept through it, pockmarking walls and sundering roofs and filling its streets with corpses; there had been murderous mobs looking for a tommy to lynch:

there had been haughty swaggering officers come to enforce some new proclamation. They could return. Through all the endless turmoil of history, they would. Kenri shivered in the wandering autumn breeze and started off along the nearest avenue.

The neighbourhood was a slum at the moment, gaunt crumbling tenements, cheerless lanes, aimlessly drifting crowds. They wore doublets and kilts of sleazy grey, and they stank. Most of them were Norms, nominally free – which meant free to starve when there wasn't work to be had. The majority were Norm-Ds, low-class manual labourers with dull heavy faces, but here and there the more alert countenance of a Norm-C or B showed briefly in the glare of a lamp, above the weaving, sliding shadows. When a Standard pushed through, gay in the livery of the state or his private owner, something flickered in those eyes. A growing knowledge, a feeling that something was wrong when slaves were better off than freemen – Kenri had seen that look before, and knew what it could become: the blind face of destruction. And elsewhere were the men of Mars and Venus and the Jovian moons, yes, the Radiant of Jupiter had ambitions and Earth was still the richest planet.... No, he thought, the Star Empire wouldn't last much longer.

But it ought to last his and Dorthy's lifetime, and they could make some provision for their children. That was enough.

An elbow jarred into his ribs. 'Outta the way, tommy!'

He clenched his fists, thinking of what he had done beyond the sky, what he could do here on Earth – silently, he stepped off the walk. A woman, leaning fat and blowsy from an upstairs window, jeered at him and spat. He dodged the fleck of spittle, but he could not dodge the laughter that followed him.

They hate, he thought. *They still don't dare resent their masters, so they take it out on us. Be patient. It cannot endure another two centuries.*

It still shook in him, though. He grew aware of the tautness in his nerves and belly, and his neck ached with the strain of keeping his face humbly lowered. Though Dorthy was waiting for him in a garden of roses, he needed a drink. He saw the winking neon bottle and turned in that door.

A few sullen men were slumped at tables, under the jerky obscenity of a live mural that must be a hundred years old. The tavern owned only half a dozen Standard-D girls, and they were raddled things who must have been bought third hand. One of them gave Kenri a mechanical smile, saw his face and dress and badge, and turned away with a sniff.

He made his way to the bar. There was a live tender who showed him a glazed stare. 'Vodzan,' said Kenri. 'Make it a double.'

'We don't serve no tommies here,' said the bartender.

Kenri's fingers whitened on the bar. He turned to go, but a hand touched his arm. 'Just a minute, spaceman.' To the attendant: 'One double vodzan.'

'I told you – '

'This is for me, Wilm. And I can give it to anyone I want. I can pour it on the floor if I so desire.' There was a thinness in the tone, and the bartender went quickly off to his bottles.

Kenri looked into a white, hairless face with a rakish cast to its skull structure. The lean grey-clad body was hunched over the bar, one hand idly rolling dice from a cup. There were no bones in the fingers, they were small delicate tentacles; and the eyes were coloured like ruby.

'Thank you,' said Kenri. 'May I pay – '

'No. It's on me.' The other accepted the glass and handed it over. 'Here.'

'Your health, sir.' Kenri lifted the glass and drank. The liquor was pungent fire along his throat.

'Such as it is,' said the man indifferently. 'No trouble to me. What I say here goes.' He was probably a petty criminal of some sort, perhaps a member of the now outlawed Assassins' Guild. And the body type was not quite human. He must be a Special-X, created in the genetic labs for a particular job or for study or for amusement. Presumably he had been set free when his owner was done with him, and had made a place for himself in the slums.

'Been gone long?' he asked, looking at the dice.

'About twenty-three years,' said Kenri. 'Sirius.'

'Things have changed,' said the X. 'Anti-Kithism is growing strong again. Be careful you aren't slugged or robbed, because if you are, it'll do you no good to appeal to the city guards.'

'It's nice of you to – '

'Nothing.' The slim fingers scooped up the dice and rattled the cup again. 'I like somebody to feel superior to.'

'Oh.' Kenri set the glass down. For a moment, the smoky room blurred. 'I see. Well – '

'No, don't go off.' The ruby eyes lifted up to his, and he was surprised to see tears in them. I wanted to sign on myself, once, and they wouldn't have me.'

Kenri said nothing.

'I would of course, give my left leg to the breastbone for a chance to go on just one voyage,' said the X dully. 'Don't you think an Earthling has his dreams now and then – we too? But I wouldn't be much use. You have to grow up in space, damn near, to know enough to be of value on some planet Earth never heard of. And I suppose there's my looks too. Even the underdogs can't get together any more.'

'They never could, sir,' said Kenri.

'I suppose you're right. You've seen more of both space and time than I ever will. So I stay here, belonging nowhere, and keep alive somehow;

but I wonder if it's worth the trouble. A man isn't really alive till he has something bigger than himself and his own little happiness, for which he'd gladly die. Oh, well.' The X rolled out the dice. 'Nine. I'm losing my touch.' Glancing up again: 'I know a place where they don't care who you are if you've got money.'

'Thank you, sir, but I have business elsewhere,' said Kenri awkwardly.

'I thought so. Well, go ahead, then. Don't let me stop you.' The X looked away.

'Thank you for the drink, sir.'

'It was nothing. Come in whenever you want, I'm usually here. But don't yarn about the planets out there. I don't want to hear that.'

'Goodnight,' said Kenri.

As he walked out, the dice clattered across the bar again.

Dorthy had wanted to do some surface travelling on Marduk, get to see the planet. She could have had her pick of the colony for escorts, but she chose to ask Kenri. One did not say no to a Star, so he dropped some promising negotiations for pelts with a native chief, hired a groundcar, and picked her up at the time she set.

They rode quietly for a while, until the settlement was lost behind the horizon. Here was stony desert, flamboyantly coloured, naked crags and iron hills and low dusty thorn-trees sharp in the thin clear air. Overhead, the sky was a royal blue, with the shrunken disc of Sirius A and the brilliant spark of its companion spilling harsh light over the stillness.

'This is a beautiful world,' she said at last. Her tones came muffled through the tenuous air. 'I like it better than Ishtar.'

'Most people don't, Freelady,' he answered. 'They call it dull and cold and dry.'

'They don't know,' she said. Her fair head was turned from him, looking at the fantastic loom of a nearby scarp, gnawed rocks and straggling brush, tawny colour streaked with the blue and red lightning of mineral veins.

'I envy you, Kenri Shaun,' she said at last. 'I've seen a few pictures, read a few books – everything I could get hold of, but it isn't enough. When I think of all you have seen that is strange and beautiful and wonderful, I envy you.'

He ventured a question: 'Was that why you came to Sirius, Freelady?'

'In part. When my father died, we wanted someone to check on the family's Ishtarian holdings. Everyone assumed we'd just send an agent, but I insisted on going myself, and booked with the Temeraire. *They all thought I was crazy. Why, I'd come back to new styles, new slang, new people . . . my friends would all be middle-aged, I'd be a walking anachronism . . . you know.' She sighed. 'But it was worth it.'*

He thought of his own life, the grinding sameness of the voyages, weeks slipping into months and years within a pulsing metal shell; approach, strangeness, the savage hostility of cruel planets – he had seen friends buried under landslides, spitting out their lungs when helmets cracked open in airlessness, rotting alive with some alien sickness; he had told them goodbye and watched them go off into a silence which never gave them back and had wondered how they came to die; and on Earth he was a ghost,

265

*not belonging, adrift above the great river of time, on Earth he felt somehow unreal.
'I wonder, Freelady,' he said.*

'Oh, I'll adjust,' she laughed.

*The car ground its way over high dunes and down tumbling ravines, it left a track
in the dust which the slow wind erased behind them. That night they camped near the
ruins of a forgotten city, a place which must once have been a faerie spectacle of
loveliness. Kenri set up the two tents and started a meal on the glower while she
watched. 'Let me help,' she offered once.*

'It isn't fitting, Freelady,' he replied. And you'd be too clumsy anyway,
you'd only make a mess of it. *His hands were deft on the primitive skillet. The
ruddy light of the glower beat against darkness, etching their faces red in windy
shadows. Overhead, the stars were high and cold.*

*She looked at the sputtering meal. 'I thought you ... people never ate fish,' she
murmured.*

*'Some of us do, some don't, Freelady,' he said absently. Out here, it was hard to
resent the gulf between them. 'It was originally tabooed by custom in the Kith back
when space and energy for growing food on shipboard were at a premium. Only a rich
man could have afforded an aquarium, you see; and a tight-knit group of nomads has
to ban conspicuous consumption to prevent ill feeling. Nowadays, when the economic
reason has long disappeared, only the older people still observe the taboo.'*

*She smiled, accepting the plate he handed her. 'It's funny,' she said. 'One just
doesn't think of your people as having a history. You've always been around.'*

*'Oh, we do, Freelady. We've plenty of traditions – more than the rest of mankind,
perhaps.'*

A hunting marcat screamed in the night. She shivered. 'What's that?'

*'Local carnivore, Freelady. Don't let it worry you.' He slapped his slug-thrower,
obscurely pleased at a chance to show – what? Manliness? 'No one with a weapon has
to fear any larger animals. It's other things that make the danger – occasionally a
disease, more often cold or heat or poison gases or vacuum or whatever hell the
universe can brew for us.' He grinned, a flash of teeth in the dark lean face. 'Anyway,
if it ate us it would die pretty quickly. We're as poisonous to it as it is to us.'*

*'Different biochemistry and ecology,' she nodded. 'A billion or more years of
separate evolution. It would be strange, wouldn't it, if more than a very few planets
had developed life so close to Earth's that we could eat it. I suppose that's why there
never was any real extrasolar colonization – just a few settlements for mining or
trading or extracting organic chemicals.'*

*'That's partly it, Freelady,' he said. 'Matter of economics, too. It was much easier
– in money terms, cheaper – for people to stay at home; no significant percentage of
them could ever have been taken away in any event – human breeding would have
raised the population faster than emigration could lower it.'*

*She gave him a steady look. When she spoke, her voice was soft. 'You Kithmen are
a brainy lot, aren't you?'*

He knew it was true, but he made the expected disclaimer.

'No, no,' she said. 'I've read up on your history a little. Correct me if I'm wrong,

but since the earliest times of space travel the qualifications have been pretty rigid. A spaceman just had to be of high intelligence, with quick reactions and stable personality both. And he couldn't be too large, physically; but he had to be tough. And a dark complexion must be of some small help, now and then, in strong sunlight or radiation. . . . Yes, that was how it was. How it still is. When women began going to space too, the trade naturally tended to run in families. Those spacemen who didn't fit into the life, dropped out; and the recruits from Sol were pretty similar in mind and body to the people they joined. So eventually you got the Kith – almost a separate race of man; and it evolved its own ways of living. Until at last you had a monopoly on space traffic.'

'No, Freelady,' he said. 'We've never had that. Anyone who wants to build a spaceship and man it himself, can do so. But it's an enormous capital investment; and after the initial glamour had worn off, the average Solarian just wasn't interested in hard and lonely life. So today, all spacemen are Kithmen, but it was never planned that way.'

'That's what I meant,' she said. Earnestly: 'And your being different naturally brought suspicion and discrimination. . . . No, don't interrupt, I want to say this through. . . . Any conspicuous minority which offers competition to the majority is going to be disliked. Sol has to have the fissionables you bring from the stars, we've used up our own; and the unearthly chemicals you bring are often of great value, and the trade in luxuries like furs and jewels is brisk. So you are essential to society, but you still don't really belong in it. You are too proud, in your own way, to ape your oppressors. Being human, you naturally charge all the traffic will bear, which gives you the reputation of being gougers; being able to think better and faster than the average Solarian, you can usually best him in a deal, and he hates you for it. Then there's the tradition handed down from Mechanoclastic times, when technology was considered evil and only you maintained a high level of it. And in the puritan stage of the Martian conquest, your custom of wife trading – oh, I know you do it just to relieve the endless monotony of the voyages, I know you have more family life than we do – Well, all those times are gone, but they've left their legacy. I wonder why you bother with Earth at all. Why you don't all just wander into space and let us stew in our own juice.'

'Earth is our planet too, Freelady,' he said, very quietly. After a moment: 'The fact that we are essential gives us some protection. We get by. Please don't feel sorry for us.'

'A stiff-necked people,' she said. 'You don't even want pity.'

'Who does, Freelady?' he asked.

On the edge of the slum, in a zone bulking with the tall warehouses and offices of the merchant families, Kenri took an elevator up to the public skyway going towards the address he wanted. There was no one else in sight at that point; he found a seat and lowered himself into it and let the strip hum him toward city centre.

The skyway climbed fast, until he was above all but the highest towers.

267

Leaning an arm on the rail, he looked down into a night that was alive with radiance. The streets and walls glowed, strings of coloured lamps flashed and flashed against a velvet dark, fountains leaped white and gold and scarlet, a flame display danced like molten rainbows at the feet of a triumphal statue. Star architecture was a thing of frozen motion, soaring columns and tiers and pinnacles to challenge the burning sky; high in that airy jungle, the spaceman could hardly make out the river of vehicles and humanity below him.

As he neared the middle of town, the skyway gathered more passengers. Standards in bright fantastic livery, Norms in their tunics and kilts, an occasional visitor from Mars or Venus or Jupiter with resplendent uniform and greedy smouldering eyes – yes, and here came a party of Frees, their thin garments a swirling iridescence about the erect slender forms, a hard glitter of jewels, the men's beards and the women's hair elaborately curled. Fashions had changed in the past two decades. Kenri felt acutely aware of his own shabbiness, and huddled closer to the edge of the strip.

Two young couples passed his seat. He caught a woman's voice: 'Oh, look, a tommy!'

'He's got a nerve,' mumbled one of the men. 'I've half a mind to – '

'No, Scanish.' Another feminine voice, gentler than the first. 'He has the right.'

'He shouldn't have. I know these tommies. Give 'em a finger and they'll take your whole arm.' The four were settling into the seat behind Kenri's. 'My uncle is in Transsolar Trading. He'll tell you.'

'Please, no, Scanish, he's listening!'

'And I hope he – '

'Never mind, dear. What shall we do next? Go to Halgor's?' She attempted a show of interest.

'Ah, we've been there a hundred times. What is there to do? How about getting my rocket and shooting over to China? I know a place where they got techniques you never – '

'No. I'm not in the mood. I don't know what I want to do.'

'My nerves have been terrible lately. We bought a new doctor, but he says just the same as the old one. They don't any of them know which end is up. I might try this new Beltanist religion, they seem to have something. It would at least be amusing.'

'Say, have you heard about Marla's latest? You know who was seen coming out of her bedroom last ten-day?'

Kenri grabbed hold of his mind and forced it away from listening. He didn't want to. He wouldn't let the weariness and sickness of spirit which was the old tired Empire invade him.

Dorthy, he thought. *Dorthy Persis from Canda. It's a beautiful name, isn't it? There's music in it. And the from Candas have always been an outstanding family.*

She isn't like the rest of the Stars.

She loves me, he thought with a singing in him. *She loves me. There is a life before us. Two of us, one life, and the rest of the Empire can rot as it will. We'll be together.*

He saw the skyscraper ahead of him now, a thing of stone and crystal and light that climbed towards heaven in one great rush. The insigne of the from Candas burned on its façade, an ancient and proud symbol. It stood for 300 years of achievement.

But that's less than my own lifetime. No, I don't have to be ashamed in their presence. I come of the oldest and best line of all humanity. I'll fit in.

He wondered why he could not shake off the depression that clouded him. This was a moment of glory. He should be going to her as a conqueror. But —

He sighed and rose as his stop approached.

Pain stabbed at him. He jumped, stumbled, and fell to one knee. Slowly, his head twisted around. The young Star grinned in his face, holding up a shockstick. Kenri's hand rubbed the pain, and the four people began to laugh. So did everyone else in sight. The laughter followed him off the skyway and down to the ground.

There was no one else on the bridge. One man was plenty to stand watch, here in the huge emptiness between suns. The room was a hollow cavern of twilight, quiet except for the endless throbbing of the ship. Here and there, the muted light of instrument panels glowed, and the weird radiance of the distorted stars flamed in the viewport. But otherwise there was no illumination, Kenri had switched it off.

She came through the door and paused, her gown white in the dusk. His throat tightened as he looked at her, and when he bowed, his head swam. There was a faint sweet rustling as she walked closer. She had the long swinging stride of freedom, and her unbound hair floated silkily behind her . . .

'I've never been on a bridge before,' she said. 'I didn't think passengers were allowed there.'

'I invited you, Freelady,' he answered, his voice catching.

'It was good of you, Kenri Shaun.' Her fingers fluttered across his arm. 'You have always been good to me.'

'Could anyone be anything else, to you?' he asked.

Light stole along her cheeks and into the eyes that turned up at him. She smiled with a strangely timid curve of lips. 'Thank you,' she whispered.

'Ah, I, well —' He gestured at the viewport, which seemed to hang above their heads. 'That is precisely on the ship's axis of rotation, Freelady,' he said. 'That's why the view is constant. Naturally, "down" on the bridge is any point at which you are standing. You'll note that the desks and panels are arranged in a circle around the inner wall, to take advantage of that fact.' His voice sounded remote and strange to his ears. 'Now here we have the astrogation computer. Ours is badly in need of

overhauling just now, which is why you see all those books and calculations on my desk – '

Her hand brushed the back of his chair. 'This is yours, Kenri Shaun? I can almost see you working away on it, with that funny tight look on your face, as if the problem were your personal enemy. Then you sigh, and run your fingers through your hair, and put your feet on the desk to think for a while. Am I right?'

'How did you guess, Freelady?'

'I know. I've thought a great deal about you, lately.' She looked away, out to the harsh blue-white stars clustered in the viewport.

Suddenly her fists gathered themselves. 'I wish you didn't make me feel so futile,' she said.

'You – '

'This is life, here.' She spoke swiftly, blurring the words in her need to say them. 'You're keeping Earth alive, with your cargoes. You're working and fighting and thinking about – about something real. Not about what to wear for dinner and who was seen where with whom and what to do tonight when you're too restless and unhappy to stay quietly at home. You're keeping Earth alive, I said, and a dream too. I envy you, Kenri Shaun. I wish I were born into the Kith.'

'Freelady – ' It rattled in his throat.

'No use.' She smiled, without self-pity. 'Even if a ship would have me, I could never go. I don't have the training, or the inborn strength, or the patience, or – No! Forget it.' There were tears in the ardent eyes. 'When I get home, knowing now what you are in the Kith, will I even try to help you? Will I work for more understanding of your people, kindness, common decency? No. I'll realize it's useless even to try. I won't have the courage.'

'You'd be wasting your time, Freelady,' he said. 'No one person can change a whole culture. Don't worry about it.'

'I know,' she replied. 'You're right, of course. You're always right. But in my place, you would try!'

They stared at each other for a long moment.

That was the first time he kissed her.

The two guards at the soaring main entrance were giants, immobile as statues in the sunburst glory of their uniforms. Kenri had to crane his neck to look into the face of the nearest. 'The Freelady Dorthy Persis is expecting me,' he said.

'Huh?' Shock brought the massive jaw clicking down.

'That's right.' Kenri grinned and extended the card she had given him. 'She said to look her up immediately.'

'But – there's a party going on – '

'Never mind. Call her up.'

The guardsman reddened, opened his mouth, and snapped it shut again. Turning, he went to the visiphone booth. Kenri waited, regretting his insolence. *Give 'em a finger and they'll take your whole arm.* But how else could a Kithman behave? If he gave deference, they called him a servile bootlicker; if he showed his pride, he was an obnoxious pushing bastard; if he dickered for a fair price, he was a squeezer and bloodsucker; if he spoke his own language to his comrades, he was being secretive; if he cared more for his skyfaring people than for an ephemeral nation, he was a traitor and coward; if –

The guard returned, shaking his head in astonishment. 'All right,' he said sullenly. 'Go on up. First elevator to your right, fiftieth floor. But watch your manners, tommy.'

When I'm adopted into the masters, thought Kenri savagely, *I'll make him eat that word.* Then, with a new rising of the unaccountable weariness: *No. Why should I? What would anyone gain by it?*

He went under the enormous curve of the door, into a foyer that was a grotto of luminous plastic. A few Standard servants goggled at him, but made no move to interfere. He found the elevator cage and punched for fifty. It rose in a stillness broken only by the sudden rapid thunder of his heart.

He emerged into an anteroom of red velvet. Beyond an arched doorway, he glimpsed colours floating, a human blaze of red and purple and gold; the air was loud with music and laughter. The footman at the entrance stepped in his path, hardly believing the sight. 'You can't go in there!'

'The hell I can't.' Kenri shoved him aside and strode through the arch. The radiance hit him like a fist, and he stood blinking at the confusion of dancers, servants, onlookers, entertainers – there must be a thousand people in this vaulted chamber.

'Kenri! Oh, Kenri –'

She was in his arms, pressing her mouth to his, drawing his head down with shaking hands. He strained her close, and the misty cloak she wore whirled about to wrap them in aloneness.

One moment, and then she drew back breathlessly, laughing a little. It wasn't quite the merriment he had known, there was a thin note to it, and shadows lay under the great eyes. She was very tired, he saw, and pity lifted in him. 'Dearest,' he whispered.

'Kenri, not here . . . Oh, darling, I hoped you would come sooner, but – No, come with me now, I want them all to see the man I've got me.' She took his hand and half dragged him forward. The dancers were stopping, pair by pair as they noticed the stranger, until at last there were a thousand faces stiffly turned to his. Silence dropped like a thunderclap, but the music kept on. It sounded tinny in the sudden quiet.

Dorthy shivered. Then she threw back her head with a defiance that was dear to him and met the eyes. Her arm rose to bring the wristphone to her lips, and the ceiling amplifiers boomed her voice over the room: 'Friends, I want to announce . . . Some of you already know . . . well, this is the man I'm going to marry –'

It was the voice of a frightened little girl. Cruel to make it loud as a goddess talking.

After a pause which seemed to last forever, somebody performed the ritual bow. Then somebody else did, and then they were all doing it, like jointed dolls. There were a few scornful exceptions, who turned their backs.

'Go on!' Dorthy's tones grew shrill. 'Go on dancing. Please! You'll all – later –' The orchestra leader must have had a degree of sensitivity, for he struck up a noisy tune and one by one the couples slipped into a figure dance.

Dorthy looked hollowly up at the spaceman. 'It's good to see you again,' she said.

'And you,' he replied.

'Come.' She led him around the wall. 'Let's sit and talk.'

They found an alcove, screened from the room by a trellis of climbing roses. It was a place of dusk, and she turned hungrily to him. He felt how she trembled.

'It hasn't been easy for you, has it?' he asked tonelessly.

'No,' she said.

'If you –'

'Don't say it!' There was fear in the words. She closed his mouth with hers.

'I love you,' she said after a while. 'That's all that matters, isn't it?'

He didn't answer.

'Isn't it?' she cried.

He nodded. 'Maybe. I take it your family and friends don't approve of your choice.'

'Some don't. Does it matter, darling? They'll forget, when you're one of us.'

'One of you – I'm not born to this,' he said bleakly. 'I'll always stick out like – Well, never mind. I can stand it if you can.'

He sat on the padded bench, holding her close, and looked out through the clustered blooms. Colour and motion and high harsh laughter – it wasn't his world. He wondered why he had ever assumed it could become his.

They had talked it out while the ship plunged through night. She could never be of the Kith. There was no room in a crew for one who couldn't endure worlds never meant for man. He would have to join her instead. He could fit in, he had the intelligence and adaptability to make a place for himself.

What kind of place? he wondered as she nestled against him. A planner of more elaborate parties, a purveyor of trivial gossip, a polite ear for boredom and stupidity and cruelty and perversion – No, there would be

Dorthy, they would be alone in the nights of Earth and that would be enough.

Would it? A man couldn't spend all his time making love.

There were the big trading firms, he could go far in one of them. (Four thousand barrels of Kalian jung oil rec'd pr. acct., and the fierce rains and lightning across the planet's phosphorescent seas. A thousand refined thorium ingots from Hathor, and moonlight sparkling the crisp snow and the ringing winter stillness. A bale of green furs from a newly discovered planet, and the ship had gone racing through stars and splendour into skies no man had ever seen.) Or perhaps the military. (Up on your feet, soldier! Hup, hup, hup, hup!... Sir, the latest Intelligence report on Mars ... Sir, I know the guns aren't up to spec, but we can't touch the contractor, his patron is a Star-Free... The General commands your presence at a banquet for staff officers.... Now tell me, Colonel Shaun, tell me what you *really* think will happen, you officers are all so *frightfully* close-mouthed.... Ready! Aim! Fire! So perish all traitors to the Empire!) Or even the science centres. (Well, sir, according to the book, the formula is...)

Kenri's arm tightened desperately about Dorthy's waist.

'How do you like being home?' he asked. 'Otherwise, I mean.'

'Oh – fine. Wonderful!' She smiled uncertainly at him. 'I was so afraid I'd be old-fashioned, out of touch, but no, I fell in right away. There's the most terribly amusing crowd, a lot of them children of my own old crowd. You'll love them, Kenri. I have a lot of glamour, you know, for going clear to Sirius. Think how much you'll have!'

'I won't,' he grunted. 'I'm just a tommy, remember?'

'Kenri!' Anger flicked across her brow. 'What a way to talk. You aren't, and you know it, and you won't be unless you insist on thinking like one all the time – ' She caught herself and said humbly: 'I'm sorry, darling. That was a terrible thing to say, wasn't it?'

He stared ahead of him.

'I've been, well, infected,' she said. 'You were gone so long. You'll cure me again.'

Tenderness filled him, and he kissed her.

'A-hum! Pardon!'

They jerked apart, almost guiltily, and looked up to the two who had entered the alcove. One was a middle-aged man, austerely slender and erect, his night-blue tunic flashing with decorations; the other was younger, pudgy-faced, and rather drunk. Kenri got up. He bowed with his arms straight, as one equal to another.

'Oh, you must meet, I know you'll like each other – ' Dorthy was speaking fast, her voice high. 'This is Kenri Shaun. I've told you enough about him, haven't I?' A nervous little laugh. 'Kenri, my uncle, Colonel from Canda of the Imperial Staff, and my nephew, the Honourable Lord

273

Doms. Fancy coming back and finding you have a nephew your own age!'

'Your honour, sir.' The colonel's voice was as stiff as his back. Doms giggled.

'You must pardon the interruption,' went on from Canda. 'But I wished to speak to ... to Shaun as soon as possible. You will understand, sir, that it is for the good of my niece and the whole family.'

Kenri's palms were cold and wet. 'Of course,' he said. 'Please sit down.'

'Thank you.' From Canda lowered his angular frame onto the bench, next to the Kithman; Doms and Dorthy sat at opposite ends, the young man slumped over and grinning. 'Shall I send for some wine?'

'Not for me, thanks,' said Kenri huskily.

The cold eyes were level on his. 'First,' said the colonel, 'I want you to realize that I do not share this absurd race prejudice which is growing up about your people. It is demonstrable that the Kith is biologically equal to the Star families, and doubtless superior to some.' His glance flickered contemptuously over to Doms. 'There is a large cultural barrier, of course, but if that can be surmounted, I, for one, would be glad to sponsor your adoption into our ranks.'

'Thank you, sir.' Kenri felt dizzy. No Kithman had ever gone so high in all history. That it should be *him* – ! He heard Dorthy's happy little sigh as she took his arm, and something of the frozenness within him began to thaw. 'I'll ... do my best – '

'But will you? That is what I have to find out.' From Canda leaned forward, clasping his gaunt hands between his knees. 'Let us not mince words. You know as well as I that there is a time of great danger ahead for the Empire, and that if it is to survive the few men of action left must stand together and strike hard. We can ill afford the weaklings among us; we can certainly not afford to have strong men in our midst who are not wholeheartedly for our cáuse.'

'I'll be ... loyal, sir,' said Kenri. 'What more can I do?'

'Much,' said the colonel. 'Considerable of it may be distasteful to you. Your special knowledge could be of high value. For example, the new tax on the Kith is not merely a device to humiliate them. We need the money. The Empire's finances are in bad shape, and even that little bit helps. There will have to be further demands, on the Kith as well as everyone else. You can assist us in guiding our policy, so that they are not goaded to the point of abandoning Earth altogether.'

'I – ' Kenri swallowed. He felt suddenly ill. 'You can't expect – '

'If you won't, then you won't, and I cannot force you,' said from Canda. There was a strange brief sympathy in the chill tones. 'I am merely warning you of what lies ahead. You could mitigate the lot of your ... former ... people considerably, if you help us.'

'Why not ... treat them like human beings?' asked Kenri. 'We'll always stand by our friends.'

'Three thousand years of history cannot be cancelled by decree,' said from Canda. 'You know that as well as I.'

Kenri nodded. It seemed to strain his neck muscles.

'I admire your courage,' said the aristocrat. 'You have started on a hard road. Can you follow it through?'

Kenri looked down.

'Of course he can,' said Dorthy softly.

Lord Doms giggled. 'New tax,' he said. 'Slap a new one on fast. I've got one tommy skipper on the ropes already. Bad voyage, debts, heh!'

Red and black and icy blue, and the shriek of lifting winds.

'Shut up, Doms,' said the colonel. 'I didn't want you along.'

Dorthy's head leaned back against Kenri's shoulder. 'Thank you, uncle,' she said. There was a lilt in her voice. 'If you'll be our friend, it will work out.'

'I hope so,' said from Canda.

The faint sweet odour of Dorothy's hair was in Kenri's nostrils. He felt the gold waves brushing his cheek, but still didn't look up. There was thunder and darkness in him.

Doms laughed. 'I got to tell you 'bout this spacer,' he said. 'He owes the firm money, see? I can take his daughter under contract if he doesn't pay up. Only his crew are taking up a collection for him. I got to stop that somehow. They say those tommy girls are mighty hot. How about it, Kenri? You're one of us now. How are they, really? Is it true that –'

Kenri stood up. He saw the room swaying, and wondered dimly if he was wobbling on his feet or not.

'Doms,' snapped from Canda, 'if you don't shut your mouth –'

Kenri grabbed a handful of Lord Doms' tunic and hauled him to his feet. The other hand became a fist, and the face squashed under it.

He stood over the young man, weaving, his arms hanging loose at his sides. Doms moaned on the floor. Dorthy gave a small scream. From Canda leaped up, clapping his hand to a sidearm.

Kenri lifted his eyes. There was a thickness in his words. 'Go ahead and arrest me,' he said. 'Go on, what are you waiting for?'

K-k-kenri –' Dorthy touched him with shaking hands.

From Canda grinned and nudged Doms with a boot. 'That was foolish of you, Kenri Shaun,' he said, 'but the job was long overdue. I'll see that nothing happens to you.'

'But this Kith girl –'

'She'll be all right too, I daresay, if her father can raise that money.' The hard eyes raked Kenri's face. 'But remember, my friend, you cannot live in two worlds at once. You are not a Kithman any longer.'

Kenri straightened. He knew a sudden dark peace, as if all storms had

275

laid themselves to rest. His head felt a little empty, but utterly clear.

It was a memory in him which had opened his vision and shown him what he must do, the only thing he could do. There was a half-human face and eyes without hope and a voice which had spoken: *'A man isn't really alive till he has something bigger than himself and his own little happiness, for which he'd gladly die.'*

'Thank you, sir,' he said. 'But I am a Kithman. I will always be.'

'Kenri –' Dorthy's tone broke. She held his arms and stared at him with wildness.

His hand stroked her hair. 'I'm sorry, dearest,' he said gently.

'Kenri, you can't go, you can't, you can't – '

'I must,' he said. 'It was bad enough that I should give up everything which had been my life for an existence that to me is stupid and dreary and meaningless. For you, I could have stood that. But you are asking me to be a tyrant, or at least to be a friend of tyrants. You're asking me to countenance evil. I can't do it. I wouldn't if I could.' He took her shoulders and looked into the unseeing bewilderment of her eyes. 'Because that would, in the end, make me hate you, who had so twisted my own self, and I want to go on loving you. I will always love you.'

She wrenched away from him. He thought that there were psychological treatments to change her feelings and make her stop caring about him. Sooner or later, she'd take one of those. He wanted to kiss her farewell, but he didn't quite dare.

Colonel from Canda extended a hand. 'You will be my enemy, I suppose,' he said. 'But I respect you for it. I like you, and wish – well, good luck to you, Kenri Shaun.'

'And to you, sir ... Goodbye, Dorthy.'

He walked through the ballroom, not noticing the eyes that were on him, and out the door to the elevator. He was still too numb to feel anything, that would come later.

Theye Barinn is a nice girl, he thought somewhere on the edge of his mind. *I'll have to go around and see her soon. We could be happy together.*

It seemed like a long while before he was back in the Town. Then he walked along empty streets, alone within himself, breathing the cool damp night wind of Earth.

Is Your Child Using Drugs? Seven Ways To Recognize A Drug Addict

RACHEL POLLACK

SPEECH: DOES YOUR CHILD's speech pattern conform with his customary actions? Look for slurring, difficulty of speech, as if drunk.

Allan and Gloria Rumsilver looked at their son standing in the doorway. The moonlight, bright to excess as it had been for nine nights, flared about Dominiq's head like an unstable aura, causing Allan to squint his eyes, then look away. 'Since when do you ring the bell?' he asked. 'You lose your key again?' Dominiq's mouth twisted. His facial muscles pushed up his nostrils to give his contorted lips, his bare teeth more room. His tongue curled and stretched with seeming indolence, experimenting in a private sexuality as it sought a proper cavity or surface to make a proper sound. He coughed, then jerked back his head. Allan and Gloria could see tremors ripple his skin's exposed areas. A moment later Dominiq squeezed between his parents and lurched upstairs (his arm muscles alone under reasonable control), only to stop at the landing and say, his back to them, 'You must know. You must find out. Something must be done.'

CHEMICAL AROMAS: Do you smell strange aromas, like glue, Carbona, Magic Marker? Does your child's breath smell of any strange chemical odour?

Dominiq's mother decided that before Dominiq came home from school she should clean out his room. For the last few days he'd denied her entrance, and this closeness, joined to his other strange behaviour, had so aggravated Allan and Gloria that for the first time since Dominiq's early puberty they had considered invading his privacy for his own good. But now Gloria decided that she could enter her son's room as a gesture of aid rather than to spy, and so she laboured upstairs with the vacuum cleaner. At the closed door she paused, her attention momentarily snagged by howling wind; earlier the day had felt calm and warm, though of course with cleaning she had not left the house in hours. A faint glow between the door and the frame further distracted her. As her hand touched the knob this glow flared up, then died, while the wind rose in pitch and volume till she felt her ears turn red trying to contain the noise. When the door did not open she

277

thought, 'Maybe God doesn't want me in there,' but then embarrassment at such a juvenile notion strengthened her arm enough to force the door.

A smell, unbearably sweet – exotic fruit left to rot – smothered her like a great bear. Her sinuses in flames, she stumbled backward from the room. But before she slammed the door (and in confusion kicked the vacuum cleaner down the thirteen steps) she saw, through the closed window, the trees, motionless from the windless day.

EATING HABITS: Is there evidence of loss of appetite? Is there unusual use of sweets, soda, sugar, etc.?

To counteract Dominiq's several days' refusal to eat dinner Gloria had spent three hours preparing an elaborate Hunter's Soup, her son's favourite. But now, once again, the boy just stared embarrassed at the final wisps of smoke from the cooling food. After ten minutes Allan said, 'Are you planning to eat anything?' Pause. 'You know, your mother worked all day on that.' He waited only a moment more, then wiped off his spoon, laid it on the tablecloth, and, crossing behind his son, said. 'You'll eat some all right.' He pried open Dominiq's mouth – the boy did not struggle – lifted a spoonful and poured it down Dominiq's throat. An archetypal revulsion jerked Dominiq's muscles, as if a hand had rapped the motor centres in the cortex. His arms flung off his father, his legs kicked back his chair as he pitched forward, spitting out his soup. Gloria saw that the clear brown liquid had turned a muddy yellow in her son's mouth.

PILLS: Are your prescription pills disappearing? Are strange coloured pills found on clothing, dressers, or on person?

Allan and Gloria first used the terms 'drugs' and 'narcotics' when they partially viewed Dominiq swallow a pill, then bury a plastic vial in the backyard – 'partially' because Dominiq stood behind a willow tree so that his parents saw only specks, spots, blotches rather than a unified form. When the boy had gone his parents scooted forward and, digging like dogs, uncovered the vial, which indeed contained some twenty pills, all black and large, about three times the size of aspirin. When Allan tried to crush one he found it harder than the carborundum it vaguely resembled. This hardness, its inappropriateness to internal medication, so fascinated Allen he did not notice immediately the pill's extreme weight, at least two ounces. Allan wished to test it, see what tools would smash it, but Gloria insisted they rebury the batch before Dominiq could discover them.

HALLUCINATIONS: User senses distortion, there may be intensification of sensory perception. There may be a loss of reality or unexplainable psychotic or antisocial behaviour. User when on LSD or hallucinogenic drug might also want to destroy himself.

Dominiq leaned his right shoulder against the garage and lifted his head towards the northeast. Twenty feet to the left Allan and Gloria watched him, certain he didn't notice them or didn't care, yet still embarrassed. Allan said, 'He seems calm.' Gloria watched Dominiq's left hand; the fingers flexed constantly, smoothly rippling the air. Just after moonrise (the moon that night appeared immense, yet dim, as if caution at close proximity shrouded its light) Dominiq collapsed their assumption of his obliviousness. With his arm pointed towards the moon he called to them, 'See them? Gathering? They're putting everything together for the trip. Just like we used to do before we went away for fishing. But they don't need boats, you know. All they need's a place to put themselves together.'

Allan shouted across the twenty feet, 'There's no one there.'

Now Dominiq turned to look directly at them. 'When you stop me,' he said, 'please do it –' he shrugged – 'softly.'

'No one wants to hurt you,' said Gloria, feeling in her voice insufficient reassurance.

'Yes, you must. But softly.'

CHANGE OF PERSONALITY: Is the child acting contrary to his known personality makeup? Is there unexplained elation? Is there erratic behaviour or unusual physical activity?

When Dominiq ran from the house at 3.00 a.m. his parents, awake to discuss his problem, decided to follow. By the time they'd put on their robes and slippers, grabbed the car keys, and got outside the boy was heading, several hundred yards down the road, for the great rock field beyond the housing development. The station wagon followed quietly, lights off, but Dominiq loped so smoothly, his head thrown back snorting the wind, that they might have cruised alongside and not penetrated his elation. At the rock field the moon, even brighter there than over their house, provided sufficient light to watch from a safe distance as their son pushed uprooted tree trunks, two feet around and eight feet high, with little more effort than if he'd handled balsa wood or cardboard. (These petrified trunks, so round and flat, like stone pillars, had always intrigued them. Gloria had once investigated scientific studies of their origin, but unsatisfactorily.) Dominiq, his superhuman strength oddly normal in the moon glare, formed with the pillars a circle two hundred yards across. After he'd set the last trunk in place he stepped to the centre, where he slowly rotated his body. 'There,' he called loudly, as if to awaken sentience in the wood, 'I've set it up for you. Just like the picture. It's all ready, so now you can let me go.'

EYES: Is there a glassy look? Are the pupils pinpointed? Do the eyes look strange to you?

Nearly paralysed above the knees, Dominiq lurched downstairs, where he swayed back and forth and said, 'It's tonight, isn't it? It's tonight.' His eyes darted back and forth like trapped insects.

'Yes,' Allan snapped, 'it certainly is. Come on, Gloria, we're not waiting till tomorrow. We're going to that drug clinic right now.'

Soon the station wagon was darting nervously through the housing development, Dominiq's sweatless body held upright between his mother and father. 'Perhaps I should look at his eyes,' Gloria ventured and took out the notebook in which they recorded Dominiq's symptoms. But when she peered into the large black pupils – now they just stared at the moon, heavy in the sky like a pregnant woman – she saw, instead of her own reflection, a strange illusion, like a photographic negative: a stony desert, cold and grey, empty and flat, with hills like chipped teeth in the distance. Slowly a face appeared within the rock, human yet not human, like a child's sculpture. As her thighs moved apart in imminent sexual arousal Gloria whined, 'Could you stop the car? I think I'm going to be sick.'

'What the hell,' Allan said, but pulled over near the rock field.

Dominiq's head poked forward to watch his mother walk stiffly towards the tree trunks. 'It's tonight,' he called after her.

Allan shouted, 'Gloria, our boy's in trouble. Will you come back here?'

The petrified circle, however, soundproofed Gloria, who only stared at the bitter face that floated out of the moon, larger and closer, like a sex criminal attacking at night. Suddenly the ground heaved and shook. On her hands and knees, Gloria saw the earth crack, deep fissures, narrow eyes, a thin nose, and a long straight mouth. The tree trunks stuck out from the edges of the face like stiff locks of hair. Her hands reached down to caress the dirt.

Right then something gripped her shoulder and she heard an alien voice jabber at her. Before she could squirm away Allan had lifted her up. 'Will you come on?' his high voice said. 'Our son needs help.'

Back in the car, Dominiq turned his tearless face towards his mother. 'I'm sorry,' he said. 'I couldn't help it.' Allan gunned the motor.

But before the car had gone fifty yards he slammed the brakes. Something was happening to the road; huge cracks split the macadam, two eyes, a mouth . . . Allan spun the car around.

Back through the development, past the houses, everywhere, lawns, schoolyards, driveways, bitter faces cracked the earth. Heaving and shaking, the car doubled back, cut around, turn after turn, searching for a hole. 'I'm sorry. I'm sorry,' Dominiq repeated.

And Allan, as he finally found an open road, shouted, 'It's all right. We'll find a doctor. It's okay. The doctor will help you.'

Gloria watched the cold, cold faces form an aisle for the speeding car.

The Ninth Symphony of Ludwig Van Beethoven and Other Lost Songs

CARTER SCHOLZ

WHEN A MAN'S HALFWAY to his death, he knows. The bones shift, the organs settle, the blood ticks out a quiet warning: time's half gone, look around, what've you done, what are you *going* to do? Every day we meet reminders of our mortality and dismiss them, uneasily ignore, turn our faces from the grave. But at that halfway mark, ignorance is impossible; a man thinks, My God, I'm thirty-five, I'm forty, and the years are relentless, I'll never be thirty or twenty or fifteen again – and was I ever? Did I ever look around, feel, really *know* eighteen or twenty-four or any of my ages? Did I make the most of them?

Charles Largens woke one morning and found himself there. He thought, I'm thirty-five years old and I won't live past seventy. My bones tell me in language I can't rebuff. Half my life is gone, and oh Lord, where?

The early years had gone into two sonatas, an unfinished symphony, a mass, an incomplete song cycle. Those were good years, good work. But since then his time had gone into research, criticism; it had been made solid, not in sounds but in vast stacks of paper, dreary essays and analyses. He did not enjoy it, and often the stuff had no meaning for him, but it took his time nonetheless. It had taken half his life.

In his voicetyper was an unfinished essay on Buxtehude; he had abandoned it last night when the fugues and inventions piled up in a baroque tangle and he could make no more sense of them. Notes had swarmed past his eyes like flies on a five-staved racetrack, the precise ordered counterpoint a frightening miniature of his own boxed and formal life. He fell asleep with that image and woke to the sudden shock of being thirty-five. And he thought of Ludwig Van Beethoven, his avatar, the one constant source of solace in his life. He wanted to be Beethoven that morning, more than he ever had before.

Such a thing was not impossible. It was not easy to be Beethoven, of course. Like most of the Lincoln Centre musicologists in the year 2016, he had been trying the greater part of his career for that distinction; and only now, after years of the lesser talents, the Couperins and Loeschorns and Bertinis, and atop that awful sense of waste and futility, did he feel ready to consider the Master.

But be honest: it was more than consideration; this morning he recognized it as an obsession. Bach and Chopin and Debussy and even old Buxtehude were fine in their places, but for him, Charles Largens, only one composer had all the balance, the power, the complete rightness that music ought to have; so as a pianist might dream of Carnegie (as he once had), or an artist of the Guggenheim, or a literary critic of *Finnegans Wake*, so Largens longed to base his lifework as musicologist on the works of Beethoven. More now; as Beethoven he might transcend the study of music, and attain the abstract itself. That was the dream that kept him going those years after his own music went dry, the dream that drove him to write essays on the preludes of Moskowski and bore himself to madness with Czerny just because he had been a student of the Master's; just because that particular essay might draw some attention, make someone cry, Hey! he's got it! and you could never tell what might attract the men with power, the men with the machines, so you did it all.

He wanted to be Beethoven, and these men could do that for him, with their machines.

The machines were windows into the past. Not doors, nor even a very clear sort of window; they more revealed the texture of the glass than the scene beyond, for what they did was transfer your consciousness into the mind of someone in the past.

After the historians found that subjective impressions of history were not very much more valuable than textbooks and records, the psychologists and scholars took over the vast banks of transfer equipment; they roamed and delved the past like archaeologists in a newly unearthed Greek library. Essays appeared psychoanalyzing Freud. The real reasons for the Emancipation Proclamation were revealed. The Shakespeare/Bacon myth was finally debunked. George Washington's real name came out. And it was inevitable that the artists, the writers, the musicians, in their mutual despair of ever taking art further than it had already gone in the barren year 2016, came forward eager to learn the inspirations for *Macbeth*, *Also Sprach Zarathustra*, *Waiting for Godot*, the Beethoven Ninth. To find out if El Greco was really astigmatic; to catch Hemingway's last thoughts as he triggered the shotgun; to study firsthand the mad genius of Van Gogh; to see the world as the great minds of history saw it. To put together in the sad flat year 2016 a world, piecemeal, from remnants of the past.

Time travel, of a sort; it was not real time travel, for that would have been magic, a kind of miracle, and there were no more miracles or magic in the world they had made. It was a world of norms and averages and no extremes, a world where everything had an explanation and a reason, where even this miraculous-seeming time travel could be expressed in hard clear terms, if you had the math. There were no paradoxes; the mind occupied seemed to have no awareness of its passengers. The passengers could only observe, could not touch the past. One might even jump back into one's own life and affect it not at all (aside perhaps from some slight *déjà vu*). Of course, the government kept the tightest of reins on the process; so only now, after ten years with the very elite Lincoln Centre Research Group, did Charles Largens feel qualified to ask for Beethoven, to accept that last resort.

It was his essay on the inspirations of Buxtehude that drew the attention of H. Grueder, chairman of the board deciding past inhabitations. Largens had been studying the lesser talents for those ten years; he had even inhabited a few. And now his patience had paid its reward: word was out that Charles Largens was a man to watch, a man on the edge of success. And the only thing dulling his sense of triumph was that ineluctable, tender realization that he had never meant to be a musicologist. He had joined the Lincoln Centre group as a pianist and composer; but the tenor of the times was research over performance, study before passion; and call it weakness, expediency, what you will, he had found himself more in the archives than in the practice rooms. After some years those quantitative changes became qualitative: he stopped even calling himself a composer; he was a musicologist (sharp Latin percussives), still a student of music, but now from the cold side: theory over practice, intellect over heart. As a boy he had dreamed of long polished grand pianos, warm and shining under bright spots, their keyboard mouths open and waiting, and beyond the stage's edge a blinding darkness filled with murmurs and the rustlings of programmes, shirts, gowns. And ovations, storms of applause like all the warm summer showers that ever were, drenching him to a blissful numbness. But his life of composing was not that way; it was drab and hungry, and he wanted so desperately the colour of a great composer's life. And what easier, directer way than the transfers? At first he told himself that his own work would profit from the contacts with past greats; but he knew it was a lie – he found that the contacts withered his own impulses. He was glutted, stuffed with music not his own. Several times in those years he had wanted to quit, get out, go back to composing – but the money was good, he was sometimes acclaimed for his critical insights as he had not been for his music, and he had a fear that perhaps he could not compose any more. And too, as his own music faded, there was the growing dream of Beethoven.

The morning that dream seemed ready to come real, the morning Grueder sent for him, he was met by George Santesson outside the conference room. The rest of the board was inside, waiting for him; the separate and personal greeting from Santesson was a surprise. The big man smiled broadly and wrung his hand with real warmth. 'Nervous?' he whispered. Largens nodded.

'Don't worry, you'll make it. I read your essay. You'll do fine.'

Largens felt warm. He fumbled for a way to extend the moment. 'I feel as nervous as I did at my conservatory tryout.'

Santesson smiled in appreciation. 'You majored in composition, didn't you?'

'Yes. I see you've been doing research on me.'

'One likes to know about one's future colleagues.' With that, Santesson pushed open the thick leather-covered door and they entered. Largens' heart surged: Santesson was head of Beethoven Studies. Such confidence was heady stuff.

He seated himself at the far end of an oval table. Grueder congratulated him on his essay, shuffled through some notes, and finally asked the long-awaited question: Who? Who would it be next? Offering him his choice of composers for extended study, with full inhabitation rights. He had the strange feeling that Grueder already knew – Santesson certainly did – the feeling that this was all formality, that the decision was already made. He had for that second the feeling of a defendant watching the jury file back in.

He said Beethoven, and there was no surprise. Grueder nodded, made a notation on a schedule, a tiny precise scratching motion with his antique pen, and said he didn't see why not, and that Largens would be permitted a preliminary occupation during the composing of the first piano sonata, 1794, full rights pending approval of the results of that study. Was that acceptable?

Largens thanked everyone several times.

Santesson was on hand the next day, too, when Largens showed up at the transfer room with a head full of anticipations, and, stupidly, a notebook. He and Santesson laughed at that. Then the older man wished him luck and left him alone with the technicians.

They asked him a number of questions about his ancestry and mental health while they took an EEG and ran some machines of which he could see only the exposed backs, and finally they brought him a paper cup full of orange juice.

'What's this?' Largens asked.

'A hallucinogen. Very mild. It prepares you for the transfer.'

'I never had to do this before.'

'You were never trying to get into Beethoven's head before. He has a tremendous alpha potential. If you didn't drink this, it'd be like mismatching audio impedances; you'd never get across.'

He was led into a thick-carpeted room more like a den than a laboratory: rich tapestry colours and subdued yellow lights instead of harsh fluorescents. Purposes of setting, he presumed. The only visible electronics were a stereo system and a tangle of multicoloured wires that spilled from a wall socket into spaghetti patterns on the couch. The silence could be felt, like the pressure preceding a storm; behind the wall hangings there must have been acoustical tiles.

'Would you undress now, Mr Largens?' someone said.

His clothes came off with more friction than usual, it seemed; his hearing seemed somehow bent, his vision slightly fragmented. They taped

284

electrodes to him: cold metal goosefleshed his neck and arms, his groin, the small of his back, behind his ears. He felt the coldness spreading to cover his skin with hallucinatory foil. He heard a thunk and a quiet hissing as someone set a phono needle down. A tickling began behind his ears and Beethoven's first piano sonata began to play in his head.

swimming in sounds that spiralled up around him, came together in his head and cancelled gravity, he could feel billions of tiny soft points of velvet grow and lift him through the liquid sky with the first piano notes rising, pulsing colours on the horizon, and each note had a texture, this C like rough dark wood, that F a silky coldness, an A like a trapped bumblebee in his hands, and the music was no longer coming into him through his ears but was bursting out from within like a spontaneous song breaking free and sailing into a clear summer sky, apart from its source, apart from time, it carried Largens and he had no sense of going forward or going back or anything other than motion itself, of shutting his eyes and feeling the gone world whirl beneath him, he was a child flat back on a grassy plain, eyes clenched tight at the sky and fingers dug into fistfuls of earth and the whole world spinning and spinning and nothing but spinning, the motion, the vertigo, circles and currents, layers of moire confusion, oceans and waves rolling and rolling, the perpetual roll and flat scream of things that change and never change, moving not moving, the seasons that spin down a spiral of time, the ocean that crawls and rolls under its mapflat surface, the planets that turn and spin, each its own clock, the moving and complete motions of the instantaneous universe. He was moving through the first movement of the first piano sonata of the beginning of a long and turbulent life full of its own movements and motions, songs wound into a soul and waiting for release, steps to be taken through meadows and woods and narrow cobbled streets, wines to be tasted ... and it all shifted and was moving him somewhere, the motion and the music becoming one and leading him into a life whose goal was their perfect union.

There was a darkness, and a light, as Largens opened his new eyes onto Vienna of 1794.

Cries and the beat of hooves and the rumble and clatter of wagons through mudpuddled streets reached him as he lurched to consciousness. The windows of the room leaned open to catch the afternoon rain-freshened air, and the sun struck rainbow brilliances off watery glass. The voices Largens heard could have been Beethoven's subconscious musings or the town's glad emergence after the storm. Beethoven went to the window and breathed deeply. Largens dizzied with the sights and sounds and smells of his dream come real, and he wept. He tried to put his hands to his face, and of course nothing happened. Foolish man, he fondly cursed himself, crying without eyes, expecting another man's body to express your joy. But if he was physically detached, the spiritual union was incredible. This was no fantasy; he *was* Beethoven, he could feel every ache and exultation of the composer's soul, and he had never before known what life could be like–! To have the world spread before you, to sense the forces of destiny shifting like banks of clouds or strata of earth – this was what it was to be great, to carry genius within you like a seed, a freight of potency. Very early in his own life

Largens had felt the hints of this. In a way, his whole life had been an attempt to recapture that lost greatness. And here, Beethoven: with no doubt of his own importance, even so young. As young as Largens had been when he entered the Centre. The drab improbable world of the future, his past.

Beethoven's mind was warm and sparkling. It idled and hummed with life like a brook in late spring; thoughts mixed and swirled in currents of warm and cool. Beethoven was content simply to be in his new lodgings and to peer out the large crystal windows overlooking the street where movers struggled in with his belongings. The sweet force of this content washed Largens.

Largens reviewed the history of the moment: it was late in the year; Beethoven had just moved to Count Carl Lichnowsky's house in Vienna, Alserstrasse 45. Here he would earn a substantial salary for composing and performing, and form a rare lasting friendship with the Count. *Dem Fursten Carl von Lichnowsky gewidmet.* He remembered the words from the top of a piano sonata he had played when young.

Beethoven paced the room, brooding. He thought rapidly, in fragments of dialect. Words, sounds, gave shape to music, which he visualized rather than heard. Once visualized, he immediately orchestrated the phrase. Only occasionally did he go to the piano to play out a bar. At last he began to play a full piece, the second movement of his first piano sonata.

Largens waited. This movement had been written piecemeal years before, but there were other things in the composer's mind, and Largens could sense syntheses occurring between what was played and what was imagined. He watched the young fingers triphammer up and down arpeggios with a certain vicarious satisfaction, a remote pride. With two final flourished chords, the movement ended, and Largens' mind leaped to full attention.

Beethoven leaned over the keyboard, pondering. Then he lifted a quill, inked it, and began to write . . .

Hours later Largens awoke in Manhattan, screaming German curses. He blinked twice and settled foolishly back onto the couch as an attendant unwound wires, disconnected meters, and handed him his clothes. He stared at them as if they had changed colour, or shrunk three sizes. He was acutely disoriented. A doctor standing near the door watched Largens and made notes on a flat glowing pad.

'I . . . he was having a tantrum,' Largens explained. 'He lost his temper at a mover for interrupting him. He . . .' His thoughts fluttered. He shook his head. 'Why am I so woozy?'

The doctor said, 'Could be the drug.'

'But I've taken them before; I never felt like this. Are you sure it's nothing serious?'

The doctor regarded him coldly. 'We are not *sure* of anything, Mr

Largens.'

'Did I say something wrong?'

'Nothing. Not a thing. It's a little idiosyncrasy of mine that I snap at people for no reason at all.'

'For what reason are you snapping at me?'

The doctor thumbed off his light-pen. 'It's a little matter of responsibility, Mr Largens. Of all the ways you could be spending this money – and for that matter, your time, though I suppose that's your business – this strikes me as the most wasteful and dangerous. If I had my way, you people wouldn't be mucking around in the past at all. We just don't know enough about it. But you've got your government lobbies, and people must have their novelties, so you're allowed to go. Let's leave it at that. But don't expect me to get too concerned over your dizziness.'

'If you feel that way, why do you work here?'

The doctor paused, and had a look Largens knew: the hard, bitter look of a man who knows just how much of himself he has sold, and how cheaply. 'I intend to start a free clinic with my salary from here.' He clipped the pen in his pocket and walked out.

The attendant put away a handful of wires. 'Don't mind him. Professional paranoia. Every week a different worry. This week it's something called a crosstalk effect.'

'What's that?'

'Well, when you have a cable or a magnetic tape or a laser carrying more than one channel of information, there's always a certain amount of leakage between channels. If one channel's quiet you can hear the others coming through. That's crosstalk. The more channels, the worse it gets. So they're especially worried about guys like Beethoven; sometimes he has a dozen or more researchers in his head at once. They're worried about that.'

'What, that Beethoven might overhear thoughts from the future?'

'Something like that.'

'Oh, but that's absurd. Even if Beethoven heard anything, he'd never guess the source. He'd think it was . . .' Largens slowed.

'Inspiration. Intuition. You begin to see?'

Largens stood silent. He thought of Da Vinci's notebooks, the visions of Blake. For a second in the murmur of the air conditioning, he thought he could hear a dozen researchers from *his* future whispering in one corner of his mind.

'Oh, but after all . . .'

The attendant held up his hand. 'I know, I know. I won't argue it. It's one of those damned paradoxes. Could be, couldn't be. That's why they're upset. Until they can *prove* any of it, there's nothing they can do. And how do you prove a paradox?'

So there were paradoxes, after all.

In the first piano sonata of Ludwig Van Beethoven, the influence of his tutor Josef Haydn is clearly felt. Haydn seems to guide the young composer's pen from time to time. But

In this, his first sonata, the young Beethoven first breaks from his classical antecedents. The second movement seems to be saying a last farewell to the 'galant' age. Breaking from the strict regimen of Haydn's instruction,

The first sonata might be called a tribute to Haydn. The composer moves with great surety through these familiar

Here the young Beethoven's craftsmanship still shows sign of immaturity, as when the splendid A-flat major catalina is prevented from fully developing by a clumsy

The second movement is not in sonata form, but is rather a rhapsody, laid out

Beethoven's originality

Yes, yes, but where did he get his ideas?

At six Santesson came in to wish him good-night. All day Largens had been working on his essay and it had gone nowhere. The older man read the desk at a glance, took in the litter of half-written pages, abandoned beginnings, and all that they meant – and gave Largens a sympathetic nod. There must have been something near desperation in the young man's face, because Santesson paused as he was leaving, and motioned Largens to follow.

They went down the empty halls, the last ones in the building. They did not speak. They reached the transfer room and only then did Largens have an intimation of their purpose. Santesson fumbled a key from his pocket, slid the door open, and sealed it after them before turning on the lights.

The room stood empty and silent. Humming.

'Do you know how to use the equipment, Charles?'

'No.'

For half an hour Santesson detailed the use of the machinery, scrupulously, completely, until Largens could have started it alone, sent himself on a retrogressive voyage – and at the end of it Santesson pressed a key into his hand. 'In case you ever need to,' he whispered. And left Largens alone in the dark building.

A tight humming excitement was in him. He walked around the room, running his hand over smooth panels, knurled knobs. He listened to his breathing and felt his pulse. His hands moved over the controls almost independently of thought. He set them for Beethoven, 1794. He stepped into the carpeted tapestried room where the Kempff recording of the first sonata still rested on the turntable. If he could live it just once more ... His hands moved, attaching wires, taping electrodes, remembering. He lay on the couch for minutes. Then he got up, went back to the main room, returned all the switches to neutral, shut the lights off and went home.

Shortly after that he had an invitation from the Santessons. A cocktail party at their home in the West Eighties. He guessed it would be wearisome, but the night of the party he dressed anyway and took a cab crosstown. He had to go. In the past few years he had obligated himself. To tell the truth, Largens relied on these social functions to advance him where his talents alone might not. Seeing the uncompleted essay in his voicetyper, thinking of the rumours of personnel cutbacks, he knew he had to go. Any gesture of support from Santesson was welcome.

The apartment was elegant. The room was lit in soft blue. All the elder members of the Centre were there, the aged coterie he had never before met informally. The elite. They had been born in the middle of the last century; some had studied with Stockhausen, Berio, Xenakis. The last legendary names of music.

Lia Santesson greeted him with a quick surprising press of her lips to his. Behind her was George Santesson, smiling warmly.

'Good of you to come, Charles.'

He had the giddy, paranoiac feeling that they were all here for him, for his imminent prominence. The feeling increased as Lia led him through a gauntlet of introductions, her small electronic earrings making windchime noises as they walked, the old men's voices barely rising above the background of the party. They treated him with courtesy. He moved tentatively past their nods and smiles, a man exploring unsure ground.

The party's tempo was *adagio*. The guests all spoke softly, like low whispering strings; they moved like ancient clockwork. After a while Largens moved to a remote corner of the room. There was fatigue from the closed world of the party, which, somewhere, he realized was the same closed world as his life. *Adagio molto e cantabile.*

'Is that *you*, Charlie?'

The wonder in the voice stopped him, He turned. 'I'm sorry?'

'David Kanigher, remember? The New Music Ensemble, what, fifteen years ago?'

'David! Of course!' Kanigher now wore glasses and an ineffective moustache, but was otherwise unchanged.

'Charlie. What have you been doing?'

And time shifted for Largens then: it stuttered and stopped and he was no longer at the Santessons' party, but somewhere liquid in his own mind, where the events of his life swept past him like a wave pulling sand from

289

under his bare feet. He was there only with Kanigher, wondering how he could possibly explain his life's turnings to this stranger from the past. He felt a sudden cold twist of remorse. It might have been the liquor or the plummet of memory, but all at once it sickened him to be standing there, just past thirty-five years old, talking with a man whose ambitions he had once shared.

Young Largens had been the Centre's *enfant terrible* in the days before he switched over to musicology. One of the few real talents. Then a criticism from Santesson had unmanned him. Though Santesson had been only forty then, he carried unmistakable authority, and what he said had struck Largens to the core: You've no heritage. No sense of the past in your music. Modern, superficial, shallow. Clever, but ultimately disappointing.

Of course it was what Largens had always feared about himself. He had been orphaned at thirteen, already an excellent pianist; he had been sent to relatives, an ancient aunt and uncle who had no piano and refused to let him waste time on music. It took him a full year to muster the courage to sue them and win the right to live in a state Montessori home. He grew up there with a hundred other youngsters, all bright and creative: artists, actors, poets. From then on, everyone in his life had been adept, but, he realized with adolescent smugness, none brilliant. That was for him. He was sure he had that spark of true greatness. And he feared that, like his playmates, he was really a talented dilettante.

So Santesson's comment had struck him to the core: *You've no heritage*. No parents, true. *No sense of the past*. But the past was those two shrivelled tyrants, the past was cracked porcelain, the smell of urine and rose water. *Even Beethoven*, yes, the god, *that great innovator, had deep respect for his forerunners*. And Largens determined then to study music, to learn the history of music so well that no one could criticize him on that score, ever. Later he found it was a lifetime job.

'I'm in Beethoven Studies now,' he said, the inside of his mouth like chalk.

'Are you composing?'

The cruel question. 'No.' Glancing around, he saw Lia Santesson watching him from fifty feet away. She smiled as their eyes met. He turned away.

'That's too bad, Charlie. You had the makings of a fine composer.'

'Perhaps I did.' Yes. The makings. Kanigher had learned the difference.

Kanigher smiled. 'Did you know I was jealous of you?'

'Yes, I knew that.' Certainly. The Ensemble playing an evening of new music: works by Stockhausen, Cage, Riley, Shapiro, and Largens. Kanigher found it so hard to work, while for Largens the music simply flowed from his pen. For that reason he had switched to musicology, believing he would always have that easy facility.

'What are *you* doing?'

'Scrambling for money. Would you believe it – I had to sell my piano last month! I've been using those dreadful Baldwin uprights in the Centre basement. I have to spend an hour tuning before I can play, it's so damp down there.'

'I don't understand. What about your salary?'

Kanigher spread his hands. 'No more. All the money is going into your research equipment. They can't afford to keep unproductive composers on the payroll.'

Largen's remorse found a small, hard comfort in that. 'Unproductive?'

'Well, yes. I suppose I've become rather avant-garde, and I don't have the carapace for it. I'm too sensitive to criticism. And my, have they been criticizing. So I'm suffering through a block.' Kanigher finished his drink. 'They offered me a job teaching music history, which I turned down, and suddenly I was without a salary. My contract had a rather clever termination clause that I never read. It states that if I turn down any Centre job when my own position is in jeopardy, I void the contract.'

'So what's wrong with teaching history.'

'Well, there's an awful lot of it going on.' Kanigher paused. '"If we carry our respect for the past too far, we are in danger of detaching ourselves from the present." Andre Hodeir said that, a twentieth-century musicologist.' He laughed. 'You can tell I'm idle: I've been reading. But Christ, Charlie, I believe that. I'm terrified of losing the present. That's what music is all about, damn it! More than anything else, it's . . . a sense of what is necessary.

'You remember how clutched up I was with the Ensemble. Couldn't write anything. I had a girl then. She was so much better than anything I'd hoped for, it made everything a little unreal. I was sure I'd lose her, and I guess it was that sureness that finally drove her away. All right, I was just a young idiot. But Christ, when I lost her, I wrote music like I was born for it! Looking back, I can see that all I was doing was trying to hold those moments I had lost.' Kanigher was quiet, and then he smiled. 'I read through some of it the other day. It was a little embarrassing.

'But – now I feel I'm in danger of losing my composing. It makes me edgy and alert to little things, but totally useless in things that count. I'm afraid that's more serious than losing the girl, because then I knew I was young, I knew I could get over it, I knew I had my music and my friends. I'm a little older now, my only friends are acquaintances in the Centre, and the music's all I have. It's too precious. I'm afraid to gamble it. I'm all too willing to take one of their jobs just to keep my muse safe and living in the style to which it's accustomed.'

Largens looked at his drink. He shut his eyes. He looked up. 'I wasn't afraid.'

Kanigher stared at him a long time.

'I'm sorry, Charlie. Christ, I'm sorry. I thought you were happy.'

'I'm all right.'

'Santesson's been after me to study Beethoven.'

'Why should he care what you do?'

'He seems to need these little conquests, displays of power. I'm sorry you're not happy, Charlie.'

Santesson came over then. Liquor moved in Largens. He felt dead drained and set upon. Santesson smiled, a slow revelation of lion's teeth, and yet – with all his instincts burning in clear flame, Largens thought, *Why, he's afraid of Kanigher.* Why should a man intimate with Beethoven know such fear? And oddly, he had his answer: because Kanigher threatens him. Beethoven does not. Because Beethoven is dead. His music is fixed, pinned to the staves. Creation is a kind of magic that lives in men, and when they die it passes from them. Only the works remain. Santesson fears the potential: the actual he can master, with notes and diagrams and rules. In that second, Largens knew Santesson's power, and consequently his weakness. He felt some small magic stir in himself with that perception.

But Kanigher did not sense control of the situation resting on him. He retreated.

'Hello, David,' Santesson said. 'How's the composing coming?'

'Not very well, I'm afraid.'

'Well, you know there's a place for you upstairs.'

'Yes. I know. I'm considering it.'

And as if that were all Santesson wanted he said, 'Come, Charles, I have someone you should meet,' and turned from Kanigher.

But Largens was aggressive. He had his first real motivation in much time. Suddenly, strangely, there was music in him. He wanted to get home and write it down. 'I don't think I'll stay,' he said.

Santesson stopped and studied him. 'Do what you like, of course. I thought you'd like to meet your competition for the Beethoven job.'

And Largen's breath left him. He followed Santesson and met a man named John Hart, a man with a feral look, and they spoke for a short time, saying nothing about the Beethoven job. It occurred to him that Santesson might have lied.

He finally broke free and made for the door, but was deftly caught by Lia Santesson. She chided him for ignoring her all evening, and started speaking in a low, oiled, intimate voice that eventually drew him out of his resolution and into an empty room with her. Into a warm, silken purgatory.

The last cry of a man dying, mad and forgotten, in the midst of a summer storm. Layers and levels and years away, the lightning flickered and the thunder rolled out of the hills over Largens as he died; then he opened his eyes and thought no: that's not me.

He raised himself on one elbow and looked panic-stricken into darkness. Then a faint numeric glow brought him back. It was just past 2 a.m. and he had been lying half under Lia Santesson's naked body for almost an hour, dozing. She was still asleep. He felt bad – seduced and soured with irresolution. Furtively he bent to whisper her awake, when he heard a gentle breathing behind him. A thin slice of light cut across the floor, over the bed and his calf. He pivoted at the waist and saw the large dark silhouette of George Santesson in the doorway. Light and the late remnants of the party were faintly behind him. Largen's mouth half opened, and he froze in that twisted stiff posture, in an agony of silence, in a waiting and a wanting to cry out, to explain, to accept punishment for his adultery if punishment were needed. He was riven by the thought of having hurt someone unaware. And then he was hotly ashamed, for *he* had been seduced, *he* had been led to this, as much by Santesson as by his wife. The big man did not move or speak. They stared at each other for almost a minute; then Santesson let out a slightly heavier breath and passed into the hall.

When Largens finally left, silent and exhausted and with no good-byes, the walk home woke him. It was much too late to go to sleep anyway, so he sat up with a single light on, reading through his old notebooks. He started to play a couple of his compositions, but they were demanding and his fingers were stiff, and the sound of the piano in the silent apartment was loud and plangent. It sounded much more assertive than he felt. He had to admit he had put it off too long.

He saw Santesson once more before the thing happened. Late one evening they passed in the hall and Largens was immediately and pointlessly embarrassed enough to rush for the elevators. Santesson stopped him and drew him gently aside and said, 'I wanted to thank you for giving my wife what I can't.'

The blood pounding through his temples turned cold. 'Oh,' he said; then 'Oh! I –' Then he said nothing, but gripped Santesson's arms and was gripped back. He felt he had been used, manipulated into it, yes – but he felt Santesson's sincerity too, the man's great deep pain and weakness. He pitied him.

'It's terribly hard sometimes,' Santesson said, 'to have to live here, now, when your soul is somewhere else; when the only thing that ever felt like home . . . is something you can't even touch. I've given so much to my music, to Beethoven.' He seemed to struggle briefly. 'You know the opening of the Ninth's third movement . . . the melodic theme?' Largens nodded. Santesson's mouth moved: 'Mine.'

'*What?*'

'I wonder what these transfers are, sometimes. What they've done to us. To the past. I sometimes think it's all one, there is no past or future, only that great timeless flow between. . . . I've had so many transfers; I've left so much of myself back there, Charles. I feel I've left my soul there.' He shook his head. 'Do you know what I mean?'

Largens could only nod.

'I'll let you go.' He dropped his arms. 'I have to do something. You're a good man, Charles.'

The next morning Largens was interrupted from work by the sounds of a hallway commotion, from the direction of the transfer rooms. He walked into the hall; a cold intuition gripped him; he started to run. The door was open; people clustered. He forced his way through and found Grueder and a dozen others surrounding the red velvet couch. As he entered the tiny room, a doctor straightened, stethoscope limp in his hand. Grueder looked at Largens and said, 'It's Santesson. He's dead.'

The doctor said, 'At your earliest convenience, Mr Grueder,' and went stiffly out. The others followed, murmuring.

Largens stared in incomprehension.

Grueder's face was strictured, a hard and ancient landscape strained by simply being. He sighed. 'An unauthorized transfer. Santesson set up the equipment late last night after everyone left. He gave himself triple the required trigger voltage. It killed him.'

'How?'

'His brain just shut off. His mind was no longer here and it couldn't come back.'

Largens trembled. Santesson's body was still, composed. His face was peaceful. 'The controls . . . where –?'

Grueder just shook his head. 'It doesn't matter, Charles, he's dead. Wherever – whenever – he is, he's dead. Come – '

'*Where?*'

Grueder looked at him strangely.

'Beethoven. 1823.'

Largens reeled. 'The Ninth . . .'

'Yes. The Ninth.' Grueder looked around, to make sure they were alone. 'This was no accident, Charles. There was a note on his desk – I haven't told anyone this – he requested that you be appointed head of Beethoven Studies. I think we can arrange to honour that wish . . .'

'My God,' Largens whispered, hardly hearing. He stared at the dead man's face, a poor snapshot exposure of a soul, a brief final connection of body and spirit. His heart, his brain, his body, were off, cold, stone; there was no way for Santesson to be alive. But Largens believed, he knew with fanatic irrationality, that some infinitesimal part of Santesson was living, almost two centuries in the past. . . .

'Did you hear, Charles? You're head of Beethoven Studies now.'

'I heard.'

'Don't mention this to anyone, Charles. Lord, if the government found out this was unauthorized, they'd shut us down in a second. The doctor suspects, but he can't prove anything, I hope. They only need a small excuse to end the programme, so for God's sake keep quiet about it, Charles!' Largens sensed a threat behind that. He just nodded.

Something in Largens' silence sparked to Grueder. The old man looked at

Santesson and sighed. 'He had a hard life, Charles.'

'So have we all.'

For some time I have been occupied with major works. Much of the music has already hatched, at least in my head. I must first get them off my neck; two important symphonies, each one different from my others . . .

– Ludwig Van Beethoven, after completion of his Eighth Symphony.

The passage was circled in Santesson's notebook. The word *two* was underlined.

Largens walked out of the office with a confidence grown from a year of authority. 'What is this stuff about a Tenth Symphony?'

Hart was there, serving as his assistant. He pushed the notebook back across the desk and snorted. 'Nonsense. Santesson's pet theory. Some fragments of an unfinished symphony were found . . .'

'Yes, I *know* that, but a musicologist of Santesson's stature wouldn't make all these notes simply on that basis.'

'Well, there they are.'

A fine antagonism had been honed between the men. True to his word, Grueder had given Largens the appointment. Hart was still resenting it. And he had learned that to cut Largens he had only to insult Santesson. He added, 'Personally I think the old boy went a bit *soft* towards the end.' Stressing the *double entendre.*

For an instant Largens wanted to whirl the little man around, slap him across the face, shut him up. But the feeling passed, and he simply sighed, and walked out, allowing Hart his small victory.

He was thirty-six. It was winter. He was bitterly unhappy. Was that all the years were good for, to add an extra sting to the remorse?

Santesson's death had affected him deeply. The poor impotent bastard – escaping not even into death, but into a life not his own. Largens had had a brief affair with Lia; three months ago he had talked Kanigher into taking a musicology job; he did not know how much further he might fill Santesson's role.

He watched the setting sun bleed New York. The day turned red, was drawn off into Jersey. Central Park stretched below, the lights just coming on, a few couples strolling. The city was livable for the first time in a century: two million people now. Buildings were coming down crosstown. But it seemed so empty to him. He had grown up here when it was five times as dense.

Hart left without saying good-night. Largens heard the elevator chime, close, suck away. He felt very alone. He stepped into the hall, looking up and down. Lights off, doors sealed for the night. He walked down the corridor, passing no one, hearing nothing. He walked faster.

A strange feeling took hold of him.

By the time he reached the transfer room he was running.

He fumbled with his key, pressed it home; the door opened. He went in, sealed it, snapped on the lights.

The machinery waited.

(*In case you ever need to.* The whisper, razoring back to him, from a year away.)

(Santesson's escape.)

Quickly then, the patch. It was not as if he were breaking regulations: he had permission for this transfer; what matter when he took it? He was going back to the Ninth, he was going to consummate that lifelong obsession. His fingers twitched. His brain raced. At the last slider, marked *trigger voltage,* his fingers paused.

(Escape.)

1.5 he needed.

He slid it to 5.

A red light blinked, blinked, blinked.

(Escape!)

His hand trembled.

He brought it back to 1.5.

He had to rest for several minutes on the couch and let the sweat dry before he could take the drug. He taped electrodes to his skin, cold square steel invasions of his nakedness. He trembled there waiting for the colours to start, knowing he was wrong, knowing why he couldn't tamper with the past this way, but he was too far gone in his need, the colours were on him, he reached for the trigger switch and *like that:* immediately went to sleep.

and the centre went away and left him spinning in a silver void, down and across cold currents of time that moved with the vast slowness of glaciers. He moved in directions he could not name. His metabolism was high with nerves and it panicked him to think what difference that might make and all the colours and the great rumbling shapes moved about him and he was afraid, God what've I done, he was climbing a wall of paranoia until he dropped off the top straight into sleep

and he shrugged it off with heavy blankets and a fear of suffocation. Bright morning sunlight was in the room. Intimations of the coming winter whispered across the sill. Beethoven stretched, rolled his legs out of bed. He quickly crossed the room, pulled on some woollen socks, and plunged his arms into a basin of icy water. Largen's consciousness seemed to splash into bright fragments at the shock and reform quivering, clearer, sharper. Beethoven started bellowing up and down scales. He towelled himself, went to the window overlooking Baden and sang a few measures from the symphony's second movement. He sang some more, paused, and made a pencil notation on the shutter, alongside a dozen others and lists of figures, sums, conversions from florins to guilders.

Then another researcher blinked into being. Santesson. Vibrations of interest, perhaps irony, reached him. Of course. This was a younger

Santesson. And he suddenly realized, that was why Santesson had been so friendly and encouraging the first time. Santesson *knew* Largens would end up here sometime later. A fragment of Largens' future had been part of Santesson's memory.

Meanwhile, Beethoven's whole train of thought went past unnoticed. Largens let it. To hell with analysis: he was here for magic. He didn't care why Beethoven was writing the symphony, only that he was a part of it.

He wanted to be more a part of it.

So when Beethoven sat at the pianoforte to start work, Largens in effect *dictated* a phrase to him.

To his utter and terrified amazement, the composer stopped. His pen wavered in midstroke; it trembled with just a hint of suspicion as Largens' phrase roiled in his mind; then he jotted it down.

Crosstalk.

Beethoven had heard.

Some chemistry, some arcane connection of blood pressures, brainwaves, *something* had bridged the gap – and now Beethoven was developing a passage from his theme. *What had he done?*

This was not the Ninth Symphony; and yet the music spattered out from the pen, not entirely his, not all Beethoven's. His panic increased. What were the mechanics of music, time, the past?

Music was articulated time. Largens always thought of it as a river. If he were lucky, relaxed and easy in his craft, a man could tap the flow, turn the currents of time to something solid, a piece of music. And rarely, so rarely, he might actually direct the flow. Time might swirl and bend around him as space bends around a point of gravity. Beethoven had that force; that was his magic. But Beethoven was unique. What of himself and the critics that with machineries, with tinkerings and tamperings dammed the flow? What were they doing to the past?

The next few hours were blurred and broken. Largens had no sense of returning to 2016. He remembered Santesson's voice, among all the other phantom voices filling Beethoven's head. The opening of the third movement – but not the way Largens remembered it. He lost all track of time then and came finally to consciousness in the dark transfer room, drained and sick with the irresponsibility of what he had done. He skirted Central Park on the way home, feeling vaguely threatened by it, watching the night sky glow faintly through layers of leaves that shifted as he walked under them. The way the layers crossed and moved stirred something in him. It reminded him of the surrealistic moments of transfer. It gave him unpleasant intimations, as if the trees were trying to tell him something; or, more accurately, his mind was searching for a way to reach him, and the trees were handy. *Something is different.* He was too tired to think about it. He stopped in a bar on Sixty-eighth Street, had three drinks and went home. He had trouble with his door key – he had to search his ring for it, which seemed far too crowded – got inside, and dropped onto the bed.

The benefit of living in a closed world was that you were effectively shielded from attack from without. The failing was that your defences weakened, and if the closed world started to come apart, you were helpless.

Charles Largens' world had showed the first weak seam. He lay drunk in his bed and cried as he hadn't since his parents died.

The afternoon before the official transfer he spent with Lia. In the same apartment on East Eighty-fourth, they traded thoughts and intimacies. He spoke as in a dream:

'Does it seem different to you?'

'What?'

'The way things are.'

'What things?'

'Everything; I don't know. You and I and

The apartment on Seventy-eighth Street was unchanged since Santesson's death; Lia lived alone there and he visited frequently. This morning

He was so confused now, the world seemed only a welter of possibilities, nothing was certain. The sense of *change* that followed each of his returns had disjointed him so

A thin drizzle greyly painted the bedroom window as they

No, no; it was not real, it couldn't be. He was dreaming, the dreams timeless monuments of time, clear and precise, their meanings faint and distant. These dreams had no more reality, no less importance, than all the music he had never written.

His dreams now, his nightdreams, were of Beethoven and the past, of music unravelling itself into spaghetti piles, and he woke frequently in sweat and fear, lying still but sliding madly into the past: time and the tide took him back, the great bulk of days he had lived weighed more heavily than days he would yet live, freighted him towards the past. It was only necessary to stand still in that awful darkness to be drawn vertiginously back.

And one morning, *that* morning he walked to the Centre in a surreal mood, living in a fantasy of the near-future which was a baroque counterpointed dream of the past since he was dreaming of where he would be in a half hour which would be two hundred years in the past, and concurrently he was remembering all the times in his past he had daydreamed of this moment, each disparate present a window on the past through the future, and how different it all was from how he had frequently thought it would be. He had now a fear of alternate presents, vague suspicions of what was happening to him, to time, to music. He thought of how hectic his time with Beethoven would be with all the researchers from past and future history converging on that most covetable moment of inspiration.

(He had spent one afternoon with Bach during the Brandenburg months, during his assistantship to Santesson, and had been so drained by the babel of thoughts from the dozen others also there that he quite forgot why he had come. His own thoughts were washed from him in the greater cataract; there was only the sound of all the critics that would ever inhabit Bach during that period – a dozen trains converging on the same terminus from different moments in time, with a tumult and a clattering and collision, Bach, the terminus, all ignorant of the chaos within.)

(Or had all that furious racket somehow fuelled the headlong counterpoint of the Brandenburg concerti? No, ridiculous, stop it.)

But he walked into the transfer room now with a growing apocalyptic sense, his every instinct so tightly wound that they had to give him a tranquillizer with the drug; and at the moment of triggering he still screamed, screamed his way into *the place without time, the place* of motion without destination, form without function, research without purpose, the floating fragments of times without order. Time without his world, times without Beethoven, times where his own life was rich and glorious; and in an instant quickly past he heard his song cycle finished, he heard half a score symphonies that were his own; he clutched at them and they vanished, and only the flat spinning emptiness remained, as distant and unreachable as the bowl of the sky. . . . The moire patterns slowed, the layers peeled back to show greater complexities, more permutations, fork upon fork of time, and then a great rending –

(there was a time as a boy he had lain by midnight railroad tracks, waiting for a train to pass, the air hot, muggy, iron-smelling; he waited till a glow appeared, distant, and grew to a full glare; and then the train was upon him and rushing past like doom and time and the endless vacuum of space wrapped in a midnight earth blackness, the air shuddering and sucking all around him, the very fabric of space torn with its force. He felt his heart clutch up, stall, and he felt the end of the world passing in that endless second. Time suspended. He felt that now, in the moment of transfer, in the region between times.)

– as blocks of time were torn by their roots, knocked free and avalanched : all past in an instant.

1823. Baden.

He was there; and the first thing was *not* a clear idyllic vision of the past, but a riot-blur of greygreen light and the assault of a thousand nightmare conversations of which he heard no words –

but Beethoven was *deaf* –

but the voices of a thousand and more men from Largens' time filled the void with their own sounds and laments, voices of pain and frustration and everything Largens saw coming to fruition in himself, voices of humanity enough to crush him –

then strangely they all fell silent –

a tense waiting hush, as before a curtainrise –

... and Beethoven thought clearly of the fourth movement of his Ninth Symphony, musing, brooding, on the proper introduction to Schiller's Ode ...

and the voices surged out of silence:

O Freunde, nicht diese Töne! Sondern lasst uns ausgenehmere anstimmen und freudevollere ...

Beethoven staggered and gasped. He tore open his notebook.

The voices – !

Beethoven's tortured mind sensed them, it caught all the thunder and roar of a thousand voices, all gabbling humanity; they struck off his mind like a scream off piano strings, fragmenting into tones and harmonies:

Freude, schöner Gotterfunken, Tochter aus Elysium ...

He scribbled frantically, desperately, and they urged him on, the minds pressed and sang and screamed, pleaded with him to say for them the things they couldn't, and Beethoven was filled with pity, understanding, a community of despair ...

Seid umschlungen, Millionen, dieser Kuss der ganzen Welt ...

and harder they pressed, each with his own personal demands and pains, each in search of his own special magic, a thousand variations of the Ninth, a thousand personal misinterpretations spilling their own lost songs into the chaos –

Deine Zauber binden wieder, was die Mode streng getheilt ...

Largens caught the roar of an electronicized version, metal resonances echoing through Beethoven's deaf mind, a confusion of sounds, reverberating, building, starting to topple this immense structure, and in the chaos he recognized Santesson's voice, and then his own, all singing with the mad intensity they had never trusted their own lives to reach, a tottering sea of sound, climbing and accelerating, oh they knew what was coming, they *knew* it! madly racing, *screaming* –

Ja, wer auch nur eine Seele, sein nennt auf dem Erdenrund!

Und wer's nie gekonnt der stehle, weinend sich aus diesem Bund ...

until it was too much, too much pressure, and there was a rending and a piercing cry of anguish that was Beethoven's own as he *saw* what was inside him, and the turmoil raged on and on, past the end of the music –

(the last cry of a man dying, mad and forgotten, in the midst of a summer storm. The lightning flickered and the thunder rolled out of the hills over Largens as he died; then he opened his eyes and thought, Oh my God, it's me, it is, it's me and Santesson and all the rest, all the failed and weak and impotent ... but it's not Beethoven.)

300

Silence . . .

Somewhere outside it was raining, fat drops hammering and spraying his face, and unheard thunder shaking the earth . . .

and inside the chaos raged on and rose over Largens as all the occupants wept and muttered about their own misspent lives (and the composer was silent, silent) and they at least rested in this dark world of grey ash, this mind burnt and made their own –

(and Largens strained to hear Beethoven, but there was silence, silence, only silence –)

until the recall, and with great relief he heard the raining silence fall away, recede like foaming surf into sand, and he heard:

'You okay?'

The lights were soft and warm: inside lights. The sky's cold grey was gone. He was back.

'Uh.' Speech was an effort. 'Yeah. Are – are you the one who strapped me in?'

'Yeah. You're all right, you're sure?'

'Uh huh.' Largens' voice was quite flat. 'You look different.'

The attendant smiled. 'They all say that after they've been through the breakdown.'

'Breakdown?'

'Yeah. The 1823 breakdown you went to study, remember?' The attendant shook his head with old amusement. 'Every time, you guys forget.'

'I . . . I went to study the Ninth . . .'

'The what?'

'The Ninth, the Ninth Symphony! The Chorale on Schiller's "Ode to Joy!"'

'Hey, take it easy. Beethoven only wrote *eight* symphonies, remember? There were fragments for the Ninth, but no more.'

'No!' Largens sat up suddenly, and the room tilted. In his vertigo he felt thoughts rushing away and he tried to hold them.

'Poor guy,' the attendant said, peeling tape from wires. 'First he loses his hearing, then his sanity. Never wrote another note.'

Largens was sick, soul-sick. The room spun without spinning.

They had killed the Ninth Symphony. All the frustrated pianists and composers and singers turned scholars had brought their frustration to the works they studied; and they had brought it to Beethoven himself. All their souls' cheapnesses summed; the faint crosstalk turned to a shout. They had brought their weakness and despair in such pent-up furious quantity that Beethoven had been swamped by it, and drowned.

Largens saw layers of reality peeling away, shifting, each one new with each new transfer, each time another subtle alteration: past present future so closely bound and interwoven there was no way *not* to change them.

301

This time they had killed the Ninth. This time Beethoven had gone mad in 1823. But next time – after the next transfer, what might happen? Would there be seven symphonies, or six, or four? As the thousands converged earlier and earlier in the master's life in coming realities, in search of unworked time, when would the breakdown occur? After a few more years of indiscriminate transfers, would the young Beethoven ever leave Bonn to study with Haydn? Or would he rebel against his tyrannical father and never touch the piano after the old man's death?

It was all so delicately balanced.

And he felt the reality of the Ninth leaving him, a great weight lifting; his memories slid and shifted and there was a great surge of loss. How, how did it go?

Freude . . .

He tried to hear, to remember, but there was only the silence, deafening and mute.

A terrible long night. Sleepless, he listened to faraway traffic and watched snow hit his window. He had dreams while he was awake. Dreams in which the building moved. In which the room filled with water, then emptied of air. The window vanished and he was left in complete blackness. He got up and walked around in the blackness. He walked at least a quarter of a mile straight into it. Then he was in bed again. He went to visit his aunt and uncle. They yelled at him. He forced open his uncle's dresser with a claw hammer and got out the pistol he kept there and shot both of them. There was a large grand piano in the living room when he tried to leave. He couldn't get past it. Later he was in a cemetery, knocking over stones. The ground was very dry and loose and they went over easily. When he saw the old composer walk stiffly around the room, lecturing, he went to sleep.

He woke at two in the afternoon and took a cold shower. Without thinking, he called the government agency. He then dressed and dictated two letters to his voicetyper. He mailed one and took the other with him. He walked directly to Grueder's office. The old man was hanging up the phone when he entered.

'Charles.' He looked pale and shaken. 'Something awful has happened. The government's found out about our unauthorized transfers.'

Largens slid his envelope across the table. Grueder only glanced at it.

'They're sending investigators. They're sure to close us down.'

'So?'

'So? No more transfers!'

'I called them.'

Grueder looked at him dumbly. 'You. I didn't trust you at first. Then I did.'

'I had a little talk with Beethoven last night. Or with myself, or with whatever remnants of Beethoven are in me. He said it might be too late, but

I'd never know if I didn't try.'

'This is incredible. You'll regret this, Largens!'

'I may.'

'You idiot! What are you going to do now, compose?'

'I think so.'

'You can't walk away from it that easily!'

'Yes I can,' Largens said.

He went outside. He was shaking. If it had gone on, all Beethoven's music might have gone. What would the world – his world – be like without Beethoven?

Still, he was afraid he had made a terrible mistake. The silence – a silence with specific dimensions, a silence in four movements – haunted him. Could he ever make up for that?

Despair rose in him as he stood there with no place to go. Then he remembered about inaction and time and the tide that wanted to draw him back. He took a step and then another and soon he was walking home, entering the second half of his life.

Why, I'm a young man, he thought. I'm two hundred years younger than I was yesterday. I can do something with that.

What was necessary was to begin.

The Electric Ant

PHILIP K. DICK

AT FOUR-FIFTEEN IN THE afternoon, TST, Garson Poole woke up in his hospital bed, knew that he lay in a hospital bed in a three-bed ward, and realized in addition two things: that he no longer had a right hand and that he felt no pain.

They have given me a strong analgesic, he said to himself as he stared at the far wall with its window showing downtown New York. Webs in which vehicles and peds darted and wheeled glimmered in the late afternoon sun, and the brilliance of the ageing light pleased him. It's not yet out, he thought. And neither am I.

A fone lay on the table beside his bed; he hesitated, then picked it up and dialled for an outside line. A moment later he was faced by Louis Danceman, in charge of Tri-Plan's activities while he, Garson Poole, was elsewhere.

'Thank God you're alive,' Danceman said, seeing him; his big fleshy face with its moon's surface of pock marks flattened with relief. 'I've been calling all – '

'I just don't have a right hand,' Poole said.

'But you'll be OK. I mean, they can graft another one on.'

'How long have I been here?' Poole said. He wondered where the nurses and doctors had gone to; why weren't they clucking and fussing about him making a call?

'Four days,' Danceman said. 'Everything here at the plant is going splunkishly. In fact we've splunked orders from three separate police systems, all here on Terra. Two in Ohio, one in Wyoming. Good solid orders, with one-third in advance and the usual three-year lease-option.'

'Come and get me out of here,' Poole said.

'I can't get you out until the new hand – '

'I'll have that done later.' He wanted desperately to get back to familiar surroundings; memory of the mercantile squib looming grotesquely on the pilot screen careened at the back of his mind; If he shut his eyes he felt himself back in his damaged craft as it plunged from one vehicle to another, piling up enormous damage as it went. The kinetic sensations . . . he winced, recalling them. I guess I'm lucky, he said to himself.

'Is Sarah Benton there with you?' Danceman asked.

'No.' Of course; his personal secretary – if only for job considerations –

would be hovering close by, mothering him in her jejune, infantile way. All heavy-set women like to mother people, he thought. And they're dangerous; if they fall on you they can kill you. 'Maybe that's what happened to me,' he said aloud. 'Maybe Sarah fell on my squib.'

'No, no; a tie rod in the steering-fin of your squib split apart during the heavy rush-hour traffic and you – '

'I remember.' He turned in his bed as the door of the ward opened; a white-clad doctor and two blue-clad nurses appeared, making their way towards his bed. 'I'll talk to you later,' Poole said, and hung up the fone. He took a deep, expectant breath.

'You shouldn't be foning quite so soon,' the doctor said as he studied the chart. 'Mr Garson Poole, owner of Tri-Plan Electronics. Makers of random ident darts that track their prey for a circle-radius of a thousand miles, responding to unique enceph wave patterns. You're a successful man Mr Poole. But, Mr Poole, you're not a man. You're an electric ant.'

'Christ,' Poole said, stunned.

'So we can't really treat you here, now that we've found out. We knew, of course, as soon as we examined your injured right hand; we saw the electronic components and then we made torso X-rays and of course they bore out our hypothesis.'

'What', Poole said, 'is an "electric ant"?' But he knew; he could decipher the term.

A nurse said, 'An organic robot.'

'I see,' Poole said. Frigid perspiration rose to the surface of his skin, across all his body.

'You didn't know,' the doctor said.

'No.' Poole shook his head.

The doctor said, 'We get an electric ant every week or so. Either brought in here from a squib accident – like yourself – or one seeking voluntary admission ... one who, like yourself, has never been told, who has functioned alongside humans, believing himself – itself – human. As to your hand – ' He paused.

'Forget my hand,' Poole said savagely.

'Be calm.' The doctor leaned over him, peered acutely down into Poole's face. 'We'll have a hospital boat convey you over to a service facility where repairs, or replacement, on your hand can be made at a reasonable expense, either to yourself, if you're self-owned, or to your owners, if such there are. In any case you'll be back at your desk at Tri-Plan, functioning just as before.'

'Except,' Poole said, 'now I know.' He wondered if Danceman or Sarah or any of the others at the office knew. Had they – or one of them – purchased him? Designed him? A figurehead, he said to himself; that's all I've been. I must never really have run the company; it was a delusion implanted in me when I was made ... along with the delusion that I am human and alive.

'Before you leave for the repair facility,' the doctor said, 'could you kindly settle your bill at the front desk?'

Poole said acidly, 'How can there be a bill if you don't treat ants here?'

'For our services,' the nurse said. 'Up until the point we knew.'

'Bill me,' Poole said, with furious, impotent anger. 'Bill my firm.' With massive effort he managed to sit up; his head swimming, he stepped haltingly from the bed and on to the floor. 'I'll be glad to leave here,' he said as he rose to a standing position. 'And thank you for your humane attention.'

'Thank you, too, Mr Poole,' the doctor said. 'Or rather I should say just Poole.'

At the repair facility he had his missing hand replaced.

It proved fascinating, the hand; he examined it for a long time before he let the technicians install it. On the surface it appeared organic – in fact, on the surface, it was. Natural skin covered natural flesh, and true blood filled the veins and capillaries. But, beneath that, wires and circuits, miniaturized components, gleamed ... looking deep into the wrist he saw surge gates, motors, multistage valves, all very small. Intricate. And – the hand cost forty frogs. A week's salary, in so far as he drew it from the company payroll.

'Is this guaranteed?' he asked the technicians as they fused the 'bone' section of the hand to the balance of the body.

'Ninety days, parts and labour,' one of the technicians said. 'Unless subjected to unusual or intentional abuse.'

'That sounds vaguely suggestive,' Poole said.

The technician, a man – all of them were men – said, regarding him keenly, 'You've been posing?'

'Unintentionally,' Poole said.

'And now it's intentional?'

Poole said, 'Exactly.'

'Do you know why you never guessed? There must have been signs ... clickings and whirrings from inside you, now and then. You never guessed because you were programmed not to notice. You'll now have the same difficulty finding out why you were built and for whom you've been operating.'

'A slave,' Poole said. 'A mechanical slave.'

'You've had fun.'

'I've lived a good life,' Poole said. 'I've worked hard.'

He paid the facility its forty frogs, flexed his new fingers, tested them out by picking up various objects, such as coins, then departed. Ten minutes later he was aboard a public carrier, on his way home. It had been quite a day.

At home, in his one-room apartment, he poured himself a shot of Jack Daniel Purple Label – sixty years old – and sat sipping it, meanwhile gazing through his sole window at the building on the opposite side of the street. Shall I go to the office? he asked himself. If so, why? If not, why? Choose one.

Christ, he thought, it undermines you, knowing this. I'm a freak, he realized. An inanimate object mimicking an animate one. But – he felt alive. Yet . . . he felt differently, now. About himself. Hence about everyone, especially Danceman and Sarah, everyone at Tri-Plan.

I think I'll kill myself, he said to himself. But I'm probably programmed not to do that; it would be a costly waste which my owner would have to absorb. And he wouldn't want to.

Programmed. In me somewhere, he thought, there is a matrix fitted in place, a grid screen that cuts me off from certain thoughts. Certain actions. And forces me into others. I am not free. I never was, but now I know it; that makes it different.

Turning his window to opaque, he snapped on the overhead light, carefully set about removing his clothing, piece by piece. He had watched carefully as the technicians at the repair facility had attached his new hand: He had a rather clear idea, now, of how his body was assembled. Two major panels, one in each thigh; the technicians had removed the panels to check the circuit complexes beneath. If I'm programmed, he decided, the matrix probably can be found there.

The maze of circuitry baffled him. I need help, he said to himself. Let's see . . . what's the fone code for the class BBB computer we hire at the office?

He picked up the fone, dialled the computer at its permanent location in Boise, Idaho.

'Use of this computer is prorated at a five frogs per minute basis,' a mechanical voice from the fone said. 'Please hold your mastercreditcharge-plate before the screen.'

He did so.

'At the sound of the buzzer you will be connected with the computer,' the voice continued. 'Please query it as rapidly as possible, taking into account the fact that its answer will be given in terms of a microsecond, while your query will – ' He turned the sound down then. But quickly turned it up as the blank audio input of the computer appeared on the screen. At this moment the computer had become a giant ear, listening to him – as well as fifty thousand other queries throughout Terra.

'Scan me visually,' he instructed the computer. 'And tell me where I will find the programming mechanism which controls my thoughts and behaviour.' He waited. On the fone's screen a great active eye, multi-lensed, peered at him; he displayed himself for it, there in his one-room apartment.

The computer said, 'Remove your chest panel. Apply pressure at your breastbone and then ease outward.'

He did so. A section of his chest came off; dizzily, he set it down on the floor.

'I can distinguish control modules,' the computer said, 'but I can't tell which – ' It paused as its eye roved about on the fone screen. 'I distinguish a roll of punched tape mounted above your heart mechanism. Do you see it?' Poole craned his neck, peered. He saw it, too, 'I will have to sign off,' the computer said. 'After I have examined the data available to me I will contact you and give you an answer. Good day.' The screen died out.

'I'll yank the tape out of me, Poole said to himself. Tiny . . . no larger than two spools of thread, with a scanner mounted between the delivery drum and the take-up drum. He could not see any sign of motion; the spools seemed inert. They must cut in as override, he reflected, when specific situations occur. Override to my encephalic processes. And they've been doing it all my life.

He reached down, touched the delivery drum. All I have to do is tear this out, he thought, and –

The fone screen relit. 'Mastercreditchargeplate number 3-BNX-882-HQR446-T,' the computer's voice came. 'This is BBB-307DR recontacting you in response to your query of sixteen seconds' lapse, 4 November 1992. The punched-tape roll above your heart mechanism is not a programming turret but is in fact a reality-supply construct. All sense stimuli received by your central neurological system emanate from that unit and tampering with it would be risky if not terminal.' It added, 'You appear to have no programming circuit. Query answered. Good day.' It flicked off.

Poole, standing naked before the fone screen, touched the tape drum once again, with calculated, enormous caution. I see, he thought wildly. Or do I see? This unit –

If I cut the tape, he realized, my world will disappear. Reality will continue for others, but not for me. Because my reality, my universe, is coming to me from this minuscule unit. Fed into the scanner and then into my central nervous system as it snailishly unwinds.

It has been unwinding for years, he decided.

Getting his clothes, he re-dressed, seated himself in his big armchair – a luxury imported into his apartment from Tri-Plan's main offices – and lit a tobacco cigarette. His hands shook as he laid down his initialled lighter; leaning back, he blew smoke before himself, creating a nimbus of grey.

I have to go slowly he said to himself. What am I trying to do? Bypass my programming? But the computer found no programming circuit. Do I want to interfere with the reality tape? And, if so, *why*?

Because, he thought, if I control that, I control reality. At least so far as I'm concerned. My subjective reality . . . but that's all there is. Objective reality is a synthetic construct, dealing with a hypothetical universalization of a multitude of subjective realities.

My universe is lying within my fingers, he realized. If I can just figure out how the damn thing works. All I set out to do originally was to search for and locate my programming circuit so I could gain true homeostatic functioning: control of myself. But with this –

With this he did not merely gain control of himself; he gained control over everything.

And this sets me apart from every human who ever lived and died, he thought sombrely.

Going over to the fone he dialled his office. When he had Danceman on the screen he said briskly, 'I want you to send a complete set of microtools and enlarging screen over to my apartment. I have some microcircuitry to work on.' Then he broke the connection, not wanting to discuss it.

A half-hour later a knock sounded on his door. When he opened up he found himself facing one of the shop foremen, loaded down with microtools of every sort. 'You didn't say exactly what you wanted,' the foreman said, entering the apartment. 'So Mr Danceman had me bring everything.'

'And the enlarging-lens system?'

'In the truck, up on the roof.'

Maybe what I want to do, Poole thought, is die. He lit a cigarette, stood smoking and waiting as the shop foreman lugged the heavy enlarging-screen, with its power supply and control panel, into the apartment. This is suicide, what I'm doing here. He shuddered.

'Anything wrong, Mr Poole?' the shop foreman said as he rose to his feet, relieved of the burden of the enlarging-lens system. 'You must still be rickety on your pins from your accident.'

'Yes,' Poole said quietly. He stood tautly waiting until the foreman left.

Under the enlarging-lens system the plastic tape assumed a new shape: a wide track along which hundreds of thousands of punch-holes worked their way. I thought so, Poole thought. Not recorded as charges on a ferrous oxide layer but actually punched-free slots.

Under the lens the strip of tape visibly oozed forward. Very slowly, but it did, at uniform velocity, move in the direction of the scanner.

The way I figure it, he thought, is that the punched holes are *on* gates. It functions like a player piano; solid is no, punch-hole is yes. How can I test this?

Obviously by filling in a number of the holes.

He measured the amount of tape left on the delivery spool, calculated – at great effort – the velocity of the tape's movement, and then came up with a figure. If he altered the tape visible at the ingoing edge of the scanner, five to seven hours would pass before that particular time period arrived. He would in effect be painting out stimuli due a few hours from now.

With a microbrush he swabbed a large – relatively large – section of tape with opaque varnish ... obtained from the supply kit accompanying the microtools. I have smeared out stimuli for about half an hour, he pondered. Have covered at least a thousand punches.

It would be interesting to see what change, if any, overcame his environment, six hours from now.

309

Five and a half hours later he sat at Krackter's, a superb bar in Manhattan, having a drink with Danceman.

'You look bad,' Danceman said.

'I am bad,' Poole said. He finished his drink, a Scotch sour, and ordered another.

'From the accident?'

'In a sense, yes.'

Danceman said, 'Is it – something you found out about yourself?'

Raising his head, Poole eyed him in the murky light of the bar. 'Then, you know.'

'I know,' Danceman said, 'that I should call you "Poole" instead of "Mr Poole". But I prefer the latter and will continue to do so.'

'How long have you known?' Poole said.

'Since you took over the firm. I was told that the actual owners of Tri-Plan, who are located in the Prox System, wanted Tri-Plan run by an electric ant whom they could control. They wanted a brilliant and forceful – '

'The real owners?' This was the first he had heard about that. 'We have two thousand stockholders. Scattered everywhere.'

'Marvis Bey and her husband Ernan, on Prox 4, control fifty-one per cent of the voting-stock. This has been true from the start.'

'Why didn't I know?'

'I was told not to tell you. You were to think that you yourself made all company policy. With my help. But actually I was feeding you what the Beys fed to me.'

'I'm a figurehead,' Poole said.

'In a sense, yes,' Danceman nodded. 'But you'll always be "Mr Poole" to me.'

A section of the far wall vanished. And, with it, several people at tables nearby. And –

Through the big glass side of the bar, the skyline of New York City flickered out of existence.

Poole said hoarsely, 'Look around. Do you see any changes?'

After looking around the room, Danceman said, 'No. What like?'

'You still see the skyline?'

'Sure. Smoggy as it is. The lights wink – '

'Now I know,' Poole said. He had been right; every punch-hole covered up meant the disappearance of some object on his reality world. Standing, he said, 'I'll see you later, Danceman. I have to get back to my apartment; there's some work I'm doing. Good night.' He strode from the bar and out on to the streets, searching for a cab.

No cabs.

Those, too, he thought. I wonder what else I painted over. Prostitutes? Flowers? Prisons?

There, in the bar's parking-lot, Danceman's squib. I'll take that, he

310

decided. There are still cabs in Danceman's world; he can get one later. Anyhow it's a company car, and I hold a copy of the key.

Presently he was in the air, turning towards his apartment.

New York City had not returned. To the left and right vehicles and buildings, streets, ped-runners, signs . . . and in the centre nothing. How can I fly into that? he asked himself. I'd disappear.

Or would I? He flew towards the nothingness.

Smoking one cigarette after another he flew in a circle for fifteen minutes . . . and then, soundlessly, New York reappeared. He could finish his trip. He stubbed out his cigarette (a waste of something so valuable) and shot off in the direction of his apartment.

If I insert a narrow opaque strip, he pondered as he unlocked his apartment door, I can –

His thoughts ceased. Someone sat in his living-room chair, watching a captain kirk on the TV. 'Sarah,' he said, nettled.

She rose, well padded but graceful. 'You weren't at the hospital, so I came here. I still have that key you gave me back in March after we had that awful argument. Oh . . . you look so depressed.' She came up to him, peeped into his face anxiously. 'Does your injury hurt that badly?'

'It's not that.' He removed his coat, tie, shirt, and then his chest panel; kneeling down he began inserting his hands into the microtool gloves. Pausing, he looked up at her and said, 'I found out I'm an electric ant. Which from one standpoint opens up certain possibilities, which I am exploring now.' He flexed his fingers and at the far end of the left Waldo a micro screwdriver moved, magnified into visibility by the enlarging-lens system. 'You can watch,' he informed her. 'If you so desire.'

She had begun to cry.

'What's the matter?' he demanded savagely, without looking up from his work.

'I – it's just so sad. You've been such a good employer to all of us at Tri-Plan. We respect you so. And now it's all changed.'

The plastic tape had an unpunched margin at top and bottom; he cut a horizontal strip, very narrow, then, after a moment of great concentration, cut the tape itself four hours away from the scanning-head. He then rotated the cut strip into a right-angle piece in relation to the scanner, fused it in place with a micro heat element, then re-attached the tape reel to its left and right sides. He had, in effect, inserted a dead twenty minutes into the unfolding flow of his reality. It would take effect – according to his calculations – a few minutes after midnight.

'Are you fixing yourself?' Sarah asked timidly.

Poole said, 'I'm freezing myself.' Beyond this he had several other alterations in mind. But first he had to test his theory; blank, unpunched tape meant no stimuli, in which case the *lack* of tape . . .

'That look on your face,' Sarah said. She began gathering up her purse, coat, rolled-up aud-vid magazine. 'I'll go; I can see how you feel about finding me here.'

'Stay,' he said. 'I'll watch the captain kirk with you.' He got into his shirt. 'Remember years ago when there was – what was it? – twenty or twenty-two TV channels? Before the Government shut down the independents?'

She nodded.

'What would it have looked like,' he said, 'if this TV set projected all channels on to the cathode-ray screen *at the same time?* Could we have distinguished anything in the mixture?'

'I don't think so.'

'Maybe we could learn to. Learn to be selective; do our own job of perceiving what we wanted to and what we didn't: Think of the possibilities, if our brain could handle twenty images at once; think of the amount of knowledge which could be stored during a given period. I wonder if the brain, the human brain – ' He broke off. 'The human brain couldn't do it,' he said, presently, reflecting to himself. 'But in theory a quasi-organic brain might.'

'Is that what you have?' Sarah asked.

'Yes,' Poole said.

They watched the captain kirk to its end, and then they went to bed. But Poole sat up against his pillows, smoking and brooding. Beside him, Sarah stirred restlessly, wondering why he did not turn off the light.

Eleven-fifty. It would happen any time, now.

'Sarah,' he said, 'I want your help. In a very few minutes something strange will happen to me. It won't last long, but I want you to watch me carefully. See if I – ' He gestured. 'Show any changes. If I seem to go to sleep, or if I talk nonsense, or – ' He wanted to say, if I disappear. But he did not. 'I won't do you any harm, but I think it might be a good idea if you armed yourself. Do you have your anti-mugging gun with you?'

'In my purse.' She had become fully awake now; sitting up in bed, she gazed at him with wild fright, her ample shoulders tanned and freckled in the light of the room.

He got her gun for her.

The room stiffened into paralysed immobility. Then the colours began to drain away. Objects diminished until, smoke-like, they flitted away into shadows. Darkness filmed everything as the objects in the room became weaker and weaker.

The last stimuli are dying out, Poole realized. He squinted, trying to see. He made out Sarah Benton, sitting in the bed; a two-dimensional figure that doll-like had been propped up, there to fade and dwindle. Random gusts of dematerialized substance eddied about in unstable clouds; the elements collected, fell apart, then collected once again. And then the last heat, energy and light dissipated; the room closed over and fell into itself, as if sealed off from reality. And at that point absolute blackness replaced everything, space without depth, not nocturnal but rather stiff and unyielding. And in addition he heard nothing.

Reaching, he tried to touch something. But he had nothing to reach with. Awareness of his own body had departed along with everything else in the universe. He had no hands and, even if he had, there would be nothing for them to feel.

I am still right about the way the damn tape works, he said to himself, using a non-existent mouth to communicate an invisible message.

Will this pass in ten minutes? he asked himself. Am I right about that, too? He waited ... but knew intuitively that this time sense had departed with everything else. I can only wait, he realized. And hope it won't be long.

To pace himself, he thought, I'll make up an encyclopedia; I'll try to list everything that begins with an *a*. Let's see. He pondered. Apple, automobile, acksetron, atmosphere, Atlantic, tomato aspic, advertising – he thought on and on, categories slithering through his fright-haunted mind.

All at once light flickered on.

He lay on the couch in the living-room, and mild sunlight spilled in through the single window. Two men bent over him, their hands full of tools. Maintenance-men, he realized. They've been working on me.

'He's conscious,' one of the technicians said. He rose, stood back; Sarah Benton, dithering with anxiety, replaced him.

'Thank God!' she said, breathing wetly in Poole's ear. 'I was so afraid; I called Mr Danceman finally about – '

'What happened?' Poole broke in harshly. 'Start from the beginning and for God's sake speak slowly. So I can assimilate it all.'

Sarah composed herself, paused to rub her nose, and then plunged on nervously, 'You passed out. You just lay there, as if you were dead. I waited until two-thirty and you did nothing. I called Mr Danceman, waking him up unfortunately, and he called the electric-ant maintenance – I mean, the organic-roby maintenance people, and these two men came about four-forty-five, and they've been working on you ever since. It's now six-fifteen in the morning. And I'm very cold and I want to go to bed; I can't make it in to the office today; I really can't.' She turned away, sniffling. The sound annoyed him.

One of the uniformed maintenance-men said, 'You've been playing around with your reality tape.'

'Yes,' Poole said. Why deny it? Obviously they had found the inserted solid strip. 'I shouldn't have been out that long,' he said. 'I inserted a ten-minute strip only.'

'It shut off the tape transport,' the technician explained. 'The tape stopped moving forward; your insertion jammed it, and it automatically shut down to avoid tearing the tape. Why would you want to fiddle around

313

with that? Don't you know what you could do?'

'I'm not sure,' Poole said.

'But you have a good idea.'

Poole said acridly, 'That's why I'm doing it.'

'Your bill', the maintenance-man said, 'is going to be ninety-five frogs. Payable in instalments, if you so desire.'

'OK,' he said; he sat up groggily, rubbed his eyes and grimaced. His head ached and his stomach felt totally empty.

'Shave the tape next time,' the primary technician told him. 'That way it won't jam. Didn't it occur to you that it had a safety factor built into it? So it would stop rather than – '

'What happens,' Poole interrupted, his voice low and intently careful, 'if no tape passes under the scanner? No tape – nothing at all? The photocell shining upward without impedance?'

The technicians glanced at each other. One said, 'All the neuro circuits jump their gaps and short out.'

'Meaning what?' Poole said.

'Meaning it's the end of the mechanism.'

Poole said, 'I've examined the circuit. It doesn't carry enough voltage to do that. Metal won't fuse under such slight loads of current, even if the terminals are touching. We're talking about a millionth of a watt along a cesium channel perhaps a sixteenth of an inch in length. Let's assume there are a billion possible combinations at one instant arising from the punchouts on the tape. The total output isn't cumulative; the amount of current depends on what the battery details for that module, and it's not much. With all gates open and going.'

'Would we lie?' one of the technicians asked wearily.

'Why not?' Poole said. 'Here I have an opportunity to experience everything. Simultaneously. To know the universe in its entirety, to be momentarily in contact with all reality. Something that no human can do. A symphonic score entering my brain outside of time, all notes, all instruments sounding at once. And all symphonies. Do you see?'

'It'll burn you out,' both technicians said, together.

'I don't think so,' Poole said.

Sarah said, 'Would you like a cup of coffee, Mr Poole?'

'Yes,' he said; he lowered his legs, pressed his cold feet against the floor, shuddered. He then stood up. His body ached. They had me lying all night on the couch, he realized. All things considered, they could have done better than that.

At the kitchen table in the far corner of the room, Garson Poole sat sipping coffee across from Sarah. The technicians had long since gone.

'You're not going to try any more experiments on yourself, are you?' Sarah asked wistfully.

Poole grated, 'I would like to control time. To reverse it.' I will cut a segment of tape out, he thought, and fuse it in upside down. The causal sequences will then flow the other way. Thereupon I will walk backwards down the steps from the roof field, back up to my door, push a locked door open, walk backward to the sink, where I will get out a stack of dirty dishes. I will seat myself at this table before the stack, fill each dish with food produced from my stomach ... I will then transfer the food to the refrigerator. The next day I will take the food out of the refrigerator, pack it in bags, carry the bags to a supermarket, distribute the food here and there in the store. And at last, at the front counter, they will pay me money for this, from their cash register. The food will be packed with other food in big plastic boxes, shipped out of the city into the hydroponic plants on the Atlantic, there to be joined back to trees and bushes or the bodies of dead animals or pushed deep into the ground. But what would all that prove? A video tape running backward ... I would know no more than I know now, which is not enough.

What I want, he realized, is ultimate and absolute reality, for one microsecond. After that it doesn't matter, because all will be known; nothing will be left to understand or see.

I might try one other change, he said to himself. Before I try cutting the tape. I will prick new punch-holes in the tape and see what presently emerges. It will be interesting because I will not know what the holes I make mean.

Using the tip of a microtool, he punched several holes, at random, on the tape. As close to the scanner as he could manage ... he did not want to wait.

'I wonder if you'll see it,' he said to Sarah. Apparently not, in so far as he could extrapolate. 'Something may show up,' he said to her. 'I just want to warn you; I don't want you to be afraid.'

'Oh dear,' Sarah said tinnily.

He examined his wristwatch. One minute passed, then a second, a third. And then –

In the centre of the room appeared a flock of green and black ducks. They quacked excitedly, rose from the floor, fluttered against the ceiling in a dithering mass of feathers and wings and frantic in their vast urge, their instinct, to get away.

'Ducks,' Poole said marvelling. 'I punched a hole for a flight of wild ducks.'

Now something else appeared. A park bench with an elderly, tattered man seated on it, reading a torn, bent newspaper. He looked up, dimly made out Poole, smiled briefly at him with badly made dentures, and then returned to his folded-back newspaper. He read on.

'Do you see him?' Poole asked Sarah. 'And the ducks?' At that moment the ducks and the park bum disappeared. Nothing remained of them. The interval of their punch-holes had quickly passed.

'They weren't real,' Sarah said. 'Were they? So how?'

'You're not real,' he told Sarah. 'You're a stimulus-factor on my reality tape. A punch-hole that can be glazed over. Do you also have an existence in another reality tape or one in an objective reality?' He did not know; he couldn't tell. Perhaps Sarah did not know, either. Perhaps she existed in a thousand reality tapes; perhaps on every reality tape ever manufactured. 'If I cut the tape,' he said, 'you will be everywhere and nowhere. Like everything else in the universe. At least as far as I am aware of it.'

Sarah faltered, 'I am real.'

'I want to know you completely,' Poole said. 'To do that I must cut the tape. If I don't do it now, I'll do it some other time; it's inevitable that eventually I'll do it.' So why wait? he asked himself. And there is always the possibility that Danceman has reported back to my maker, that they will be making moves to head me off. Because, perhaps, I'm endangering their property – myself.

'You make me wish I had gone to the office after all,' Sarah said, her mouth turned down with dimpled gloom.

'Go,' Poole said.

'I don't want to leave you alone.'

'I'll be fine,' Poole said.

'No, you're not going to be fine. You're going to unplug yourself or something, kill yourself because you've found out you're just an electric ant and not a human being.'

He said, presently, 'Maybe so,' Maybe it boiled down to that.

'And I can't stop you,' she said.

'No,' he nodded in agreement.

'But I'm going to stay,' Sarah said. 'Even if I can't stop you. Because if I do leave, and you do kill yourself, I'll always ask myself for the rest of my life what would have happened if I had stayed. You see?'

Again he nodded.

'Go ahead,' Sarah said.

He rose to his feet. 'It's not pain I'm going to feel,' he told her. 'Although it may look like that to you. Keep in mind the fact that organic robots have minimal pain circuits in them. I will be experiencing the most intense – '

'Don't tell me any more,' she broke in. 'Just do it if you're going to, or don't do it if you're not.'

Clumsily – because he was frightened – he wriggled his hands into the microglove assembly, reached to pick up a tiny tool: a sharp cutting-blade. 'I am going to cut a tape mounted inside my chest panel,' he said, as he gazed through the enlarging-lens system. 'That's all.' His hand shook as it lifted the cutting-blade. In a second it can be done, he realized. All over. And – I will have time to fuse the cut ends of tape back together, he realized. A half-hour at least. If I change my mind.

He cut the tape.

Staring at him, cowering, Sarah whispered, 'Nothing happened.'

'I have thirty or forty minutes.' He reseated himself at the table, having drawn his hands from the gloves. His voice, he noticed, shook; undoubtedly Sarah was aware of it, and he felt anger at himself, knowing that he had alarmed her. 'I'm sorry,' he said, irrationally; he wanted to apologize to her. 'Maybe you ought to leave,' he said in panic; again he stood up. So did she, reflexively, as if imitating him; bloated and nervous, she stood there palpitating. 'Go away,' he said thickly. 'Back to the office where you ought to be. Where we both ought to be.' I'm going to fuse the tape-ends together, he told himself; the tension is too great for me to stand.

Reaching his hands towards the gloves, he groped to pull them over his straining fingers. Peering into the enlarging-screen he saw the beam from the photoelectric gleam upward, pointed directly into the scanner; at the same time he saw the end of the tape disappearing under the scanner ... he saw this, understood it; I'm too late, he realized. It had passed through. God, he thought, help me. It has begun winding at a rate greater than I calculated. So it's *now* that –

He saw apples and cobblestones and zebras. He felt warmth, the silky texture of cloth; he felt the ocean lapping at him and a great wind, from the north, plucking at him as if to lead him somewhere. Sarah was all around him, so was Danceman. New York glowed in the night, and the squibs about him scuttled and bounced through night skies and daytime and flooding and drought. Butter relaxed into liquid on his tongue, and at the same time hideous odours and tastes assailed him: the bitter presence of poisons and lemons and blades of summer grass. He drowned; he fell; he lay in the arms of a woman in a vast white bed which at the same time dinned shrilly in his ear: the warning noise of a defective elevator in one of the ancient, ruined downtown hotels. I am living, I have lived, I will never live, he said to himself, and with his thoughts came every word, every sound; insects squeaked and raced, and he half-sank into a complex body of homeostatic machinery located somewhere in Tri-Plan's labs.

He wanted to say something to Sarah. Opening his mouth he tried to bring forth words – a specific string of them out of the enormous mass of them brilliantly lighting his mind, scorching him with their utter meaning.

His mouth burned. He wondered why.

Frozen against the wall, Sarah Benton opened her eyes and saw the curl of smoke ascending from Poole's half-opened mouth. Then the roby sank down, knelt on elbows and knees, then slowly spread out in a broken, crumpled heap. She knew without examining it that it had 'died'.

Poole did it to itself, she realized. And it couldn't feel pain; it said so itself. Or at least not very much pain; maybe a little. Anyway, now it is over.

I had better call Mr Danceman and tell him what's happened, she decided. Still shaky, she made her way across the room to the fone; picking it up, she dialled from memory.

It thought I was a stimulus-factor on its reality tape, she said to herself. So it thought I would die when it 'died'. How strange, she thought. Why did it imagine that? It had never been plugged into the real world; it had 'lived' in an electronic world of its own. How bizarre.

'Mr Danceman,' she said, when the circuit to his office had been put through. 'Poole is gone. It destroyed itself right in front of my eyes. You'd better come over.'

'So we're finally free of it.'

'Yes, won't it be nice?'

Danceman said, 'I'll send a couple of men over from the shop.' He saw past her, made out the sight of Poole lying by the kitchen table. 'You go home and rest,' he instructed Sarah. 'You must be worn out by all this.'

'Yes,' she said. 'Thank you, Mr Danceman.' She hung up and stood, aimlessly.

And then she noticed something.

My hands, she thought. She held them up. Why is it I can see through them?

The walls of the room, too, had become ill-defined.

Trembling, she walked back to the inert roby, stood by it, not knowing what to do. Through her legs the carpet showed, and then the carpet became dim, and she saw, through it, further layers of disintegrating matter beyond.

Maybe if I can fuse the tape-ends back together, she thought. But she did not know how. And already Poole had become vague.

The wind of early morning blew about her. She did not feel it; she had begun, now, to cease to feel.

The winds blew on.

'Arena'

FREDRIC BROWN

CARSON OPENED HIS EYES, and found himself looking upwards into a flickering blue dimness.

It was hot, and he was lying on sand, and a rock embedded in the sand was hurting his back. He rolled over to his side, off the rock, and then pushed himself up to a sitting position.

'I'm crazy,' he thought. 'Crazy – or dead – or something.' The sand was blue, bright blue. And there wasn't any such thing as bright blue sand on Earth or any of the planets. Blue sand under a blue dome that wasn't the sky nor yet a room, but a circumscribed area – somehow he knew it was circumscribed and finite even though he couldn't see to the top of it.

He picked up some of the sand in his hand and let it run through his fingers. It trickled down on to his bare leg. *Bare?*

He was stark naked, and already his body was dripping perspiration from the enervating heat, coated blue with sand wherever sand had touched it. Elsewhere his body was white.

He thought: then this sand is really blue. If it seemed blue only because of the blue light, then I'd be blue also. But I'm white, so the sand *is* blue. *Blue sand*: there isn't any blue sand. There isn't any place like this place I'm in.

Sweat was running down in his eyes. It was hot, hotter than hell. Only hell – the hell of the ancients – was supposed to be red and not blue.

But if this place wasn't hell, what was it? Only Mercury, among the planets, had heat like this and this wasn't Mercury. And Mercury was some four billion miles from . . . From?

It came back to him then, where he'd been: in the little one-man scouter, outside the orbit of Pluto, scouting a scant million miles to one side of the Earth Armada drawn up in battle array there to intercept the Outsiders.

That sudden strident ringing of the alarm bell when the rival scouter – the Outsider ship – had come within range of his detectors!

No one knew who the Outsiders were, what they looked like, or from what far galaxy they came, other than that it was in the general direction of the Pleiades.

First, there had been sporadic raids on Earth colonies and outposts; isolated battles between Earth patrols and small groups of Outsider spaceships; battles sometimes won and sometimes lost, but never resulting in the capture of an alien vessel. Nor had any member of a raided colony ever survived to describe the Outsiders who had left the ships, if indeed they had left them.

Not too serious a menace, at first, for the raids had not been numerous or destructive. And individually, the ships had proved slightly inferior in armament to the best of Earth's fighters, although somewhat superior in speed and manœuvrability. A sufficient edge in speed, in fact, to give the Outsiders their choice of running or fighting, unless surrounded.

Nevertheless, Earth had prepared for serious trouble, building the mightiest armada of all time. It had been waiting now, that armada, for a long time. Now the showdown was coming.

Scouts twenty billion miles out had detected the approach of a mighty fleet of the Outsiders. Those scouts had never come back, but their radiotronic messages had. And now Earth's armada, all ten thousand ships and half-million fighting spacemen, was out there, outside Pluto's orbit, waiting to intercept and battle to the death.

And an even battle it was going to be, judging by the advance reports of the men of the far picket line who had given their lives to report – before they had died – on the size and strength of the alien fleet.

Anybody's battle, with the mastery of the solar system hanging in the balance, on an even chance. A last and *only* chance, for Earth and all her colonies lay at the utter mercy of the Outsiders if they ran that gauntlet –

Oh yes. Bob Carson remembered now. He remembered that strident bell and his leap for the control panel. His frenzied fumbling as he strapped himself into the seat. The dot in the visiplate that grew larger. The dryness of his mouth. The awful knowledge that this was *it* for him, at least, although the main fleets were still out of range of one another.

This, his first taste of battle! Within three seconds or less he'd be victorious, or a charred cinder. One hit completely took care of a lightly armed and armoured one-man craft like a scouter.

Frantically – as his lips shaped the word 'One' – he worked at the controls to keep that growing dot centred on the crossed spiderwebs of the visiplate. His hands doing that, while his right foot hovered over the pedal that would fire the bolt. The single bolt of concentrated hell that had to hit – or else. There wouldn't be time for any second shot.

'Two.' He didn't know he'd said that, either. The dot in the visiplate wasn't a dot now. Only a few thousand miles away, it showed up in the magnification of the plate as though it were only a few hundred yards off. It was a fast little scouter, about the size of his.

An alien ship, all right!

'Thr –' His foot touched the bolt-release pedal....

320

And then the Outsider had swerved suddenly and was off the crosshairs. Carson punched keys frantically, to follow.

For a tenth of a second, it was out of the visiplate entirely, and then as the nose of his scouter swung after it, he saw it again, diving straight towards the ground.

The ground?

It was an optical illusion of some sort. It *had* to be: that planet – or whatever it was – that now covered the visiplate couldn't be there. Couldn't possibly! There *wasn't* any planet nearer than Neptune three billion miles away – with Pluto on the opposite side of the distant pinpoint sun.

His *detectors*! *They* hadn't shown any object of planetary dimensions, even of asteroid dimensions, and still didn't.

It couldn't be there, that whatever-it-was he was diving into, only a few hundred miles below him.

In his sudden anxiety to keep from crashing, he forgot the Outsider ship. He fired the front breaking rockets, and even as the sudden change of speed slammed him forward against the seat straps, fired full right for an emergency turn. Pushed them down and *held* them down, knowing that he needed everything the ship had to keep from crashing and that a turn that sudden would black him out for a moment.

It did black him out.

And that was all. Now he was sitting in hot blue sand, stark naked but otherwise unhurt. No sign of his spaceship and – for that matter – no sign of *space*. That curve overhead wasn't a sky, whatever else it was.

He scrambled to his feet.

Gravity seemed a little more than Earth-normal. Not much more.

Flat sand stretching away, a few scrawny bushes in clumps here and there. The bushes were blue, too, but in varying shades, some lighter than the blue of the sand, some darker.

Out from under the nearest bush ran a little thing that was like a lizard, except that it had more than four legs. It was blue, too. Bright blue. It saw him and ran back again under the bush.

He looked up again, trying to decide what was overhead. It wasn't exactly a roof, but it was dome-shaped. It flickered and was hard to look at. But definitely, it curved down to the ground, to the blue sand, all around him.

He wasn't far from being under the centre of the dome. At a guess, it was a hundred yards to the nearest wall, if it was a wall. It was as though a blue hemisphere of *something* about two hundred and fifty yards in circumference was inverted over the flat expanse of the sand.

And everything blue, except one object. Over near a far curving wall there was a red object. Roughly spherical, it seemed to be about a yard in diameter. Too far for him to see clearly through the flickering blueness.

But, unaccountably, he shuddered.

He wiped sweat from his forehead, or tried to, with the back of his hand.

Was this a dream, a nightmare? This heat, this sand, that vague feeling of horror he felt when he looked towards that red thing?

A dream? No, one didn't go to sleep and dream in the midst of a battle in space.

Death? No, never. If there were immortality, it wouldn't be a senseless thing like this, a thing of blue heat and blue sand and a red horror.

Then he heard the voice.

Inside his head he heard it, not with his ears. It came from nowhere or everywhere.

'Through spaces and dimensions wandering,' rang the words in his mind, *'and in this space and this time, I find two peoples about to exterminate one and so weaken the other that it would retrogress and never fulfil its destiny, but decay and return to mindless dust whence it came. And I say this must not happen.'*

'Who ... what are you?' Carson didn't say it aloud, but the question formed itself in his brain.

'You would not understand completely. I am – ' There was a pause as though the voice sought – in Carson's brain – for a word that wasn't there, a word he didn't know. *'I am the end of evolution of a race so old the time cannot be expressed in words that have meaning to your mind. A race fused into a single entity, eternal. . . .*

'An entity such as your primitive race might become' – again the groping for a word – *'time from now. So might the race you call, in your mind, the Outsiders. So I intervene in the battle to come, the battle between fleets so evenly matched that destruction of both races will result. One must survive. One must progress and evolve.'*

'One?' thought Carson. 'Mine or – ?'

'It is in my power to stop the war, to send the Outsiders back to their galaxy. But they would return, or your race would sooner or later follow them there. Only by remaining in this space and time to intervene constantly could I prevent them from destroying one another, and I cannot remain.

'So I shall intervene now. I shall destroy one fleet completely without loss to the other. One civilization shall thus survive.'

Nightmare. This had to be nightmare, Carson thought. But he knew it wasn't.

It was too mad, too impossible, to be anything but real.

He didn't dare ask *the* question – *which?* But his thoughts asked it for him.

'The stronger shall survive,' said the voice. *'That I cannot – and would not – change. I merely intervene to make it a complete victory, not'* – groping again – *'not Pyrrhic victory to a broken race.*

'From the outskirts of the not-yet battle I plucked two individuals, you and an Outsider. I see from your mind that, in your early history of nationalisms, battles

between champions to decide issues between races were not unknown.

'You and your opponent are here pitted against one another, naked and unarmed, under conditions equally unfamiliar to you both, equally unpleasant to you both. There is no time limit, for here there is no time. The survivor is the champion of his race. That race survives.'

'But –' Carson's protest was too inarticulate for expression, but the voice answered it.

'It is fair. The conditions are such that the accident of physical strength will not completely decide the issue. There is a barrier. You will understand. Brain-power and courage will be more important than strength. Most especially courage, which is the will to survive.'

'But while this goes on, the fleets will –'

'No, you are in another space, another time. For as long as you are here, time stands still in the universe you know. I see you wonder whether this place is real. It is, and it is not. As I – to your limited understanding – am and am not real. My existence is mental and not physical. You saw me as a planet; it could have been as a dust-mote or a sun.

'But to you this place is now real. What you suffer here will be real. And if you die here, your death will be real. If you die, your failure will be the end of your race. That is enough for you to know.'

And then the voice was gone.

Again he was alone, but not alone. For as Carson looked up, he saw that the red thing, the sphere of horror that he now knew was the Outsider, was rolling towards him.

Rolling....

It seemed to have no legs or arms that he could see, no features. It rolled across the sand with the fluid quickness of a drop of mercury. And before it, in some manner he could not understand, came a wave of nauseating hatred.

Carson looked about him frantically. A stone, lying in the sand a few feet away, was the nearest thing to a weapon. It wasn't large, but it had sharp edges, like a slab of flint. It looked a bit like blue flint.

He picked it up, and crouched to receive the attack. It was coming fast, faster than he could run.

No time to think out how he was going to fight it; how anyway could he plan to battle a creature whose strength, whose characteristics, whose method of fighting he did not know? Rolling so fast, it looked more than ever like a perfect sphere.

Ten yards away. Five. And then it stopped.

Rather, it *was stopped*. Abruptly the near side of it flattened as though it had run up against an invisible wall. It bounced, actually bounced back.

Then it rolled forward again, but more cautiously. It stopped again, at the same place. It tried again, a few yards to one side.

323

Then it rolled forward again, but more cautiously. It stopped again, at the same place. It tried again, a few yards to one side.

There was a barrier there of some sort. It clicked, then, in Carson's mind, that thought projected by the Entity who had brought them there: ' – accident of physical strength will not completely decide the issue. There is a barrier.'

A force-field, of course. Not the Netzian Field, known to Earth science, for that glowed and emitted a crackling sound. This one was invisible, silent.

It was a wall that ran from side to side of the inverted hemisphere; Carson didn't have to verify that himself. The Roller was doing that, rolling sideways along the barrier, seeking a break in it that wasn't there.

Carson took half a dozen steps forward, his left hand groping out before him, and touched the barrier. It felt smooth, yielding, like a sheet of rubber rather than like glass, warm to his touch, but no warmer than the sand underfoot. And it was completely invisible, even at close range.

He dropped the stone and put both hands against it, pushing. It seemed to yield, just a trifle, but no farther than that trifle, even when he pushed with all his weight. It felt like a sheet of rubber backed up by steel. Limited resiliency, and then firm strength.

He stood on tiptoe and reached as high as he could and the barrier was still there.

He saw the Roller coming back, having reached one side of the arena. That feeling of nausea hit Carson again, and he stepped back from the barrier as it went by. It didn't stop.

But did the barrier stop at ground-level? Carson knelt down and burrowed in the sand; it was soft, light, easy to dig in. And two feet down the barrier was still there.

The Roller was coming back again. Obviously, it couldn't find a way through at either side.

There must be a way through, Carson thought, or else this duel is meaningless.

The Roller was back now, and it stopped just across the barrier, only six feet away. It seemed to be studying him although, for the life of him, Carson couldn't find external evidence of sense organs on the thing. Nothing that looked like eyes or ears, or even a mouth. There was though, he observed, a series of grooves, perhaps a dozen of them altogether, and he saw two tentacles push out from two of the grooves and dip into the sand as though testing its consistency. These were about an inch in diameter and perhaps a foot and a half long.

The tentacles were retractable into the grooves and were kept there except when in use. They retracted when the thing rolled and seemed to have nothing to do with its method of locomotion; that, as far as Carson could judge, seemed to be accomplished by some shifting – just *how* he

324

couldn't imagine – of its centre of gravity.

He shuddered as he looked at the thing. It was alien, horribly different from anything on Earth or any of the life forms found on the other solar planets. Instinctively, he knew its mind was as alien as its body.

If it could project that almost tangible wave of hatred, perhaps it could read his mind as well, sufficiently for his purpose.

Deliberately, Carson picked up the rock that had been his only weapon, then tossed it down again in a gesture of relinquishment and raised his empty hands, palms up, before him.

He spoke aloud, knowing that although the words would be meaningless to the creature before him, speaking them would focus his own thoughts more completely upon the message.

'Can we not have peace between us?' he said, his voice strange in the stillness. 'The Entity who brought us here has told us what must happen if our races fight – extinction of one and weakening and retrogression of the other. The battle between them, said the Entity, depends upon what we do here. Why cannot we agree to an eternal peace – your race to its galaxy, we to ours?'

Carson blanked out his mind to receive a reply.

It came, and it staggered him back, physically. He recoiled several steps in sheer horror at the intensity of the lust-to-kill of the red images projected at him. For a moment that seemed eternity he had to struggle against the impact of that hatred, fighting to clear his mind of it and drive out the alien thoughts to which he had given admittance. He wanted to retch.

His mind cleared slowly. He was breathing hard and he felt weaker, but he could think.

He stood studying the Roller. It had been motionless during the mental duel it had so nearly won. Now it rolled a few feet to one side, to the nearest of the blue bushes. Three tentacles whipped out of their grooves and began to investigate the bush.

'O.K.,' Carson said, 'so it's war then.' He managed a grin. 'If I got your answer straight, peace doesn't appeal to you.' And, because he was, after all, a young man and couldn't resist the impulse to be dramatic, he added, 'To the death!'

But his voice, in that utter silence, sounded silly even to himself. It came to him, then, that this *was* to the death, not only his own death or that of the red spherical thing which he thought of as the Roller, but death to the entire race of one or the other of them: the end of the human race, if he failed.

It made him suddenly very humble and very afraid to think that. With a knowledge that was above even faith, he knew that the Entity who had arranged this duel had told the truth about its intentions and its powers. The future of humanity depended upon *him*. It was an awful thing to realize. He had to concentrate on the situation at hand.

There had to be some way of getting through the barrier, or of killing through the barrier.

Mentally? He hoped that wasn't all, for the Roller obviously had stronger telepathic powers than the undeveloped ones of the human race. Or did it?

He had been able to drive the thoughts of the Roller out of his own mind; could it drive out his? If its ability to project were stronger, might not its receptivity mechanism be more vulnerable?

He stared at it and endeavoured to concentrate and focus all his thought upon it.

'*Die,*' he thought. '*You are going to die. You are dying. You are –* '

He tried variations on it, and mental pictures. Sweat stood out on his forehead and he found himself trembling with the intensity of the effort. But the Roller went ahead with its investigation of the bush, as utterly unaffected as though Carson had been reciting the multiplication table.

So *that* was no good.

He felt dizzy from the heat and his strenuous effort at concentration. He sat down on the blue sand and gave his full attention to studying the Roller. By study, perhaps, he could judge its strength and detect its weaknesses, learn things that would be valuable to know when and if they should come to grips.

It was breaking off twigs. Carson watched carefully, trying to judge just how hard it worked to do that. Later, he thought, he could find a similar bush on his own side, break off twigs of equal thickness himself, and gain a comparison of physical strength between his own arms and hands and those tentacles.

The twigs broke off hard; the Roller was having to struggle with each one. Each tentacle, he saw, bifurcated at the tip into two fingers, each tipped by a nail or claw. The claws didn't seem to be particularly long or dangerous, or no more so than his own fingernails, if they were left to grow a bit.

No, on the whole, it didn't look too hard to handle physically. Unless, of course, that bush was made of pretty tough stuff. Carson looked round; within reach was another bush of identically the same type.

He snapped off a twig. It was brittle, easy to break. Of course, the Roller might have been faking deliberately but he didn't think so. On the other hand, where was it vulnerable? How would he go about killing it if he got the chance? He went back to studying it. The outer hide looked pretty tough; he'd need a sharp weapon of some sort. He picked up the piece of rock again. It was about twelve inches long, narrow, and fairly sharp on one end. If it chipped like flint, he could make a serviceable knife out of it.

The Roller was continuing its investigations of the bushes. It rolled again, to the nearest one of another type. A little blue lizard, many-legged like the one Carson had seen on his side of the barrier, darted out from under the bush.

A tentacle of the Roller lashed out and caught it, picked it up. Another tentacle whipped over and began to pull legs off the lizard, as coldly as it had pulled twigs off the bush. The creature struggled frantically and emitted a shrill squealing that was the first sound Carson had heard here, other than the sound of his own voice.

Carson made himself continue to watch; anything he could learn about his opponent might prove valuable, even knowledge of its unnecessary cruelty – particularly, he thought with sudden emotion, knowledge of its unnecessary cruelty. It would make it a pleasure to kill the thing, if and when the chance came.

With half its legs gone, the lizard stopped squealing and lay limp in the Roller's grasp.

It didn't continue with the rest of the legs. Contemptuously it tossed the dead lizard away from it, in Carson's direction. The lizard arced through the air between them and landed at his feet.

It had come through the barrier! The barrier wasn't there any more!

Carson was on his feet in a flash, the knife gripped tightly in his hand, leaping forward. He'd settle this thing here and now! With the barrier gone – but it wasn't gone. He found that out the hard way, running head on into it and nearly knocking himself silly. He bounced back and fell.

As he sat up, shaking his head to clear it, he saw something coming through the air towards him, and threw himself flat again on the sand, to one side. He got his body out of the way, but there was a sudden sharp pain in the calf of his left leg.

He rolled backwards, ignoring the pain, and scrambled to his feet. It was a rock, he saw now, that had struck him. And the Roller was picking up another, swinging it back gripped between two tentacles, ready to throw again.

It sailed through the air towards him, but he was able to step out of its way. The Roller, apparently, could throw straight, but neither hard nor far. The first rock had struck him only because he had been sitting down and had not seen it coming until it was almost upon him.

Even as he stepped aside from that weak second throw Carson drew back his right arm and let fly with the rock that was still in his hand. If missiles, he thought with elation, can cross the barrier, then two can play at the game of throwing them.

He couldn't miss a three-foot sphere at only four-yard range, and he didn't miss. The rock whizzed straight, and with a speed several times that of the missiles the Roller had thrown. It hit dead centre, but hit flat instead of point first. But it hit with a resounding thump, and obviously hurt. The Roller had been reaching for another rock, but changed its mind and got out of there instead. By the time Carson could pick up and throw another rock, the Roller was forty yards back from the barrier and going strong.

His second throw missed by feet, and his third throw was short. The Roller was out of range of any missile heavy enough to be damaging.

Carson grinned. That round had been his.

He stopped grinning as he bent over to examine the calf of his leg. A jagged edge of the stone had made a cut several inches long. It was bleeding pretty freely, but he didn't think it had gone deep enough to hit an artery. If it stopped bleeding of its own accord, well and good. If not, he was in for trouble.

Finding out one thing, though, took precedence over that cut: the nature of the barrier.

He went forward to it again, this time groping with his hands before him. Holding one hand against it, he tossed a handful of sand at it with the other hand. The sand went right through; his hand didn't.

Organic matter versus inorganic? No, because the dead lizard had gone through it, and a lizard, alive or dead, was certainly organic. Plant life? He broke off a twig and poked it at the barrier. The twig went through, with no resistance, but when his fingers gripping the twig came to the barrier, they were stopped.

He couldn't get through it, nor could the Roller. But rocks and sand and a dead lizard.... How about a live lizard?

He went hunting under bushes until he found one, and caught it. He tossed it against the barrier and it bounced back and scurried away across the blue sand.

That gave him the answer, so far as he could determine it now. The screen was a barrier to living things. Dead or inorganic matter could cross it.

With that off his mind, Carson looked at his injured leg again. The bleeding was lessening, which meant he wouldn't need to worry about making a tourniquet. But he should find some water, if any was available, to clean the wound.

Water – the thought of it made him realize that he was getting awfully thirsty. He'd *have* to find water, in case this contest turned out to be a protracted one.

Limping slightly now, he started off to make a circuit of his half of the arena. Guiding himself with one hand along the barrier, he walked to his right until he came to the curving sidewall. It was visible, a dull blue-grey at close range, and the surface of it felt just like the central barrier.

He experimented by tossing a handful of sand at it, and the sand reached the wall and disappeared as it went through. The hemispherical shell was a force-field, too, but an opaque one, instead of transparent like the barrier.

He followed it round until he came back to the barrier, and walked back along the barrier to the point from which he'd started.

No sign of water.

Worried now, he started a series of zigzags back and forth between the barrier and the wall, covering the intervening space thoroughly.

No water. Blue sand, blue bushes, and intolerable heat. Nothing else.

It must be his imagination, he told himself, that he was suffering *that* much from thirst. How long had he been there? Of course, no time at all, according to his own space-time frame. The Entity had told him time stood still out there, while he was here. But his body processes went on here, just the same. According to his body's reckoning, how long had he been here? Three or four hours, perhaps. Certainly not long enough to be suffering from thirst.

Yet he was suffering from it; his throat was dry and parched. Probably the intense heat was the cause. It was *hot*, a hundred and thirty Fahrenheit, at a guess. A dry, still heat without the slightest movement of air.

He was limping rather badly and utterly fagged when he finished the futile exploration of his domain.

He stared across at the motionless Roller and hoped it was as miserable as he was. The Entity had said the conditions here were equally unfamiliar and uncomfortable for both of them. Maybe the Roller came from a planet where two-hundred-degree heat was the norm; maybe it was freezing while he was roasting. Maybe the air was as much too thick for it as it was too thin for him. For the exertion of his explorations had left him panting. The atmosphere here, he realized, was not much thicker than on Mars.

No water. That meant a deadline, for him at any rate. Unless he could find a way to cross that barrier or to kill his enemy from this side of it, thirst would kill him eventually.

It gave him a feeling of desperate urgency, but he made himself sit down a moment to rest, to think.

What was there to do? Nothing, and yet so many things. The several varieties of bushes, for example; they didn't look promising, but he'd have to examine them for possibilities. And his leg – he'd have to do something about that, even without water to clean it; gather ammunition in the form of rocks; find a rock that would make a good knife.

His leg hurt rather badly now, and he decided that came first. One type of bush had leaves – or things rather similar to leaves. He pulled off a handful of them and decided, after examination, to take a chance on them. He used them to clean off the sand and dirt and caked blood, then made a pad of fresh leaves and tied it over the wound with tendrils from the same bush.

The tendrils proved unexpectedly tough and strong. They were slender and pliable, yet he couldn't break them at all, and had to saw them off the bush with the sharp edge of blue flint. Some of the thicker ones were over a foot long, and he filed away in his memory, for future reference, the fact that a bunch of the thick ones, tied together, would make a pretty serviceable rope. Maybe he'd be able to think of a use for rope.

Next, he made himself a knife. The blue flint *did* chip. From a foot-long splinter of it, he fashioned himself a crude but lethal weapon. And of tendrils from the bush, he made himself a rope-belt through which he could thrust the flint knife, to keep it with him all the time and yet have his hands free.

He went back to studying the bushes. There were three other types. One was leafless, dry, brittle, rather like a dried tumbleweed. Another was of soft, crumbly wood, almost like punk. It looked and felt as though it would make excellent tinder for a fire. The third type was the most nearly woodlike. It had fragile leaves that wilted at the touch, but the stalks, although short, were straight and strong.

It was horribly, unbearably hot.

He limped up to the barrier, felt to make sure that it was still there. It was. He stood watching the Roller for a while; it was keeping a safe distance from the barrier, out of effective stone-throwing range. It was moving around back there, doing something. He couldn't tell what it was doing.

Once it stopped moving, came a little closer, and seemed to concentrate its attention on him. Again Carson had to fight off a wave of nausea. He threw a stone at it; the Roller retreated and went back to whatever it had been doing before.

At least he could make it keep its distance. And, he thought bitterly, a lot of good *that* did him. Just the same, he spent the next hour or two gathering stones of suitable size for throwing, and making several piles of them near his side of the barrier.

His throat burned now. It was difficult for him to think about anything except water. But he *had* to think about other things: about getting through that barrier, under or over it, getting *at* that red sphere and killing it before this place of heat and thirst killed him.

The barrier went to the wall upon either side, but how high, and how far under the sand?

For a moment, Carson's mind was too fuzzy to think out how he could find out either of those things. Idly, sitting there in the hot sand – and he didn't remember sitting down – he watched a blue lizard crawl from the shelter of one bush to the shelter of another.

From under the second bush, it looked out at him.

Carson grinned at it, recalling the old story of the desert-colonists on Mars, taken from an older story of Earth – 'Pretty soon you get so lonesome you find yourself talking to the lizards, and then not so long after that you find the lizards talking back to you. . . .'

He should have been concentrating, of course, on how to kill the Roller, but instead he grinned at the lizard and said, 'Hello, there.'

The lizard took a few steps towards him. 'Hello,' it said.

Carson was stunned for a moment, and then he put back his head and roared with laughter. It didn't hurt his throat to do so, either; he hadn't been *that* thirsty.

Why not? Why should the Entity who thought up this nightmare of a place not have a sense of humour, along with the other powers he had? Talking lizards, equipped to talk back in my own language, if I talk to them – it's a nice touch.

He grinned at the lizard and said, 'Come on over.' But the lizard turned and ran away, scurrying from bush to bush until it was out of sight.

He had to get past the barrier. He couldn't get through it, or over it, but was he certain he couldn't get under it? And come to think of it, didn't one sometimes find water by digging?

Painfully now, Carson limped up to the barrier and started digging, scooping up sand a double handful at a time. It was slow work because the sand ran in at the edges and the deeper he got the bigger in diameter the hole had to be. How many hours it took him, he didn't know, but he hit bedrock four feet down: dry bedrock with no sign of water.

The force-field of the barrier went down clear to the bedrock.

He crawled out of the hole and lay there panting, then raised his head to look across and see what the Roller was doing.

It was making something out of wood from the bushes, tied together with tendrils, a queerly shaped framework about four feet high and roughly square. To see it better, Carson climbed on to the mound of sand he had excavated and stood there staring.

There were two long levers sticking out of the back of it, one with a cup-shaped affair on the end. Seemed to be some sort of a catapult, Carson thought.

Sure enough, the Roller was lifting a sizable rock into the cup-shape. One of his tentacles moved the other lever up and down for a while, and then he turned the machine slightly, aiming it, and the lever with the stone flew up and forward.

The stone curved several yards over Carson's head, so far away that he didn't have to duck, but he judged the distance it had travelled, and whistled softly. He couldn't throw a rock that weight more than half that distance. And even retreating to the rear of his domain wouldn't put him out of range of that machine if the Roller pushed it forward to the barrier.

Another rock whizzed over, not quite so far away this time.

Moving from side to side along the barrier, so the catapult couldn't bracket him, he hurled a dozen rocks at it. But that wasn't going to be any good, he saw. They had to be light rocks, or he couldn't throw them that far. If they hit the framework, they bounced off harmlessly. The Roller had no difficulty, at that distance, in moving aside from those that came near it.

Besides, his arm was tiring badly. He ached all over.

He stumbled to the rear of the arena. Even that wasn't any good; the rocks reached back there, too, only there were longer intervals between them, as though it took longer to wind up the mechanism, whatever it was, of the catapult.

Wearily he dragged himself back to the barrier again. Several times he fell and could barely rise to his feet to go on. He was, he knew, near the limit of his endurance. Yet he didn't dare stop moving now, until and unless he could put that catapult out of action. If he fell asleep, he'd never wake up.

One of the stones from it gave him the glimmer of an idea. It hit one of the piles of stones he'd gathered near the barrier to use as ammunition and struck sparks.

Sparks! Fire! Primitive man had made fire by striking sparks, and with some of those dry crumbly bushes as tinder...

A bush of that type grew near him. He uprooted it, took it over to the pile of stones, then patiently hit one stone against another until a spark touched the punklike wood of the bush. It went up in flames so fast that it singed his eyebrows and was burned to an ash within seconds.

But he had the idea now, and within minutes had a little fire going in the lee of the mound of sand he'd made. The tinder bushes started it, and other bushes which burned more slowly kept it a steady flame.

The tough tendrils didn't burn readily; that made the fire-bombs easy to rig and throw; a bundle of faggots tied about a small stone to give it weight and a loop of the tendril to swing it by.

He made half a dozen of them before he lighted and threw the first. It went wide, and the Roller started a quick retreat, pulling the catapult after him. But Carson had the others ready and threw them in rapid succession. The fourth wedged in the catapult's framework and did the trick. The Roller tried desperately to put out the spreading blaze by throwing sand, but its clawed tentacles would take only a spoonful at a time and its efforts were ineffectual. The catapult burned.

The Roller moved safely away from the fire and seemed to concentrate its attention on Carson. Again he felt that wave of hatred and nausea – but more weakly; either the Roller itself was weakening or Carson had learned how to protect himself against the mental attack.

He thumbed his nose at it and then sent it scuttling back to safety with a stone. The Roller went to the back of its half of the arena and started pulling up bushes again. Probably it was going to make another catapult.

Carson verified that the barrier was still operating, and then found himself sitting in the sand beside it, suddenly too weak to stand up.

His leg throbbed steadily now and the pangs of thirst were severe. But those things paled beside the physical exhaustion that gripped his entire body.

Hell must be like this, he thought, the hell that the ancients had believed in. He fought to stay awake, and yet staying awake seemed futile, for there was nothing he could do while the barrier remained impregnable and the Roller stayed back out of range.

He tried to remember what he had read in books of archaeology about the methods of fighting used back in the days before metal and plastic. The stone missile had come first, he thought. Well, that he already had.

Bow and arrow? No; he'd tried archery once and knew his own ineptness even with a modern sportsman's dura-steel weapon, made for accuracy. With only the crude, pieced-together outfit he could make here, he doubted if he could shoot as far as he could throw a rock.

Spear? Well, he *could* make that. It would be useless at any distance, but would be a handy thing at close range, if he ever got to close range. Making one would help keep his mind from wandering, as it was beginning to do.

He was still beside one of the piles of stones. He sorted through it until he found one shaped roughly like a spearhead. With a smaller stone he began to chip it into shape, fashioning sharp shoulders on the sides so that if it penetrated it would not pull out again like a harpoon. A harpoon was better than a spear, maybe, for this crazy contest. If he could once get it into the Roller, and had a rope on it, he could pull the Roller up against the barrier and the stone blade of his knife would reach through that barrier, even if his hands wouldn't.

The shaft was harder to make than the head, but by splitting and joining the main stems of four of the bushes, and wrapping the joints with the tough but thin tendrils, he got a strong shaft about four feet long, and tied the stone head in a notch cut in one end. It was crude, but strong.

With the tendrils he made himself twenty feet of line. It was light and didn't look strong, but he knew it would hold his weight and to spare. He tied one end of it to the shaft of the harpoon and the other end about his right wrist. At least, if he threw his harpoon across the barrier, he'd be able to pull it back if he missed.

He tried to stand up, to see what the Roller was doing, and found he couldn't get to his feet. On the third try, he got as far as his knees and then fell flat again.

'I've got to sleep,' he thought. 'If a showdown came now, I'd be helpless. He could come up here and kill me, if he knew. I've got to regain some strength.'

Slowly, painfully, he crawled back from the barrier.

The jar of something thudding against the sand near him wakened him from a confused and horrible dream to a more confused and horrible reality, and he opened his eyes again to blue radiance over blue sand.

How long had he slept? A minute? A day?

Another stone thudded nearer and threw sand on him. He got his arms under him and sat up. He turned round and saw the Roller twenty yards away, at the barrier.

It rolled off hastily as he sat up, not stopping until it was as far away as it could get.

He'd fallen asleep too soon, he realized, while he was still in range of the Roller's throwing. Seeing him lying motionless, it had dared come up to the barrier. Luckily, it didn't realize how weak he was, or it could have stayed there and kept on throwing stones.

He started crawling again, this time forcing himself to keep going until he was as far as he could go, until the opaque wall of the arena's outer shell was only a yard away.

Then things slipped away again....

When he awoke, nothing about him was changed, but this time he knew that he had slept a long while. The first thing he became aware of was the inside of his mouth; it was dry, caked. His tongue was swollen.

Something was wrong, he knew, as he returned slowly to full awareness. He felt less tired, the stage of utter exhaustion had passed. But there was pain, agonizing pain. It wasn't until he tried to move that he knew that it came from his leg.

He raised his head and looked down at it. It was swollen below the knee, and the swelling showed even half-way up his thigh. The plant tendrils he had tied round the protective pad of leaves now cut deeply into his flesh.

To get his knife under that imbedded lashing would have been impossible. Fortunately, the final knot was over the shin bone where the vine cut in less deeply than elsewhere. He was able, after an effort, to untie the knot.

A look under the pad of leaves showed him the worst: infection and blood poisoning. Without drugs, without even water, there wasn't a thing he could do about it, except *die* when the poison spread through his system.

He knew it was hopeless, then, and that he'd lost, and with him, humanity. When he died here, out there in the universe he knew, all his friends, everybody, would die too. Earth and the colonized planets would become the home of the red, rolling, alien Outsiders.

It was that thought which gave him courage to start crawling, almost blindly, towards the barrier again, pulling himself along by his arms and hands.

There was a chance in a million that he'd have strength left when he got there to throw his harpoon-spear just *once*, and with deadly effect, if

334

the Roller would come up to the barrier, or if the barrier was gone.

It took him years, it seemed, to get there. The barrier wasn't gone. It was as impassable as when he'd first felt it.

The Roller wasn't at the barrier. By raising himself up on his elbows, he could see it at the back of its part of the arena, working on a wooden framework that was a half-completed duplicate of the catapult he'd destroyed.

It was moving slowly now. Undoubtedly it had weakened, too.

Carson doubted that it would ever need that second catapult. He'd be dead, he thought, before it was finished.

His mind must have slipped for a moment, for he found himself beating his fists against the barrier in futile rage, and made himself stop. He closed his eyes, tried to make himself calm.

'Hello,' said a voice.

It was a small, thin voice. He opened his eyes and turned his head. It *was* a lizard.

'Go away,' Carson wanted to say. 'Go away; you're not really there, or you're there but not really talking. I'm imagining things again.'

But he couldn't talk; his throat and tongue were past all speech with the dryness. He closed his eyes again.

'Hurt,' said the voice. 'Kill. Hurt – kill. Come.'

He opened his eyes again. The blue ten-legged lizard was still there. It ran a little way along the barrier, came back, started off again, and came back.

'Hurt,' it said. 'Kill. Come.'

Again it started off, and came back. Obviously it wanted Carson to follow it along the barrier.

He closed his eyes again. The voice kept on. The same three meaningless words. Each time he opened his eyes, it ran off and came back.

'Hurt. Kill. Come.'

Carson groaned. Since there would be no peace unless he followed the thing, he crawled after it.

Another sound, a high-pitched, squealing, came to his ears. There was something lying in the sand, writhing, squealing. Something small, blue, that looked like a lizard.

He saw it was the lizard whose legs the Roller had pulled off, so long ago. It wasn't dead; it had come back to life and was wriggling and screaming in agony.

'Hurt,' said the other lizard. 'Hurt. Kill. Kill.'

Carson understood. He took the flint knife from his belt and killed the tortured creature. The live lizard scurried off.

Carson turned back to the barrier. He leaned his hands and head

335

against it and watched the Roller, far back, working on the new catapult.

'I could get that far,' he thought, 'if I could get through. If I could get through, I might win yet. It looks weak, too. I might – '

And then there was another reaction of hopelessness, when pain sapped his will and he wished that he were dead, envying the lizard he'd just killed. It didn't have to live on and suffer.

He was pushing on the barrier with the flat of his hands when he noticed his arms, how thin and scrawny they were. He must really have been here a long time, for days, to get as thin as that.

For a while he was almost hysterical again, and then came a time of deep calm and thought.

The lizard he had just killed *had crossed the barrier, still alive.* It had come from the Roller's side; the Roller had pulled off its legs and then tossed it contemptuously at him and it had come through the barrier.

It hadn't been dead, merely unconscious. A live lizard couldn't go through the barrier, but an unconscious one could. The barrier was not a barrier, then, to living flesh, but to conscious flesh. It was a *mental* protection, a *mental* hazard.

With that thought, Carson started crawling along the barrier to make his last desperate gamble, a hope so forlorn that only a dying man would have dared try it.

He moved along the barrier to the mound of sand, about four feet high, which he'd scooped out while trying – how many days ago? – to dig under the barrier or to reach water. That mound lay right at the barrier, its farther slope half on one side of the barrier, half on the other.

Taking with him a rock from the pile nearby, he climbed up to the top of the dune and lay there against the barrier, so that if the barrier were taken away he'd roll on down the short slope, into the enemy territory.

He checked to be sure that the knife was safely in his rope belt, that the harpoon was in the crook of his left arm and that the twenty-foot rope fastened to it and to his wrist. Then with his right hand he raised the rock with which he would hit himself on the head. Luck would have to be with him on that blow; it would have to be hard enough to knock him out, but not hard enough to knock him out for long.

He had a hunch that the Roller was watching him, and would see him roll down through the barrier, and come to investigate. It would believe he was dead, he hoped – he thought it had probably drawn the same deduction about the nature of the barrier that he had. But it would come cautiously; he would have a little time –

He struck himself.

Pain brought him back to consciousness, a sudden, sharp pain in his hip that was different from the pain in his head and leg. He had, thinking things out before he had struck himself, anticipated that very pain, even hoped for it, and had steeled himself against awakening with a sudden movement.

He opened his eyes just a slit, and saw that he had guessed rightly. The Roller was coming closer. It was twenty feet away; the pain that had awakened him was the stone it had tossed to see whether he was alive or dead. He lay still. It came closer, fifteen feet away, and stopped again. Carson scarcely breathed.

As nearly as possible, he was keeping his mind a blank, lest its telepathic ability detect consciousness in him. And with his mind blanked out that way, the impact of its thoughts upon his mind was shattering.

He felt sheer horror at the *alienness*, the *differentness* of those thoughts, conveying things that he felt but could not understand or express, because no terrestrial language had words, no terrestrial brain had images to fit them. The mind of a spider, he thought, or the mind of a praying mantis or a Martian sand-serpent, raised to intelligence and put in telepathic *rapport* with human minds, would be a homely familiar thing, compared to this.

He understood now that the Entity had been right: Man or Roller, the universe was not a place that could hold them both.

Closer. Carson waited until it was only feet away, until its clawed tentacles reached out....

Oblivious to agony now, he sat up, raised and flung the harpoon with all the strength that remained to him. As the Roller, deeply stabbed by the harpoon, rolled away, Carson tried to get to his feet to run after it. He couldn't do that; he fell, but kept crawling.

It reached the end of the rope, and he was jerked forward by the pull on his wrist. It dragged him a few feet and then stopped. Carson kept going, pulling himself towards it hand over hand along the rope. It stopped there, tentacles trying in vain to pull out the harpoon. It seemed to shudder and quiver, and then realized that it couldn't get away, for it rolled back towards him, clawed tentacles reaching out.

Stone knife in hand, he met it. He stabbed, again and again, while those horrid claws ripped skin and flesh and muscle from his body.

He stabbed and slashed, and at last it was still.

A bell was ringing, and it took him a while after he'd opened his eyes to tell where he was and what it was. He was strapped into the seat of his scouter, and the visiplate before him showed only empty space. No Outsider ship and no impossible planet.

The bell was the communications plate signal; someone wanted him to switch power into the receiver. Purely reflex action enabled him to reach forward and throw the lever.

The face of Brander, captain of the *Magellan*, mother-ship of his group of scouters, flashed into the screen. His face was pale and his black eyes glowing with excitement.

'*Magellan* to Carson,' he snapped. 'Come on in. The fight's over. We've won!'

The screen went blank; Brander would be signalling the other scouters of his command.

Slowly, Carson set the controls for the return. Slowly, unbelievingly, he unstrapped himself from the seat and went back to get a drink at the cold-water tank. For some reason, he was unbelievably thirsty. He drank six glasses.

He leaned there against the wall, trying to think.

Had it happened? He was in good health, sound, uninjured. His thirst had been mental rather than physical; his throat hadn't been dry.

He pulled up his trouser leg and looked at the calf. There was a long white scar there, but a perfectly healed scar; it hadn't been there before. He zipped open the front of his shirt and saw that his chest and abdomen were criss-crossed with tiny, almost unnoticeable, perfectly healed scars.

It *had* happened!

The scouter, under automatic control, was already entering the hatch of the mother-ship. The grapples pulled it into its individual lock, and a moment later a buzzer indicated that the lock was airfilled. Carson opened the hatch and stepped outside, went through the double door of the lock.

He went right to Brander's office, went in, and saluted.

Brander still looked dazed. 'Hi, Carson,' he said. 'What you missed; what a show!'

'What happened, sir?'

'Don't know, exactly. We fired one salvo, and their whole fleet went up in dust! Whatever it was jumped from ship to ship in a flash, even the ones we hadn't aimed at and that were out of range! The whole fleet disintegrated before our eyes, and we didn't get the paint of a single ship scratched!

'We can't even claim credit for it. Must have been some unstable component in the metal they used, and our sighting shot just set it off. Man, too bad you missed all the excitement!'

Carson managed a sickly ghost of a grin, for it would be days before he'd be over the impact of his experience, but the captain wasn't watching.

'Yes, sir,' he said. Common sense, more than modesty, told him he'd be branded as the worst liar in space if he ever said any more than that. 'Yes, sir, too bad I missed all the excitement....'

The Man Who Came Back

ROBERT SILVERBERG

NATURALLY, THERE WAS a tremendous fuss made over him, since he was the first man actually to buy up his indenture and return from a colony-world. He had been away eighteen years, farming on bleak Novotny IX, and who knew how many of those years he had been slaving and saving to win his passage home?

Besides, rumour had it that a girl was involved. It could be the big romance of the century, maybe. Even before the ship carrying him had docked at Long Island Spaceport, John Burkhardt was a systemfamed celebrity. Word of his return had preceded him – word, and all manner of rumour, legend and myth.

The starship *Lincoln*, returning from a colony-seeding trip in the outer reaches of the galaxy, for the first time in its history was carrying an Earthward-bound passenger. A small army of newsmen impatiently awaited the ship's landing, and the nine worlds waited with them.

When he stepped into the unloading elevator and made his descent, a hum of comment rippled through the gathered crowd. Burkhardt looked his part perfectly. He was a tall man, spare and lean. His face was solemn, his lips thin and pale, his hair going grey though he was only in his forties. And his eyes – deepset, glowering, commanding. Everything fit the myth: the physique, the face, the eyes. They were those of a man who could renounce Earth for unrequited love, then toil eighteen years out of the sheer strength of that love.

Cameras ground. Bulbs flashed. Five hundred reporters felt their tongues going dry with anticipation of the big story.

Burkhardt smiled coldly and waved at the horde of newsmen. He did not blink, shield his eyes, or turn away. He seemed almost unnaturally in control of himself. They had expected him to weep, maybe kneel and kiss the soil of Mother Earth. He did none of those things. He merely smiled and waved.

The Global Wire man stepped forward. He had won the lottery. It was his privilege to conduct the first interview.

'Welcome to Earth, Mr Burkhardt. How does it feel to be back?'

'I'm glad to be here.' Burkhardt's voice was slow, deep, measured, controlled like every other aspect of him.

'This army of pressmen doesn't upset you, does it?'

'I haven't seen this many people all at once in eighteen years. But no – they don't upset me.'

'You know, Mr Burkhardt, you've done something special. You're the only man ever to return to Earth after signing out on an indenture.'

'Am I the only one?' Burkhardt responded easily. 'I wasn't aware of that.'

'You are indeed, sir. And I'd like to know, if I may – for the benefit of billions of viewers – if you care to tell us a little of the story behind your story? Why did you leave Earth in the first place, Mr Burkhardt? And why did you decide to return?'

Burkhardt smiled gravely. 'There was a woman,' he said. 'A lovely woman, a famous woman now. We loved each other, once, and when she stopped loving me I left Earth. I have reason to believe I can regain her love now, so I have returned. And now, if you'll pardon me – '

'Couldn't you give us any details?'

'I've had a long trip, and I prefer to rest now. I'll be glad to answer your questions at a formal press conference tomorrow afternoon.'

And he cut through the crowd towards a waiting cab supplied by the Colonization Bureau.

Nearly everyone in the system had seen the brief interview or had heard reports of it. It had certainly been a masterly job. If people had been curious about Burkhardt before, they were obsessed with him now. To give up Earth out of unrequited love, to labour eighteen years for a second chance – why, he was like some figure out of Dumas, brought to life in the middle of the 24th century.

It was no mean feat to buy one's self back out of a colonization indenture, either. The Colonization Bureau of the Solar Federation undertook to transport potential colonists to distant worlds and set them up as homesteaders. In return for one-way transportation, tools and land, the colonists merely had to promise to remain settled, to marry and to raise the maximum practical number of children. This programme, a hundred years old now, had resulted in the seeding of Terran colonies over a galactic radius of better than five hundred light-years.

It was theoretically possible for a colonist to return to Earth, of course. But few of them seemed to want to, and none before Burkhardt ever had. To return, you had first to pay off your debt to the government – figured theoretically at $20,000 for round-trip passage, $5000 for land, $5000 for tools – plus 6 per cent interest per year. Since nobody with any assets would ever become a colonist, and since it was next to impossible for a colonist, farming an unworked world, to accumulate any capital, no case of an attempted buy-out had ever arisen.

Until Burkhardt. He had done it, working round the clock, outproducing his neighbours on Novotny IX and selling them his surplus, cabling his extra pennies back to Earth to be invested in blue-chip securities, and finally – after eighteen years – amassing the $30,000-plus-accrued-interest that would spring him from indenture.

Twenty billion people on nine worlds wanted to know why.

The day after his return, he held a press conference in the hotel suite provided for him by the Colonization Bureau. Admission was strictly limited – one man from each of the twenty leading news services, no more.

Wearing a faded purplish tunic and battered sandals, Burkhardt came out to greet the reporters. He looked tremendously dignified – an overbearing figure of a man, thin but solid, with enormous gnarled hands and powerful forearms. The grey in his hair gave him a patriarchical look on a world dedicated to cosmetic rejuvenation. And his eyes, shining like twin beacons, roved around the room, transfixing everyone once, causing discomfort and uneasiness. No one had seen eyes like that on a human being before. But no one had ever seen a returned colonist before, either.

He smiled without warmth. 'Very well, gentlemen. I'm at your disposal.'

They started with the peripheral questions first.

'What sort of planet is Novotny IX, Mr Burkhardt?'

'Cold. The temperature never gets above sixty. The soil is marginally fertile. A man has to work ceaselessly if he wants to stay alive there.'

'Did you know that when you signed up to go there?'

Burkhardt nodded. 'I asked for the least desirable of the available colony worlds.'

'Are there many colonists there?'

'About twenty thousand, I think. It isn't a popular planet, you understand.'

'Mr Burkhardt, part of the terms of the colonist's indenture specify that he must marry. Did you fulfil this part of the contract?'

Burkhardt smiled sadly. 'I married less than a week after my arrival there in 2319. My wife died the first winter of our marriage. There were no children. I didn't remarry.'

'And when did you get the idea of buying up your indenture and returning to Earth?'

'In my third year on Novotny IX.'

'In other words, you devoted fifteen years to getting back to Earth?'

'That's correct.'

It was a young reporter from Transuniverse News who took the plunge toward the real meat of the universe. 'Could you tell us why you changed your mind about remaining a colonist? At the spaceport you said something about their being a woman ––'

'Yes.' Burkhardt chuckled mirthlessly. 'I was pretty young when I

341

threw myself into the colonization plan – twenty-five, in point of fact. There was a woman; I loved her; she married someone else. I did the romantic thing and signed up for Novotny IX. Three years later, the newstap from Earth told me that she had been divorced. This was in 2322. I resolved to return to Earth and try to persuade her to marry me.'

'So for fifteen years you struggled to get back so you could patch up your old romance,' another newsman said. 'But how did you know she hadn't remarried in all that time?'

'She did remarry,' Burkhardt said stunningly.

'But – – '

'I received word of her remarriage in 2324, and of her subsequent divorce in 2325. Of her remarriage in 2327, and of her subsequent divorce in 2329. Of her remarriage in the same year, and her subsequent divorce in 2334. Of her remarriage in 2335, and of her divorce four months ago. Unless I have missed the announcement, she has not remarried this last time.'

'Did you abandon your project every time you heard of one of these marriages?'

Burkhardt shook his head. 'I kept on saving. I was confident that none of her marriages would last. All these years, you see, she's been trying to find a substitute for me. But human beings are unique. There are no substitutes. I weathered five of her marriages. Her sixth husband will be myself.'

'Could you tell us – could you tell us the name of this woman, Mr Burkhardt?'

The returned colonist's smile was frigid. 'I'm not ready to reveal her name just yet,' he said. 'Are there any further questions?'

Along toward mid-afternoon, Burkhardt ended the conference. He had told them in detail of his efforts to pile up the money; he had talked about life as a colonist; he had done everything but tell them the name of the woman for whose sake he had done all this.

Alone in the suite after they had gone, Burkhardt stared out at the other glittering towers of New York. Jet liners droned overhead; a billion lights shattered the darkness. New York, he thought, was as chaotic and as repugnant to him as ever. He missed Novotny IX.

But he had had to come back. Smiling gently, he opaqued the windows of his suite. It was winter, now, on Novotny IX's colonized continent. A time for burrowing away, for digging in against the mountain-high drifts of blue-white snow. Winter was eight standard months long, on Novotny IX; only four out of the sixteen standard months of the planet's year were really livable. Yet a man could see the results of his own labour, out there. He could use his hands and measure his gains.

And there were friends there. Not the other settlers, though they were

342

good people and hard workers. But the natives, the Euranoi.

The survey charts said nothing about them. There were only about five hundred of them left, anyway, or so Donnoi had claimed. Burkhardt had never seen more than a dozen of the Euranoi at any one time, and he had never been able to tell one from another. They looked like slim elves, half the height of a man, grey-skinned, chinless, sad-eyed. They went naked against their planet's bitter cold. They lived in caves, somewhere below the surface. And Donnoi had become Burkhardt's friend.

Burkhardt smiled, remembering. He had found the little alien in a snowdrift, so close to dead it was hard to be certain one way or the other. Donnoi had lived, and had recovered, and had spent the winter in Burkhardt's cabin, talking a little, but mostly listening.

Burkhardt had done the talking. He had talked it all out, telling the little being of his foolishness, of his delusion that Lily loved him, of his wild maniac desire to get back to Earth.

And Donnoi had said, when he understood the situation, '*You will get back to Earth. And she will be yours.*'

That had been between the first divorce and the second marriage. The day the newstapes had brought word of Lily's remarriage had nearly finished Burkhardt, but Donnoi was there, comforting, consoling, and from that day on Burkhardt never worried again. Lily's marriages were made, weakened, broke up, and Burkhardt worked unfalteringly, knowing that when he returned to Earth he could have Lily at last.

Donnoi had told him solemnly, '*It is all a matter of channelling your desires. Look: I lay dying in a snowdrift, and I willed you to find me. You came; I lived.*'

'But I'm not Euranoi,' Burkhardt had protested. 'My will isn't strong enough to influence another person.'

'*Any creature that thinks can assert its will. Give me your hand, and I will show you.*'

Burkhardt smiled back across fifteen years, remembering the feel of Donnoi's limp, almost boneless hand in his own, remembering the stiff jolt of power that had flowed from the alien. His hand had tingled for days afterward. But he knew, from that moment, that he would succeed.

Burkhardt had a visitor the next morning. A press conference was scheduled again for the afternoon, and Burkhardt had said he would grant no interviews before then, but the visitor had been insistent. Finally, the desk had phoned up to tell Burkhardt that a Mr Richardson Elliott was here, and demanded to see him.

The name rang a bell. 'Send him up,' Burkhardt said.

A few minutes later, the elevator disgorged Mr Richardson Elliott. He was shorter than Burkhardt, plump, pink-skinned, clean-shaven. A ring glistened on his finger, and there was a gem of some alien origin mounted on a stickpin near his throat.

343

He extended his hand. Burkhardt took it. The hand was carefully manicured, pudgy, somehow oily.

'You're not at all as I pictured you,' Burkhardt said.

'You are. Exactly.'

'Why did you come here?'

Elliott tapped the newsfax crumpled under his arm. He unfolded it, showing Burkhardt the front-page spread. 'I read the story, Burkhardt. I knew at once who the girl – the woman – was. I came to warn you not to get involved with her.'

Burkhardt's eyes twinkled. 'And why not?'

'She's a witch,' Elliott muttered. 'She'll drain a man dry and throw the husk away. Believe me, I know. You only loved her. I married her.'

'Yes,' Burkhardt said. 'You took her away from me eighteen years ago.'

'You know that isn't true. She walked out on you because she thought I could further her career, which was so. I didn't even know another man had been in the picture until she got that letter from you, postmarked the day your ship took off. She showed it to me – laughing. I can't repeat the things she said about you, Burkhardt. But I was shocked. My marriage to her started to come apart right then and there, even though it was another three years before we called it quits. She threw herself at me. I didn't steal her from anybody. Believe me, Burkhardt.'

'I believe you.'

Elliott mopped his pink forehead. 'It was the same way with all the other husbands. I've followed her career all along. She exists only for Lily Leigh, and nobody else. When she left me, it was to marry Alderson. Well, she killed him as good as if she'd shot him, when she told him she was pulling out. Man his age had no business marrying her. And then it was Michaels, and after him Dan Cartwright, and then Jim Thorne. Right up the ladder to fame and fortune, leaving a trail of used-up husbands behind her.'

Burkhardt shrugged. 'The past is of no concern to me.'

'You actually think Lily will marry you?'

'I do,' Burkhardt said. 'She'll jump at it. The publicity values will be irresistible. The sollie star with five broken marriages to millionaires now stooping to wed her youthful love, who is now a penniless ex-colonist.'

Elliott moistened his lips unhappily. 'Perhaps you've got something there,' he admitted. 'Lily might just do a thing like that. But how would it last? Six months, a year – until the publicity dies down. And then she'll dump you. She doesn't want a penniless husband.'

'She won't dump me.'

'You sound pretty confident, Burkhardt.'

'I am.'

For a moment there was silence. Then Elliott said, 'You seem determined to stick your head in the lion's mouth. What is it – an obsession to marry her?'

'Call it that.'

'It's crazy. I tell you, she's a witch. You're in love with an imaginary goddess. The real Lily Leigh is the most loathsome female ever spawned. As the first of her five husbands, I can take oath to that.'

'Did you come here just to tell me that?'

'Not exactly,' Elliott said. 'I've got a proposition for you. I want you to come into my firm as a Vice President. You're system-famous, and we can use the publicity. I'll start you at sixty thousand. You'll be the most eligible bachelor in the universe. We'll get you a rejuvenation and you'll look twenty-five again. Only none of this Lily Leigh nonsense. I'll set you up, you'll marry some good-looking kid, and all your years on Whatsis Nine will be just so much nightmare.'

'The answer is no.'

'I'm not doing this out of charity, you understand. I think you'll be an asset to me. But I also think you ought to be protected against Lily. I feel I owe you something, for what I did to you unknowingly eighteen years ago.'

'You don't owe me a thing. Thanks for the warning, Mr Elliott, but I don't need it. And the answer to the proposition is No. I'm not for sale.'

'I beg you – – '

'No.'

Colour flared in Elliott's cheeks for a moment. He rose, started to say something, stopped. 'All right,' he said heavily. 'Go to Lily. Like a moth drawn to a flame. The offer remains, Mr Burkhardt. And you have my deepest sympathy.'

At his press conference that afternoon, Burkhardt revealed her name. The system's interest was at peak, now; another day without the revelation and the peak would pass, frustration would cause interest to subside. Burkhardt told them. Within an hour it was all over the system.

Glamorous Lily Leigh, for a decade and a half queen of the solido-films, was named today as the woman for whom John Burkhardt bought himself out of indenture. Burkhardt explained that Miss Leigh, then an unknown starlet, terminated their engagement in 2319 to marry California industrialist Richardson Elliott. The marriage, like Miss Leigh's four later ones, ended in divorce.

'I hope now to make her my wife,' the mystery man from Novotny IX declared. 'After eighteen years I still love her as strongly as ever.'

Miss Leigh, in seclusion at her Scottsdale, Arizona home following her recent divorce from sollie-distributing magnate James Thorne, refused to comment on the statement.

For three days, Lily Leigh remained in seclusion, seeing no one, issuing no statements to the press. Burkhardt was patient. Eighteen years of waiting teaches patience. And Donnoi had told him, as they trudged through the grey slush of rising spring, *'The man who rushes ahead foolishly forfeits all advantages in a contest of wills.'*

Donnoi carried the wisdom of a race at the end of its span. Burkhardt remained in his hotel suite, mulling over the advice of the little alien. Donnoi had never passed judgment on the merits and drawbacks of Burkhardt's goal; he had simply advised, and suggested, and taught.

The press had run out of things to say about Burkhardt, and he declined to supply them with anything new to print. So, inevitably, they lost interest in him. By the third day, it was no longer necessary to hold a press conference. He had come back; he had revealed his love for the sollie queen, Lily Leigh; now he was sitting tight. There was nothing to do but wait for further developments, if any. And neither Burkhardt nor Lily Leigh seemed to be creating further developments.

It was hard to remain calm, Burkhardt thought. It was queer to be here on Earth, in the quiet autumn, while winter fury raged on Novotny IX. Fury of a different kind raged here, the fury of a world of five billion eager, active human beings, but Burkhardt kept himself aloof from all that. Eighteen years of near-solitude had left him unfit for that sort of world.

It was hard to sit quiet, though, with Lily just a visi-call away. Burkhardt compelled himself to be patient. She would call, sooner or later.

She called on the fourth day. Burkhardt's skin crawled as he heard the hotel operator say – in tones regulated only with enormous effort – 'Miss Leigh is calling from Arizona, Mr Burkhardt.'

'Put the call on.'

She had not used the visi-circuit. Burkhardt kept his screen blank too.

She said, without preliminaries, 'Why have you come back after all these years, John?'

'Because I love you.'

'Still?'

'Yes.'

She laughed – the famous LL laugh, for his benefit alone. 'You're a bigger fool now than you were then, John.'

'Perhaps,' he admitted.

'I suppose I ought to thank you, though. This is the best publicity I've had all year. And at my age I need all the publicity I can get.'

'I'm glad for you,' he said.

'You aren't serious, though, about wanting to marry me, are you? Not after all these years. Nobody stays in love that long.'

'I did.'

'Damn you, what do you want from me?' The voice, suddenly shrill, betrayed a whisper of age.

346

'Yourself,' Burkhardt said calmly.

'What makes you think I'll marry you? Sure, you're a hero today. The Man Who Came Back From The Stars. But you're nothing, John. All you have to show for eighteen years is callouses. At least back then you had your youth. You don't even have that any more.'

'Let me come to see you, Lily.'

'I don't want to see you.'

'Please. It's a small thing – let me have half an hour alone with you.'

She went silent.

'I've given you half a lifetime of love, Lily. Let me have half an hour.'

After a long moment she said, simply, hoarsely, 'All right. You can come. But I won't marry you.'

He left New York shortly before midnight. The Colonization Bureau had hired a private plane for him, and he slipped out unnoticed, in the dark. Publicity now would be fatal. The plane was a chemically powered jet, somewhat out of date; they were using photon-rockets for the really fast travel. But, obsolete or no, it crossed the continent in three hours. It was just midnight, local time, when the plane landed in Phoenix. As they had arranged it, Lily had her chauffeur waiting, with a long sleek limousine. Burkhardt climbed in. Turbines throbbed; the car glided out towards Lily's desert home.

It was a mansion, a sprawled-out villa moated off – a *moat*, in water-hungry Arizona! – and topped with a spiring pink stucco tower. Burkhardt was ushered through open fern-lined courtyards to an inner maze of hallways, and through them into a small room where Lily Leigh sat waiting.

He repressed a gasp. She wore a gown worth a planet's ransom, but the girl within the gown had not changed in eighteen years. Her face was the same, impish, the eyes dancing and gay. Her hair had lost none of its glossy sheen. Her skin was the skin of a girl of nineteen.

'It's like stepping back in time,' he murmured.

'I have good doctors. You wouldn't believe I'm forty, would you? But everyone knows it, of course.' She laughed. 'You look like an old man, John.'

'Forty-three isn't old.'

'It is when you let your age show. I'll give you some money, John, and you can get fixed up. Better still, I'll send my doctors to you.'

Burkhardt shook his head. 'I'm honest about the passing of time. I look this way because of what I've done these past eighteen years. I wouldn't want a doctor's skill to wipe out the traces of those years.'

She shrugged lightly. 'It was only an offer, not a slur. What do you want with me, John?'

'I want you to marry me.'

Her laughter was a silvery tinkle, ultimately striking a false note. 'That made sense in 2319. It doesn't now. People would say you married me for my money. I've got lots of money, John, you know.'

'I'm not interested in your money. I want *you*.'

'You think you love me, but how can you? I'm not the sweet little girl you once loved. I never was that sweet little girl. I was a grasping, greedy little girl – and now I'm a grasping, greedy old woman who still looks like a little girl. Go away, John. I'm not for you.'

'Marry me, Lily. We'll be happy. I know we will.'

'You're a stupid monomaniac.'

Burkhardt only smiled. 'It'll be good publicity. After five marriages for profit, you're marrying for love. All the worlds love a lover, Lily. You'll be everyone's sweetheart again. Give me your hand, Lily.'

Like a sleepwalker, she extended it. Burkhardt took the hand, frowning at its coldness, its limpness.

'But I don't love you, John.'

'Let the world think you do. That's all that matters.'

'I don't understand you. You – – '

She stopped. Burkhardt's grip tightened on her thin hand. He thought of Donnoi, a grey shadow against the snow, holding his hand, letting the power flow from body to body, from slim alien to tall Earthman. *It is all a matter of channelling your desires*, he had said. *Any creature that thinks can learn how to assert its will. The technique is simple.*

Lily lowered her head. After a moment, she raised it. She was smiling.

'It won't last a month,' Richardson Elliott grunted, at the sight of the announcement in the paper.

'The poor dumb bastard,' Jim Thorne said, reading the news at his Martian ranch. 'Falling in love with a dream-Lily that never existed, and actually marrying her. She'll suck him dry.'

On nine worlds, people read the story and talked about it. Many of them were pleased; it was the proper finish for the storybook courtship. But those who knew Lily Leigh were less happy about it.

'She's got some angle,' they said. 'It's all a publicity stunt. She'll drop him as soon as the fanfare dies down. And she'll drop him so hard he won't ever get up.'

Burkhardt and Lily were married on the tenth day after his return from space. It was a civil ceremony, held secretly. Their honeymoon trip was shrouded in mystery. While they were gone, gossip columnists speculated. How could the brittle, sophisticated, much-married Lily be happy with a simple farmer from a colony-world?

Two days after their return to Earth from the honeymoon, Burkhardt and his wife held a joint press conference. It lasted only five minutes. Burkhardt, holding his wife's hand tightly, said, 'I'm happy to announce that Miss Leigh is distributing all of her possessions to charity. We've both signed up as indentured colonists and we're leaving for Novotny IX tomorrow.'

'Really, Miss Leigh?'

'Yes,' Lily said. 'I belong at John's side. We'll work his old farm together. It'll be the first useful thing I've ever done in my life.'

The newsmen, thunderstruck, scattered to shout their story to the waiting worlds. Mr and Mrs John Burkhardt closed the door behind them.

'Happy?' Burkhardt asked.

Lily nodded. She was still smiling. Burkhardt, watching her closely, saw the momentary flicker of her eyes, the brief clearing-away of the cloud that shrouded them – as though someone were trapped behind those lovely eyes, struggling to get out. But Burkhardt's control never lapsed. Bending, he kissed her soft lips lightly.

'Bedtime,' he said.

'Yes. Bedtime.'

Burkhardt kissed her again. Donnoi had been right, he thought. Control was possible. He had channelled desire eighteen years, and now Lily was his. Perhaps she was no longer Lily as men had known her, but what did that matter? She was the Lily of his lonely dreams. He had created her in the tingling moment of a handshake, from the raw material of her old self.

He turned off the light and began to undress. He thought with cosy pleasure that in only a few weeks he would be setting foot once again on the bleak tundra of Novotny IX – this time, with his loving bride.

Acknowledgments

The Publishers gratefully acknowledge permission granted by the following to reprint the copyright material included in this volume:

Harrison Bergeron by Kurt Vonnegut Jr. Excerpted from the book 'Welcome to the Monkey House'. Copyright © 1961 by Kurt Vonnegut Jr. Originally published in 'Fantasy and Science Fiction'. Reprinted by permission of Delacorte Press/Seymour Lawrence, Kurt Vonnegut Jr and his attorney, Donald C. Farber.

The Engine at Heartspring's Centre by Roger Zelazny. Copyright © Roger Zelazny. Reprinted by permission of the Author and the Author's Agents, Kirby McCauley Ltd.

Twilight by John W. Campbell. Reprinted by permission of the Author and the Author's Agents, Scott Meredith Literary Agency, Inc., 845 Third Avenue, New York, New York 10022.

Mysterious Doings in the Metropolitan Museum by Fritz Leiber. © 1974 by Terry Carr for 'Universe 5' and reprinted by permission of the Author and E. J. Carnell Literary Agency.

The Crystal Egg by H. G. Wells. Reprinted by permission of the Estate of the late H. G. Wells and A. P. Watt Ltd.

The Gioconda of the Twilight Noon by J. G. Ballard. Copyright © 1964 by J. G. Ballard. From 'The Twilight Beach', published by Victor Gollancz Ltd and Penguin Books Ltd. Reprinted by permission of the Author and his Agents, C. & J. Wolfers Ltd.

The Tunnel Under the World by Frederik Pohl. © 1954 by Galaxy Publishing Corporation and reprinted by permission of the Author and E. J. Carnell Literary Agency.

The Coffin Cure by Alan E. Nourse. From 'Tiger by the Tail'. Copyright © 1965 by Alan E. Nourse. Reprinted by permission of Brandt & Brandt Literary Agents Inc.

Castaway by Arthur C. Clarke. Reprinted by permission of the Author, the Publishers, Victor Gollancz Ltd, and the Author's Agents, David Higham Associates Ltd and Scott Meredith Literary Agency, Inc., 845 Third Avenue, New York, New York 10022.